by the
STARS

PRAISE FOR *BY THE STARS*

"*By the Stars* is an enchanting tale that transports readers to a not-so-bygone time when honor and duty shaped the world and bravery defined a generation. Like Cal and Kate's relationship, the story blossoms from a charming will they, won't they romance, perseveres through the hardships and horrors of war, and matures into a transformative tale of faith, destiny, and the life-changing power of enduring love." —Lindsay Maxfield, editor, Deseret Media Companies

❧

"Present and past meld together in this richly crafted story, including the difficulties of life during WWII, the highs and lows of first loves, and having to leave behind the thing you want most. *By the Stars* is a heartwarming tale showing that with faith and determination, all things are possible. . . . As I finished the last page, I closed the cover, hugged the book close to my chest, and sighed with contentment as my new friend Cal finished telling me his story, and oh, what a story." —Kelly Dearth, founder of DeliciousReads.com

❧

"A tender tale of the endurance of love and the hardships of war. Sweet and heartfelt. Cal and Kate's love story is one to remember." —Teri Harman, author of the Moonlight Trilogy

by the
STARS

Lindsay B Ferguson

BONNEVILLE
BOOKS

An imprint of Cedar Fort, Inc.
Springville, Utah

ISBN 13: 978-1-4621-1815-1

Published by Bonneville Books, an imprint of Cedar Fort, Inc.
2373 W. 700 S., Springville, UT, 84663
Distributed by Cedar Fort, Inc. www.cedarfort.com

LIBRARY OF CONGRESS CATALOGING-IN-PUBLICATION DATA

Names: Ferguson, Lindsay, 1984- author.
Title: By the stars / Lindsay Ferguson.
Description: Springville, UT : Bonneville Books, [2016]
Identifiers: LCCN 2015040025 | ISBN 9781462118151 (perfect bound : acid-free
  paper)
Subjects: LCSH: World War, 1939-1945--Fiction. | Love stories. | Christian
  fiction.
Classification: LCC PS3606.E7258 B9 2016 | DDC 813/.6--dc23
LC record available at http://lccn.loc.gov/2015040025

Cover design by Michelle May Ledezma
Cover design © 2016 by Cedar Fort, Inc.
Edited and typeset by Justin Greer

Printed in the United States of America

10 9 8 7 6 5 4 3 2 1

Printed on acid-free paper

To my mom, for always believing in me
and for being there every step of the way.

To Cory, for his steadfast encouragement, support, and love.

Inspired by a true story

Prologue

Standing on the front porch of the long-standing brown-brick rambler, I lifted my hand to meet the door. With my fist clenched, I paused for a moment. I was looking forward to feeding my curiosity. But a few moments earlier, walking up the drive, glancing around the front yard and the large plot of land surrounding the home, a slight feeling of nervousness had begun to slowly sneak over me.

I knew it was silly. He was expecting me, and I was sure he had talked to many people interested in hearing about his experiences before. Plus, he was really old! Even if he was "with it" for a man of his age, what could the chances be that he would even remember my visit a few hours later?

My fist met the door.

Thump, thump, thump.

I stood there waiting, anticipating the door swinging open at any second.

Nothing.

A few more seconds. Still nothing.

I wondered how long I should wait before knocking again.

What if he wasn't home? But he was ninety-three years old. Where would a ninety-three-year-old man even go?

Standing there pondering where my visitee might be, I felt my muscles slowly relax, my uneasiness trickling away. Letting out a breath, I glanced from side to side and studied the house and property I was standing on. The home seemed old, probably built at least fifty-some-odd years earlier. But it had been nicely kept up. Red rosebushes flanked the garden beds bordering the house and the grass appeared to have been freshly mowed. But mostly it was quiet. The place felt slow paced, peaceful even. The cheerful song of a few birds chirping nearby floated on the air, and I suddenly noticed what a beautiful day it was. The temperature was moderate and the air was still. A perfect summer afternoon.

Turning my attention back to the door, I realized a minute or so had passed by. I lifted my hand to knock again.

Thump, thump, thump.

Nothing.

Maybe, because of his age, it was taking him an excruciating amount of time to answer the door. I began thinking of all that must go into the task of door-answering for a person of ninety-three. I envisioned an aged, decrepit-looking man struggling for seconds, even minutes, to push his feeble little body up from sitting position to standing, and then more agonizing seconds, maybe even minutes, to get situated at his walker before making the slow and shaky trek across the room to the door. Poor old man; no wonder he was taking so long!

Or maybe he had forgotten all about my visit. Of course he had! Or his hearing was completely gone and he couldn't even hear my knocking. Oh dear. How would it be to be that old?

I began knocking again, this time with much more force. I had to be sure he would hear me.

THUMP, THUMP, THUMP.

Suddenly the door swung open. A shiny peachy-bald head with a pair of sparkling, crystal blue eyes and a friendly smile appeared in front of me. "Well, hello!" he said with much-unexpected energy. "You're here! I hope I didn't keep you waiting long."

"No, not at all!" I replied, a bit startled to have him actually standing in front of me, and with such enthusiasm at that.

I quickly took in his image. To my surprise, he didn't appear frail and decrepit at all. On the contrary, he seemed quite robust. Dressed in a button-down shirt neatly tucked into slacks, he was standing upright with a sincere, welcoming smile spread across his face—a face that seemed to have far too few wrinkles for a man of ninety-three. There I was, standing in front of the oldest person I had ever met, quickly realizing he truly didn't look or seem it.

"I had a water pipe break in the backyard," he began to explain, his friendly eyes smiling at me. "A maintenance man from the city is here taking a look at it and I was back there giving him a hand." He pointed a finger out the door toward a vehicle parked on the road alongside his property with the city insignia on its door. Why hadn't I noticed the truck parked there before?

In more of a hushed tone, he continued, "You know how these types of appointments go." A wry smile was spread across his face. "They never quite show up when they say they will, and it always takes longer than you think."

"I know what you mean," I responded with a laugh, still in awe at his astuteness, both mentally and physically.

"Well, anyhow," he continued, "As you know, I am Cal." He extended his hand out toward me, which I met with mine.

"Thank you so much for having me over," I said as he shook my hand with a steady grip.

"Of course," he responded, his eyes twinkling.

"I've heard a lot about you," I continued.

He chuckled. "Oh, well, all good things, I hope."

"Definitely good things," I replied with a smile.

"Well, come on in and take a seat," he said, waving me in through the door.

"Thank you," I said. Stepping from the porch into his house I entered what looked to be the home's main living area. Soaking in my surroundings, I immediately felt like I had been transported back in time. Not in a dingy, outdated way you might feel in an older home that hadn't been well kept up, but in a cozy, homespun, comfortable sort of way. Like warm pumpkin pie on Thanksgiving Day.

The home didn't appear to have had much updating done in recent years as far as modern trends go, but I quickly realized that was part of the charm of it. The living area had wood-paneled walls, dark-green carpet, and a floral-patterned couch with a few vintage-looking sitting chairs placed around the room. Heavy, sweeping mauve-colored drapes hung from the windows and picturesque paintings of landscapes and old photographs with ornate frames decorated the walls.

While the home's classic décor and old-fashioned flair were charming, the most enchanting part was the photographs. Gazing around the room I felt enveloped by them. Some black and white, others in faded 1970s color, and several in the crisp, vibrant quality of modern cameras—they were everywhere. Scattered across shelves, lining bookcases, adorning decorative tables, and hanging on the walls, photographs seemed to cover every spare inch of the room. The wall directly in front of me was covered with a gigantic wooden bookcase filled with volumes of beautifully aged, leather-bound books, and the empty spaces at the bookends were filled with more photographs.

"Go ahead and take a seat," he said, his words startling me a little.

"Thanks," I responded, taking a few steps toward a seafoam-green sitting chair in front of me. I lowered myself to sit on it.

Cal was making himself comfortable in a cushy brown leather recliner across from me.

"I really like all your photos," I said, gesturing around the room.

"Aren't they something?" he responded with a smile, seemingly pleased with my observation. "I know there are a lot of them, but there are just so many good ones and it's hard to pick and choose, so I keep out as many as I can. I like having them where I can see them."

"They're great," I replied, my eyes still scanning the room. My gaze fell upon one placed on a small side table next to the couch a couple feet to my left. Encased in a simple gold frame, it pictured a handsome young man in a World War II–era soldier's uniform. He was standing next to a middle-aged woman, his arm wrapped around her shoulder.

"Is that you?" I asked, pointing to the man in the photo.

"It is. I was standing with my mother there. That picture was taken the morning I was sent off to the war."

I nodded and looked back to the photo, its significance bearing a little more meaning to me now. It captured the last time his mother would see her son for months, most likely years. For all she knew, it could be the last time she would ever see him. The thought made my stomach curl with the thought of ever having to send my own son off to war. Staring at the woman in the photo, I noticed her mouth formed a slight smile. But as I looked a little closer, I realized it was tight-lipped, forced even, and of course I understood why.

My focus shifted to the young man standing beside her. I took a moment to study him. He stood tall and sure, his lean, muscular frame outlined by a perfectly pressed uniform. A smile curled in the corner of his mouth. His dark, slightly wavy hair was combed neatly to the side underneath his soldier cap, making him look quite official. What stood out most to me were his eyes. Although the photo was in black and white, the lightness of his eyes shone through the photo. Gleaming with determination, there was something resolute and sure about them, yet unpretentious and honest.

"Well now, I understand you'd like to hear a little bit about my life," Cal said.

"Yes," I replied, nodding, bringing myself back to our conversation. "I've heard so much about you, and I'd love to hear about some of your experiences firsthand."

He smiled and leaned forward on his chair, resting his arms on his lap in front of him. "You know, it's interesting to me that people want to hear about my life. To me, my life is very normal. Now, I realize I came from a different era and served in the war and all of that, but that's just what we did back then. It was our duty. Now, to me, I'm sure your life would seem rather interesting. The way the kids nowadays send text message on phones and surf the Internet. The way you all get all sorts of college degrees and travel the world at a young age. That just didn't happen in my day. Now, to me, that's interesting." He paused for a moment, shrugged, and with a chuckle added, "But those are just the ramblings of an old man."

"Perspective is a funny thing, isn't it?" I said. "See, to me it's so interesting that you lived during so many important events in history, like the Depression and the war. And you were able to see all that has changed over the last century. It must be incredible to think back on all that has happened."

"Oh, yes. It is," he replied with a far-off look in his eyes. "And my, how times have changed. It's a different world today, there's no question about that." His blue eyes gleamed as he spoke, reminding me of the young man in the photo. "You know, to this day if I come across a penny on the sidewalk I still lean down to pick it up. When I was a boy, a penny could buy you an all-day sucker. Finding a penny was like hitting the jackpot! I never passed one up then, and I still can't now." He let out a low chuckle.

I found myself liking this old gentleman more and more by the minute. There was a calm, content nature about him that was endearing. Somehow I could already tell he seemed to understand things a little better than most people. He had lived a long life, and judging by his photos and what I already knew so far, it had been full.

"But of course," he continued, "I'd be happy to share with you whatever you'd like to hear about my life."

I felt a sense of satisfaction, honor even, with his response. "Thank you. I'd really like that."

"Where would you like to start?"

I was unsure of how to answer. "The beginning?"

He nodded and cleared his throat. "Well, let me warn you, I might think of the beginning of my story a little differently than what many people would. For me, the real beginning was her." He paused, his gaze slowly wandering past me. There was a far-off look in his eyes, something like fondness, perhaps longing. He looked back at me. "Of course, there are many memories before her: small details perhaps, but still, events that shaped my life."

I nodded, urging him to continue.

He cleared his throat. "I remember being a boy of about, oh, six years old, and being put in charge of driving our family's wagon. Can you imagine that? Six years old!" His head tilted back and a rolling laugh resonated out of his mouth. "These days I'm sure that would be considered child labor or some sort of nonsense."

I smiled. "You're probably right."

"I was so short that I had to lift my hands way up high above my head to steer those darn horses." His eyes filled with amusement and he raised both his hands up above his head as if he were holding reigns. Chuckling, he dropped them back down to his lap. "I remember those horses pulling me every which way, nearly pulling

6

me up and out of the wagon a few times." He shrugged. "But the job had to be done."

He sighed and his smile faded.

"Now, there's something important you need to know about my story before I begin." Suddenly his expression and tone had changed from lighthearted to serious. I was a little surprised at the abrupt shift.

"Okay," I responded. I sat up a little straighter in my chair.

"If there's one thing I've learned throughout my experiences, it's that in life there are no coincidences. In my life there have been no coincidences. God's hands are in everything. As I have given my life to Him, He has shaped it."

The room was suddenly very still and quiet. Reverent even. The old phrase *I could have heard a pin drop* was an entirely appropriate description of the moment.

"There are no coincidences," he continued, a little more slowly now.

I looked into his eyes, those wonderful, piercing blue eyes, enveloping sincerity and intensity all at once.

"And for that," he continued, "I am forever grateful."

Chapter One

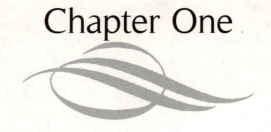

SEPTEMBER 1934

Weaving his way through the crowded hallway, Cal treaded around a boisterous cluster of students talking and laughing over each other, their jovial sounds reverberating across the corridor. He made it a few strides further before having to take a swift step to the side to avoid a curly, blonde-headed girl bouncing her way out a classroom door, obliviously chatting with a friend glued to her side, nearly crashing into his chest. Cal let out a sigh, having bypassed the near-collision.

As the girl continued forward, her shoulder bumped into his arm. "Oops, sorry, Cal!" she cried out through a fit of giggles, offering him an embarrassed shrug.

"It's fine," he murmured with a wave of his hand. He had known the girl, Ruby Paskins, since the first grade. Ruby had always been a bit on the silly side, but for some reason he had noticed that trait coming out in many girls his age lately when conversing with him.

Turning to continue toward his destination down the hallway, his gaze reached out over the bustling sea of adolescents. He was still surprised his summer growth spurt had left him standing almost a head taller than most all the other kids at school.

The energy radiating through the building was almost palpable. Cal could understand why the likes of Ruby Paskins would have a little extra spring to her step this morning. Even a steady, levelheaded youth such as himself, who didn't get riled up about much of anything, had to admit there was something exciting about today. After all, the first day of school only happened once a year.

The students had just dispersed from their first period classes. Cal was about to make his first stop by the place he would get to know better than any other that year: his locker. After being handed the slip of paper revealing his assigned number earlier this morning, he knew right where his locker would be without having to think about it. The school wasn't all that large, plus Cal had a knack for easily navigating his way around places.

This year things at school would be a little different. Most of his closest friends, his friends his own age, had gone onto high school as ninth-graders. Cal would be left in eighth grade at the junior high with kids a calendar year younger than himself. Usually he didn't mind it much that he was a year behind in school, but now many of his friends were an entire school away. That, combined with his summer growth spurt, left him feeling the age gap more than ever.

"Hey, Morgan!" The call came from a yard or so behind him.

Cal turned to follow the shout of his last name. His eyes met those of a freckle-faced boy with wild, sandy-colored hair and a large gap between his two front teeth. The boy took a few steps toward Cal, reached over, and gave him a friendly slap on the back. He smacked the gum he was chewing in his mouth as he spoke. "A group of us are playing ball after school at the park field. You oughta come!"

The boy's name was Billy Haymond. Cal had gotten to know him last year when the two of them had a couple of classes together. Billy was a happy-go-lucky type; perhaps a bit reckless even, but never meant any harm by it. In class Cal had been amused by Billy's outgoing, borderline unruly personality, and had been entertained sitting back watching the boy cause ruckus, although he never joined in it. Cal wasn't a goody two-shoes by any means, but naturally followed rules simply because that's what he knew he should do.

"Sounds like fun," Cal responded. "I'll see if I can make it."

"Ah, we've heard that before. Tell your old man to lay off and give you a break from the farm for once, eh?"

Cal nodded and let out a chuckle. "I'll see what I can do."

"All right, see you around, Morgan." Billy turned, swaggering back into the throng of students.

Cal smiled and shook his head as he watched his friend walk away. He knew Billy was right; he was rarely given a break. But it was his duty to his dad and to his family. He also knew he wouldn't be meeting Billy and the boys to play ball after school today. Work on the farm couldn't wait, and if he and his siblings didn't do their part to get it done, who would?

Continuing on, Cal made a few long strides toward the wall of lockers in front of him. He glanced down at the paper in his hands to double check the exact number and looked back up. Yes, he was in the right place. Locker 124 was directly in front of him. He twisted the combination and opened it, placed the book he received in first period inside, and pushed the door shut.

He turned to begin walking toward his next class, but as he looked up an image caught his eye, stopping him in his tracks. It was a girl.

Walking slowly toward him, she was focused on a slip of paper in her hands, her head tilted downward. Her steps were light and her features soft. She was wearing a dainty lavender dress with a matching ribbon tied in her hair, complementing the curl to her soft brown locks.

An instant later she looked up, right in his direction. Cal had to catch his breath as he took in a full look at her. She could right well been the loveliest thing he had ever laid eyes on.

He stood for a moment frozen and staring as her chocolate-brown eyes scanned the row of lockers behind him. Quickly he caught himself and realized how foolish he must look standing there gaping. He forced himself to look away before she noticed him watching her. Glancing to his side, he felt his face growing hot, but he quickly pushed his reserved tendencies away, regaining composure.

Glancing back toward the girl, he saw she had moved a few feet to his right now. She had a questioning look in her eyes, like she was trying to find something. Cal knew exactly what he needed to do. He took in a deep breath, cleared his throat, and took a step toward her. "Looking for your locker?" he asked, trying his best to sound steady and sure.

Her head snapped around to him. "Yes, actually." She met his eyes with confidence. "It has to be right around here somewhere," she continued, her eyes darting back to the row of lockers behind him.

Cal noticed her self-assured demeanor right away. She wasn't all that tall but stood very straight and held herself in a poised fashion that Cal wasn't familiar with when it came to girls his age. Although he wasn't necessarily shy around girls, Cal tended to be more on the reserved side in general. He hadn't had a lot of experience with the opposite sex, mainly because there hadn't been many girls that had caught his interest. Sure, there were gals that were good looking at school, but most of them he had grown up with, and it simply didn't interest him much to think romantically about a girl he could remember sneaking globs of goo out of the paste jar to eat. But this girl was different; he could tell that already.

"I made it to the 100s," she continued, looking back at him with a helpless shrug. "And my locker number is 125, so I guess that's a start." She thrust the locker slip in her hand out toward him. "See if you can make heads or tails of it."

"125?" He looked up at her, into her striking eyes. "Mine is 124. That means our lockers are right next to each other."

She raised an eyebrow. "Well, aren't you just in the right place at the right time."

There was a flirtatious tone in her voice, another thing Cal wasn't familiar with. He felt his face beginning to flush. She grinned back at him with a teasing look in her eyes, seeming to like the effect she was having on him.

Cal was trying to keep his wits about him, but inwardly he was ecstatic about what this meant. With their lockers being side by side, he would get to see this enchanting girl every day of the school year! Maybe this wouldn't shape up to be such a boring year after all.

"Aren't you going to ask me my name?" she asked, tilting her head to the side, the playful look still in her eyes.

Cal stood a little straighter. He may not have known how to flirt, but if she wanted to tease he could certainly tease back. "Nah. I figured you'd be the type of girl to tell it to me before I had a chance to ask," he replied nonchalantly.

She smiled in satisfaction. "You're right, I am. And it's Kate."

❧

Books in arms, Cal and Kate walked side by side along the road away from the school. All day long Cal had been scheming how he could strike up conversation with Kate if he were to run into her after school at their lockers again. Sure enough she had been there, and it hadn't been as difficult as he expected. After a few moments of chatting, they realized they were headed in the same general direction to walk home, and to Cal's delight, they began walking together.

It was a pleasant early-September day. Cal looked down the road lined with large trees canopying its sides, their leaves in varying bright shades of green. Soon those leaves would be transforming to vibrant yellows, oranges, and reds, something Cal looked forward to every year.

"How was your first day of school?" Cal asked.

"Not too bad," Kate responded. "Yours?"

Cal shrugged. "Fine," he breathed, and paused for a moment. There were so many questions he wanted to ask her, things he had been wondering about her all day. But where to start?

"School is definitely different here from my old school in California, though," Kate continued, before Cal had a chance to start with his questions. "But a lot of things are different here."

She had answered one of his biggest questions before he even had a chance to ask. "So, you moved from California, then," he said.

"Yes."

No wonder she stood out so much. Not only was she beautiful, she was from a whole other state, a state that might as well have been another country, as far Cal was concerned. He had never traveled out of about a thirty-mile radius from his hometown.

Cal realized he had been rather tongue-tied. "That's a big move," was all he could think to say.

"It was," Kate agreed.

"What's so different about it here?"

"Well, first off, it's a lot smaller. More slow-paced. And the people here seem more . . . how do I put it . . . simple, maybe?"

"Sounds like a nice way of saying we're boring," Cal teased.

Kate shot him a smile and laughed. "Maybe."

"Well, we do know how to have a little fun."

"Oh really?" she responded with a grin, looking over at him poignantly. "And what do you like to do for fun?"

Cal cleared his throat. What did he like to do for fun? He couldn't tell her he spent almost every waking moment of his life outside school working on his family's farm. He would definitely seem like a backward, small-town boy to her then.

"You know, the usual stuff," he replied, clearing his throat. "Sports. Collecting cards. Those kinds of things."

"Hmm. Do you have a job?"

"A job? Well, no. I mean, sort of. I . . . I work my family's farm."

"Your family has a farm?" she asked. To Cal's surprise, she sounded interested, enthusiastic even. "Do you have farm animals?"

"Oh, sure," he responded with a chuckle. "All sorts of them."

"How about pigs? I love pigs! They're awfully cute!"

"Pigs, cute? Yeah, we have a few pigs. The only time a pig is cute is when it's about to be served up for breakfast."

"Eww!" Kate squealed with laughter.

Cal smiled in satisfaction, pleased to have amused her.

"One thing I do like about the farm is driving the wagon," he said, holding his head a bit higher. "It's giving me practice for when I get my driver's license."

"Aren't you at least another year away from that?"

"Nah, I'll be fifteen in a couple months."

Kate looked surprised. Cal was used to this, so he began his explanation. "When I was eight I got real sick and missed most of third grade, so I had to do it over again. That put me a year behind in school."

She appeared interested. "What kind of sickness did you have?"

"Well, I reckon it was more of an injury. I was out in the field one day tending our sheep herd and my appendix burst. It was awfully painful. No one knew. I just sat out there scrunched up in a little ball all day long moanin' and cryin'. When I wasn't home by dark, my younger brother finally came out looking for me. He found me lying there on the ground. By that time I was barely conscious."

"How scary," Kate breathed. For the first time her large brown eyes held in them a serious look.

"I can't remember a whole lot after that. Pa rushed me to the hospital and said about seven or eight doctors told him I was a goner. But they opened me up anyway and saw that the poison hadn't spread yet. So they did an emergency surgery and another surgery the next morning. I was so sick and weak it took me a whole year to get back to normal. I had to relearn how to walk and everything. The doctors said it was a miracle I survived." He paused for a moment and let out a breath. "So anyway, that's why I'm in eighth grade and not ninth."

Cal had been focusing on the road ahead as he told the story, but now he glanced over at Kate to see her reaction. She was staring at him wide-eyed. "Golly. Well, I'm glad you are okay."

The sincerity in her voice caught Cal off guard. "Thanks," he replied softly, suddenly feeling a bit shy. He looked back toward the open road. He could see out of the corner of his eye that she had done the same.

It was quiet for a few moments. For the first time Cal noticed the sound of the gravel crunching beneath their feet as they walked. He wondered why she wasn't saying anything. Maybe he had said too much. Or maybe he had mistaken her for being interested when she was actually bored. He hoped not. He hadn't had a conversation like this with a girl like her in, well, ever.

He looked up at the sky. A few light, wispy clouds dappled across the pale blue background like brushstrokes of watercolors from the paintings he admired in his schoolbooks. He wondered what it would be like to fly in an airplane up in the clouds.

"Cumulus or cirrus?" he asked with a nod toward the sky.

"Easy. Cirrus," Kate shot back.

Cal nodded. He liked her spunk. "I think you're right. So . . . ," he continued, clearing his throat. "Why'd you move here from California?"

"My parents got a divorce," she said without hesitation, look-ing straight ahead. Her eyes were unwavering from the road. She appeared impassive, but Cal thought he might have heard a slight quiver in her voice when she said the words. "Mother grew up here, Father in California," she continued. "When they got married they moved to California for his job. I lived there my whole life. But after the divorce, Mother wanted to move back here to be close to my grandparents. And that's why we're here now. Well, that's the short version, at least."

Cal nodded. "I'm sorry about the divorce," he said slowly. "That must be . . . tough."

"It's all right," she replied quickly. "It was for the best." Her eyes darkened a bit, and he thought she seemed a little more guarded than she had been a few short moments before.

"Do you miss California?"

"Of course."

"What part do you miss the most?"

"Most? Hmm," she responded thoughtfully. "Well, everything is so beautiful there. The buildings, the streets, the clothes. The people are so modern and fashionable. But . . . " She let out a sigh. "I'd say most of all, I miss the ocean."

The ocean. How interesting. Cal had never seen an ocean in person. He wondered if he would ever get to see one in his lifetime. "I've never seen an ocean other than what I've seen in pictures and paintings in books and things," he inserted. "They look real pretty, though."

"Oh, they are," Kate assured. "I think the ocean is the most exquisite place in the world, especially at sunset. I love sitting on a blanket on the beach and looking out into the ocean. It looks like it just keeps going and going forever and ever."

Cal enjoyed watching Kate's face light up in excitement. There was silence for a couple moments.

"Do you miss your pa?" Cal asked.

Kate shrugged. "Sometimes, I guess. He was never around much, though. And even when he was, I never really felt like he cared to get to know me much. So it's not too different now."

Cal nodded. He saw his own dad plenty, although oddly enough, he felt like he could relate to what Kate was saying in his own way.

"Mostly I feel bad for my mother. It's been pretty hard on her. Well, hard on the both of us." Kate stopped abruptly, her eyes darting over to Cal's, her expression quickly transforming from relaxed to hesitant. "I'm sorry, I don't know why I'm telling you all this."

"Don't be sorry. I don't mind."

Cal had never thought much about what it might be like to have parents get divorced. But even more interesting to him was the emotion he saw trickle through Kate's poised persona as she spoke about her family. It was curious to him that a girl who could be so confident could quickly turn into someone who had vulnerabilities.

There was silence for a couple moments.

"Well, we may not have any oceans here," Cal said, breaking

15

the quiet, "but how about our mountains?" He nodded toward the towering mountain range to the east. "You have to admit that they are pretty spectacular."

"Oh, I completely agree," Kate replied ardently. "The mountains just about took my breath away when we got off the train in Salt Lake."

Cal smiled with pride. He knew the mountains here were something special. He loved to look up to them while working out on the fields, admiring their rugged beauty.

"See that mountain with the peak clear up there to the top," he said, pointing to the eastward mountain range. "That's Lone Peak . . . "

Cal continued telling Kate the names of the surrounding mountains. Soon their conversation turned back to school and homework. They continued walking and talking until they came the fork in the road that would split their journeys.

After waving goodbye, Cal continued down the dirt road with a new spring in his step.

⁓

The first few weeks of school passed by quickly. Cal and Kate continued seeing each other in passing, usually while making stops at their lockers. Kate would wave in her coy way, which usually caused Cal to blush a bit, but he would soon recover and strike up conversation.

But a few days into school, Cal kept hearing the same excited conversation spread around the hallways as he walked by different groups of students. Had they met the new girl in school, Kate Clayton? She was so stylish. So fun and friendly. So pretty. Cal agreed, but had an inkling where this was going.

Soon Kate had made friends with all the most popular girls at school. She was the new "it" girl. But her popularity didn't just come from her being pretty, or stylish, or outgoing, although Cal observed she was all of those things and more. She was nice to everyone, no matter what their interests were or what social groups they ran around with. Not many kids their age had the confidence to do that. Every girl wanted to be friends with her, and every boy had special interest in her.

As the year went on, Cal's interactions with Kate seemed to come less and less frequently. When he would see her at their lockers, she always had friends swarming around her, and he didn't feel comfortable interjecting into their conversations. He would watch her pass by in the hallways, talking and laughing with the other kids like she hadn't a care in the world, and he would remember the girl he talked with walking home that first day of school. The girl who could tell a cirrus cloud from a cumulous. The girl who loved the ocean. The girl who was dismayed by her parents' divorce. He began to feel the Kate Clayton he knew wasn't the same girl everyone else at school knew. They were all getting to know the surface-level Kate Clayton, but Cal knew more.

One day, about halfway through the school year, Cal was walking toward his locker when he saw Kate standing alone near hers. Instantly excited that for once he had caught her alone, he quickly planned out something he could say to her to begin conversation.

As he approached, she looked over in his direction and a wide smile spread across her face. Elated she had noticed him and that she looked happy to see him, he took in a breath. He was about to open his mouth to say hi when he heard a boy's voice to the right of him speak up. "Hey, Kate."

Kate giggled and waved back at the boy. Cal instantly recognized him as the loudmouth on the football team. And then Cal realized something. Kate hadn't been smiling at him. In fact, he was pretty sure she hadn't even noticed him standing there.

He watched as the boy strutted confidently toward Kate. The pair began talking and laughing. Cal looked away.

At that moment a hard realization hit Cal, something he figured he should have realized a long time ago. Kate was out of his league.

Chapter Two

APRIL 1938

Three and a half years later

Sitting at his desk Cal leaned forward, anxiously bouncing one leg and tapping on the desktop with the eraser of his pencil. He glanced toward the clock hanging on the wall. It was eleven forty-five.

Brrnnngg.

There it was—the lunch bell. Cal grabbed for the notepad and textbook off his desk, tucked them under his right arm, and began walking swiftly toward the door.

"Don't forget to study chapter twenty-three of your textbook over the weekend!" his teacher called as the students rushed out of the classroom.

Cal wasn't usually in such a hurry to get to the lunchroom, but today he wanted his timing to be just right. He knew from past experience that if he left class quickly, his chances of running into her on his way to the lunchroom were much higher.

He hurried down the hallway without bothering to stop at his locker to drop off his book. Walking toward the lunchroom door, he glanced around. No sign of her yet. But there was still a chance he could catch her inside. He passed through the door and slowed to a stop a few feet beyond it, taking a moment to quickly scan the room. Still no sign of her.

He let out a sigh. Students were filing through the door, a few bumping his shoulders in their hurried walks past him. He was out of luck. He turned and slowly walked to the lunch line. Today lunch consisted of a small cut of beef, a biscuit, an apple, and a carton of milk. School lunch had been instituted not long before as a federal program to make sure kids were still eating during the Depression.

A few moments later, Cal was sitting at a table in his usual spot in the lunchroom across from his two friends, Jimmy and David. They were making small talk while eating, but Cal's thoughts were preoccupied, still thinking about his attempt at trying to run into Kate.

Although he hadn't spoken to her much the whole year long other than an occasional "hi," or "how's it going" and of course the customary head nod while passing each other in the hallway, he was determined to catch her in a moment where she wasn't surrounded by her endless entourage of friends or slew of admiring high school boys so they could have a real conversation. He had heard she recently split from the school's quarterback she had been dating for the better part of the year and figured this could be his chance to talk with her without having to try and make chatter with the big oaf glued to her side. And once he did, if the topic of prom happened to come up Cal definitely wouldn't mind, especially if she was to mention that she didn't have a date yet. Cal had thought many times about what his response to her would be given this scenario, running it over and over in his head. *"You don't have a date for the prom yet? Golly, neither to do I. Maybe we could go together?"*

He had strategically thought it out so what he said would sound casual, yet still direct, not wanting her to think he had pre-planned it, although basically he had. He wanted to sound like he was simply asking her because the topic came up, and neither of them had plans yet, so why not?

"What are you gonna do, Cal?"

Cal's head shot up from looking down at his lunch tray. He realized he had been lost in his thoughts and hadn't been paying any attention to the conversation his friends sitting across from him were having.

"Huh?" he asked.

"Prom. Are you thinking about going or what?"

Cal couldn't help but smile to himself. "Uh, I don't know," he answered casually. "I haven't thought about it too much." He lifted his milk carton to his lips and took a swig as he glanced away. Yes, he was telling a small fib. But he couldn't admit to his friends that he had been considering asking Kate Clayton to the prom. Their reaction would probably be to laugh, tell him he was crazy, and then tease him about her every day until school let out. Unless, by some great stroke of luck or blessing sent from above, the perfect circumstance to ask her presented itself and he mustered up the guts to actually do it. But furthermore, the caveat was that she would miraculously have to say yes.

"You outta go," Jimmy said. "You've never gone to a school dance. And if you're going to choose a dance to go to, prom should be it."

Cal chugged another gulp. "Sounds like you guys are thinking of going. Who are you gonna ask?"

The boys threw out some names of girls they were considering.

"What about you?" David asked, turning the conversation back to Cal.

Cal paused for a moment and then slowly shook his head. "Ah, I don't know. I need some ideas."

"How about Kate Clayton?"

"What?" he stammered. "Why her?"

Jimmy shrugged. "You've always been keen on her, right? Prom would be a good time to do something about it."

Cal was trying to hide his surprise. How did his friends know this? He had never told them he had interest in Kate. Cal was a private person and liked to think that certain things in his life were left personal. "What makes you think I am keen on Kate Clayton?"

Jimmy and David glanced at each other, exchanging knowing smirks.

"Oh, I don't know," answered David with a chuckle. "Just the way you look at her, I guess. Always seems you've been sort of stuck on her."

"It's no big deal, Cal," Jimmy injected. Having been friends with Cal since he was young, Jimmy understood Cal's reserved nature and how a discussion like this would most likely make him feel uncomfortable. "Most the guys at school are probably in your same boat wanting to ask her out."

"Yeah," Cal muttered, looking down at his tray. But after stopping to think about Jimmy's comment, he began feeling a little uneasy. Could that many other guys have the same feelings for Kate as he did? He had always liked her, had felt a special connection with her from the very first time he talked to her in eighth grade. But what if all the guys felt that way? What if they all thought they had something special with her just as he did? It suddenly occurred to him that this could be a very real possibility. *Get in line, Cal, you're one of the many,* he thought with frustration.

At that moment the boys heard an excited squeal followed by a chorus of giggles coming from behind Cal and echoing across the lunchroom. David and Jimmy instinctively looked up. Cal turned, following their gazes to the source of the commotion.

There she was. Kate was standing near the entrance of the lunchroom holding a large bouquet of brightly colored flowers. It seemed half the girls in the school were gathered around her admiring the striking assorted bunch in her hands with "oooh"s and "ahhh"s.

"They're beautiful!" Cal heard one voice yelp in a high-pitched squeal.

"Who are they from?" another asked in a hushed tone.

"Peter Johnson," Kate responded matter-of-factly.

"Peter Johnson?" another voice cried. "He's a dream!"

Cal turned back toward his friends. He took a bite of his apple and grunted. Peter Johnson was the star of the school's basketball team. Of course he would be next in line.

Cal didn't play on any of the school sports teams, although if he had a choice he would have liked to play baseball. And he was pretty good at it too. He had started going to some of the tryout practices last year. The coach told him he was a natural, that he had some real potential. But when he arrived home from school an hour or so late two, three, and then four days in a row, his father started questioning him. Where had he been? Why had he been slacking off on his work around the farm? Cal reluctantly answered that he was considering trying out for the school baseball team. And he wasn't at all surprised with his father's discouraging response. The farm would suffer if Cal missed out on working hours, and they couldn't have that.

Cal had been disappointed but wasn't one to dwell on things. He understood he played an important role in keeping their family's livelihood afloat. The Depression had hit the entire country hard and their small town of Crescent, Utah, on the southern end of the Salt Lake Valley, was no exception. In fact, many were saying the economy in Utah was one of the worst hit in all of the US states. Cal's parents reminded him and his siblings that they were lucky to have the farm, and Cal understood why. His family raised sheep and cattle. With four to five thousand heads of sheep at any given time, and hundreds of cattle spread out across the acres of land they leased, it was no small farm.

They also had acres of fields around their house for farming grains and crops, but agriculture wasn't their main source of income—the animals were. This had unexpectedly proved advantageous during the Depression and the terrible drought, and had probably saved them. The drought was the worst it had been in years and spread across the entire country for nearly a decade. They could keep livestock alive during the drought, but the farmers whose main focus was agriculture couldn't keep crops alive without water. Trading had become a regular way of life for many, including Cal's family. Although they didn't have much, they had been able to keep food on the table, and when it came down to it, that's all that mattered.

But sometimes while out working around the farm Cal would let his mind wander to what it would be like to have a more normal high school experience. To play on the school baseball team. To get involved in the social scene at school. To have a more carefree adolescent life like many of his classmates seemed to have. At times it sounded appealing, but usually Cal was just fine with his life the way that it was. He was glad he could focus on learning while he was at school and leave all the drama and immaturity of high school kids behind him when the afternoon bell rang. He'd walk out the school doors and get away to the fields. But today he was surprised to find himself a little bit jealous of those popular sports stars at his school he usually found rather laughable.

Cal heard the sound of Kate's voice drifting across the room. "He pulled these flowers out of his locker and gave them to me. Then right after that he asked me to prom!"

Cal's eyes had been focused on a wall hanging of the school's mascot across the room when he overheard what Kate said. Instinctively feeling both his friend's eyes on him, he glanced over to them, already knowing what they were thinking.

"Sorry, Cal," Jimmy said with a sympathetic shrug.

Cal shook his head. "Nah, it's no big deal. I wasn't that interested in going, anyway. It was just a thought."

The thought hadn't been so much about rom as it was about Kate. And then and there he decided it was a thought that had no use anymore.

Chapter Three

JUNE 1941
Three years later

Sitting in the pew, holding an aged, leather-bound hymnbook between the two of them, Cal sang along softly with the congregation. Although he was following the words, he wasn't paying much attention to the music or what he was singing. It was hard to focus with her sitting so close.

Out of the corner of his eye, he noticed her head move slightly in his direction. He glanced over to meet her gaze. Her eyes danced and the corners of her mouth turned up, forming a playful smile, while her lips moved along with the words of the song. It was hard to imagine that he would soon have to leave her, and everything else, behind.

When the hymn was over, there was a benediction. Following that they both stood, anxious to stretch their legs.

"Nice service, don't you think?" Marlene commented as they began filing out of the pew.

Cal nodded, although he was trying to remember just what the topic of the sermon had been. Between sitting next to her and his mind constantly wandering off imagining what his life might look like in a couple weeks from now, he had been more than a little distracted during the service.

He rested his hand on the small of her back and leaned his head over her shoulder. "I don't know about the service, but it sure was nice sitting next to you."

A giggle escaped Marlene's mouth as she glanced back at him adoringly.

They exited the chapel and began walking toward the front doors to exit the building. As they were about to reach the door, Marlene abruptly turned to Cal. "I just remembered the tour of the church house that was going to be held after the service today. I thought maybe we could go."

"Oh, right . . . ," Cal trailed off, trying not to let the reluctance come through in his voice. It wasn't that it sounded all that bad; he was just ready to get out of the hot, stuffy building. After sitting in the chapel for the last hour, he would have preferred doing something outdoors, perhaps a nice Sunday stroll.

"But we don't have to," Marlene added quickly. "If you'd rather leave now, that's fine too."

Cal knew she meant it, but he also knew Marlene enjoyed learning about the history of the valley, and this was one of the longest standing chapels around. He quickly decided that for her he could endure another half hour or so being cooped up indoors.

"Nah, it's fine. I think it sounds . . . swell."

Marlene shot Cal a questioning smile. "Are you sure?"

"Yes." He reached for her hand. "Let's go."

The couple made their way down the hall and to the east end of the building; the tour's designated meeting spot.

As they approached, they noticed a group of fifteen or so people clumped together in the hallway waiting. Cal and Marlene instantly recognized a familiar face of a former schoolmate and began chatting with him about what they had all been up to since high school graduation a couple years earlier.

A few moments later, a young woman's voice began speaking over the crowd. "Ahem. Is everyone ready to begin?" the velvety yet assertive voice began.

The group instantly quieted and turned toward the woman. Cal thought the voice sounded familiar, but an unusually tall man was standing directly in front of him blocking his view. Curious to put a face with the voice, Cal shifted his weight to his other foot and moved his head to the side, just enough to get a good look at the woman leading the tour. He caught his breath with the sight of her. He was right. He did know the woman. Of course it was her voice.

Marlene leaned in to Cal. "Why look, it's Kate Clayton," she whispered. "You remember Kate, don't you, Cal?"

"Sure," Cal replied, swallowing hard.

"Thank you all for coming to the tour today," Kate began steadily. A self-assured smile rested on her mouth as she spoke. Her voice and presence radiated a sort of poised confidence not many could exude, but that sort of thing had always come naturally to Kate. "As many of you may already know, this church house is one of the oldest structures still standing on this end of the valley. It is a classic example of the detail and craftsmanship the pioneers put into building their places of worship."

Cal and Marlene listened as Kate continued her introduction. She hadn't offered any sort of gesture indicating she recognized the two of them, which didn't surprise Cal, although a part of him wanted her to. More than a few times since graduation, Cal had wondered where life had taken Kate Clayton.

When Kate finished the introduction she asked the group to walk in the opposite direction down the hall toward the foyer. As instructed, Cal began to turn. As he was turning his head, he unexpectedly caught Kate's gaze. Their eyes met and he couldn't help but stare back at her for a moment. He noticed the recognition in her dark eyes. She smiled and lifted her head in a slight nod as if to say hello, her chestnut curls bobbing with the movement.

Cal lifted his hand, returning the gesture. He felt a sense of satisfaction as he turned and began walking down the hall. She remembered him.

He quickly felt his face flush realizing how silly that sounded, even to himself. Of course she remembered him. They were school-mates starting in the eighth grade spanning all through high school. But still, to have a girl like Kate Clayton acknowledge his existence in the world, well, that didn't happen every day.

He looked over to his side and remembered Marlene walking

alongside him, instantly feeling a pang of guilt about how he had let his mind wander. Marlene hadn't seemed to notice the exchange between Cal and Kate. Although she probably wouldn't have cared, Cal didn't want Marlene to have any reason to feel bad. He had grown to care about her quite a bit over the past year they had been going steady. He reached out for her hand. She looked over at him and smiled as they continued walking down the corridor.

Soon they reached the foyer. Standing close together, Cal and Marlene watched as Kate sauntered around the crowd to the center of the room. She began talking about the craftsmanship of the entrance, pointing out the woodwork in the moldings along the wall next to the ceiling.

Cal was having a hard time focusing. The tour was the sort of thing he might normally enjoy under the right circumstances, but his impending departure on the forefront of his thoughts combined with the warmth of the building under the hot summer sun certainly wasn't making it easy, and the unexpected meeting with Kate Clayton had caught him a bit more off guard than he'd like to admit. His shirt felt warm and sticky against his back and his collar tight and constraining around his neck. He tilted his head from side to side, wishing he could loosen his tie, or better yet be rid of it altogether. He had never been one much for ties.

Trying to take his mind off the heat, Cal glanced around the room at the faces of those standing and listening. Some were familiar, some not. Eventually his gaze was brought back to the center of the room where Kate was standing. She was addressing a question about where the stones on the exterior of the building were brought from during construction. Cal watched and listened as she answered with knowledge and grace. He noticed how her dark eyebrows furrowed in concentration as she spoke, and how her stylish black dress, dotted with tiny white polka dots, gathered at her thin waist and swished against her legs as she shifted her weight from one foot to the other. He found himself not only admiring her delicate features and striking beauty, but also the confidence she held as she spoke, something he had admired about her from the day he first met her back in the eighth grade. If he was being honest with himself, she was, simply, enchanting.

Then something happened. For the second time that day Kate

27

looked directly at Cal, meeting his gaze. But this time when their eyes met they locked and neither of them looked away. She kept her focus on him as she continued talking to the group. Cal was surprised and even a little uncomfortable at her zoning in on him. He began wondering if everyone else in the room, including Marlene, might notice they were staring at each other. But he kept his eyes on her. He couldn't compel himself to look away.

A few moments passed and it soon felt like they were the only two people in the room. Completely engaged in her, he had no idea what she was actually saying or how much longer their lingering gaze would continue, but he knew he wasn't going to be the one to look away. He no longer cared that the room was hot. He was oblivious to that now. He no longer cared what others might think. He was lost. Lost in those deep brown, beautiful eyes.

Then suddenly, as clear as day, Cal heard a voice inside his head speak to him.

That is the girl you are going to marry.

Cal's head jerked to the side in a quick, surprised response.

Marry? Kate Clayton? Why on earth would he think that? He was with Marlene. She was the girl he was going to marry. It only made sense.

He dropped his eyes to the floor and began mulling over the words that had entered his mind. An uncomfortable tightness began forming in his throat, and he started to remember just how darn hot it was in that building.

After a moment he slowly raised his head back up and glanced over to the girl at his side and then ahead to the girl standing in front of the crowd. A strange feeling was beginning to settle over him.

Why didn't that thought enter his mind when he looked at Marlene? And more importantly, why, when the voice spoke those words to him, had it not sounded like his own?

Chapter Four

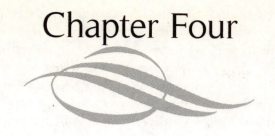

His heart pounding from exertion and entire upper body wet with perspiration, Cal brought the shovel down hard and fast, meeting the ground with a *thwack*. Pushing the spade forward, he scooped a large load of dirt and tossed it out of the ditch. A couple dozen more of these and he would be done with this portion of the new irrigation ditch. It was important he finished it up before he left next week. Although he knew one of his brothers or even his father could complete the project if he wasn't able to, he would rather leave knowing all that he had set out to finish before departing was complete. He'd feel better about things that way.

Placing the shovel down, he climbed out of the ditch. Taking a deep breath, he swiped his arm across his forehead wiping the beads of sweat away before they trickled into his eyes and glanced toward the sky to the hot summer sun. It was a hot one. Not only was it hot, but a light humidity pressed upon him making the heat seem more enveloping than usual. And now he knew why. From his blocked view down in the ditch he hadn't been able to see it, but a cluster of dark gray clouds were rolling in from the western mountains. Although he didn't necessarily like humidity, he was looking forward to what those clouds would bring. Rain. Blessed rain. It was amazing what comfort the sight of dark clouds could bring.

With the beginning of the new decade, it seemed the terrible drought spell of the 1930s had finally come to an end. Cal and his family, along with the rest of the country, were rejoicing that the "dust bowl" and the "dirty thirties" seemed to be behind them.

So far it had been a good year for rainfall. But still each time Cal saw a hint of a rain cloud he couldn't help but feel a bit giddy. He supposed that feeling would never go away after living through what they had in the past decade. Although the economy was looking up along with farming and agriculture, there were many things Cal would never take for granted again. Among those, of course, was food. Although his family never had to go completely without, there were times when food had been scarce enough that Cal understood what it was like to not have enough. Not only that, but variety had been nonexistent. They had to eat what they could get, which was usually the same simple things over and over again and as bland as could be with no salt to season or sugar to sweeten. For Cal it wasn't just about what he and his family had gone through, it was what he knew so many others much worse off than them had to endure.

Yes, Cal had learned that food was a precious commodity. But everything seemed to gradually be getting better. He wondered if the place he would be traveling to next week would be better off too. The newspapers and radio reported economic growth throughout the entire country, so he assumed that would be the case.

He couldn't wrap his mind around the fact that he would soon be living somewhere entirely new on the other side of the country. It was so unexpected and seemed entirely foreign. What would day-to-day life be like? He had been working on the farm his whole life. He had lived in Crescent, Utah, his whole life.

And what would come of he and Marlene? It would be difficult to leave her behind. But for as long as they had been going together his feelings for her had always felt reserved and he could never quite pinpoint why. And now Sunday's occurrence had only complicated matters in his mind more, leaving him feeling more confused about their relationship than ever.

Why? Why would he have had that thought about Kate when it should have been Marlene he was thinking about marrying?

Cal heard a crackle overhead, followed shortly by a burst. Instantly he felt the patter of cool, small raindrops on his face and arms. He let out a sigh, the interruption from his perplexed thoughts welcomed.

Turning to again inspect his work, everything looked as it should. He began walking back toward the house with the shovel in hand. A slight grin formed on his lips as he heard the pitter-patter of raindrops falling on the open field surrounding him.

The rainfall started out light but by the time he had made it halfway back to the house it was coming down more strongly, and when he was within a hundred yards of the back porch had become a full on downpour. Cal raced to the backdoor with a smile at the delightful feeling of his rain-soaked clothes.

Now he needed to change and get ready for his date.

An hour later he had bathed, dressed, combed his hair, and was ready to head out to meet Marlene. He thudded down the stairs of his parents' quaint yet comfortable home and into the kitchen. His father was sitting at the round kitchen table reading a newspaper while his mother stood at the stove stirring a wooden spoon in a pot.

Cal glanced around the room and noticed his youngest brother, Jack, hunched in the corner huddled over the radio likely listening to his favorite radio program, The Lone Ranger. Cal smiled to himself thinking about how his fourteen-year-old brother practically lived and died by listening to the popular program about the old west Texas Ranger.

Cal was number four of six children. Anna was the oldest, followed by Mary. Both sisters were now married and moved out of the house. Then there was Curtis who lived at home still, working the farm. Cal came next, followed by his younger brothers George and Jack.

"I'm heading out to meet Marlene for dinner over at her house tonight," Cal announced as he walked into the room.

"All right," his mother answered over her shoulder. "Have a good time."

His father didn't look up from his paper.

Cal cleared his throat. "Pa . . . would it be all right if I borrowed the car tonight? I was thinking about taking Marlene to a picture show after dinner."

His dad looked up to meet Cal's eyes. He wasn't a very talkative man, even to his own children. But that didn't bother Cal much. Cal tended to be more on the reserved side himself, so he somewhat understood it. But sometimes he wished his father would look at him with more assurance, or trust, even.

After all, Cal had been working alongside his father on the farm practically his whole life, for as long as he could remember. And since graduating two years earlier he had been working the farm full-time. Cal had graduated at the perfect time, right when things with the economy were beginning to turn around. He had been a tireless worker and always tried hard to show his father that. He figured that his father did appreciate it, but the truth was that he rarely showed it.

"That should be fine," his father said in a rather stern tone. But he always sounded a little stern.

"Thanks, Pa." Cal turned and began toward the door.

"You've only got a few days left . . . ," his father continued.

Cal stopped. He found the comment a little ironic. Did his father really think he really needed reminding of that? He turned back toward his father to hear the rest of what he was going to say.

Clearing his throat, his father finished. "Have a nice time."

"Yes, do," his mother piped in.

Cal nodded. "I will. I mean, we will."

It wasn't just about him anymore. It was we. He and Marlene.

He turned back around and walked to the door, grabbed the keys off the wall hook, and walked out the front door.

❧

Cal rocked his feet forward a bit, keeping the porch swing moving at a steady, slow motion. He sat next to Marlene within proper distance, but still close. They were holding hands, resting them on his knee in between them.

The rain had ceased while they had been in the picture show and it had turned out to be quite a nice night. The fresh smell of rainfall lingered in the air.

"It was so sweet of you to take me to see *The Wizard of Oz* again," Marlene said, smiling at Cal.

"I enjoyed it."

"Oh, so did I. Maybe even more the second time. Of course it has been months since we first saw it." She squeezed his hand. "You know how I love that show."

Cal nodded. "Well, I was hoping we could do something special tonight with it being one of our last nights together and all."

"Yes," she replied, her eyes suddenly melancholy. "I can't believe how fast it came."

"Me neither."

Marlene let go of his hand and hugged an arm around Cal's arm next to her, and then leaned her head to rest against his shoulder. "I'm going to miss you so much."

"I'll miss you too," Cal replied quietly.

She pulled her head away from his shoulder and tilted her face up toward him. He leaned down and gave her a quick kiss on the lips and pulled back.

"Cal, do you ever . . . think about us, you know, after you get home? Do you ever think about what might happen?"

Cal felt a nervous lump forming in his throat. The truth was he'd thought about it a great deal but still wasn't sure how to answer. He had told Marlene he loved her a handful of times and he believed he did. But when he had said the words "I love you" it sometimes felt almost obligatory, forced even, and he wondered if she sensed that. In the past he had told himself it only felt that way because he was shy and it didn't come naturally to him to express his feelings, but now he was beginning to ask himself why he had never been able to bring up marriage with her. He knew that's what she wanted. But because she was proper she would wait for him to bring it up first. He could tell simply by the way she looked at him that she loved him, and after dating for almost a year it seemed natural that he should feel ready for that next step.

But now his thoughts kept wandering to Kate—a girl he hadn't seen or talked to in years. The experience Sunday had jolted him, and he couldn't clear her from his thoughts.

Inwardly he wanted to let out a groan. It was ridiculous. There was no reason for him to be thinking of Kate. It was only complicating matters and that wasn't something he needed right now. The best thing to do would be to push her from his thoughts and focus on what was real and right in front of him—his relationship with Marlene.

He cleared his throat. "You know I love you, Marlene. And I . . . I just want you to know that I think the world of you, and . . . I'm really going to miss our time together."

Marlene nodded and rested her head back against his shoulder.

He wished he could bring himself to tell her he wanted to marry her, but the words just wouldn't come out. Maybe it was because he knew he would be gone for a long time, three years to be exact, and the future seemed too far off to make any promises.

Suddenly Marlene's head popped up. "What if you weren't going?"

Cal was quiet for a moment. "But I am."

"But what if you weren't?"

He paused a moment longer. "Then I still wouldn't want to lose you."

Marlene smiled.

He knew it wasn't exactly what she wanted to hear, but it seemed close enough.

❧

Driving home from Marlene's house, Cal began thinking about their earlier conversation. When he told Marlene he didn't want to lose her he was telling the truth. He didn't. He and Marlene got along nicely. They had similar interests and similar backgrounds, they carried on conversations nicely, and he knew she would make a good companion. She was the type that had been preparing her whole life to be a wife and a mother, and she was a pretty girl to boot. He counted himself lucky to have been going steady with her.

Cal was twenty-one years old and Marlene was twenty. Even if they were to go off and get married tomorrow they weren't all that young to be married compared to others their age, and the possibility of marriage was still three years off. Many of their friends were already married and he knew Marlene had some friends who even had children already. So why couldn't he bring himself to tell her he wanted to marry her when he returned?

After pondering on it for a few minutes, he decided it must be the nature of their upcoming separation. The duration itself was daunting enough. He couldn't imagine how it would be to be gone away from her for that long. How did couples make distances like that, both in miles and in time, work? He knew there would be letters, but would letters be enough?

He sighed. A mission. His whole life he had heard of young men in his church getting asked, or "called" as they put it, to serve a mission. But the thought that he might someday be one of them had never crossed his mind. He had always assumed missionaries were the outgoing, uninhibited types. They needed to be comfortable striking up conversation with anyone at anytime, anywhere, which wasn't necessarily his personality. Sure, he could carry on a conversation just fine and could find almost anyone interesting. But the thought of approaching someone that may not be at all interested in talking to him and bringing up a point, that point being religion, which wasn't the easiest of topics to bring up out of thin air in the first place, was incredibly daunting.

So why had he been asked to go? He had been very surprised when he'd been pulled aside after church one day by a church leader asking to meet with him the following Sunday, and even more surprised after walking out the doors of the man's office. Cal was to spread the word of God's love of his children to the people in the southeastern United States. His church, The Church of Jesus Christ of Latter-Day Saints, wasn't asking many young men to serve missions these days. Hardly any were serving international missions with growing tensions overseas. Stateside missionaries were still being sent out but it wasn't common. Surprised and caught off guard, Cal had accepted the call to serve. At the time it felt like the right thing to do. But now he wasn't so sure.

Cal pulled up the dirt drive to his home and parked the car. After turning off the ignition he leaned his head forward, resting his forehead against the steering wheel.

What was he doing? Did God really want *him* to serve a mission? Weren't there so many other young men more qualified, more polished, more prepared to serve than him?

He closed his eyes and offered up a simple, silent prayer to the Lord expressing his concerns.

When he was finished he lifted his head, and a feeling slowly settled upon him. It was peace.

He would go.

Chapter Five

Staring out the bus window, Cal watched the landscape pass by in a blur. Although he was seated aboard the most comfortable and modern ride of his life, his nerves were on edge and he was having a hard time relaxing. He rarely got nervous and hadn't expected to feel this way. But then again he had never experienced anything like this before. Not only was this his first time aboard a bus, but it was his first time leaving home. He had never been outside the Salt Lake Valley before in his life. And now he was busing across the country to live in a place he had never been with people he didn't know.

But mostly it was the time that had his head spinning. *Three whole years.*

He could hardly believe it. It sounded like a lifetime. Who would he be then? What would become of everyone back home? And what about the war that had begun to break out overseas? There were so many unknowns. He shook his head as if trying to shake off the nervousness. He leaned his head back against the cushy headrest of the seat and closed his eyes, trying to relax.

He thought back to his departure at the bus station in Salt Lake City. His whole family had been there, along with Marlene. Everyone had been huddled around him chatting. Then the bus conductor had rung the bell. It was time to board.

Cal hugged his siblings one by one. They each gave him sincere goodbyes and well wishes. He was touched when he noticed his youngest brother Jack's eyes well up with tears after their embrace.

Then he had turned to his father, who was holding out his hand. "Good luck, son," he said with a strong grip. It didn't surprise Cal that his father didn't offer a hug. It just wasn't his way. But the handshake felt approval enough. "We'll miss you around here," he said as their hands locked. Cal noticed a glint of affection in his father's eyes, which was something rare. But as quickly as it came he was back to business. "Make sure to watch your things when you get to the Louisville station. I've heard of fellows getting their luggage stolen when they're not looking in those big cities."

"I will."

His father nodded his head once swiftly. "Good luck."

"Thanks, Pa."

Then Cal turned to his mother. Her eyes were glistening. She took a step forward and gently wrapped her arms around him. "I love you, son," she said softly as she gave him a rather timid embrace. The sound of those words coming from his mother instantly shot a pang to his heart. He hugged her back, lingering in the comfort of her embrace. It wasn't something he felt often. For some reason he didn't entirely understand, his family had never been very affectionate. Hugging was a rare occurrence and the words "I love you" were as rare as his father showing any signs of affection. His mother wasn't a cold person, but for some reason seemed to struggle showing affection. Cal had wondered before if his mother would have been more affectionate and soft with her children had his father been more comfortable with it. But his father seemed to set the tone of the family and the household and that's just how things were. They were a no-nonsense farming family.

"I love you too," he replied back to her.

"You'll do wonderfully," she said as she pulled back, wiping at the corner of one of her eyes.

"Thanks, Ma." He appreciated her words of encouragement. He knew it didn't come easy to her.

Last, he had turned to Marlene. They had already said their

goodbyes the night before. "Good luck," Marlene murmured while hugging him, sniffing. "I meant everything I said . . . about us," she continued, her voice catching.

"Me too," Cal responded, feeling more sadness with this final goodbye than he had expected. "I'll miss you, Marlene."

She nodded and turned and kissed him on the cheek. Then she let go of him and backed up. He watched as she swiped at a tear trickling down her cheek. He felt slightly embarrassed knowing his whole family was watching, but he also knew it didn't matter. They knew Marlene and him were serious. But his feelings for her still felt muddled and confused.

The rest was foggy. He had picked up his two suitcases and walked to the line that had formed next to the shiny silver, white, and blue bus with its signature leaping greyhound insignia on its sides. He handed his luggage over to be stored in the under-bus storage, walked on board, found his seat, and waved out the window one final time before departing.

Still resting his head against the headrest his breathing slowed. Going over the earlier events of the day helped him relax. He wasn't sure how long he had been riding. It could have been an hour, or it could have been three. All he knew was he had many more to go before arriving to Louisville. Gazing out the window, he couldn't believe how much land there seemed to be. It looked as if they could keep going and going forever. He let his eyes close and slowly drifted off to sleep.

❧

After three tired days of travel, Cal finally arrived in Louisville. The ride across the country had been long and tiresome, but also rather remarkable.

During the nights he slept on and off, trying to make himself comfortable while sitting up straight and leaning his head against the vibrating window. Every so often his body would jerk awake and he would remember, with a strange feeling, where he was before dozing off again.

Along the way the bus made a stop in Topeka, Kansas. While there, Cal had some time to de-board the bus and stretch his legs. As he walked around the bus station he noticed a shoe shining booth. He had seen men in picture shows get their shoes shined. On a whim he decided to indulge in the small luxury and paid fifteen cents for his first shoeshine. He had felt quite swanky getting a shoeshine while wearing a suit in a nice bus station.

This morning Cal woke in the early hours feeling groggy and weary, but now, hours later, all that was gone. Any nervousness left over from the day before had now melted away and was replaced with something else. Excitement.

He had heard people talk about the thrill of traveling and had never quite understood what they meant. But he was getting the idea of it now. He was in a new place with new people and a different culture than what he had experienced in life back home. The Louisville bus station was much larger than Salt Lake City's and walking around it had been rather invigorating. Cal glanced around, watching people of all sorts bustling around the busy station, everyone apparently with somewhere important to be. He found it ironic that among all these seemingly important business travelers and well-to-do individuals who could afford traveling by bus, there was him, a backward farm boy from small-town Utah. He felt as though he stood out like a sore thumb but realized he probably blended right in as another busy traveler.

He was wearing a suit, standard missionary attire, and had already noticed the difference in how people acted around him wearing it. It was like a suit automatically demanded a certain level of respect. When he approached a man working at the station with a question, just as he stepped off the bus, for the first time in his life he had been addressed as "sir."

But it wasn't just the way regular passers-by assessed him. He noticed something else. The gals kept eyeing him too. But maybe it was just in his head.

There had been six other missionaries on board his bus. None of whom he knew, but at least they were fellows from back home. All seven of them stood waiting where they had been told they would be met by their mission president, who would direct where they would be going next. Cal looked at the others and noticed most seemed to be having the same feelings as him, a little nervous and jittery, but mostly excited.

"What do you think?" one of the missionaries next to him asked. He had learned the young man's name was Sam a little earlier.

"Not sure what to think," Cal responded with a slight smile. "It's kind of exciting though, isn't it?"

"Yeah, this place is really big. Lots of people."

"Sure is," Cal agreed.

"Have you noticed the gals?" injected Stuart, a tall, polished young man from Salt Lake City. "There are a lot of lookers around here." A bit earlier Stuart told all the others about how his dad owned one of the biggest car dealerships in Salt Lake and how business was booming. Of all of them, Stuart seemed the most city-savvy.

"Yeah, there are," Sam responded under his breath with a smirk.

"But that won't do us much good seeings how we're not supposed to go with gals while servin' as missionaries," piped in Johnny, a farm boy from a small town in northern Utah.

"It doesn't hurt to look," Stuart pointed out.

"Suppose not," Johnny mumbled.

Cal smiled to himself. Some of the guys probably had girlfriends back home waiting for them like he did, and some didn't. Either way, it was going to be a long three years.

Stuart loudly cleared his throat and nodded his head to the right. The boys glanced toward his gesture and noticed an attractive blonde stewardess about their age sauntering toward them. She glanced over to the group of young men and, surprising Cal, made eye contact with him. She offered him a wink. Startled and unsure of how to react, Cal quickly looked away as she walked past. He could feel his face getting warm.

Once she was out of hearing range, Sam turned to Cal. "Morgan, did you get a load of that? She winked right at you!"

"Nah," Cal responded, embarrassed.

"He's right," Stuart replied with a smirk. "She did."

Just then a tall man with receding silver hair wearing a deep-gray suit approached them. A pretty older woman wearing bright red lipstick and a suit dress was at his side.

"Hello, Elders," the man said. At first the title startled him, but then Cal reminded himself that as a missionary he would be known as Elder Morgan for the next three years. The man had a strong voice and rather commanding presence while still seeming friendly and approachable.

"I'm President Jensen, your mission president, and this is my wife, Sister Jensen. Good to see you boys all here safe and sound. Now, let's get to work."

Chapter Six

Another bus station. But this time, Cal was alone. In Louisville the missionaries had been split up into pairs and sent off to the area they would be serving in, spread throughout a handful of states in the southeast. But with seven new missionaries, there was one left to travel alone, and that one happened to be Cal.

Cal had arrived at the Lexington bus station and had been standing in the same spot inside the station for about twenty minutes now. It was after nine thirty in the evening and getting dark. With his small bag slung over his shoulder holding a few books and personal items, and his large bag holding everything else he would need to live for the next three years at his feet, he glanced around, searching for three young men in suits that should be there to retrieve him as he was instructed. But there was no sign of them.

He had been traveling for forty hours and was flat exhausted. He expected to see the missionaries that were supposed to meet him here as soon as he walked off the bus, but instead all he found was crowds of people walking by without anyone giving him so much as a second glance. Rather than wandering around looking for the missionaries, he decided he would try and stay put so they didn't miss each other—a tactic he had learned from his mother when he was young. Thinking of his mother and home now while in the middle of this foreign place he had never seen, traveling all alone for the first time in his life, he suddenly felt extremely homesick. He hadn't expected to feel it so soon. But then he hadn't expected to get lost before he even found where he was supposed to be going.

In the beginning he was hoping the missionaries were just running late. But now he wasn't so sure. He glanced around, wondering what to do next. He saw a man walking in his direction wearing a Grayhound uniform. "Excuse me?" he asked.

"Yes?" the man replied, slowing to a stop. He was an older gentleman with a southern accent. He seemed a bit tired and worn down, but polite enough.

"I am looking for some . . . well . . . some friends I was supposed to meet here after my bus." Cal decided it might be a little difficult to explain the background of the missionaries at this point. "I've been waiting for awhile now and I'm not sure what to do. I'm not familiar with this city at all."

"Hmph," the man grunted, looking Cal up and down. "Have you tried calling them?"

"Calling?"

"Yes, we have a payphone right over there." The man pointed to the far wall of the station. Sure enough, there was a payphone booth in the corner.

"Oh." Cal stared at the booth. He had never used a telephone before in his life. Of course he knew what a telephone was, but the idea of calling had never occurred to him. He wasn't sure if he had a phone number to call, but he supposed there might be one in the papers he had been sent and brought along with some mission information. "I haven't tried that, but I will. Thank you."

The man offered Cal a tired nod and went on his way.

Cal began digging around in his small bag for a few moments before locating the envelope that had his mission information in it. Once he found it, he opened it up and began thumbing through the papers. There was the bus information for his initial ride from Salt Lake, a packing list, and a study guide. Finally he came to the letter from President and Sister Jensen welcoming him to the mission he had received shortly after being asked to serve. His eyes moved to the bottom of the page. Below their names was an address and a phone number.

Relief flooded over his body. He would call them. They were back in Louisville, but they should have more details on where he needed to go. If he could just ask them the address of his apartment, he could take a taxi there.

He approached the large black rotary pay telephone mounted to the wall and set down his bags. On the upper portion of the telephone, there were the numbers one through nine fanned out in a circular shape. The receiver hung next to it. He had a pretty good idea of how to work a rotary phone having seen them used on picture shows before, but he wasn't sure how to insert money to use it. He sighed with relief as he quickly noticed instructions listed below the numbers.

REMOVE RECEIVER
DEPOSIT DIME (OR TWO NICKELS)
LISTEN FOR DIAL TONE
IF BUSY OR NO ANSWER HANG UP
MONEY WILL BE RETURNED

Luckily he had some change along with a bit of the money he'd saved up over the past couple years. Besides the money his dad had begun paying him for working on the farm, Cal had also been working alongside his uncle over the past year running the threshing machine he owned, which had earned Cal a bit of extra money. The thresher automatically separated grain from stalks and husks which was a valuable service to many farmers. Cal, his uncle, and his cousin would arrange to rent their services, towing the machine around and running it for farmers who didn't have their own threshers. The little business had turned out to be fairly profitable.

Cal reached into his pocket and thumbed for a dime. Holding the paper with the phone number on it out in front of him, he brought the receiver to his ear. The first number he needed to dial was 3. He placed his finger in the number 3 spot and slowly rotated the wheel all the way to the left until it hit the finger stop. He pulled his hand back and watched as the rotary wheel slowly spun backward and returned with a clank to its starting position.

He let out a breath of satisfaction. It appeared his first dialed number had worked. He continued with the following numbers, picking up speed and confidence in working the machine as he went. Now finished, he waited and listened, curious to see the number buttons had actually worked. Suddenly he heard a low, dull *hummm. This must be the ringtone,* he thought. He had heard people refer to the ringtone but had never actually heard one himself. Again, he heard the low *hummm.* He waited, wondering how long it usually took people to answer the phone. *Hummm. Hummm. Hummm.*

He couldn't be certain since he had never done this before, but he was pretty sure they should have answered by now. He let it ring a few more times for good measure, but still there was nothing. With a sigh, he set the receiver back on the phone. A moment later his change clanked into the dispenser. He scooped it up and placed it back in his pocket.

Glancing around, Cal was unsure of what to do next. It was only getting later and he knew he needed to get somewhere soon.

Then, out of nowhere, he heard the echo of President Jensen's voice in his head. *"Three missionaries will be meeting you at the station to take you to the apartment on Elm Street."*

Elm Street.

He had no idea where Elm Street was, but the only thought in his mind now was that he needed get there.

He picked up his bags and walked out of the station to the front of the building where he had noticed taxicabs picking up passengers earlier. Standing on the curb, he watched for one for a few minutes and lifted his hand to wave one down.

Soon a car pulled up alongside him. "Where to?" the driver hollered out the rolled-down passenger window.

Cal cleared his throat. "Well, the problem is I don't have the exact address where I'm going."

The cab driver stared back at him blankly.

"But I know the street name," he offered. "Elm Street. Do you happen to know where that is?"

There was recognition in the driver's eyes. "Sure do. That's about, oh, twelve miles or so from here. That ride will cost you about eighty-five cents."

Cal paused. Eighty-five cents was round about what he made in an hour of working his uncle's threshing machine on farms back home. It was a lot of money for a twelve-mile drive, but this was about his only choice. "All right then," he said.

Just as Cal had never spoken on a phone before, he most certainly had never ridden in a taxicab before. But over the past two days he had learned there was a first time for everything. The driver helped him put his luggage in the cab, Cal stepped into the backseat, and they sped off.

Ten minutes later the cab had reached a residential looking area. The driver made a turn and glanced back at Cal over his shoulder. "Almost there."

They made one more turn and the cab slowed to a stop along the side of a darkened street. "This is Elm."

"Okay," Cal replied, looking out his window. The dark street was lined with small houses that appeared nicely kept from what he could make out. Gigantic, lush, deep-green trees were everywhere. He could already tell the area was going to be much greener than the landscape he was used to back home.

"You getting out here?" the cab driver asked.

Cal took a breath. He was trying to stay calm, but the truth was he was quite worried. What if he didn't find where he needed to be? He could end up stranded on this dark street with nowhere to go far away from the bus station. But he couldn't think of any other options. His instincts were telling him to get out, so he decided to follow them.

"Yes, I'll get out here."

The cab driver raised his eyebrows. Cal realized the man probably thought he was plumb crazy, but he stuck with his impromptu plan. What else could he do?

He got out of the cab and paid the driver, and was soon watching the taxi's taillights fade into the darkness. He looked down at his luggage at his feet. Warily, he picked them up again, swinging the small one over his shoulder and holding the large one by its handles.

While on his taxi ride he thought through what he'd do once he reached Elm Street, and he decided he had no other choice but to walk until he found a home that felt right to approach. Then he would knock on the door and ask if they knew the whereabouts of the Mormon missionaries in this area.

He walked along the sidewalk and passed a few houses until

he approached a small red-bricked home with white shutters and flowers in planter boxes under the two front windows. It looked like a friendly house. There were no lights on, but there were no lights on in any of these houses. He swallowed. This was as good as any.

His stomach did a flip-flop as he walked up the sidewalk leading to the front door. What would someone think of a strange man with luggage approaching their door at ten o'clock at night? Would they even be awake? What if he woke them out of their beds? Would they be angry?

He made it to the front porch and shut his eyes in one final quick prayer. *Please, God, help me.*

He lifted his hand to the door and knocked. After about ten seconds the front window to the left of him lit up. A moment later the front door cracked open five or six inches. A pleasantly plump older woman was on the other side of it, peeking through the opening at him with a questioning, slightly perturbed look in her eyes. She was dressed in a nightgown with a robe over the top and her hair was wrapped in large curlers stacked high on her head.

Quickly Cal began his explanation. "Hello, ma'am, I'm very sorry for knocking on your door so late at night, but would you happen to know of any Mormon missionaries in this area, and where I might be able to find them?"

Her eyes instantly lit up and a welcoming smile spread across her face. She opened the door wider. "You're in luck. Those boys rent my basement apartment."

Minutes later Cal found himself in the apartment downstairs being introduced to the two young men who were the missionaries he would be serving with and would be his roommates for the time being. Companions, as they called it. Usually companions were in pairs, but because there was currently an uneven number of missionaries in this mission area, Cal's first arrangement would be a three-person companionship.

The young men were friendly and animated, and as apologetic as ever about the mix-up. There had been a misunderstanding when the boys had spoken to President Jensen about Cal's arrival. They thought they were supposed to meet him at 9:30 the next morning at the bus station, not 9:30 that evening.

They welcomed him in, gave him a snack, and empathized, and laughed, with Cal about the situation.

Later Cal was finally able to lie down and rest his tired body on the rather short and hard twin bed that would be his. It would be for the next few months, he assumed, until being transferred to a different city within the mission parameters. He didn't mind that the bed wasn't all that soft or comfortable. He simply couldn't imagine feeling any more relieved or happy at the moment than to be lying down, about to get some rest, no longer feeling lost or alone.

This wasn't home, but it felt like the place he needed to be. And he couldn't help but feel that as small and insignificant as he knew his life was in the grand scheme of things, that there was someone watching over him, helping guide him to the very place he needed to be. And that made him feel more significant than he had in a long time.

Chapter Seven

JUNE 1944

As Cal sat in the comfortable chair across President Jensen's office desk he was struck with a thought. Time was a funny thing. In some ways it felt like hardly any time had passed at all since first meeting the man sitting across from him at the Louisville bus station, but in other ways that day three years earlier seemed almost a lifetime ago.

He had been not much more than a boy then, just beginning to learn about how life worked and how he would make his way in it. He knew now he had been young, naive, and inexperienced, although at the time he thought he was anything but that. But the past three years had taught him a great deal. He had thought he knew what hard work meant before, having worked on the farm his whole life, and the farm had been laborious, physically wearing work. But this work was different. There was the walking miles and miles pounding doors each day, which ninety percent of the time led to rejection. There was waking up at the crack of dawn and going to bed late. There were the numerous service projects doing work for others that they couldn't do for themselves. The many hours spent cleaning up yards, working on farms, helping people move, even cleaning homes, and once organizing and carrying out a funeral for a family the missionaries barely knew but were asked to conduct on account of the family being too devastated by the death of their young daughter to do it themselves. Not only had his mission taught Cal to work harder than he ever had before, it taught him to look outside of himself, and had required of him confidence, self-reliance, and leadership even when he didn't know he had it in him. He had learned more and grown more than he ever expected.

"Well, Elder Morgan, it's been a true pleasure serving with you these three years," President Jensen boomed across the desk in his friendly yet assertive way.

"Thank you, President. The pleasure has been all mine. I've learned a great deal in my time here and am grateful to have had this opportunity."

The corner of President Jensen's mouth turned up in a slight smile and he suddenly had a curious look in his eyes. "How grateful?" he asked with a low chortle.

The question caught Cal off guard, and he quickly searched for the words to respond.

President Jensen leaned back on his chair and lifted his hand at Cal. "You don't need to answer that; it was just a perfect lead into what I was about to ask you next." He paused for a moment contemplatively and then continued. "I know you are eager to get home. But with how small this mission has dwindled down to due to all the young men getting called home to go serve in the war, we have a lot of loose ends that need to be tied up here. Granted, we still have a few other missionaries left who are all scheduled to go back to Utah in six weeks. But there's a lot of work we need to get done in those six weeks." He cleared his throat and continued, "Basically, what I'm proposing is this—how would you feel about extending your time with us for another six weeks?"

It only took Cal a moment to process what President Jensen was saying. He had wondered how the mission would continue functioning with all the missionaries they had lost, so it didn't entirely shock him that he was being asked to stay longer. There wasn't anything extremely pressing causing Cal to want to get home right away. Of course there was his family. He longed to see his mother and give her a great big hug, and was surprised how much he looked forward to seeing his father again face to face. He felt that with all the people he had interacted with over his mission and all he had learned about the complexities of personalities and families through seeing it lived out in the lives of the people he served, he somehow understood his father more.

As much as he had originally thought she would be there when he returned, Marlene was now out of the picture. They had written faithfully every week for the first year or so, but then it began dwindling to every couple weeks and less and less. At about eighteen months into his mission she had written asking if he would be okay with her going out with other men, just for fun, she had added. Cal was a bit surprised at her asking, having assumed she had been doing that already with the way her letters had been waning. He wrote her back and assured her that was fine. The next letter he received she told him she was moving to Texas to live with her sister for a while. But since then he hadn't heard anything from Marlene.

Cal knew that after returning home he would be called to serve in the war very soon. He had reported to the government when he would be returning from his mission and was sure to get orders soon after he returned. Cal's brother George, who was just a year his junior, had been serving in the war for close to a year now. After basic training, George had been deployed to Western Europe, but according to his letters hadn't seen much battle yet. Cal's older brother, Curtis, had a hearing impairment that deemed him unable to serve in the military. Although Jack was barely coming of age to serve, he wouldn't be permitted to serve due to the same hearing problem.

But Cal had nothing holding him back. The last letter he had received from his mother a week ago said she hadn't received any instruction on Cal's impending service yet.

Quickly considering all these factors, Cal nodded his head. "Sign me up for another six weeks."

❧

Across the country back in Crescent, Utah, a flustered young woman hurried up the dirt driveway leading to the Morgan household. It was midday, about noon, and the warm June sun beamed down brightly on her as she inhaled the freshness of the summer blooms while walking up the drive.

When she reached the doorstep, she took a deep breath. But before she had a chance to lift her hand to knock, the door burst open, almost smacking her in the face. A pair of young children sprung out the door.

"Can't catch me!" a young boy of about five years old called back to a little girl, who looked to be about three or so. She giggled and toddled after the boy, who walked right into Marlene's skirt.

"Oh, hello!" Marlene exclaimed, smiling down at them. She assumed these must be the children of Cal's oldest sister, Anna, who was likely visiting for the day.

"Who are you?" the boy asked with a twisted expression, bright blue eyes staring up at her. His eyes reminded her of Cal's.

"I'm your uncle's . . . um, his . . ."

Just then Cal's mother appeared at the door, with Anna just behind her.

"Why, hello, Marlene!" Mrs. Morgan's expression looked genuinely pleased to see her. The two children scuttled past Marlene and out into the yard to play.

"Hello, Mrs. Morgan, and Anna, how are you?"

"We're well," Anna answered with a smile.

Mrs. Morgan nodded. "It's nice to see you, dear."

"Nice to see you too."

"So you're back in town from Texas, are you?" Mrs. Morgan asked.

"I am."

"Are you visiting or back for good now?"

"Well, I . . . I do love it in Texas. But I miss home too. I can see myself ending up either place, really. No permanent plans yet."

Mrs. Morgan and Anna exchanged knowing glances. "Well, that's nice to have options," Mrs. Morgan said.

"Yes," Marlene said quietly, a hint of nervousness crackling through her voice.

There was a pause in the conversation for a moment, and then Marlene cleared her throat. "So, is Cal home?"

Mrs. Morgan arched her eyebrows in a surprised expression. "Oh, I assumed you knew. No, he won't be back for, well, about four weeks now."

"What? Why?" Marlene said in a surprised gasp, her heart

sinking a bit. Realizing she might have sounded overly dramatic or disappointed, she steadied her voice and then continued, "I thought he would have been home at least two weeks ago . . ."

"He would have, but his mission president asked him to extend six weeks," Mrs. Morgan explained, with Anna nodding behind her.

"Extend?" Marlene's heart fell even more, although she tried to mask her emotions. She had made a special trip back to Utah to see Cal and thought she had timed it perfectly. She came two weeks after he should have returned to make sure he would be back. She thought about writing a letter to his family to check when his return date was, but there was no reason she could think of that he would come home past the three-year mark, especially with the war.

Marlene thought of Bobby, her beau in Texas. Bobby was good-looking and well to do, and he wanted to marry her. They had been going steady for quite awhile, but the truth was a piece of her heart was still with Cal. He had always been so sweet and respectful, and there was something so strong and steady about him. Something she couldn't quite put her finger on. Not only that, but she had never been attracted to someone like she was to Cal. He was built lean and strong and had wonderful wavy brown hair and piercing blue eyes that would make any girl swoon. But Cal was so unassuming. He seemed to have no idea of his good looks and what a catch he really was.

Bobby had told Marlene he was ready to settle down and that he knew she was the one for him, and Marlene thought he might be right. But with a piece of her still with Cal, she felt she needed to give him one last shot before saying yes to Bobby.

Her sister thought she was crazy for questioning Bobby's marriage proposal. But Marlene told her she needed to see Cal once more, to find out if there was any spark left. Her sister begrudgingly approved of Marlene's travel back to Utah but made her promise to give it no more than a week. She told Marlene that if the spark wasn't there after a week together, it wouldn't be there at all. Marlene knew she was probably right. She wouldn't need much time. Not only that, but she needed to get back for her job working as an office assistant at her brother-in-law's accounting firm.

Now Marlene had a dilemma. She would have to explain to her

sister *and* her brother-in-law why she needed to stay another four weeks until Cal got home, and at least a week past that so they could actually spend some time together.

"Are you all right, Marlene?" Mrs. Morgan asked in a concerned tone, noticing the girl's distressed expression.

"Oh, I'm fine," Marlene stammered. "I'll just . . . drop by again in four weeks or so then."

"All right," Mrs. Morgan replied in an apologetic tone. "Take care, dear."

Forcing a smile, Marlene nodded and turned to walk back down the drive, trying to hide the disappointment in her steps.

Chapter Eight

Cal rested his arm on the rolled down window of the front passenger seat, letting a warm gust of muggy air blow into his face. He had never felt more alive and free as he did now, cruising along the scenic east coast highway with his three friends.

They had just finished their visit to New York City, a grand and thrilling adventure. It had been a dazzling display of lights, buildings, and people, and a glimpse into a whole new way of life.

But as much as Cal enjoyed visiting the city, during their stroll through Central Park he had realized something. Reaching the park's edge, gazing up at the stunning Plaza Hotel with endless yellow taxis, shiny black street cars and old fashioned horse-drawn carriages passing by, Cal had felt a longing deep down in his soul. He missed looking out to glittering open fields of a green landscape. He missed the shimmer of golden waves of cornstalks, and the scent of freshly cut grass and chicken feed. Most of all, he missed the sight of the towering, strikingly picturesque snowcapped mountains always there to stop and gaze at as he worked.

Before his mission, he sometimes questioned if he wanted to continue with the farming business when he returned. He hadn't worked in any other occupation and wondered if he would someday want to do something different for a living. But that moment a few days earlier in Central Park had unexpectedly solidified his plans in mind. The farm, working the land, raising the animals, tending and nurturing them, was his first love.

Well, almost his first love. He had another first love once, and sometimes her name tiptoed its way into his thoughts and danced its way across his unconscious mind in his dreams.

Kate.

As he went from house to house in the southeast working tireless hours of service, and even as he walked past little corner cafés in New York and elegant skyscraping structures on his final detour before returning home, for some reason his mind wandered to her memory. He often thought about that strange encounter he had with her at the church a few days before leaving on his mission. He found himself wondering, asking himself why. But before he could begin to answer that question, he forced himself to push her out of his thoughts. There was no use thinking about her now. She was sure to be married by now, moved onto that next phase of life.

And then there was Marlene. Sometimes he thought about what her situation would be when he returned. Last he heard she was still in Texas living with her sister. He held her out as a possibility. Perhaps they would still end up together. But most likely she would be married by now too. At this point his life was an open road, like the highway they were headed down now.

He was glad he had agreed to stay on for an extra six weeks after his mission, and it had also created an unexpected opportunity. A member of the church in the area had asked President Jensen if there were any missionaries headed back to Utah that might be willing to drive his car back to Salt Lake for him instead of taking their usual bus rides home, also offering the young men full permission to take detours to whatever sights and stops they wanted on their way home. President Jensen asked Cal and the other three missionaries headed back to Salt Lake if they were interested in the arrangement, to which they all readily volunteered. Cal had been thrilled. For him, this was the chance of a lifetime. He'd get to visit places he had never dreamed of being able to see, alongside the other returning missionaries he had become good friends with during their time serving together.

The men planned and mapped out their trip home, deciding to take a two-week detour to visit various cities and sites along the way. They had already made a stop in Washington, DC, had just left New York, and were headed to Boston next. There were a few more stops they planned to make over the next week, but then they would be headed home.

There were a lot of ifs and maybes in Cal's future. He hoped it would lead to a wife and a family and continuing in the farming business. But there was one thing he knew would undoubtedly be in his future, something that could alter everything. It left in his mind many uncertainties about what his future could hold, and if he would even have one.

War.

Chapter Nine

Again Marlene found herself at Cal's front doorstep. She had come two weeks ago, which had been four weeks after her first visit. Mrs. Morgan had informed her that the family had received a telegram from Cal a few days earlier explaining he was going to be another couple of weeks out. He and some friends were driving a car home and planned to make some stops at some sites along the way.

"Two more weeks!" Marlene had exclaimed, no longer trying to hide her disappointment. Cal's mother nodded back with sympathetic eyes.

Marlene had phoned her sister and explained the situation. Her sister told her it must have been a sign. If she was meant to be with Cal, it shouldn't have to be so difficult. Marlene responded that was nonsense, but she was starting to wonder herself. Then there had been trying to explain the predicament to her brother-in-law and convincing him to hold her job. In the beginning he had understood, although she could tell he was annoyed with the situation. But now he was growing impatient. The last she spoke to him he explained the office work was piling up and he'd have to hire someone else soon if she wasn't able to return. She had told her beau, Bobby, she was simply back in Utah visiting family and had decided to extend her stay, but she could tell he was now growing suspicious.

Mrs. Morgan was again standing at the doorstep looking into Marlene's eyes with an apologetic expression. Marlene didn't need her to speak to know what she was about to say.

"I'm sorry, dear; he still isn't back."

Marlene let out a sigh and was quiet for a few moments. Finally, she nodded and said, "It's all right, Mrs. Morgan. Thank you for your patience with me this last month or so."

She paused again, and then with tired eyes continued, "I have a lot waiting for me back in Texas—my sister, my job, and, actually, a beau. I told myself that if I came by today and Cal still wasn't back yet I would go back to Texas. I don't think I can wait any longer."

Mrs. Morgan nodded. "I understand. I'm sure Cal will understand too. I'll let him know you came by when he gets back. I wish I would have known with certainty just when that would be so I could have told you. I am truly sorry about that."

"There's no need to apologize," Marlene responded. "It's not your fault."

They stood in silence for a moment longer. Marlene glanced around the front yard of the Morgan home, wondering if this would be the last time she would see this quaint yet lovely place.

"Well, I better be on my way. I'm going to catch today's train. It leaves this afternoon."

"All right, have a safe travel, dear."

"Thanks, I will."

❧

About two hours later, hot and sweaty from the smoldering heat of the car ride on the hot August day, with his small bag slung over his shoulder and larger bag heavy in his other hand, Cal waved goodbye to his friends, the other returning missionaries left in the car, as they backed out of the dirt drive. He turned, his shoes crunching the dirt below his feet, and began walking toward the front porch of the home he grew up in.

As he approached the front doorsteps, he stopped and stood for a moment taking in his surroundings. He looked over at the large apple tree in the front yard he had spent many hours climbing as a boy and picking off juicy green apples. He would sit on its limbs munching on the tart apples and spitting out their middle seeds until he felt sick. He glanced up to the window of his room above the front porch, where he had spent many cool nights gazing out, watching the stars. His eyes wandered to the black shutters he painted every summer that framed the home's windows. This was a scene he had imagined many days and nights over the past few years, and he was finally here.

After a deep breath, the anticipation of seeing his family beginning to well up in his stomach, he walked toward the door, twisted the front doorknob, and stepped into the home. Instantly he heard the excited yelp of his mother.

❧

"She was here, today?" Cal asked in surprise.

"Yes, just a couple hours ago," his mother replied.

Cal had only been home for all of five minutes. After they said their teary-eyed hellos, his mother explained about Marlene. They were the only ones home with his father and the boys out checking on their herds of sheep a few miles up the road.

"She said her train left this afternoon," his mother added.

"Well, do you suppose I should try to stop by her house and see if she's left yet?"

This was the last thing Cal had expected to happen. He was actually quite surprised Marlene had gone to such lengths to see him. He felt he owed it to her to try and track her down, and thinking back to his time with her now, he longed to have her with him again. He realized now this could be the path for him. He thought of how wonderful it would be to have someone to be with before going off to war. Perhaps they would even have time to marry if he wasn't sent off too soon. He had heard of many couples who hurried the marriage so they could have time together before leaving off to war. He knew Marlene well, and if she had enough faith in what they had together to go to these lengths to see him again, then maybe this was it.

Cal had made up his mind. He hadn't waited for an answer from his mother. "I'm going to go to her house to see if I can catch her."

His mother nodded. "Very well. Take the keys to the truck; they are in the same spot by the door as always."

Cal smiled. "Thanks, Ma." He gave her a hug. "See you soon."

Cal arrived at Marlene's parents' house. Another door to knock. He had knocked so many doors over the course of his mission, but the answer on the other side of this one bared much greater consequence for him personally than it ever had before.

He knocked. A few seconds later, the door swung open. It was Marlene's mother. He could see the instant shock in her face upon seeing him.

"Is Marlene here?" Cal asked, out of breath. He had ran up to the doorstep, somehow his impulses telling him the quicker he moved the better chance he had at not missing her.

Her eyes instantly fell. "I'm sorry, Cal. You just missed her. We just got home from dropping her off at the train station. Her train left about fifteen minutes ago."

Chapter Ten

Cal sat on the wooden rocker on the back porch of his home, rocking back and forth, sipping on a glass of milk while watching the sunrise. A light rainfall the night before had left a skiff of dewy moisture over the acres of grassy fields. The sky was an elegant painting of gold and orange with the morning sunlight shimmering off the few scattered rain clouds that were dissipating. In the background were the mountains, even more striking and magnificent than he remembered. He realized now that he had never fully appreciated them.

But maybe he had been that way with a lot of things before—the farm, his family, and even Marlene. Yesterday's scramble trying to catch her before she left had got him thinking, and he wondered if he hadn't tried hard enough with her. Maybe he should have kept writing her after she stopped and tried more earnestly to keep their romance going. But for some reason, at the time, he hadn't been all that concerned with the realization that their relationship seemed to be fading.

He sighed. Maybe he was just getting caught up in the emotion of it all. She was gone, and everything was sure to work out the way it needed to. He kept telling himself that if there was anything he learned on his mission, it was that some things happen for a reason, and that God's hands are in the way things work out. Maybe there was some greater reason he didn't understand now of why he had missed her.

The day before, word had gotten around town that Cal had returned. Some extended family came by to welcome him home, including his uncle Raymond. Uncle Raymond had been made bishop of a congregation in Draper, a neighboring town of Crescent, and asked Cal if he would like to stop by his chapel the next morning for church services. Cal agreed to visit his uncle's congregation, which was ironically to be held in the same chapel he had visited with Marlene the Sunday before he left for his mission. The day he had taken a tour after the service and had a chance meeting with an unexpected tour guide—the same girl that he had first met back in the eighth grade and could never quite free from his thoughts.

He leaned back in his rocker once more, its hinges squeaking beneath him, and rocked forward, lifting himself out of the chair. It was time to get dressed and ready for church.

❧

Cal walked into the church house a few minutes late. He had gotten caught up talking with his family over breakfast of pancakes, eggs, and bacon his mother made and lost track of the time. As he walked through the building's foyer he remembered that strange thought that had entered his mind as he had stared into Kate's eyes with her gazing back at him so earnestly that day. An unexpected feeling of anticipation ran through his veins. He shook his head as if trying to shake it off. There was no reason to bring his thoughts and feelings back to the emotions of that odd day three years earlier.

The sound of the congregation singing the opening hymn trailed out the chapel and into the foyer. They were singing one of Cal's favorite hymns, "Come Thou Fount of Every Blessing." He continued forward until he came to the two large wooden doors that were propped open leading into the chapel. He stopped at the doors, scanning the rows of pews for a spot to sit.

The chapel was fairly full with not many spots available. Cal's eyes focused in on a row about halfway to the front of the room that had an open space on the end of the bench. That would do. He began walking toward it, aware of eyes on his back as he walked.

When he was a few feet away from the row he noticed from behind a young woman sitting next to the spot he was soon to claim. Her brown hair was curled in the popular wavy fashion, cascading elegantly down hitting just above shoulders. As he approached the bench, her head was turned away from him. It looked as though she was chatting with someone seated on the opposite side of her. She seemed to sense him there, and before he had a chance to interrupt and ask if the seat was available just to be sure, she turned to him.

The sight of her sparkling deep-brown eyes gazing up at him sent an electrifying jolt through his body. Although logically he knew the mere glance of a woman had no real power or force, he could have sworn the sight of her nearly knocked him off his feet.

It was Kate.

Chapter Eleven

Standing speechless, breathless, Cal was searching for words but couldn't think of any, let alone spit them out. The echo of the song continued floating around him, the congregation now singing the hymn's final line, "Here's my heart, O, take and seal it . . ."

As the congregation concluded singing and the organ played the last few measures of the song, Cal opened his mouth to speak, but she beat him to it.

"Go ahead, Cal, the seat is yours," Kate whispered. Her lips were pursed in a subtle grin so stunning it was almost cruel.

Cal could do nothing but offer a swift nod. As he sat down next to her, he cleared his throat. "Thanks," he murmured in a low, husky voice. He stole a glance over at her and noticed a slight smile resting on her lips as she folded her arms and closed her eyes for the opening prayer. For a quick moment he let himself stare at the loveliness of her face with her eyes closed and head tilted downward, her long eyelashes curling upward. Her creamy, smooth cheeks were slightly flushed, and her lips were bright red and plump. Her features were soft and delicate, like the porcelain dolls his sisters collected when they were young. He had to force himself to look away. As he sat with his eyes closed, he didn't hear a word of the prayer. His mind was racing with thoughts, images, and memories, all of her.

The next thing he knew he heard "amen" in unison. Feeling a bit dizzy, he opened his eyes and looked directly forward. But he wasn't seeing anything. All he could think of was her sitting next to him.

His heart was pounding so loudly he knew she must be able to hear it. Although he wanted to, he didn't dare look over at her again. The last thing he wanted to be was a gawker.

A moment later he felt a nudge against his arm, sending him nearly jumping upwards. He looked over as she leaned her head in closer to his.

"Welcome back," she whispered, the smooth sound of her voice floating over to him, leaving him feeling jittery and strangely tranquil all at once.

An hour later, the meeting was coming to an end. Cal had been thinking about what he would say to her after the service ended the entire time but still wasn't sure.

They both looked up after the benediction and Cal turned to her, about to begin a conversation. He had so many questions. What was she up to these days? Where was she living? Most important, was she married? He hoped against all odds the answer to the latter question would be no. He had snuck a peek at her left hand resting on her lap during the service and saw that her ring finger was bare, but this strange twist of fate placing her directly in front of him seemed almost too good to be true, and he had to make sure fate wasn't just playing a heartless trick on him.

She was turned toward him now. With the two of them sitting side by side, he quickly scanned her lovely face once again. "Hi," he simply said.

"Hi," she responded back with a grin.

The next few minutes went by in a blur. Cal had planned to walk up to the stand and say hello to his uncle after the service but had completely forgotten about that now. The two of them stood from their seats and filed out of the chapel side by side, maneuvering around the people in the crowded room until they were finally out of the building.

Soon they were standing on the front walk of the church house facing each other, with the morning sun spilling down on them.

"How have you been?" Cal asked, his heart pounding.

"Good," she responded, the corner of her mouth turning up in a playful smile. "And you? You must have just recently gotten home from your mission?"

"Yeah." He was surprised she even knew he had been gone. "I got back yesterday, actually."

Her eyebrows rose. "Wow, just yesterday? How was it?"

"It was great. I mean, there were good times and hard times, but I'm glad I went."

"Well, that's good. Especially after being gone for three years."

He paused for a moment, surprised again that she knew how long he'd been gone. "I suppose you're right," he said with a chuckle. "And how about you?" he asked, trying to not sound overly eager. "What have you been up to lately?"

"Oh, you know, just this and that," she responded nonchalantly tilting her head to the side, studying him playfully.

"I'd like to know more," Cal answered steadily, looking into her eyes. "It's been too long." The words came flowing out of his mouth smoothly, naturally, almost surprising himself. He wouldn't have dared talk to her so straightforwardly in their school days or before his mission, but things were different now. They were both grown up, past the silliness of adolescent drama and boundaries.

He could see a glint of surprise in her eyes with his response. "Want to walk me back to my mother's house?" she offered.

Cal paused for a moment, considering. "I drove my truck over here, but I could give you a ride home. Unless you'd rather walk . . ."

"I prefer walking to driving," she quickly retorted, eyeing him flirtatiously, as if challenging him. "Especially on a lovely day like today."

"So do I," he shot back.

"Is that right?"

"It is." Cal was enjoying this back and forth game they were playing. "I'll just leave the truck here and come back for it after," he added casually.

Kate pursed her lips in a pleased smile. "Very well," she said, turning on her heel. She ambled forward a few steps, her knee-length skirt bouncing as she walked. Watching her from behind, his eyes traveled from her bright-red high heels to her matching red skirt flaring out at her knees and gathering at her tiny torso with a thick black ribbon. From the waist up, she wore a fitted white blouse, showing off the slenderness of her figure.

She glanced back over her shoulder, her curls bouncing with the movement, and shot him another sparkling grin. "You coming?"

Catching his breath, he grinned back at her and took a few strides forward.

He wasn't sure where this might lead, but for some reason his instinct told him he was in for something unexpected.

❧

They had been walking for about fifteen minutes now, their flirtatious exchange slowing down to a steady, paced conversation. Kate had told Cal how she now lived in downtown Salt Lake City at the Beehive House dormitory. She was taking courses on and off at the LDS University, although right now she was off for summer break, and worked in Salt Lake as a secretary at a dentist's office. Today she was home visiting her family for the weekend.

"How's working at the dentist's office?" Cal asked.

"I like it," Kate replied. "The office is a nice, professional environment, and I feel like it's giving me good experience."

Cal nodded. "And how do you like living in the city?"

"It's been fun. I've met a lot of entertaining people and there's always something to do. But I don't plan on staying much longer. I've been wanting to move away out of state for a while now."

"Really?" Cal asked, trying to hide the disappointment in his voice. Of course she wouldn't be staying around long. That seemed to be just his luck with women. He remembered how on their walk home on the first day of eighth grade she had said she wanted to move to California someday. But he didn't want to tell her he remembered all that now.

"Where are you headed?" he asked.

"Well, I don't have any set plans yet, but I'd really love to move to a city. Preferably New York." Her eyes lit up in excitement with the words.

"New York City, huh?" Cal smiled to himself, remembering how he had thought about her a number of times as he walked through the streets of the enchanting city just last week, never imagining he would soon be walking with her by his side.

"Yes. I think it's just the place I would love to live. Full of life and excitement." Her voice had become wistful, her eyes holding in them some kind of longing.

Cal took a step forward. "Yeah, New York's a neat place, that's for sure. I can see you liking it there."

Kate whipped her head around to him. "You've been there?"

Cal nodded. "Yeah, I visited there on a detour me and some of the guys from my mission took on our drive back to Utah. It was just last week, actually."

Out of nowhere Cal felt a swift swat at his upper arm.

"Ouch!" he exclaimed, his arm tingling with momentary numbness of the slap.

He looked over at Kate, whose eyes were laughing at him and wide with envy. "You were not!" she cried, shaking her head at him. "I am incredibly jealous of you right now."

Cal let out a chuckle while massaging his arm with his other hand. "Well, I wouldn't have told you if I knew I was going to get a punch for it."

"Oh, don't be a baby," she said as they continued walking forward. She glanced over at him with a smirk, a flash of amusement in her eyes. "That was just a little swat. I can do much worse than that."

"I'm sure you can," he said under his breath. He glanced over at her and found himself in awe of her appealing combination of beauty, spunk, and unabashed self-assurance.

Kate let out a sigh. "So tell me, what was it like?"

Cal began telling her about the fascinating city, which he admitted he enjoyed more than he expected he would. "But," he continued, "being there did do one thing for me. It made me realize that as much as I loved visiting that city, I am a small-town man at heart."

"Really?" she answered, her eyes quizzical. "And why is that?"

He shrugged. "I don't know. I suppose it's in my blood. This morning I sat on my parents' back porch watching the sunrise over the mountains, and I felt it again. The land, the farming—I think it's what I was born to do. And this is where I am meant to end up."

"Hmm," she said, looking over at him, a hint of envy in her eyes.

"That must be nice to know, with such surety, what you want in life."

He noticed a momentary falter in her ever-confident eyes. But as quickly as it came it went, and she had brushed it off and was back to her normal assured self.

They walked in silence for a few moments. Then Kate broke the quiet. "You know what this reminds me of?"

Cal shook his head. "What?"

"That day back in eighth grade, you and I walking home from school together. It was the first day of school, wasn't it?"

Her mentioning that day made his heart skip a beat. He had thought back to that day so many times that hearing her speak of it almost seemed surreal.

"I'm surprised you remember that," he said, glancing over to catch her reaction.

"Why would that surprise you?"

He shrugged. "I don't know. It just does."

She looked back over at him, her smile soft yet inviting, trusting even.

And just then he noticed something. Saw it in her eyes. She liked him. He wasn't sure just what that meant, and what kind of "like" that might be, but he could tell she was enjoying their time together, as was he. But her flirtatious, teasing nature was difficult to read. For all he knew she acted this way with all the guys. Did she consider him just a friend, an old acquaintance that was fun catching up with? Or perhaps, was there something more?

"Well, I think we should go there someday," Kate said.

"Go where?" Cal asked, caught off guard.

"New York, of course!" she exclaimed. "I need someone to go with me, and I think you would make an excellent tour guide."

He could tell she was teasing to see what his reaction would be.

"I *would* make an excellent tour guide," he played back with her.

She nodded and smiled, looking pleased. They walked for a few more moments in comfortable silence.

Soon they reached Kate's mother's house. Cal walked her to the doorstep where they paused for a moment. Suddenly there was an uncomfortable stillness in the air. Cal wasn't sure what to do from here. "Well, I had a nice time on our walk," he offered, curious to see if she would give him any clues toward wanting to see him again.

"Are you sure you had a nice time, even with your hurt arm?" she asked innocently.

"Even with that."

"Well, good. Because I was wondering if you would go dancing with me tomorrow night."

Cal couldn't hide the surprise from his face. He had hoped she enjoyed the walk but certainly wasn't expecting her to ask him out. He quickly resolved to assume it was safe to expect the unexpected with Kate.

"Sure," he replied, surprised and pleased all at one.

They made arrangements for him to meet her the following night at the Beehive House dormitory downtown where she was living. From there she would direct him to the dance hall downtown.

After saying their goodbyes, Cal walked down the driveway and away from her house, his thoughts on her and the conversation they had.

She was exactly the girl he remembered from their walk that day back in eighth grade, but somehow a whole other person. She was no longer the pretty young girl he had always been keen on in his school days; she'd grown into a woman, a charming and beautiful one at that, and her spunky, engaging way had him in awe.

He sunk his hands into his pockets and let out a deep breath, thinking over all that had transpired over the past couple of hours. He'd happened to sit next to Kate at the very same chapel where he had that strange encounter with her three years ago, walked her home, and then *she* had asked *him* out. He shook his head in wonder. And tomorrow night, they would be going dancing.

Dancing.

Dancing?

He finally realized what he had gotten himself into.

Chapter Twelve

One block east of Salt Lake City's literal city center of Temple Square, a charming white colonial-styled structure stood positioned along the street. The two-story old-time mansion with its white pillars and sweeping upper deck had a crowning beehive atop the highest point of its roof symbolizing industry, an important concept and value in the LDS culture. The Beehive House had been constructed close to one hundred years earlier and was home to a number of LDS church presidents up until about twenty-five years earlier, when it had become the Home Economics wing for the LDS University. A few years later, the university decided to take advantage of the many rooms of the Beehive House and turn it into a dormitory for young women.

Cal had parked his truck a couple blocks down the street and was walking toward the Beehive House to pick up Kate. He hadn't bothered locking the truck; he knew there was no need to in Salt Lake. The city was known for being impeccably safe.

Cal had always enjoyed going downtown and joining in the hustle and bustle of the city. Although he now knew how much it failed in comparison as far as size went to cities such as New York, Salt Lake City still had an undeniable charm and classiness about it that Cal thought met those of the larger cities he had come across.

He had just driven by the downtown trolley, hearing the clang of its bell out his rolled down window as he whisked by. Then he drove down the renowned Main Street shopping row including the elegant Auerbach's department store, the jewel of all the downtown stores and shops in Cal's mind. Once when he was a young teenager he had accompanied his mother downtown to Penny's to pick out some new Sunday clothes. They had decided to take a walk into Auerbach's just to see what all the fuss was about. As soon as they stepped through the impressively large doors, the ambience and elegance of the store nearly knocked Cal's socks off. He could remember feeling as though he had been transported from Salt Lake to some sort of exquisite, luxurious, far-off location. The store was adorned with rich red carpets and magnificent large glass chandeliers. Not only did the ambience exude sheer elegance, but everyone that worked there was dressed exquisitely. It was a truly grand store.

As much as Cal and his mother enjoyed perusing, they didn't stay very long, knowing there wouldn't likely be anything in their budget range carried there. Soon they made their way down the street to Kresses five and dime for a five-cent ice cream cone to top the day off.

Cal smiled to himself, remembering the fond memory of the outing with his mother. But soon his thoughts wandered back to what had been dominating, or more like plaguing, his thoughts over the past twenty-four hours or so: his upcoming outing with Kate. Or more precisely: dancing.

With the thought of the two of them soon swinging and jiving and twisting, Cal told himself that realistically he could be saying goodbye to Kate much sooner than he would have liked due to his dancing skills, or lack thereof. A fashionable girl like her would surely have all the latest dances and moves down. Cal knew dancing was a big part of the life and social scene of young people. If he wouldn't have just been away for three years living in a situation where he had never so much as set foot on a dance floor, he might not have felt so intimidated by it. But the truth was even before his mission Cal hadn't been one much for dancing. He and Marlene had gone to a local dance hall a handful of times because she wanted to, but Marlene only liked dancing enough to dabble in it and then go back to something she was more comfortable with. He and Marlene actually had quite similar personalities—careful, calm, with a tendency to be a little reserved. But Kate, on the other hand, was a whole new personality. Although he had never seen her dance, Cal knew in his gut she was going to be great at it, and he figured she'd want a skilled dancing partner at her side. If they were to go dancing, he was sure he would end up looking and feeling like a buffoon.

Cal reached the front sidewalk of the Beehive House and paused at the crest of the walkway leading to the porch of the house. He was wearing his dark-gray felt fedora hat; the one his mother had bought for him the Christmas before, and wrote him saying it would be waiting for him back home. She had said it was the latest fashion and would be ready for him to wear out as soon as he was back. At the time he had chuckled at her letter, but now he was thankful for his mother's uncanny foresight. Along with his hat he wore a deep-gray suit, the one suit from his mission that was actually still in rather decent condition, a white dress shirt, and black tie. He knew that going dancing called for gussying up but that didn't bother him—he was used to wearing suits. It was his stiff legs and the thought of moving awkwardly on the dance floor that had him worried.

Still looking toward the Beehive house, he took his hat off with one hand and ran a nervous hand through his hair with the other. Then he sighed, placed the hat back on top of his head, and began walking forward.

When he was about halfway up the walk to the house his thoughts were interrupted by the squeak of the front door of the house swinging open. He paused as a group of four or five gals sprung out of the door, talking and laughing. They continued down the stairs in a huddled group and quickly brushed by Cal, a couple of the girls giving him eyes as they walked past. Cal began walking forward again but soon heard an eruption of laughter from behind him. He turned to see the group of girls walking down the street, their heads looking back at him smiling through giggles.

"My friend thinks you're dreamy!" one girl called, the group instantly breaking into laughter.

Cal turned back around, embarrassed, again facing the house.

Standing in the doorway, there she was.

Kate wore a shiny golden-yellow satin dress. With capped sleeves and a scooped neck, the dress was fitted down the bodice and around her middle until flaring off at her waistline and cutting off just below her knees. She had on dainty black high heels showing off her slender legs. Her hair was elegantly swooped to one side, flowing down in brown curls.

"Found yourself some other girls to take dancing tonight?" Kate called from the door.

Cal let out a nervous laugh. "No, they just . . . I mean I didn't . . ." He trailed off, unsure of what to say.

Kate stepped out from the doorway. She began walked toward him, the shimmer of her dress and her glossy curls catching the evening sunlight. Now she was standing right in front of him. "I was just teasing," she said, a glint of amusement in her eyes.

Cal caught his breath. "You look . . . very pretty," he said. Her beauty left him almost breathless, searching for words.

"Thank you," Kate responded with a grin. "You don't look too shabby yourself. I can see why those girls were making a fuss."

Cal felt his cheeks flush, surprised with her boldness.

She raised her eyebrows at him. "I like the hat."

"Oh, thanks," he responded, silently thanking his mother again. "Christmas present from my mom."

"Ah, very nice," Kate said with a smile.

Cal could tell they were off to a good start. Now if only he could breach the topic of the dancing, or better yet, suggest something else they could go do.

"So, the Coconut Grove dance hall is just down this way at the end of Main Street," Kate began explaining, gesturing to the right. "We can walk there from here. That's what I love about living downtown—everything is within walking distance."

"About that . . . ," Cal began, his face twisting uncomfortably. "Is there anything else you'd rather do instead?"

"Instead?" Kate asked, her eyebrows furrowing.

"Yeah. I'm just . . . well, to be honest . . . I'm just not all that comfortable with dancing. I haven't danced in years, and I was never very good at it before, anyway," he finished with a shrug.

Kate let out a burst of laughter. "Oh, Cal, don't be silly! Anyone can dance! You'll catch on just fine."

Cal gave her a sideways glance. "I don't think so. I'm not . . . made to move like that."

Kate shook her head with a giggle, her eyes laughing at him. Then she took a step in closer to him and continued in a softer tone. "Don't worry about it. I'll teach you! You've just got to let loose a little and you'll do fine," she said reassuringly.

Cal looked down at her. Looking up at him with her large, encouraging eyes, and standing close to him, he just couldn't resist. "Well, okay. I suppose I could give it a try."

Kate smiled widely. "All right, let's go!"

Chapter Thirteen

During their stroll down Main Street on their way to the Coco-nut Grove, Cal and Kate meandered past shops and stores he had driven by just a few minutes earlier, but this time his mind wasn't wandering to memories of previous visits downtown. All his thoughts were on the girl beside him.

They walked at a steady pace within close distance of one another. As they ambled Cal would glance over at her every so often, desperately wanting to link his arm through hers, or better yet, hold her hand. But he knew it was much too soon. He had no idea how or what she really thought of him, and he had made his mind up not to set his expectations too high. They were just friends, and if he let himself think otherwise, he might be setting himself up for disappointment.

As they walked and chatted having her close to him made his stomach flutter. Soon he decided there was one positive to how the evening was shaping out. Although he hadn't been able to get out of the dancing nonsense, it did mean he would be standing close to Kate the entire night. Not only that, he would likely get to hold her hand during a dance, and maybe rest his arm around her waist as they moved to a song. Just the thought of it sent a zing through him.

But all that depended on if they made it that far into the night. He still had bets that he'd feel like such a fool attempting the first dance that he would end up calling it quits from the get-go. And from there he wasn't sure where the night would go. He could imagine Kate being sympathetic and even agreeing to go and do something else. But at the same time he could picture her teasing and laughing at him, and him cowering off of the dance floor and disappearing out of the hall while she stayed dancing her heart out till all hours of the night, a slew of other guys around pining for her, just like it had always been in their school days.

Inwardly, Cal tried to shake his nervousness off. He needed to relax, to loosen up like she said. Why was he so anxious, anyway? He had never worried what a gal thought about him before, never once let anything get to him so much. He was a levelheaded guy, and actually had learned to recognize and appreciate that characteristic about himself during his mission. So why was he acting all funny and nervous now?

But he knew the answer. It was simple. It was Kate. She just did it to him.

"Here it is," Kate said, gesturing toward the building they were approaching. It was much larger than Cal expected. It reached down the block and far back with an upper level balcony running down the entire side of it. Palm trees adorned every pillar along the balcony and stood springing up around the front entryway. Cal knew the trees had to be artificial but had to admit they looked pretty darn realistic.

It was now dusk. A sign on the front of the building lit in bright lights read *Coconut Grove* at the top, and then *Dancing* much larger down vertically, lighting up the evening sky. The riotous sound of a big band song drifted out to the street.

A couple of signs were hanging in the front windows. One read: LARGEST—MOST COMPLETE BALLROOM IN AMERICA. WHERE DANCING REIGNS SUPREME. The other read: WHERE HAPPINESS ABOUNDS—MEET OLD FRIENDS, MAKE NEW ONES.

"Looks nice," Cal responded, looking up at the building. Then he nodded to the sign in the window. "Is it really the largest ballroom in America?"

"That's what they say," Kate responded matter-of-factly. "And it really is quite grand. Come on, I'll show you."

A few minutes later they were through the doors and standing on the perimeter of the main ballroom, the music loud in their ears, looking into the sea of people on the dance floor. The dance hall was a gigantic open space of shiny hardwood floors. Its ceiling was trimmed with red-brown wood and curved into a slight arch forming rows of pillars on the sides of the hall. Numerous large ceiling fans hung down, spinning rapidly round and round. A large stage was set on one end of the dance floor, heavy-looking, velvety, gold-colored drapes adorning its sides. In one corner of the room a cascade of three small waterfalls was flowing, with palm trees and flowers adorning the small island scene. Palm trees were placed sporadically around the perimeter of the dance hall, tying in the tropical theme to the modern-day ballroom. Cal was surprised that although there were so many people inside, the dance hall felt surprisingly cool on this warm summer night.

"This place is real swanky," Cal remarked.

Kate nodded and leaned in closer to him. "They sell postcards up front, and one time I was looking through them and read on the back of one that this ballroom can hold up to eight thousand people!"

Cal's eyebrows rose. "Now that's a lot of dancers all under one roof."

Kate let out a laugh. "Yeah. And see those ceiling fans?" She pointed to the ones that Cal noticed a few moments ago. "Those are giant airplane fans. The card said there's fifty-one fans that circulate a half million feet of cubic air a minute. I counted once, and it's true. I counted exactly fifty-one fans."

Cal nodded slowly, impressed. "Wow. Giant airplane fans, huh?" Now that was something that interested him. He smiled to himself, not surprised that Kate would count each and every one of them just to make sure the number on the postcard was right. "No wonder it stays so cool in here."

Kate smiled. "I thought you'd like that." She paused for a moment and then turned toward him with a curious look in her eye. "Do you know what else it said?"

"What?"

She took a step in closer to him. "It said the romantic atmosphere of the South Sea Isles permeates this dance hall." She arched an eyebrow at him with a giggle. "Would you agree?"

Cal let out a laugh and shifted his weight over to his other foot nervously, his hands in his pockets. He cleared his throat. "Uh, yeah. I'd have to agree with that one."

Kate's crimson-red lips were pursed in the same playful grin she wore the day before, and Cal found himself wondering how she had such a knack of transforming a completely normal conversation to a flirtatious one so quickly. He could feel his heart beginning to thump in his chest.

The song that had been playing just ended and a new tune was starting up.

"All right then, enough talk." Kate grabbed a hold of Cal's arm and tugged him forward, leading him out to the dance floor. "Come on! And you must take your hands out of your pockets; you can't dance like that!"

"Well, I know that . . . ," Cal muttered sheepishly, pulling his hands out and resting them at his sides.

They were now out on the dance floor facing one another. Cal glanced around at the energetic, chaotic scene. Couples around them were moving to the music, their feet clapping against the floor, their bodies swinging back and forth.

Here goes nothing.

"All right, Cal. Look at me." Cal's snapped his head back to Kate's, his eyes meeting hers. "Ready?"

"I'm here, aren't I?" Cal responded, hollering over the crowd and music.

"Don't get smart with me," Kate shot back with a laugh. "Do you recognize this one?"

"Sort of," Cal replied.

Kate nodded her head. "It's the jitterbug." She reached her arms out in front of her.

"Take hold of my hands."

Cal followed her instructions. He lifted his hands from his sides and took a hold of hers. With the contact he felt immediate warmth, a heat, between them. Her hands felt soft and dainty in his, yet her grip was firm and sure.

The corner of Kate's mouth turned up in a slight smile. "All right, now this one is fairly easy."

Cal raised his eyebrows at her, unconvinced.

"Just watch and follow." She leaned to one side slightly and stepped with one foot. "This is just a simple back and forth rock. Step to the side, then to the other side, and repeat . . ." Holding his hands in hers, she began doing the motions, stepping and rocking back and forth. "Side, side, side, side."

Cal followed along, their hands still grasped together in between them, moving with the rhythm of the song.

This wasn't too bad, basically just stepping to the side with a little sway. If the whole dance was this easy, maybe he'd be okay.

"See, you're doing great!" Kate exclaimed with a pleased grin as they continued with the movement.

"Thanks," Cal called back to her.

"This is the basic move of the dance we'll keep going back to."

He nodded.

"Now here's the next step." She let go of his right hand and brought her arm up on his shoulder and around his neck. Resting it there, she leaned her side into his. "Now we're at an angle, and we're both going to rock back on our outside leg." They rocked back. "Then we step forward and triple step." She was doing the footwork as she explained. "Then I turn . . ." She let go of his right hand and led him to lift his other hand with hers up high. Gracefully, she turned in a circle under their arched arms doing a triple step with the twirl. Now she was facing him again square and grabbed back a hold of his right hand so they were again holding hands in between them. "Now a final rock back." She did the move and Cal followed. "And that's it! Now do you think you can do that in real time?"

Cal let out a low, hesitant chuckle. His mind was beginning to blur now. "That was a lot more complicated than the first move . . . "

"Don't let that get to you!" she shouted above the crowd, noticing his reluctance. "You mustn't overthink it. Just move with the music!"

He could tell she had confidence in him, and although he had none in his dancing ability, he suddenly wanted very much to show her that he could do this. He could let down his guard and learn something new, something that got him out of his comfort zone, if it was for her.

"Let's try it," he said, his forehead wrinkled in concentration.

She nodded, pleased.

They rocked back on their outside legs and then stepped forward. Cal was nervous for the next part but followed along with her, moving his feet quickly to the triple step.

One, two, three.

"Very good!" Kate exclaimed. Then she let go of one of his hands and turned in a circle stylishly under his arm. Soon she was facing him again and grabbed hold of both his hands. They ended in the final rock back.

Cal looked up to Kate and saw the excitement in her eyes. "That was perfect! See, you're a natural!"

Cal could feel a wide smile spread across his face. He realized it was a little silly that he felt such pride in accomplishing a simple dance move, but at that moment nothing else seemed to matter but the two of them standing there together on the dance floor.

"That was fun!" Cal called back to her.

She threw her head back in a laugh. "See, I told you you'd like it! Want to start from the beginning?"

Cal nodded, and they began.

They continued practicing the steps. After a few times they were doing the dance in full swing along with all the other couples around them.

With the new songs that followed came new dances, and Kate taught Cal all of them: the Charleston, the East Coast Swing, the waltz, the fox-trot, and other variations of them all. Once Cal had the first few down he was able to catch on to most the others pretty easily.

As the evening progressed, Cal was becoming more and more enchanted with Kate. If someone would have told him that he would soon find her even more beautiful and enchanting than he did the day before, he wouldn't have believed them. But dancing with her tonight, holding her hands, feeling her body close to his, Cal was completely enthralled with her. The way she moved so gracefully to the music, the way her eyes lit up the room as she smiled, the way she threw back her head and laughed as they danced—it was an enlivening experience. One Cal never expected to enjoy as much as he had, and one he knew he'd never forget.

Chapter Fourteen

The late summer night air was surprisingly crisp as they strolled along the streets of Salt Lake City. It felt nice to cool off after their lively night of dancing. After a few blocks Cal could tell Kate was chilled and offered his suit coat for her to wear as they walked, which she gladly accepted. As he glanced over at her, he was suddenly taken back at the sight: Kate Clayton, the girl of his dreams, was wearing his jacket and walking beside him. Less than two weeks ago, as he drove across the country back to Utah, staring out the passenger window at the rolling hills and endless flat horizon of the Midwest, imagining his future, never would he have imagined that he would soon find himself here, next to her, like this.

They were walking down the shopping portion of Main Street now, all the stores closed up and darkened for the night. The usual bustling streets of the city felt strangely quiet, yet peacefully abandoned and still, like a picture-show set of a perfect summer night scene.

"See, after all that fuss, you weren't such a dead-hoofer after all," Kate said, smiling over at Cal.

"Well, I didn't trip," Cal pointed out. "That's something."

"No, you definitely didn't," Kate replied. "I do have to say, you surprised me." She eyed Cal curiously. "I didn't know if you had it in you."

Cal shrugged, hands in his pockets. "Neither did I."

"I think you might just sneak out and go dancing at night and keep it a secret," she continued, her eyes twinkling in jest.

"Oh yeah, you know me," Cal responded with a chuckle. He paused for a moment and then continued, "I've got to be honest, I was dreading dancing all day long. Thought I'd make a complete fool of myself. But I really did end up enjoying it."

"So did I," she said with a smile. "And you did great."

"Thanks to my instructor," Cal responded, tilting his head as he looked at her.

"All right, fine," she laughed, lifting her hands up in the air. "If you want to give me the credit I'll take it."

"You can have it," Cal laughed. "You're the only girl I'd go out on a limb like that for." He didn't mean to say it so frankly, but the words just came. He instantly cringed inside, hoping what he said hadn't been too much, and glanced over at her to check her reaction. To his surprise, he found her eyes large and warm looking back at him.

"Thanks, Cal. I'm flattered." Her voice was softer than usual, her tone sincere.

They walked in silence for a few moments.

"I was surprised how many guys were in there," Cal injected, thoughtfully. "Must have been just about all the guys left around here that aren't serving in the war yet."

Kate nodded. "Yeah. The war." Her voice sounded full of dread. "What about you? Will you go?"

"Oh, sure. I'm just waiting for them to tell me when."

Kate nodded. "Well, I hope it isn't for a while," she said, looking over at him.

"Me too."

Cal had thought about it a lot over the last few days and decided that knowing he was going to be going off to the war, he'd almost rather it come sooner than later. The waiting game was tough, and knowing his brothers and so many of his childhood friends and others he knew were out there fighting, it just felt like he needed to be out there too. But now, here with Kate, he was beginning to feel an inclination in the other direction. Suddenly he had something to potentially stay for, something holding him back from wanting to go.

They were walking close to each other, their arms brushing against each other every few strides or so. Cal wanted to reach out for her hand now more than ever, but just couldn't muster up the courage to do it. He found it funny that although he had been holding her hand practically all night while they danced, it seemed like much more of an intimate gesture now walking all alone along the darkened street.

Soon they reached the Beehive House and were standing on the front doorstep.

"Thanks again for asking me to come tonight," Cal said.

"Of course," Kate replied. "I had a swell time."

"Me too." Gazing down into her eyes, he suddenly felt like what was happening between the two of them had somehow elevated to a new level. Their gaze seemed to hold in it something deeper than friends. It reminded him of looking into her eyes that day at the church house before his mission, when their eyes had met in a few prolonged, intense moments. Again, right now their connection felt extremely strong. Cal felt it and hoped she felt it too.

Then, abruptly, she interrupted his thoughts. "I don't know if you saw the signs in the dance hall tonight, but there is a big band from New York coming into town on Saturday night to play there."

Cal nodded. "I did see that."

A smile crossed Kate's lips. "Want to be my date?"

Her request shot through Cal, instantly leaving him feeling like he was floating. "Of course," he responded back. Quickly thinking it over, Cal realized that with today being Monday, Saturday seemed forever away. He couldn't wait that long before seeing her again. "Maybe we should practice mid-week, you know, so I don't get too rusty before the big night," he suggested, trying not to let his real intentions shine through too obviously. A part of him cared if she saw through his attempt to see her sooner, but a part of him could care less. "Good idea," she replied with a smile. "Thursday night?"

"That works," Cal said.

"All right. Oh, and don't forget this." She shrugged her shoulders, his jacket still weighing them down.

"Oh, yeah," he responded, realizing he had almost forgotten it.

She turned on her heel so her back was turned to him, making it easy for Cal to pull it off her shoulders. Lifting the coat off again revealed her stunning gold dress, which was now shimmering off her slight figure in the dark.

She was facing him again. "Good night, Cal," she said with a grin.

"Good night," he responded.

She nodded and turned her back to him, glancing over her shoulder at him once more before slipping through the door.

Soon it was closed and Cal was left alone on the steps. He turned and began walking down the sidewalk, making his way back to the truck. As he walked, he let out a long sigh. A combination of relief and surprise was coming over him realizing how well the dancing and the night as a whole had gone. "Who would have thought . . . ," he murmured to himself with a chuckle under his breath as he walked alone down the darkened street.

He knew he was smiling to himself now; he felt as giddy as a schoolboy. Being with Kate was different than anything he had ever experienced. She brought excitement and life into him that he didn't before know existed. He found himself missing her and longing to be with her again in the short time they had already been apart. He had never felt that way with anyone before.

He glanced up at the stars. It was a clear night, and they glittered brightly above him. He hadn't always been one to believe in fate or that something could be meant to be. Life was life, and things happened the way they would happen. But over the past few years he had learned that some situations worked out too perfectly to be coincidence. Some things in life, it seemed, just might have a greater purpose.

As he looked up to the sky, the stars twinkling down on him, he couldn't help but wonder, and hope, that the way Kate had suddenly walked into his life so unexpectedly could be one of those unexplained coincidences that was meant to be.

Then and there he gazed up at the stars and made a simple wish.

Chapter Fifteen

The following day Cal and Jack were finishing up the rounds checking on the animals around the property and had gotten caught up in it longer than expected. Walking side by side, they made their way through the field behind their home heading back to the house for lunch.

Cal felt a shove to the side from his brother. "Race you back!" Jack called, already sprinting ahead of Cal.

"You're on!" Cal replied, chasing after him.

A minute or so later, the two erupted through their home's back door, launching into the kitchen and practically toppling over the table.

"Tie," Cal huffed to his brother, out of breath.

"No way! I had you by at least two steps!"

Cal shook his head, hands on his knees, his body bent at the waist still trying to catch his breath.

"Ma?" Jack said in a worried tone.

Cal's head shot up. He saw his mother standing at the doorway of the kitchen. She stood very still, her face white as a sheet.

"Is something wrong, Mother?" Cal asked, taking a few swift strides toward her.

As he reached her, she lifted up her hand, revealing a yellow telegram she was holding.

"For you," she said somberly, handing it over to Cal. "It was delivered a few minutes ago."

Cal gulped, knowing what it was going to be without even having to look at it. He turned the telegram over and read it.

He was to report to Camp Roberts in California on Monday, August 23. Today was Tuesday the 10th.

He quickly did the math. He had less than two weeks.

Chapter Sixteen

Waiting for Thursday to come was almost like torture. All Cal could think about was Kate, and all he wanted to do was be with her again. And now he had his departure date looming over him like a dark cloud.

He wasn't sure how Kate would react to him leaving. He wanted to talk to her all about it, but wondered if leaving so soon would make her less interested. In any case, it would probably help him glean some insight on her feelings sooner. Perhaps he'd be able to better gauge if she thought of him as just a friend or potentially something more.

When he picked her up to go dancing that evening, everything went as it had a few nights earlier. She looked as lovely as ever, and conversation flowed smoothly walking to the Coconut Grove. They enjoyed another night of dancing and laughing and flirting, and Cal's feelings for her were escalating with every song they danced.

But he still hadn't found the right moment to tell her about his departure. He figured the war would come up at some point but it hadn't yet. And it felt strange to say, out of nowhere, "Well, hey, I'm off to war in a week and a half." He knew it shouldn't be so difficult, but he didn't want to damper the evening by bringing it up when the timing wasn't right.

Their walk home had been delightful. It was another serene summer night. Cal couldn't help but think of how perfect everything seemed, except for one very aggravating detail: he would soon be gone.

They began walking down the sidewalk that led toward the front door of the Beehive House.

"This really is a beautiful house," Cal said.

"It is," she responded, and then turned to him quickly. "Want to see my favorite part?"

Cal instantly felt nervous, afraid she was going to ask him to come inside, which he knew would be inappropriate given the time of night, not to mention the house was an all girls dormitory.

"Well, I would, but I don't know if I should come in . . ."

"Oh, Cal, don't be such a fuddy-duddy!" Kate giggled in a hushed tone. "It's not inside, it's around back!"

"Oh . . . ," he began, his face getting hot. What a stupid thing to say. Of course she wasn't inviting him in. She knew the meaning of propriety.

Kate didn't seem to notice, or care, about his blunder for long. "Follow me," she said, linking her arm in his and pulling him forward. Her touch caught him off guard and his stomach did a somersault with the contact.

They were making their way along the side of the house now, dark bushes and trees surrounding them. When they had made their way around back, they found themselves at a circular rock patio made of large pieces of light-colored sandstone surrounded by beds of all sorts of flowers. Although it was dark, Cal could still make out the variety of bright colors that filled the area along with the greenery. On the patio was elegant white iron patio furniture, looking like a perfect spot to host a charming lunch or dinner party.

"This is nice," Cal commented, glancing around.

"It is, but this isn't it either," Kate said, and began tugging him along. They walked across the patio and to the backend of the yard. In the back corner along the fence, with vines and bushes surrounding it, sat a single white bench of the same style as the furniture on the patio.

Kate let go of Cal's arm and sat down on the bench. "This is my favorite spot. It's just sort of hidden back here, away from everything." She patted her hand on the spot next to her. "Come on, take a seat."

"All right." Cal sat beside her.

"I love this view, sitting here looking out into the garden of flowers. You almost feel hidden from the world beneath all the greenery. It reminds me of *The Secret Garden*. That used to be one of my favorite books when I was younger. I love to read, you know."

"Do you? I didn't know that."

"Oh, yes. I adore reading."

"What kinds of books do you like?"

"All sorts, really. I like the old classics and the modern ones as well." She let out a laugh, and then continued. "Some of the girls here tease me saying I'm always reading a tragedy. But I like those kinds of books. Happy endings just aren't always realistic, you know?"

Her comment caught Cal off guard. "But they can be," he pointed out after a moment.

"I suppose . . . ," she trailed off. "I just think they are more far and few between than most people would like to admit."

"Maybe. But I do think happy endings are out there."

Kate paused thoughtfully and then shrugged. "I will admit I enjoy fairy tales as much as the next girl. But I'm not going to be one to just expect that in life."

Cal watched her carefully, trying to get a grasp at what she was getting at. "Why's that?"

"I guess it just seems like as soon as girls around here graduate from high school they begin pining away, wishing to be swept off their feet and be married. Like it's their ultimate goal and nothing else matters."

Their turn of conversation was beginning to puzzle Cal even more now. But the subject of marriage had never come up before either, and Cal was curious to know more about how Kate felt about it. He was still baffled that she wasn't married. He knew she must have had guys vying for her hand and was surprised she had made it this long. He was twenty-four years old now, and she was twenty-three. She wasn't old by any means, but most girls he knew wanted to get married, and in his experience someone like Kate would usually get snatched up quickly. He had come to assume she just hadn't met the right one yet, but he was beginning to wonder if there was more to it than that. "Maybe those girls are just ready to move on. Ready to find the one they want to settle down with."

Kate hesitated. "I suppose so," she finally answered.

After a few moments of silence, Cal continued, "You know, I have to admit, I was surprised to see you at church on Sunday without a ring on your finger."

Kate's head spun around to him. "And why is that?" There was a hint of both amusement and slight defense in her voice.

Cal hurried to explain himself. "It's just that when I thought of you when I was gone, I figured someone would have swept you off your feet by now. I'm sure many guys have tried."

"You thought of me?" she asked, her eyes peering back at him, a glint of a smile turning the corner of her lips.

As soon as the comment escaped his mouth, he knew he had said too much. He could feel his face growing warm. Why was he always stumbling over his words with her?

"Well, you know . . . maybe in passing a time or two."

Kate looked satisfied but didn't press it any further. She looked down at her hands. "So you thought I'd be married, huh?" She looked back up at him but didn't wait for a response. "Well, you're partially right. I don't know if you remember Peter Johnson from high school. He was my boyfriend for most of senior year, played on the basketball team?"

Cal nodded. "Yeah, I think I remember him." Cal knew exactly who Peter Johnson was. He was the guy Kate had ended up going to the prom with that time he had tried to muster up the guts to ask her to go with him that day in the lunchroom, only to be dejected when she showed up with a fancy boutique of flowers exclaiming to all her friends that Peter had just asked her to the prom.

"Yes, well, I had fun with him in high school, but the moment we graduated he was determined to keep things steady with us. I didn't want to get too serious, but we continued going out. I went with other guys too. But after a year or so, Peter tried to convince me to marry him. He was going to be a doctor, you know, and my mother couldn't understand why I wouldn't want to be a doctor's wife." She shook her head. "But Peter got on my nerves. Looking back, I can't believe I let it go on as long as I did." She paused and sighed. "There have been a lot of others. Guys I've gone steady with, but then they spring marriage on me like it's something to do on their checklist. And that just doesn't interest me." She shrugged her shoulders and then looked off toward the flower garden with a resolute look in her eyes. "I've come to decide that I'm just not the marrying type. I doubt I'll ever marry."

Cal thought his heart couldn't feel any heavier than it already was with the thought of leaving Kate and going off to war in the forefront of his mind, but her words brought on a whole new level to his dismay. "Really?" he asked, his voice cracking. "Why not?" All his hopes of what his and Kate's relationship could be were suddenly being dashed away. He had thought she might be the one for him. But now he realized how foolish he had been.

"There is just too much unknown with marriage," she answered. "This is how I see it. I can live my life comfortably, knowing what to expect, and can be happy without having to rely on someone else. But with marriage you bring in another person your happiness depends on. And I don't like that. I like to be able to know that I plan my life. I determine my happiness, not someone else."

Cal was quiet for a few moments, taking in what she was saying. He had thought about Kate's parents' divorce before, wondered how it had affected her. He figured it had been rough on her, could tell that much by the look in her eyes the first time she told him about it on their walk home clear back in eighth grade. But now he was beginning to think it had been much harder for her to cope with than she ever let on.

"So is it love or marriage or both that you are doubtful about?"

Kate's eyebrows knitted together as if she was searching for the answer herself. "Both, I guess."

It was quiet for several seconds. Finally, Cal spoke up. "It sounds like you're not sure if you can trust your heart to someone else."

"I'm not afraid of my heart being broken because I won't let it happen," she answered quickly.

"I didn't say you were. I just mean that sometimes it's hard to trust. And love, and especially marriage, require a great deal of trust."

She nodded slowly. "Yes, they do."

They sat for a few seconds in silence. Then the seconds turned into minutes. It wasn't an uncomfortable silence, more of a contemplative one. Both knew the other was thinking on what they had just been talking about and both probably wanted to say more, but weren't exactly sure how to say what was on their minds.

Cal had more questions. But he didn't want to make her feel uncomfortable. He thought it might be good if he had some time to think more about it before continuing the conversation.

"The stars are beautiful tonight," he finally said, looking toward the sky.

"They certainly are," Kate responded.

He pointed out the Big Dipper, and Kate pointed out some other constellations she had discovered from reading an astronomy book.

All the while they were talking, in the back of Cal's mind he was thinking about what Kate had said, still trying to register it all. Finally, when their conversation had again died down, Cal looked over at her. "So, I heard from the Army about the war. I've been asked to report to Camp Roberts in California a week from Monday."

"What?" Kate exclaimed, her eyes wide with surprise. "Why didn't you tell me sooner?"

Cal shrugged. "It just never came up, I guess."

Kate shook her head. "Well, of course it didn't; you never mentioned it."

"I didn't want to put a damper on the night by bringing it up."

Kate paused for a moment. "So soon," she said softly.

"I know."

"How are you feeling about it?" she asked.

Cal shrugged. With everything Kate had told him tonight he wasn't sure how to feel about much of anything anymore. He thought he had something to lose by leaving her behind so soon but was beginning to realize she thought of him as nothing more than a friend. And even if there was a chance for something more, he couldn't imagine she was going to open her heart up to him in such a short amount of time. "I'm a little disappointed I'm leaving so soon," he answered. "I hoped I would have a little more time to spend at home before leaving again. But I do want to be out there serving. It's awful the things that are going on all over the world right now. As difficult as I know it will be, I could never just sit back and do nothing while thousands of guys are out there fighting, and dying, to protect our country—and the world, for that matter. It just wouldn't be right. I feel strange here, sort of in limbo just waiting, when I know my duty is out there."

Cal hadn't been looking at Kate as he spoke, his eyes had wandered out into the dark yard ahead of him, but he looked back over at her now. Her eyes were lit up, wide and tenacious. "I know exactly what you mean. Honestly, if women were allowed to, I would be out there fighting along with the men, as unladylike as that sounds."

Cal smiled. "I believe you would."

"I feel the same way you do. I find your answer . . . admirable."

Cal was caught off guard by the sudden warmth in her voice. "Thanks." The way she talked to him and looked at him made Cal feel like there was potential for something more than just a friendship. But she claimed she wasn't interested in love, so why would she want their relationship to develop beyond friendship? But her demeanor, even the way she looked at him, had gradually become more affectionate over the past couple nights as they spent more time together. It felt like more than mere flirtation. It felt like there was something deeper there. But the things she was telling him implied just the opposite.

As Cal left that evening he felt perplexed. Maybe Kate wasn't the one for him after all. Perhaps he should just give up on the idea of her. He could take her out dancing one last time Saturday night for the big band that was coming to town but detach himself from there. If he invested his time and his feelings any further, wouldn't it just end up all the more disappointing in the end?

But he couldn't shrug off the connection he felt with her. He wished he knew just how closed off she really was. Was it just marriage or love altogether she feared? And if he decided to continue seeing her, would the little time they had left to spend together be enough?

Chapter Seventeen

The sound of shoes clapping against the wood floor and occasional hollers and yelps of delight reverberated through the dance hall as the crowd of couples danced the East Coast Swing. The energy flooding through the hall was unlike any of the other nights Cal and Kate had come dancing. The famous band from New York brought a whole new vibe of liveliness and excitement to the floor. Not only that, but the place was chock-full. It seemed to Cal that practically all of Salt Lake must be packed under this roof, dancing the night away.

The dances were coming naturally to him now, to the point where most of the time he could just let loose without having to think about the steps or moves. He was having a grand time and beginning to see why Kate enjoyed dancing so much.

But the dancing and the entertainment was just a small part of his enjoyment. Mostly, it was being there with her. Holding her hands and looking into her eyes delightfully gleaming, wide and alive, soaking in the thrill of it all. She wore a stylish deep-purple satin dress along with matching purple heels. Cal thought the color was very becoming on her, contrasting against her light skin and complementing her dark hair.

When the dance ended, they stopped for a moment to catch their breath. "That was a fun one!" Kate exclaimed.

"Yeah, it was," Cal replied, catching his breath. "Want to take a break for a couple minutes and grab a drink?"

"Sounds wonderful."

They made their way off the dance floor and over to the beverage station along the perimeter of the room. Cal ordered two glasses of sparkling peach punch and handed Kate hers. "Want to step out onto the balcony and cool off?"

"Good idea."

They weaved through the crowds and were soon standing on the balcony next to the railing looking out to the city into the night sky.

"You're really getting the hang of it in there," Kate grinned before taking a sip of her punch.

"It's coming more easily now."

"I can tell you're not having to think about it so much anymore. You're as good as any guy in there!"

"Oh, I don't know about that," Cal chuckled between taking sips.

"So what do you think of the band? Pretty neat, huh?"

"They are great. And it's such a large setup. I think I counted five saxophones and eight trumpets and trombones. Plus they have that whole drum set up and all the other musicians."

"Yes, I believe it's a full seventeen-piece jazz band."

"Wow." Cal had never realized so many parts and instruments went into making music.

"Kind of makes you forget about everything else that's going on in the world being here, doesn't it?" Kate commented, looking off over the balcony.

"It does," Cal agreed.

"I think that's part of the reason I love dancing so much. You can leave your worries aside for a while and just have fun."

"I hadn't thought about it that way before," Cal said, realizing she had a point to what she was saying. "It's probably a good way for people to get their minds off their worries with the war and all."

"Definitely."

With every conversation Cal felt he was gleaning a little more insight and understanding to the person Kate was. She undoubtedly had a strong personality, a zest for life that was contagious. But she had a sensitive side as well, and some guarded feelings as Cal had discovered a couple nights earlier. He realized that her ever-confident persona really wasn't the person she always was down deep. She had some fragile feelings, some difficult things in her past that she hadn't been able to overcome, and distrust seemed to be at the root of her vulnerabilities.

He was no longer thinking of himself and how what she had said affected him. He felt sorry for her that she had carried the hurt of her parents' divorce with her all these years. He wished he could help her open her heart up after it being locked up for so long. Cal understood that relationships could be difficult, had seen it in his own family dynamic, and even on his mission with the many families he had gotten to know. But he also knew that fear shouldn't be a reason to block off one's heart. If Kate truly never wanted to fall in love, never wanted that because it didn't interest her and that wouldn't make her happy, then Cal could accept that. But if it was the fear of trust that was holding her back and he simply gave up on her because of that, he was afraid it would haunt him for the rest of his life.

Although he wasn't exactly sure how he should proceed, he decided he was too far in to back away now. He wanted to build upon what they had, wanted to see if there was something more there. Trying to hold back his mind and heart from leaping forward would be difficult. And he could end up getting hurt in the end. But it was a risk he was willing to take. They had a short time left together now, only a week, so he would make the most of the time they had and simply see what happened.

"So what are your plans for this fall?" Cal asked, looking over at her. "Are you signed up for any classes?"

Kate nodded. "Yes. I'm taking basic accounting and an office management course."

"Sounds interesting."

She nodded. "And how about the dentist's office? Do you plan to stay there?"

"Sure, for now. I enjoy working with the patients and keeping the books."

"I can see you being good at that. You're smart and good with people."

She smiled. "Thanks."

"So, what about long-term? Do you think you'll stay there?"

"I'm not sure. I think I'd like to move into more of an office manager position. I've heard the money can be good working in an attorney's office, but I've also heard the work load and office atmosphere can be a little much to bear. With my experience, I've also thought about being an office manager at a doctor's office or something like that."

"Well, I don't doubt you could do any of those things," Cal responded. "It sounds like you have things figured out."

Kate leaned forward into the railing. "Like I said before, I'd really like to move to a bigger city. New York would be grand." She paused, her eyes narrowing a bit thoughtfully. "But it would be hard leaving my mother. We're really close, you know."

"Are you?"

"Yes. She would never want to hold me back, but I know there's a part of her that probably wishes I would stay close. I have to admit, I'd miss her a lot. And I'd miss it here."

"Sometimes you don't realize how much you love a place until you leave it," Cal said. "I discovered that on my mission."

"I'm sure. I can't imagine being thrown out into a new place like that, especially when you didn't plan it yourself. You're braver than I, I'm afraid."

Cal laughed out loud. "I doubt that."

"Well, I think so." She paused for a moment, eyeing him with intrigue. "You plan to stay in the farming business, right?"

"Yeah, I do," he answered assuredly. "I know the ropes, I've been doing it my whole life. I've really come to realize I enjoy it." He paused for a moment. "Well, let me take that back. Work is work. Of course I don't enjoy every second of it, but I feel satisfaction from it. The livestock business has proved to be advantageous the longer my father has been doing it, and I think I can make a pretty decent living that way.

"I'd still like to raise some crops, but I think the real money-maker is in the animals."

Kate nodded. "I think it's great that you have things figured out."

Cal shrugged. "I'd like to think I do. But the war . . . it could change everything."

"Yeah," Kate sighed thoughtfully. "It's difficult when things feel out of your control, isn't it?"

Cal nodded. "It is."

Kate paused and looked down at her drink in her hands. "You know, my mother knows I don't want to marry. She says she understands why, although I think it disappoints her a little. I know she'd love for me to find a companion, and of course she would love to have grandchildren." Kate stopped and looked up abruptly, her face turning a light shade of red. "I'm sorry, I've said too much."

Cal shook his head. "No, it's fine. You haven't."

She peered at him. "I don't know why I'm talking like this. I'm not one to . . . share about personal things." Her eyes flickered away from him, looking momentarily unsure. Then she looked back at him, meeting his eyes. "It's just that, for some reason, I feel so comfortable with you." Her eyes were quizzical, like she was surprised herself to be saying this.

"I'm glad you do," Cal said, looking back at her steadily.

There was a warm silence between them for a few moments. Then Cal broke the quiet. "Want to go back in for a few more dances?"

Kate smiled. "I'd love to."

Later that evening, the pair ambled back to Kate's dormitory. Kate casually linked her arm through Cal's as she had a couple nights earlier. Cal's heart skipped a beat with the contact and also felt great satisfaction with the gesture. It wasn't as intimate as holding hands, but he felt like they were getting closer. After what she told him on Thursday, he didn't want to rush things, although all he longed for was be close to her.

When they reached the doorstep of the Beehive House, Kate unlinked his arm and walked toward the door. Cal wasn't exactly sure what to do next. But he did know he wanted to see her again, and soon. "Will you be coming out south again tomorrow?" he asked.

"Yes, I usually go home on Sundays. It's a good day to visit my mother."

Cal nodded. He wanted to see her tomorrow but didn't want to take away from her time at home. But he had only a week left. He wanted to take the opportunity to see her when he could. "Maybe we could go on another walk tomorrow, like last Sunday."

"That would be nice, but I had something else in mind."

"Oh?" Cal asked. He could never quite anticipate what she was going to say or do next.

"Would you come have dinner with my mother and me tomorrow night? We like to cook together on Sundays."

Cal couldn't hold back his grin. "That sounds great."

Chapter Eighteen

After attending church services the next morning, Cal returned home and spent some nice downtime with his family. Anna came to visit with her husband and their two young children. His nephew, Matthew, had dark floppy hair and light-blue eyes. Anna told Cal the boy reminded her of him. The little girl, Grace, had beautiful shiny golden locks and a smile that melted Cal's heart. He enjoyed watching the children bound around with endless energy.

Mary had also come to visit with her husband and recently announced they were expecting their first child. As Cal watched his older sisters arrive with their families and his youngest brother, Jack, greet them with a smile, he was suddenly stuck with the thought of how quickly the years had gone by. It was only yesterday he and his siblings were out running around the farm, chasing chickens and trying to scare cows. But now George was gone off to the war and Cal would be soon too. He hoped someday they would all be together again.

While Anna and Mary were busy practicing braiding little Grace's hair, Cal took Matthew out to see the chickens. After their stop by the chicken coop, Matthew rode on Cal's shoulders around the property. Cal pointed out the animals and machinery around the farm. The young boy seemed fascinated with it all. Last, they made a stop by the old tree in the front yard that Cal had loved climbing as a boy.

"See this? It's an apple tree," Cal told Matthew. He lifted the boy up off his shoulders and placed him on the tree's lowest branch.

"Uncle Cal, I'm climbing a tree!"

"You sure are. And you look to be pretty good at it too."

"Yeah, I'm good at lots of things. Momma says."

"She's right," Cal agreed. "Just don't go any higher than this branch here till you're a little older."

"All right, I won't."

Cal smiled at the boy's serious expression. "Did you know this tree used to be my very favorite tree to climb when I was a little boy like you?"

Matthew's eyes were wide with interest.

"It's a great climbing tree for a boy your size," Cal continued. "Has all the right branches. But let me show you the best part." He reached above Matthew's head and plucked off a round, bright-green apple and brought it down to the boy's level. "This tree grows apples. So during the summer you can come out and pick apples right off it and eat them all you want." Cal handed the apple to Matthew, whose eyes were wide with delight. "There you go."

"Yum!" Matthew exclaimed, taking a nibble out of the shiny green fruit.

"Tasty, isn't it?" Cal remarked.

The boy grinned up at Cal. "Tasty, isn't it!" he repeated with a laugh.

A few minutes later Cal and Matthew walked back to the house. They entered the living room where most of the family was sitting. Matthew instantly ran over to Grace and they began entertaining themselves with some small play wooden animals on the floor.

"We were just watching you out the window walking around the yard with Matthew," Anna said to Cal. She was sitting next to the children playing on the floor. "You're really good with him."

Cal shrugged. "I enjoy the kids."

"Yes, I know. Mary and I were just discussing what a great father you'll be someday."

Cal let out a laugh. "Oh, I know where this is going."

"It's not going anywhere," Mary injected. "Just an observation. You do have a great way with the children. Don't you think he does, Father?"

Cal's dad grunted. "Reckon so."

Mary smiled wryly. She had always been the tease in the family. "So, I suppose that means we need to find you a girl," she continued cheekily.

"I was waiting for that," Cal said. "Surprised it took you this long to bring it up, actually."

"You had to know it was coming with two older sisters."

At that moment Cal's mother walked through the door. "What's this talk I hear coming from the kitchen?" she asked, looking amused. She was holding a kitchen rag in her hands, drying them as she spoke.

"We're just trying to help Cal find a girl," Mary smiled.

Suddenly Jack piped in from down on the floor. "Cal doesn't need any help with the gals; he's been going out dancing downtown nearly every night this week."

Anna and Mary's heads whirled in Cal's direction.

"You, Cal Morgan, dancing?" Mary exclaimed. "I don't believe it."

Cal could feel his face beginning to flush, but he quickly shrugged it off. The other day while out working on the farm Jack asked Cal where he had been taking off to at night, and Cal told him about the Coconut Grove. He also told Jack a little about Kate. He wondered if she would be his brother's next announcement. "Guilty as charged," Cal replied with a smile, eyeing Jack.

"How did you learn to dance?" Mary asked.

Cal hesitated. "A girl taught me."

He glanced over at Anna, who was a little less invasive. Her eyebrow turned up in surprise. "And who, might as I ask, is this girl you've been taking dancing?"

"Her name is Kate," Jack announced, grinning at Cal.

"Kate? Kate who?" Mary demanded.

Cal hesitated. He didn't mind sharing details with his family, but telling them her name suddenly made it seem more real. "Kate Clayton," he answered after a moment.

Mary's eyes widened and her jaw nearly dropped to the floor. "Kate Clayton?"

Cal had forgotten that Mary might know who Kate was. Mary had been two grades ahead of Cal in school, so they had attended high school together Cal's freshman and sophomore year. But their school hadn't been that large, and a girl like Kate didn't go unnoticed. She had the reputation of being the pretty, popular girl, and with a personality like hers, of course she would cause a stir.

"Um, yes. That would be her," Cal answered.

"Nice going, Cal!" She looked genuinely impressed. "How did you snatch her up?"

Cal let out a laugh. "Don't act so surprised. Can't I date a pretty girl?"

Cal's mother cut in. "Well, of course you can, dear. Marlene was a very pretty girl."

"Yes, but Mother, you don't know Kate," Mary injected. "She's beautiful and so friendly and fun, not to mention modern and stylish. I sort of always wanted to pick her brain and ask her where she found clothes. Anyhow, well done for yourself, Cal!"

Cal was beginning to feel uncomfortable. In a normal situation this would probably be how conversation would go when a brother started going with a girl. But Cal knew his and Kate's relationship was different and didn't want his family assuming too much when he truly had no idea where it might be going himself.

"We're just friends," he said. "We ran into each other at church last week and ended up talking afterwards. She asked if I would go dancing and I said yes." He was feeling a little on the spot now, all eyes in the room on him. He noticed even his brothers-in-law were honed in on him, looking entertained with the conversation.

"Well, as long as she's a nice girl," his mother chimed in. "I think it's just fine that you've found someone to spend time with before . . . you go." Her eyes faltered.

Suddenly the mood in the room felt different. It had gone from lighthearted and playful to somber in a matter of seconds. Cal glanced around, noticing that everyone's expressions had now changed. He didn't like the foreboding feeling, and knew just what to do to change it.

"Well, Mary, here's something to stew on. She asked me over to have dinner tonight. She and her mother cook together every Sunday."

"What?" she replied, taking Cal's cue to lighten up the tone. "Why didn't you tell us sooner? Dancing, and then dinner with the family?"

Cal noticed his mother smiling at him knowingly. He had already told her earlier that day that he wouldn't be eating dinner with the family tonight, that he had been asked to dinner by a friend. His mother had said that was fine and hadn't pried any further, but now he could see she was putting it together.

Mary smiled. "Sounds like this is shaping up to be more than just a friendship, Cal."

Chapter Nineteen

Kate placed the glass pitcher of water and fresh baked rolls on the table. Then she straightened the tablecloth underneath once more. The table was all set and the chicken was about finished baking.

Her mother had been rather surprised when Kate told her she had invited a guest, in particular a young man, over for dinner. Kate hadn't done that since her high school boyfriend. Sure, there had been plenty of guys, but none of them seemed important enough to take the step and invite them into the home she grew up in. She hadn't been seeing Cal for long, but he was leaving soon and she didn't want to miss an opportunity to spend time with him before he was to go.

Kate took off her apron and set it on the kitchen counter as she watched her mother open the oven, pulling out the chicken dish. "I'll go look out the window and see if there is any sign of him."

"All right, honey," her mother replied with a smile.

Kate walked down the short hallway toward the front door. It was a couple minutes before six and Cal was always right on time. She paused at the mirror at the end of the hallway and took a look at herself. Tucking one side of her chestnut hair behind her ear, she smoothed the other side of wavy curls down. Her hair was cooperating rather well today. Pursing her lips together, she noticed the color on them had faded a bit since she had applied the red lipstick an hour or so before. She rushed into the kitchen, retrieved the miniature bottle from the small basket of odds and ends on the kitchen counter, and brought it back to the mirror. Deftly, she reapplied the color and pressed her lips together in a final touch. Much better.

A moment later she heard a knock at the door. She quickly returned to the kitchen, placed the lipstick back in the basket, and turned to her mother. "That must be him. I'll be right back."

Her mother nodded encouragingly.

Kate turned and made her way to the door, her heels clicking against the hardwood floor as she walked. As she reached for the doorknob, her stomach fluttered. She flinched. It wasn't like her to get butterflies.

She opened the door to see Cal on the doorstep. The butterflies persisted. Cal looked handsome in his navy collared shirt, and his crystal-blue eyes contrasted wonderfully against it.

"Come on in," she said, waving him through the door.

He smiled, revealing the dimples in his cheeks she found quite endearing. "Thanks." He stepped into the small entryway of the home and turned to her. "This is from my mother."

She hadn't noticed until now, but in his hands he held out a pie toward her.

"Thank you," she responded, taking the tin into her hands. She lowered her nose a bit closer to it, taking in the sweet aroma. "Apple?"

Cal nodded as he smiled back at her. His eyes were glinting with something—was it excitement or slight apprehension? He wasn't all that difficult to read, and that was part of why she liked him so much. She could tell that when he was with her he wanted to be. The prospect of what he might expect from their developing friendship had her rather apprehensive, but she was enjoying herself and knew he didn't have much time left, so she wasn't too worried. As much as she liked him she didn't want to get wrapped up in a serious relationship or romance. She'd written herself off that long ago. But she felt safe with Cal. Partially because she knew he was good person, but also because the fact that he was leaving soon and that gave her an easy out. But even so, she found herself wanting to be with him. To get to know him more.

Just then Kate's mother walked around the bend of the hall. "Hello," she said in a pleasant voice.

"Hello, Mrs. Clayton," Cal responded, shifting his gaze from Kate to her mother. He extended his hand out toward her.

She took Cal's hand in hers and gave it a quick, gentle shake. "Nice to meet you."

"Likewise," he replied warmly.

"Look what Cal brought us," Kate injected, holding the pie up.

"How lovely," her mother smiled. "We didn't prepare a dessert, so this will be perfect."

Kate noticed Cal seemed comfortable, yet slightly nervous, upon her mother's arrival. He seemed to care about the little things much more than men she had gone with in the past, and she liked that.

"Well, let's go sit down," her mother said.

Kate looked at Cal and smiled. They turned and followed her mother into the kitchen.

❧

An hour later they sat at the table, spoons clinking against their dessert dishes as they indulged in the apple pie Cal's mother had baked just hours before.

Kate's mother listened intently while Cal talked about growing up on the farm and how he would soon be leaving for training camp in California. Kate could tell her mother liked Cal. She was a polite and tactful woman, but Kate knew her well enough to be able to tell when she was pleased. And with Cal, she was.

"Well, it was very kind of your mother to send this pie," Kate's mother said. "She needn't have gone to the work of making a pie just to send it off."

"Oh, it was no trouble," Cal assured her. "We have an apple tree in our front yard at home and mother is doing everything she can to use up those apples before they go to waste. I believe she has three more pies back at home." He smiled crookedly.

"Well, tell her thank you from us nonetheless," she responded, her eyes smiling.

When they finished eating and were ready to clear the table

Kate and her mother stood and began reaching for the dishes. Cal stood up and began to help, gathering dishes as well.

Kate reached out to him next to her and grabbed hold of his lower arm. "Let us clear the table," she said to him with a raised eyebrow. "You're our guest." She knew she was keeping her hold on him a few moments longer than she needed to, but she liked having an excuse to touch him.

Cal looked over at her and took hold of her hand, lowering it back down. The feel of his hand against hers sent a wave of warmth through her body. "I'd like to help, if you don't mind," he said with a smile.

He wasn't easy to argue with, which was something Kate wasn't used to. Usually she was all but champing at the bit to find a reason to put a person in their place, whether playfully or in a serious context. But she found herself continually derailed by Cal's sincere, straightforward nature. Strangely, she found it made her want to be more sincere herself.

"How thoughtful of you," Mrs. Clayton chimed in, eyeing Kate.

Kate watched Cal as he gathered dishes and took them to the sink pleasantly, not a hint of aversion on his face. She found herself realizing that his gracious, respectful attitude made him just as attractive as his good looks.

After they finished clearing the table, Cal and Kate chatted with Kate's mother a little longer before excusing themselves. They decided to take a walk along the dirt lane outside Kate's home. She had somewhere she wanted to take him.

They began walking, fields of tall golden cornstalks surrounding them. Purple and yellow wildflowers were scattered along the border of the lane, adding dabs of vibrant color to the serene landscape.

Kate's eyes were focused on the western mountains where the sun was lowering in the evening sky close to the horizon. Thus far their conversion had been light and casual.

"We're almost to the spot," she said. They walked around a bend and followed the path down the slight curve of a hill to approach the gigantic weeping willow tree. Graceful sweeping branches of light green leaves cascaded down as the evening sun shimmered through its foliage.

"This tree is huge," Cal commented with awe. "Must be forty feet tall."

"Yeah," Kate responded. "This is what I wanted to show you. My favorite spot." She walked toward the tree to just below its branches hanging down and turned around to look at Cal.

Cal nodded, looking up at the tree. "I can see why."

"I haven't been out here in awhile. But it's just as I remember it." She turned and began walking under the branches, and then glanced back to Cal and waved him forward. "Want to come sit under it with me?"

Cal's eyebrows rose. "You don't mind sitting on the ground in your dress?"

A laugh escaped Kate's lips. "I'm not afraid of a little dirt if you aren't."

He grinned. "Fine with me."

They walked together and sat side by side. Cal propped his back against the thick trunk with his knees up. Kate sat next to him with her legs tucked to the side.

"The sun's starting to set," Cal commented, nodding toward the horizon. Pink and orange were beginning to dust the sky.

Kate nodded. "I love sunsets. And this is the perfect place to watch one."

"So when did you first start coming here, to this favorite place of yours?" Cal asked.

"Oh, not too long after we moved here." Kate paused for a moment, her mind flashing back to the day that she first discovered this spot.

She could remember the fiery feeling in her veins as she had stormed out the door of her house and escaped down the dirt lane, desperate to find somewhere she could be alone.

She chuckled. "My poor mother. I'm afraid that at times I was quite the dramatic teenage girl to deal with. We had gotten in an argument that day—I can't remember what about exactly. Probably something about moving, or . . . the divorce." She felt herself choke on the word as it came out, and was surprised it still stung a little. "Anyhow, I ran out of the house and down this lane just trying to get away. And I found this tree. I sat here and cried and cried. But it felt good to get it all out." Kate realized she had been looking at the ground in front of her, fidgeting with a loose string on her dress. She looked over to Cal.

He was looking back at her with understanding eyes. "I'm sorry. It makes me feel bad to know you had such a hard time back then."

Kate waved her hand toward him and laughed. "Oh, it was fine. I was being overly sensitive, not to mention a royal pain for my mother." She smirked. "But, as time went on, things got better." Better, or had she just learned to shut it out? She wasn't quite sure herself. "But from then on, I would come here. Not just on bad days, but on good days too. Sometimes I brought books to read, sometimes my journal to write in. A lot of times I would just come to sit."

Cal nodded. "It's nice to have a place to escape to."

They were silent for a few moments. Her thoughts went back to her early teenage years when she had been young and hopeful. She remembered countless times sitting against this tree imagining what her future husband would be like. She had always pictured a dashing, tall, dark, and handsome man sweeping her off her feet. They would live an adventurous life yet stable in love. Perhaps have a child or two. But as she grew into her older teenage years she couldn't reconcile her dream man with the hurt from her parents' divorce, and eventually the latter won out. As she gained experience and understanding of how the world really worked, how love stories in the books and picture shows really weren't all that realistic, she decided love was something she could live without.

But the problem was, she liked going out with beaus too much to keep completely away from them. She couldn't deny she enjoyed the attention the boys always gave her in her school years, so she went out with many of them. They always swooned over her, told her she was beautiful, and many professed their love for her. But in the end, they were all the same.

She'd had the same experience after graduating high school. At first the thrill of going out with older, graduated men had been new and exciting. But soon it became repetitive, and sometimes boring. Although courting was sometimes tiresome, she still enjoyed the attention, and found she usually had the upper hand in relationships. They always seemed hurt but not all that surprised when she broke up with them. She supposed many of them probably expected it; she had sort of gained that reputation. But she didn't really mind. She never had the desire or attention span to keep any of the relationships going for too long, anyway.

But now, sitting here with Cal, she found herself a little perplexed. She didn't know why she was carrying on with him other than because she simply enjoyed his company. And of course there was the undeniable attraction between the two of them. She felt it, and she knew he felt it too. But more than that she found herself wanting to be with him, to find out more about him. And that was a foreign feeling for her.

"So," she began, directing her eyes back to him. "What about you?"

Cal let out a chuckle. "What about me?" he asked, his face amused. He leaned forward a bit closer.

"Oh, I don't know. What makes you you?" she said in a half teasing, half serious tone.

"Hmm . . . ," Cal responded, looking as if he was searching for what to say next. "Well, I'd like to tell you I'm the most exciting guy you've ever met, but I think we both know that's not the truth."

She laughed. "No, I don't mean that. I know who you are, and I think you give yourself too little credit by the way. It's just . . . " She paused, looking into his eyes. What was it she was searching for? An answer to why she was intrigued with this small town farm boy? Or perhaps a reason to run? "Well, what about your mission? I feel like we haven't talked much about that, and you were there for three whole years."

Cal nodded. "What do you want to know?"

"Let's see. What was your most memorable experience while you were there?" Kate heard of people who had served missions that had experienced everything from being fed strange, sometimes downright disgusting food to being chased off the doorsteps of houses they had knocked by rabid dogs and even men with guns. It seemed that missions always produced a few amusing stories.

"It's kind of hard to narrow it down to just one story," Cal began. "But there was this one time . . ." He paused for a moment, looking out over the field. He shifted his eyes back toward Kate's. "The experience I'm thinking of, it probably isn't your typical favorite mission story. It actually happened under really sad circumstances. But for me, it kind of defines what the mission experience was to me."

Kate nodded, urging him on. She wasn't expecting this serious side of him, but was curious to hear what he had to say all the same.

"There was a family we got acquainted with while we were out there, the Hammond family," he continued. "We didn't know them very well, but our mission president did. They were really good people. They weren't members of our church but were friendly toward the missionaries. We sort of just had a mutual understanding with them. We had different beliefs, but they respected us and appreciated that we were trying to do good and spread God's word." He paused for a moment. "Anyway, one day we got a phone call from our mission president." Cal looked down at the ground, as if what he was about to say next was difficult. "And he told us that the Hammond's twelve-year-old daughter had been killed in an automobile accident."

Kate inhaled sharply. "Oh, how awful."

"Yeah, it was. The whole family was devastated." He looked out over the field again, a far-off look in his eyes, as if he was taking himself back to that day. "Our mission president told us what happened and explained that the family had a funeral to prepare, but they were too stricken and devastated to do it themselves. They didn't have any family or close friends that could help them with it. So me and my companion at the time . . . we did it."

Kate peered at Cal. "You . . . prepared a funeral?"

Cal nodded and looked back over at him. "Yeah, we did. But it wasn't just the arranging of the funeral. They also wanted us to speak at it." He sighed, a daunted look in his eyes. "Now, you have to understand, I had never even attended a funeral before. The idea of funerals, and really death altogether, was new to me. Kind of like something you hear about, but doesn't really affect you, you know? I had no idea what a funeral was even like." He rocked back and shook his head, and then leaned against the tree. "But, amazingly, it all worked out. Our arrangements came together nicely and our talks went well." He paused for a moment and then looked at her, his eyes suddenly intense. "I prayed so hard that I could say something that would comfort them, something that would give them some hope during that dark time." He shook his head. "I don't remember much of what I said except that I told them that I knew one day they would be reunited with their daughter, that they would see her again." He paused for a few moments. "After the service the family was so appreciative of everything we had done. Just so grateful. And they told me what I said was just what they needed to hear. It's something I'll never forget."

He stopped and looked away for a moment, and then back at Kate. "Anyway, like I said, not your typical favorite mission story. It was probably the saddest thing I ever saw out there. But at the same time, we were able to do something for that family that they weren't able to do for themselves. We were able to ease their burden, and that meant a lot to me."

The look in Cal's eyes held a sort of sadness and sincerity all at once. And at that moment something struck Kate. Cal was a truly good person. He had the best interest of others at the core of his intentions. She knew there weren't many people like that out there, and certainly not many men she had gone with. It was a trait she found greatly respectable and appealing. Not only that, but there was a depth to him she hadn't recognized before. He wasn't just the nice, good-looking farm boy she had grown up with. Over the years he had grown into a man of great moral character with an intensity and deepness that surprised her. Or maybe this was the person he had always been, but up until now Kate had just been too blind to see it?

When they began walking back to Kate's home, it was dusk. The sun had set and the fields surrounding them felt tranquil and still. Kate felt more at ease than she had in a long time.

Walking side by side in comfortable silence, their arms brushed against each other. Kate continued forward slowly, liking the closeness at which they were walking. Then suddenly she felt Cal gently take hold of her hand. Her heart skipped a beat with the contact. For the first few moments she held her breath, surprised at the effect the small yet intimate gesture was having on her. It wasn't like her to get flustered by something so simple. She had held hands with plenty of guys before.

But this felt different. It felt easy and comforting. And it wasn't just the rush of the contact that left her feeling almost breathless; it was the thought that she knew his touch was imparting something more.

He brushed his thumb over the top of her hand and looked over at her, giving her a subtle smile. Even through the dim light, his piercing blue eyes gleamed in the darkness. She imagined they were the color of the ocean in some warm and exotic location, like the Caribbean or the French isles.

She smiled back at him and then looked forward. Then she felt a familiar, gnawing knot in her stomach and closed her eyes for a moment.

We are just friends. This is nothing. I've gone out with a hundred guys before. Why should this be any different?

But something deep inside her told her that this wasn't like the others. He wasn't like the others. The way she felt with him wasn't like the others.

She couldn't deny it, but at the same time wasn't quite sure what to make of it, either.

All she knew was that in this moment she couldn't have felt more content.

Chapter Twenty

The week went by much too fast. As Cal prepared to leave, he worked during the day on the farm as usual and began to get his things put together that he would be taking with him, although there wasn't much. But mostly, his priority was Kate. He wanted to spend as much time with her before he left as possible.

Their relationship had escalated into something more, but what that was, he wasn't sure. All he knew was that he wanted to be with her while he still could, because in all reality it could be the last time he would ever get to spend with her. Cal was an optimistic person but also a realist, and he realized there was a good chance that she wouldn't be around when he returned from the war. Who knew what a year or two, or more than that, would bring. She could be moved off to some city far away, content in her new life, or in a new relationship. She told Cal she never wanted to marry, but at the root of his fears was that she would find someone while he was gone and that he would return only to find he lost out to another.

That is, if he did return at all.

Cal was continually hearing of guys he knew, or knew through mutual friends and acquaintances, that had been killed in the war. Each time he heard the news, it made him sick to his stomach, especially when he thought of his own brother out there. In George's letters, he still said he hadn't faced much battle yet, but there was no telling when he might. And now there was a looming feeling hanging over Cal, knowing that could very well be him.

Throughout his remaining week Cal spent a lot of time with Kate. They went dancing at the Coconut Grove a couple more times. One night they went to a picture show at the beautiful Capitol Theater downtown, enjoying the elegant architecture and design of the theater, and of course the wonderful live entertainment that preceded the show. One evening he took her out to eat at the Mayflower Café downtown on Main Street for fish-and-chips, which were new to the city and relatively unknown until the restaurant's chef had brought them to town. A recipe straight from England, the chef had said. Cal and Kate both thought the meal was divine.

Soon Saturday rolled around, which would be their last night out together. Cal wanted to take her to do something different, something special. He decided they would spend the evening at Liberty Park.

First they rode a rowboat out on the lake, talking and laughing as they went. Cal teased Kate, giving the small boat a shake as if it was about to tip, making her yelp and laugh in delight. Cal knew that whatever they might be doing, it would be exciting and memorable with Kate. He loved that about her.

After finishing the boat ride, they headed to the park's Ferris wheel. They sat side by side and held hands as they rode the gigantic wheel up and down. After a few moments Cal reached his arm around Kate and held her close as they rode. As Cal looked over at her, he focused in on her lips. He longed to kiss her, had been wanting to all week, but hadn't quite worked up the nerve to do it. Although they had come to know each other very well, Kate was still Kate, and she still intimidated him a little. Not only that, but he was also afraid what she might think. Would it scare her away?

Since they had held hands almost a week ago walking down the lane outside Kate's house, they had become closer and closer. It felt more like they were a couple now than just friends. They had held hands each time they spent together since and were becoming more comfortable together.

"Such a beautiful night," Kate commented as they looked out

over the darkening park. The Ferris wheel's colorful lights glowed, lighting up the dimming night sky.

Cal nodded as he looked over at Kate, admiring her beauty. Something he always did when he was with her.

When he dropped her off the night before after dancing, they had been facing each other holding hands. They lingered that way for a few moments, looking into each other's eyes. The moment seemed perfect and he began to lean in, thinking it was the opportunity he had been waiting for. But, at the very last moment, he second-guessed himself, turned, and kissed her lightly on the cheek instead.

But now, tonight, he knew he wanted to kiss her. He had to. Their time was running out. Although he wasn't sure exactly where they stood, he knew he'd regret it if he didn't take the chance to. But the anticipation had built up so much, Cal was almost hesitant to make the move for merely the worry that it wouldn't live up to either of their expectations. He knew she was probably expecting it, hoping she was at least, but he wasn't sure where or when that should be. He wanted it to be special, something they would both remember. And now here on the Ferris wheel, looking over the beautiful park at dusk, seemed like the perfect time.

He scooted over to her a bit closer. They were going down the turn of the wheel now. She turned toward him, her lips curling up in a slight smile. He took in a breath. This was it. He began leaning in closer to her, so close he could anticipate the feel of her lips against his. Suddenly the Ferris wheel came to an abrupt stop. The small cart they were riding in jolted forward and then back. Cal looked up. They were at the bottom of the wheel.

"Next!" he heard the boy directing the Ferris wheel line shout out while waving Cal and Kate out.

Inwardly Cal sighed. He offered Kate his hand from behind as she stepped off the contraption. He followed her and shook his head to himself. Well, that hadn't turned out how he wanted.

But there was still time.

❧

Kate wrapped her arms around herself as a gentle, cool breeze brushed by. She and Cal had just stood from the rod iron bench where they had been sitting watching the picture show. Saturday night movies at

Liberty Park shown on one of the two stages in the park were rather famous in the Salt Lake Valley.

They caught the tail end of the cartoons after riding the Ferris wheel and then the main film began. It was the mega-hit romantic comedy that had been released nearly a decade earlier, *It Happened One Night*, staring the handsome Clark Gable and elegant Claudette Chauchoin. Both Cal and Kate thoroughly enjoyed the show, sitting close and smiling and laughing through the film.

Kate had visited Liberty Park and watched picture shows before with friends, but never before had a beau brought her here. She hadn't thought of it before, but it really was quite a romantic setting.

The pair meandered side by side across the park on their way back to Cal's truck in no real hurry to get there. The trees in the park were large and their branches spread out low to the ground. As they weaved through the giant, lush, dark greenery, Cal reached out and took hold of her hand. His touch was welcomed and comforting to her, although she still felt a wave of excitement each time she felt it.

The crowds were dispersing, the movie watchers heading home for the night, and the park was beginning to feel more and more secluded. Wandering through the dark canopying trees, they were walking alongside the lake now. The stars glimmered off the water, looking like magical dancing lights reflecting off the night sky.

They paused for a moment, standing hand in hand, looking out over the lake. Kate glanced up at Cal and could see the glow of the moon catch his crystal-blue eyes. He was staring out over the water, seeming to be lost in thought.

"What are you thinking about?" she asked. Playfully eyeing him, she continued, "How I almost dunked you into the lake when we were out on the row boat?"

A subtle smile formed on his lips. "Something like that." Then he turned to her. "But if I recall correctly, it was me who almost had you in the water."

"True. But you know if you would have, I would have pulled you in right after me."

Cal nodded. "I know. I like that about you."

Kate felt her cheeks flush. He was increasingly having this effect on her.

But she knew what he must have really been thinking about

looking out over the lake. What she knew had been in the back of both of their minds the whole evening. That he would be leaving Monday morning. He had invited her over to his family's house for dinner the next night, which she was looking forward to. She felt a sweeping sense of sadness knowing this would be their last night out together, and the sadness surprised her.

"Are you nervous?" Kate asked softly.

Cal shrugged. "A little. It's not nerves so much as this dreading feeling."

Kate nodded. "It must be really hard to have to turn around and leave your family right after you just got back to them. It's only been a few weeks since you returned from your mission, after all."

Cal glanced down for a moment, let out a short chuckle, and shook his head. Then he looked back at her. "I'll miss my family, but it's not them my mind is on." He was looking into her eyes intently.

It was quiet for a few moments, but then he slowly reached his hand to her face and lightly stroked the side of her cheek with his thumb. She could feel her heart beating faster with the gentle touch of his fingers against her skin. She held her breath.

"It's you," he whispered, his voice rough.

Then he stepped in closer to her, so close that she could hear the steady sound of his breathing. Still lightly cradling her face in one hand, he gently tilted her head up toward him. She waited, breathlessly, for what she knew would be coming next.

She closed her eyes and felt his lips meet hers, soft and tenderly. She reached her arms up around his neck, pulling herself into him.

Secluded from all but the stars and the moon in the sky, their reflection dancing off the lake, they were both completely lost. Lost in the moment, and lost in each other.

Chapter Twenty-One

Cal breathed a sigh of relief. Dinner had gone wonderfully with his family and Kate. Of course she had charmed them as she always did everyone, but he had been slightly worried his large and rather rambunctious family might overwhelm her.

But it seemed quite the opposite. Kate kept up with all their friendly banter and got along very well with all of them. He enjoyed having her around with them more than he realized he would.

After everyone left, Cal and Kate were sitting in the living room next to each other on the couch. They were finally alone.

Cal looked over at Kate and took a hold of her hand. "Ready to head back?"

"No," she said, scooting a bit closer to him, resting her head against his shoulder.

Cal's heart thudded, a strange mixture of happiness and gloom rushing over him. He loved having her near, sitting close to him. But soon that would all be over.

They sat for a few moments in silence, simply enjoying one another's company. A few moments later, Kate's head popped up. "Will you show me around the farm?"

A crooked smile crossed Cal's mouth. "I guess so. What do you want to see?"

"Oh, I don't know. We could just walk around the property. You talk about it so often, I want to see where it is you do all this work of yours. Make sure you're not making it all up." She grinned at him, her eyes teasing.

"All right. Let's go."

Soon they were standing on the property behind the Morgan's home. Hand in hand, Cal led her around. First he took her by the small barn where they kept a few pigs and chickens. As they walked away from the barn and through tall grass toward the Morgan's field, the sun was setting behind the western mountains, leaving the sky dimly glowing and dusted with pastel colors. Cal looked over at Kate. "So now you've seen the pigs. Smelly, huh?"

"Yes, they are," she agreed, amused.

"If I recall correctly," he continued, "when we were walking home from school on the first day of eighth grade you said you thought pigs were cute. Still think so now?"

Kate's tilted her head back and laughed. "I did, didn't I?" Then she paused for a moment. "You remember that I said that?"

"Of course," he answered. He wanted to tell her he remembered every word she had said that day, and every day following that he had been lucky enough to talk with her. He had thought back over their conversations hundreds of times, replaying them all in his head. But he worried what she might think if he divulged all that. "I remember more than just that," he said carefully. "I remember you said the ocean was your favorite place in the world."

She nodded, eyeing him with a curious expression. "I did say that."

"Is it still?" he asked.

"Definitely," she replied without hesitation. "You'll probably get to see a lot of the ocean in California. And wherever they send you after that."

"Yeah, I guess you're right." He turned to her. "I wish I could see it with you."

"Me too," she replied.

Looking down at her, he could think of only one thing. He hadn't kissed her since the night before. Although he'd wanted to all day, there hadn't been any chance to with his family around all night, until now. He thought back to the night before, when they had shared that first kiss under the stars on the bank of the lake at Liberty Park. He had kissed her again on her doorstep when he dropped her off afterward. Since the moment he left the night before, and all day today, his mind kept wandering to kissing her again.

He thought back to the times he had kissed Marlene, which he thought he had enjoyed up until now. It didn't come close to comparing to last night with Kate. Kissing her was different: full of emotion and passion, and so much more meaningful than he had realized a simple kiss could be. But everything was different with Kate.

He reached his arm around her waist and slowly stepped in closer to her. Then he tilted his head downward, toward hers. At first their lips brushed lightly. He moved his head back slightly and could feel her smile between their kiss. He moved in again, more forcefully this time, scooping her into his arms and kissing her firmly for a few prolonged seconds. Then he pulled back. "I've been waiting for that all day," he murmured.

She laughed. "Me too."

They continued their walk around the farm, pausing every so often for a kiss along the way. He walked her by the shed where they stored all their machinery and supplies, past the fields where they kept the cows, and pointed up the road toward the five acres of land they raised their thousands of heads of sheep on.

When they finished and were walking back to the house, Cal looked over at Kate. "Thanks. That was a lot of fun showing you around." He squeezed her hand. It amazed him how much he enjoyed having her here, showing her around his life, his world.

"I like seeing you in your element," she said, smiling up at him.

"I'm glad."

Soon they were sitting side by side in Cal's truck, driving back downtown for Cal to drop her off. He tried swallowing down the nervous, hard lump that was beginning to form in his throat. It had started when he first picked her up that afternoon. But then they had been with his family and had walked around the farm, and he was able to forget their situation for a moment, pretend he wasn't about to leave the next morning. But now there was no getting around it—tonight was the last time he would see her before leaving in the morning, and possibly ever.

He had told her the time his train was departing but she hadn't said anything about coming and he didn't want her to feel obligated to. He knew she had to work. It might be just as well they say good-bye tonight in private instead of in the busy setting of the train station in front of his whole family.

Cal pulled up the street next to the Beehive House and parked his truck. It was dark now, past eleven o'clock. He stepped out of the truck and walked around her side to open her door.

They began walking up the sidewalk to the door in silence. Cal's feet felt like they weighed a hundred pounds each as he walked, dreading this moment. Dreading saying goodbye.

When they reached the porch, Kate turned to Cal.

"Well . . . ," he began, letting out a nervous breath. His stomach was twisting. He wished he could feel calm, but he felt just the opposite. It was an unnerving feeling knowing he was leaving her behind.

Suddenly he felt cheated, robbed even. Robbed of time with her. *It shouldn't have to be like this,* he thought. *I shouldn't have to leave her right as things are going so well.*

But there was no getting around it. This, he knew, could be the last time he would ever see her. Looking into her eyes he let out a regretful sigh. "I guess this is it."

Kate lifted an eyebrow at him, and the corner of her mouth turned up. "You don't think I'm going to let you off that easy, do you?"

Her response surprised him. He let out a nervous chuckle. He paused and glanced down, and then looked back up at her. "I'm just trying to be realistic here, Kate. You've told me how you feel about . . . relationships. In the beginning I just sort of figured that us going out together was, I don't know, just for fun. But for me these past two weeks have meant so much more than that." He was looking into her eyes trying to read her, to get some sort of grasp on how she was feeling.

He continued, "Going away right now is the last thing in the world I want to do. And like I said last night, that's because of you." He reached out and gently took hold of her hands. Looking down at their hands intertwined, he could think of nothing but that being with her just felt right. It was that simple. He ran his thumbs over the top of her hands and then looked up at her and took a deep breath. "I'm not sure where we stand in your mind, Kate. But if you have any hopes that someday, if I was to return, we could be something more, please let me know. Because that's all I want."

He held his breath, waiting for her response. Her eyes had been cast downward making him unable to see her reaction to what he said. But as soon as she lifted her head, slowly looking up at him, he could see the shadow of reluctance in her eyes.

Kate bit her lower lip and then breathed out a sigh. "I have so enjoyed our time together, Cal. And thank you for everything. For putting up with the dancing, taking me to the movies, and last night at the park . . . ," she trailed off. He knew last night stuck out in both their minds as something they would never forget. "And mostly for what a gentleman you have been. But I just . . . I can't make any commitments. You know that a long-term relationship isn't what I want." She paused and looked down. "I'm sorry, I just—"

He shook his head and lifted a hand up to stop her, letting go of their grasp. A sinking feeling in his stomach was taking over. "It's okay; you don't have to explain. I understand."

Her eyes were wide and despondent and suddenly glistening with tears. Her face and expression were telling him one thing, and her words was telling him another. But he wasn't going to try to persuade or convince her of what she was feeling.

They stood in silence. The air between them suddenly felt thick and slightly uncomfortable. Cal didn't like it. This was the last way he wanted to leave things off between them. But there was no turning around the conversation now, and he didn't want to drag it out.

He leaned forward and placed a gentle kiss on her right cheek. He longed to turn and meet her lips, to have one last departing kiss, but he knew now that would only make things more difficult.

He took a step backward and swallowed hard. "Take care, Kate," he said. Then he turned and began walking down the sidewalk, away from her.

His body felt tingly and numb. He couldn't comprehend how things could change so quickly, how he could go from feeling so alive and hopeful to a complete feeling of disappointment so fast. With each step he took, he could feel his heart sinking lower.

"Wait, Cal!" he heard Kate's voice call from behind him.

The sound of her voice sent a chill through his body. He turned around slowly, meeting her gaze. It was difficult to make out her expression through the darkness, but he thought he could see the glisten of a teardrop slowly running down her cheek.

She stood there silent, looking as if she was searching for what to say. The seconds he waited for what was about to escape her lips felt like an eternity. Finally the sound of her voice floated through the darkness to him. "Please, be safe."

He paused for a moment, trying to muster up something to say back to her. For those few moments, he hoped she was going to tell him she had got it wrong, that she felt the same way he did. They were meant to be together. But that wasn't it at all.

He took a deep breath. "I'll try," he replied back.

He stood looking at her for a few seconds longer, waiting to see if she had anything left to say. But she stood still, unspeaking. He took a moment to take in her image, knowing this would undeniably be the last time he would see her. Then he turned and began walking in the direction of his truck, telling himself not to look back.

After a couple steps, he fell into a steady stride, knowing the sooner he reached his truck and drove away the sooner he could leave behind the haunting image of her standing there on the porch, watching him walk away.

After getting into the truck, he sat with his hands rested on the wheel for a few moments, lost in thought.

As he pulled away, he knew he was about to begin the most slow and difficult, and likely impossible process, of his life. Forgetting her.

Chapter Twenty-Two

Camp Roberts, California

Cal stood straight and tall with his arms tight against his torso. To both sides of him a line of soldiers fanned out, forming one long line. It was hot and dry, and Cal's mouth felt parched. He wasn't exactly sure what time it was but he knew it was nearing midday, and the blazing desert sun was beating down on him. He was wearing his full army uniform—boots, pants, shirt, jacket, and cap—which wasn't exactly ideal attire for a hot day in the California desert. He knew a drink of water wasn't a possibility until they reached the mess hall for lunch, so he tried to push the thirst from his mind.

He was beginning week two of his seventeen-week training at Camp Roberts. He had traveled there on Union Pacific, his train crossing the Great Salt Lake, jetting across Utah and Nevada, and then onto California. Camp Roberts was located about halfway between San Francisco and Los Angeles. Cal had never been to California but knew from maps that this put them about smack dab in the middle of the state.

The men were told Camp Roberts was one of the largest military training facilities in the world. At 42,784 acres, the facility was capable of housing 30,000 trainees at once. Upon arrival Cal had been in awe at the large, sprawling property with miles of training fields and endless rows of two-storied whitewashed wooden barracks for housing soldiers. There were hundreds of privates' barracks, each of which housed eighty soldiers and were accompanied by mess halls, chapels, supply rooms, and an administration office. He hadn't been sure what to expect when arriving at training camp, and had no idea he was about to enter something of this size and magnitude. Camp Roberts was home to the world's largest parade field. It was the length of fourteen football fields and used for drilling and marching, which had been mentioned to Cal's unit numerous times by the drill sergeants there. They seemed rather proud of that fact.

The camp hosted a replacement training center for infantry and field artillery. The men knew that once they completed the training they would be shipped off as replacements to various infantry divisions within the army—infantry referring to the branch of the army that fights on foot. As infantry soldiers they would be trained to engage in face-to-face combat with the enemy. They could be sent anywhere in the world, wherever the army needed replacements. They would replace soldiers that had fallen and join companies of soldiers that had already been fighting.

The men were now about to begin a training drill, although they hadn't been told yet what that would be. Cal looked out ahead at the flat desert landscape of dirt and sagebrush dotted with trees every so often. It definitely was one of the more desolate places he had ever seen. He had thought the Salt Lake Valley seemed rather barren after returning from the south, but this had his hometown beat by a long shot.

A drill sergeant slowly walked down the line of soldiers, scrutinizingly eyeing them as he went. His boots heavily crunched the dirt beneath his feet with every step. "All right, soliders," he called out in an authoritative voice. "It's time for our next training drill. You will now be instructed on how to pitch a tent."

Cal heard snickers from a few soldiers around him. "We need training in weapons, not some measly tents," said a scoffing whisper a few men down.

The drill sergeant was twenty or so feet down the line. Cal wasn't sure if he had been within range to hear the grumblings of the men, but as the sergeant slowly turned on his heel to face them, Cal could see his eyes were narrowed, an indignant expression on his face. Yes, he must have heard them.

"It appears there are a few of you who think this exercise is some kind of joke." He spat on the words as they came out of his mouth. He was facing them full on now, his voice growing louder with each word. "But in less than three months when you are out on the frontlines of some wretched battlefield and night falls, and freezing rain begins pouring down on you soaking your sorry carcass to the bone, and you're more miserable than you ever thought you could be, you're going to thank your lucky stars we taught you to pitch a measly tent in basic training." He stopped, glaring over the faces of the men. Then he continued in a low, aggravated voice. "Is there anyone who still thinks this exercise is something to laugh about?"

There was nothing but silence.

"That's what I thought," he remarked. He turned and gestured to a drill sergeant standing behind him and off to the side. "Sergeant Parker is going take over the demonstration from here."

The sergeant stepped forward and began showing them the materials they'd be given to pitch tents with and demonstrated how to do it. They broke into groups and began.

A lot of the guys grumbled about the stringent nature of the camp, but coming into it Cal had expected as much. He had known hard work and a strict set of rules his whole life. The soldiers had their hair cut in short matching military cuts, wore identical uniforms expected to be perfectly pressed at all times, and made their beds just so with crisp hospital corners and the covers tucked in so tight that if their commanding officer were to throw a quarter on the bed it had better bounce. Cal had to admit, the atmosphere was fairly rigid. Not to mention the exhaustive daily drills they were to perform with precision.

Cal often thought about his brother George and how he might have handled the training camp having never been away from home before. George had also been sent to Camp Roberts for basic training, and Cal regularly found himself wondering if his brother had participated in the same drills he had and even walked the same grounds he had been. It was comforting to know George's upbringing and experience with hard work on the farm would have helped him out here.

It hadn't been as hard of an adjustment for Cal to be away from home as it was for some of the others. He had already been away from home so long, it hadn't fazed him much. In the short time he had been at camp, he was already beginning to see a change among many of the soldiers, making the transformation from boys to men. Some of them were just that—boys, likely barely graduated from high school.

For Cal, the hardest part was leaving Kate the way he did. He hadn't talked to or heard from her since that last night on her doorstep when he had said goodbye and walked away. He didn't regret what he had done. There hadn't been many other options of how he could have reacted to what she said. But he still wished things could have ended differently between them. He had held out hope that she would decide to see him off at the train station. Then maybe they could have patched up what had happened the night before. But she hadn't.

He had really thought, or maybe just hoped, she felt something more for him. But he was working hard to accept the fact that he had likely been wrong all along.

Chapter Twenty-Three

Kate was sitting on the wooden bench on the front porch of her mother's home with a book on her lap. She was trying to concentrate on the novel, but her mind kept wandering off. Finally she clapped the book shut with a sigh.

She hadn't noticed her mother standing behind her at the doorway. "Not up for reading today?" she asked.

Kate shook her head and turned to face her. "I suppose not." She had come home for the weekend because she hadn't felt up to going out with her friends dancing like they had talked about. She felt more tired than usual and decided she simply needed a weekend home with the comforting companionship of her mother. She was sure that could cheer her spirits.

"Your eyes look a bit dark," he mother commented. "Do you have a headache?"

Kate shook her head. "No. Just a little tired." She paused. "I haven't been sleeping very well the past few nights."

Her mother's expression turned a bit concerned. "Perhaps you should lie down for a nap."

"No, I'm fine," Kate responded with a shake of her head, forcing herself to impart a subtle smile.

Her mother took a few steps forward and sat on the bench next to Kate. "Really?" she asked, her eyes studying her daughter's face. The concern hadn't left her voice.

"Really," Kate answered, looking back at her mother, trying to reassure her. But she could hear the hint of doubt in her own voice.

She looked forward as they sat together in silence. Kate knew what her mother must think. It was unlike Kate to be so downbeat, to not be able to lift her spirits. She had been trying to hide the unusual bout of gloominess that had befallen her, but she should have known her mother would see through it. She could always read how Kate was feeling.

"What's really wrong, Kate? Does it have anything to do with Cal leaving?"

Kate looked away, knowing her mother would be able to read her expression. She hadn't admitted it to herself up until that point, hadn't even wanted to entertain the idea that her distracted, melancholy mood over the past week and a half could be attributed to him. She was fine. It wasn't her personality to dwell on a romantic fling that had come to an end. She could pick up and move on from any beau.

After a few moments of silence, Kate finally answered her mother. "He was a good friend," was all she could think to respond. "And . . . I just hope he will be all right."

Her answer was twofold. She hoped she hadn't hurt him too badly with the way things had ended between the two of them, and she sincerely hoped he would be safe. That the war wouldn't claim his life like it had so many others. The mere thought of that possibility made her stomach turn, and each time her mind wandered there she had to force herself to think of something else. But what did that mean?

She told herself it was only natural to worry about him. He had become a good friend. This was merely the natural reaction of a friend sending a friend off to war. It was unsettling. Of course it would be.

But now, sitting on the porch with her mother, Kate was allowing herself to think on what she was feeling more freely. Why was it that whenever her thoughts went to him, she had to try so hard to push them away? It was becoming tiring. Exhausting even.

Should it be this difficult? Should I really have to try so hard to not worry about him? To forget him?

She leaned her head against her mother's shoulder and felt tears prick at her eyes. "I miss him," she simply said.

Her mother nodded understandingly.

≈

The next morning Kate woke with newfound fervor and determination inside of her. She wasn't going to let herself feel this way anymore.

Lying awake in bed last night she finally admitted something to herself. She did care for Cal. A lot. More than any man she had ever gone out with before, in fact. And what was bothering her, she decided, was that she hadn't done anything about it. She had left things undone and unsaid, and that wasn't okay. She could live with sending him off to war, as hard as it was, if she had been honest with herself and with him about the way she felt about him. She wasn't about to jump to any conclusions about what her feelings might mean, but lying to herself wasn't going to solve it. Running away from her feelings wasn't the answer.

She shook her head. Their time together hadn't been long enough.

She walked downstairs to the kitchen to find her mother already seated at the table, sipping on her usual morning cup of hot cocoa and glancing over the Sunday paper.

"Good morning, Mother," Kate said as she walked in.

Her mother glanced up. "Hi, honey." Her eyes quickly looked Kate over. "You look like you're feeling better this morning."

Kate nodded as she sat at the table across from her mother. "I am."

"You slept well?"

Kate shrugged and smiled. "Sort of. I was up half the night thinking, but once I figured something out, I finally fell asleep and slept like a rock the rest of the night."

Her mother peered at her, seeming to try and understand what her daughter was getting at. "Well, that's good, I suppose. And what was it you figured out?"

Kate gulped. She wasn't sure how her mother would respond to what she was about to say next. "I . . . I really like him, Mother. More than I let on. More than I wanted to admit to anyone, especially myself." She found herself smiling, almost giddy that she was actually saying the words out loud.

"I wondered as much," her mother said. "You sure seemed happy when you were with him. And my, the way he looked at you. You could just tell that boy was plain smitten. But mostly the way you two were together just seemed so . . . natural."

Kate thought on that for a moment. "You're right. It was so easy with him. Nothing ever felt forced or scripted. Honestly, with a lot of the men I have gone steady with in the past it's almost been like a game to me. Like I'm playing along for some part in a play or something. Isn't that ridiculous?" She let out a laugh. "But with Cal it felt so . . . real. I never felt like I was pretending, or even trying. It just . . . happened." Kate shook her head and let out a chuckle. "That sounds so odd, I know."

Her mother's lips were pursed in a gentle smile. "Not odd, just honest."

Kate let out a breath. "I just wish I could spend more time with him. That I could have a chance to be with him a little longer."

Her mother looked back at her with sympathetic eyes. "I know, honey. But he'll be back. You'll have your chance. I know that doesn't make it any easier that he is gone now, though."

Kate shook her head. "No."

A thought had entered Kate's mind last night as she was thinking about how much she wished she could be with him again, and she had entertained it for a moment. But soon she had pushed it away. Far too outlandish.

But there it was again, creeping up on her from the back of her mind, pulling her in. And suddenly she had made her decision. This time she wasn't going to push it away. She was going to grasp onto it. She wasn't the type of person who wallowed in her sadness, who let unfortunate circumstances, however much they were a consequence of her own doing;,decide her fate. She was the kind of person that faced problems head on and took action. Took chances.

Kate's eyes darted to her mother's, and a mischievous smile slowly formed across her lips.

Decidedly, she cleared her throat. "Well, Mother. He's not gone . . . yet."

Chapter Twenty-Four

Cal stood straight as usual, with his arms at his sides, observing the demonstration.

CRACK!

The drill sergeant pulled the M1 Garand rifle away from his shoulder momentarily to inspect the circular shooting target. He had hit the third ring from the center on the upper left side. His mouth tensed and his eyebrows turned down slightly, seemingly unsatisfied with his performance. He brought the rifle back up to his shoulder and looked back into the barrel.

A few moments passed and another shot rang out, followed by four more quick shots. Peering at the target the sergeant was shooting at from one hundred yards away, Cal could make out a small hole shot through the outer left edge of the bull's-eye and one on the top edge of it. The other holes appeared to be scattered around the target on the first and second rings.

Cal glanced back to the drill sergeant, who had paused again to quickly inspect the target. The sergeant gave a small swift nod of approval, apparently pleased he had hit the center. *Well, almost the center,* Cal thought to himself with a smirk.

The drill sergeant raised the rifle back to his shoulder and shot off the remaining three rounds. Following the last crack, the clip ejected, pinging against the dirt ground. The sergeant lowered the gun to his side and turned toward the platoon of privates observing. "If you've never handled a gun before, don't be surprised if it takes a clip or two before you are able to hit the target at all," he called out. "And don't expect to hit the bull's-eye until you've had quiet a bit of practice."

The sergeant paused for a moment, glancing around at the men. Cal felt as though he was sizing them up, as if this was some sort of test to how they would measure as a soldier. Really, that wasn't fair. He was sure many of these men had never even held a gun before, let alone shot one. They'd have time to sharpen their shooting skills. But Cal had to admit, he was a little glad he'd had some experience in this area.

"Break!" the sergeant shouted.

The men lined up as instructed in four separate lines beginning at the markers on the ground indicating one hundred yards away from each line's target. For their turn they would be given one clip, which was eight rounds of shots.

Cal was four soldiers back in his line. He watched as the first in line walked up to the mark. He recognized the soldier but wasn't sure of his name. He remembered the soldier because he always appeared to conduct himself rather awkwardly and seemed generally out of place at camp. He looked young, couldn't have been more than eighteen or nineteen, and was probably better suited behind a book or a desk than a gun.

With his hands slightly wobbly, the boy began loading the clip. Cal was fairly certain this must have been his first time handling a gun. *The rifle is probably much heavier than he expected*, Cal thought to himself. The boy was struggling getting the clip loaded. He was undoubtedly feeling the pressure of all the other soldier's eyes on him. Cal silently hoped that the boy could get through the drill without embarrassing himself.

After the private fumbled with the clip for a few seconds, Cal heard a snap. Good. He had loaded it correctly. Just then Cal heard a shot ring off to the side of them. Suddenly multiple shots began ringing out, the soldiers in the other lines beginning to shoot off their clips.

The boy in Cal's line glanced around momentarily at the noise around him, his expression somewhere between uncertain and daunted. Nervously, he proceeded forward to his mark and lifted the rifle up to his shoulder, readying the weapon. He hesitated for a couple seconds, but then Cal saw the boy's finger slowly pull back on the trigger, his body tensing up anticipating the shot. Nothing sounded. A confused expression crossed the boy's face. He pulled the trigger again. Again, silence followed.

"It's the safety catch," Cal called out to the boy.

The others in the line all turned and looked at Cal. He cleared his throat. "You need to release the trigger guard," he continued.

"Oh, okay," the boy fumbled, a grateful look in his eyes.

Cal had made a couple friends in his time at camp, and he would talk and make conversation with the others, but he definitely wasn't one of the more boisterous soldiers in his platoon. The men must have been a little surprised at his offering instruction. But if there was a good reason to speak up, Cal saw no reason not to.

The boy lowered the rifle, made the adjustment, and then brought it back up to his shoulder. Cal could see his finger press against the trigger. A moment later a shot rang out. Cal's eyes tried to follow the bullet. It appeared to have gone quite a bit over the target. That was all right. At least he had got the shot out of the gun.

The boy fired off three more rounds, all with the same outcome. Cal could tell he was beginning to get frustrated. "You need to aim lower," Cal again hollered out.

The boy looked back at Cal and offered him a nod of appreciation before turning back toward the target. A moment later Cal heard another shot fire off and watched as it grazed the top of the target.

Cal clapped his hands together in encouragement. "Well done!"

The boy's mouth turned up in a slight smile. He shot off his last two rounds, one hitting the middle of the top ring and the other again whizzing over the target altogether. But Cal was satisfied. The boy had two bullets hit the target, albeit barely, but that was much better than none.

The next two soldiers each took their turns. Both seemed not much more experienced than the first boy, but were a little older and appeared less intimidated than the vulnerable boy. They each hit the target a couple times.

Soon it was Cal's turn. The soldier who had just finished his rounds handed him the rifle. Cal walked up to the mark and loaded the clip into the rifle swiftly. The click of the bolt snapped forward. He lifted the gun to rest against his shoulder and crouched down just a bit. Looking down the barrel, he aimed at the center of the target. He took a breath and pulled his finger carefully against the trigger. The shot rang out, piecing his ears. He glanced to the side of the barrel and noted the hole on the target. He had hit the outer edge of the right side of the ring closest to the bull's-eye.

He heard someone whistle from behind him and couldn't help but allow his mouth to twitch in a slight smile. He had always enjoyed target shooting.

He shot off three more rounds and glanced up. Two had hit the same ring he had already hit, one just below the bull's-eye and one to the left of it. One had hit the second ring out on the upper right side. The other had hit the bull's-eye, barely to the right of being dead center.

"We've got a bull's-eye over here!" Cal heard a soldier in his line holler. In his peripheral vision he noticed the drill sergeant approaching his line, apparently to observe Cal's remaining rounds.

Cal shot off his final four rounds and heard the clip clink to the ground. He lowered the rifle to his side and inspected the target. Another bull's-eye.

"You've got a sharp shot, private," the drill sergeant called to Cal from behind him.

Cal noticed the men in his line and others from surrounding lines were watching him with apparent interest. "That's what growing up on a farm will do to you," Cal responded back with a smile.

The sergeant nodded. "Nice work."

❧

A week had gone by and Cal and his platoon were again in the middle of another training drill. But this was a different sort.

"On your mark, get set, go!"

Cal took off in a bolt down the four-foot wide lane, his leg muscles taut as his feet hit the ground. He was running in one of the middle lanes of the eight-lane sixty-yard length sprint-training course. Altogether, the soldiers would run the length of the course five times, making up the three-hundred-yard run. Already almost halfway down his first of five back and forth lengths of the course, he and the runner in the lane to the left of him were leading the group. They had been told to run at nine-tenths their full capacity for the practice run, so Cal was pushing to nearly a full speeded sprint. As he reached the end of the first length of the course, he made a left-hand turn around the wooden stake sticking out of the ground about a foot and a half high without touching it, as instructed.

He continued down the lane in the opposite direction and inhaled, feeling his upper thighs tighten with the turn. Normally a three-hundred-yard sprint wouldn't require a great deal of exertion for Cal, but already having completed multiple sets of pull-ups, squat jumps, push-ups, and sit-ups this afternoon training for the fitness test he would have to pass at the end of basic training, and being pushed to do each exercise with the utmost precision, his body was becoming fatigued.

Cal noticed he was completing the exercises with a bit more ease than many of the men around him. He figured his time doing physical labor out on the farm, although it had only been for two short weeks before he left, had helped prepare his body for this. And he was pushing himself. He figured he might as well try and improve upon his strength and speed. It was worth the effort if there was any chance it could help him once he got out to combat.

Soon he was completing his last turn around the stake at the end of his lane. He and the soldier to his left were still at a dead heat. As they neared about twenty yards away from the finish line, the private standing at the sidelines keeping time began to count the seconds out loud, "Forty-five hup, forty-six hup, forty-seven hup, forty-eight hup, forty-nine . . ." At that moment Cal ran across the finish line, right in sync with the soldier next to him.

Cal slowed to a stop and bent over at the waist, resting his arms on his knees and catching his breath. He lifted a hand and swiped it across his forehead, brushing off drips perspiration. From behind him he felt a slap on his back. "We're supposed to keep walking for a few minutes, remember?" a friendly voice said. It was Private Walker, one of the soldiers in Cal's platoon.

Cal nodded. "Oh yeah." He started walking alongside Walker, both men catching their breath.

"You're pretty fast," Walker commented. "Run track in high school?"

Cal let out a chuckle. "Nah. I'm more experienced chasing down cattle and sheep than anything else."

"Did you grow up on a farm?" Walker asked.

Cal nodded. "I did."

"Same here," Walker responded. "From Boise, Idaho. How about you?"

"Outskirts of Salt Lake City," Cal answered.

A look of recognition entered Walker's face. "I have some cousins that live north of Salt Lake City. I've been down to visit them a couple times. Nice place, Salt Lake is. Reminds me a lot of Boise."

Cal nodded. "Are you still in the farming business?"

"Yeah. I have plans to take over my father's potato farm when I get back from the war, now that me and the wife are looking to settle down."

"You're married?" Cal asked.

A grin spread across Walker's face. "Sure am. Eight months this week."

"That's great," Cal responded.

Just then Private Bernard walked up to them. He had been in charge of recording sprint times. "Here's your scorecards," he said, handing them each a small piece of paper.

Cal read his. Forty-nine seconds.

"Nice job, Morgan," Bernard said. "You and McKenzie there were tied for first."

Cal nodded. "Thanks."

Cal, Walker, and the rest of the men made their way back toward the mess hall. When they reached their barrack along the way, they realized they had about fifteen minutes to spare before dinner was to be served. A few of them, including Cal, decided to take a quick shower before heading to the mess hall for supper.

They filed into the barrack and took turns quickly rinsing off in the one shower that all eighty of the men who occupied the barrack shared. The shower was located in a corner of the first floor and wasn't walled off, making privacy practically non-existent for the soldiers. But Cal was grateful they at least had a shower. In a couple of months such accommodations would most likely be much harder to come by.

As Cal dressed himself in his soldier's attire, feeling refreshed and rejuvenated from the shower, he thought back to the afternoon's fitness drills. Although they had been strenuous, it had been a surprisingly nice change of pace from holding guns and weapons in his hands. He had had training in machine guns, heavy weapons, mortars, and even aerial training with remote control airplanes the soldiers would shoot down. While he enjoyed target practicing and found weapon drills interesting and at times entertaining, it was becoming more and more real to him. Soon these drills wouldn't be just for practice. At least the exercise drills made it almost feel like he was out running track or doing physical conditioning with a bunch of buddies rather than training to go to war.

Cal finished dressing and walked across the wooden floor of the barrack to the door. Bernard and Walker were waiting for him there. Cal followed them out. As they were walking down the steps of the barrack, a beep of the loudspeaker rang out and an announcement began: "Private Clayton, please report to the front gate. Your wife is here to see you. Private Clayton." It beeped again, indicating an end to the announcement, and clicked off.

The other men continued walking, but Cal stopped dead in his tracks.

"Morgan, you coming?" Bernard asked.

Cal couldn't move. Clayton. Clayton was Kate's last name. Just the mere sound of her name had sent a jolt through him, bringing back a flood of memories.

"Morgan?" Bernard repeated. "Is something wrong?"

"Oh, it's nothing," Cal fumbled, realizing his friend was talking to him. He forced himself to clear his head and stepped forward, catching up. Bernard gave Cal a confused nod but didn't ask any questions.

They continued toward the mess hall, but Cal couldn't shake the thought of Kate from his mind. His thoughts wandered to the announcement. Clayton wasn't all that uncommon of a last name, but still, it was a coincidence. He wondered who this Clayton fellow was and thought how lucky he was that he had a wife to come visit him. Cal shook his head, forcing himself to think of other things. Letting his mind go there now would do no good.

Just then the familiar beep of the loudspeaker rang out again, and another announcement followed: "Repeat. Private Clayton, please report to the front gate. Your wife is here to see you. Private Clayton." Beep, and over.

Cal continued forward. Suddenly a thought entered his mind. What if? No . . . it couldn't be. Or could it?

His mind and heart began racing. If Kate were to come visit him she would have to show her ID, therefore having to use her last name, which was Clayton. But visitors were rarely permitted. Girlfriends certainly weren't allowed to visit soldiers at the camp, and from what Cal understood a visit from a wife could be authorized but was a very rare occurrence, unless she was the wife of a member of the staff or of an officer. But Cal also knew that if for some reason Kate wanted to come see him she would find a way around the rules. And, of course, the only possible way she could do that would be to pretend she was married to him.

But it couldn't be her. Not with the way they left things off. She showed no sign of ever wanting to see him again. But as small of a chance it was, what if?

Cal slowed his steps and cleared his throat. "I . . . you know, I actually realized I forgot something back in the barrack," he said to Walker and Bernard. "I'll meet you guys in the mess hall in a little bit."

The men hesitated for a moment, giving Cal a puzzled look. But they didn't press him any further. "All right," Walker said with a nod. "See you in a bit."

The men turned and began walking forward.

Cal swallowed hard, turned the other direction, and began making his way to the main gate. He knew it was farfetched. Borderline absurd. But what if it *was* Kate coming to see him and he missed that chance? He would never forgive himself. He had to check.

A few minutes later he found himself at the main front gate. He approached the guard stationed there.

"I . . . I believe I have a visitor," Cal said to the guard. "I was told to report to the main gate."

The guard nodded and opened the gate to let Cal through. Then he motioned toward a small office to the side of the gate. "Your visitor is waiting in the office," he said.

"Thanks," Cal said to him, turning toward the office building.

He approached the door of the office and reached toward its handle. The wooden door creaked as he slowly pushed it open. He was halfway into the office when his eyes met with a middle-aged, cheerful looking woman sitting behind a desk a few feet in front of him. She raised her eyebrows at him inquisitively. "May I help you?" she asked.

Reluctantly, Cal stepped through the door, already feeling sheepish for going on this wild goose chase. "Yes. I, um . . ."

Just then Cal was interrupted by a yelp of delight. "Cal!"

His head jerked around to meet the sound of her voice.

There, standing a few feet to his side, was Kate.

Chapter Twenty-Five

Cal inhaled sharply. What on earth was she doing here?

"Sweetheart!" Kate called out dramatically. Before he had a chance to say anything, let alone try to make sense of what was happening, she ran toward him and threw her arms around his neck. "I've missed you so much!"

He stood in stunned silence, in a complete state of shock. He was incapable of conjuring up something to say back to her.

After a moment of standing there dumbstruck and speechless, he realized he must have looked like a complete dimwit. He hadn't even hugged her back! Slowly he reached his arms around her, his heart thudding loudly within his chest. So loudly it was drowning out everything else in the room. He was utterly confused, his mind a cloud of fog. What was going on?

She leaned back and placed a quick, hard kiss on his lips. Then she stepped away from him and playfully exclaimed, "Don't tell me you haven't missed your wife!" She offered him a sly wink.

Suddenly it came to his realization to that his jaw was nearly dropped to the floor. He clapped his mouth shut. Finally he stammered out, "I'm just . . . surprised to see you." The end of the sentence came out more like a question then an answer.

"Surprises are always the best," she replied smoothly, shoot-ing the woman working at the desk a knowing smile. The woman shrugged her shoulders upward excitedly and let out a giggle, seem-ing to be thoroughly enjoying the show. Kate turned back to Cal and continued, "I simply couldn't pass up the opportunity to come and visit my husband this week, what with it being our first anniversary and all." She widened her eyes at him, urging him to play along.

Cal had finally gathered his wits and quickly realized it was cru-cial he played along. "I'm so glad you did . . . dear," he replied, trying to sound as husbandly as possible. "You know how I love surprises." He was suddenly finding it rather difficult not to let out a laugh at the absurdity of the situation.

Up until now he hadn't done much else but blankly stare in awe at Kate standing in front of him. But the reality of her presence was finally setting in. He took in her image, the mere sight of her leav-ing him awestruck. She was wearing a stylish crimson-red suit jacket and matching pencil skirt with red heels. Her dark hair was perfectly curled above her shoulders. Her lips were bright red, matching her striking outfit. She was so very beautiful.

He suddenly felt an overwhelming urge to pull her back into him and continue where they left off with the kiss she had planted on his lips a few moments ago. But he quickly reminded himself he didn't know what her full intentions of coming and visiting him were. The kiss was likely just part of her act pretending to be his wife.

Cal glanced downward. He hadn't noticed until now, but sit-ting on the ground behind her were two large suitcases and a small traveling bag.

"You . . . brought luggage?"

She shook her head. "You didn't think I came all this way just to say hello, did you?"

"I wasn't sure . . ." Luggage meant she planned on staying—or was going to try, at least. That was a good sign. But he was afraid her intentions would quickly be dashed. Most likely they would only get a talk for a few minutes and she would have to leave. He glanced over at the woman sitting at the desk, wondering what she would tell them to do next.

The woman was all smiles and seemed to have no clue of the charade they were putting on. "We've decided you're lovely wife here will be permitted to stay at the wives' barracks for a short time," she chimed in, beaming at Kate and then looking back to Cal.

Cal could feel his jaw again dropping and worked to keep it shut. "What? But how . . . ?"

"Dear," Kate injected, "I must tell you that Evelyn here has been an absolute miracle worker! When I first arrived, the two of us hit it off right away. We had so much to talk about, didn't we?"

Evelyn nodded reassuringly. "We certainly did!"

Cal could tell Kate had the woman practically eating out of the palm of her hand.

Kate continued, "I told her about how I had spent all of our savings, what little there was, on my ticket here to surprise you with a visit for our anniversary. And then I learned the dreadful news. Sweetheart, did you know wives aren't permitted to visit husbands here unless there are extenuating circumstances?"

Cal stared back at her blankly. He wasn't sure if he was supposed to answer the question or not. "Well, I . . ."

"Well, I sure didn't," she continued, cutting him off before he had a chance to formulate his response. "I was so devastated when I found there would be little chance I would even be allowed to see you, let alone stay. I felt so foolish. Never did I wish to inconvenience anyone. But to come all this way and to spend all our hard-earned money to not even get to see you, it would be simply tragic!"

Evelyn nodded soberly. "A very unfortunate misunderstanding is what it was, Kate." The woman turned her attention to Cal. "Normally I would have never attempted such a thing, but Kate's story of planning to surprise you on your anniversary and spending all that money to get here, well, I found it very touching. And . . . ," she said, pausing with an excited grin, "let's just say I pulled some strings for you and your adorable wife here."

Kate's smile was wide, her eyes large and full of gratitude. "Isn't it one of the kindest things you have ever heard of, Cal? What a perfect anniversary present! We are truly indebted to you, Evelyn."

Cal stared at Kate, amazed at her performance. He would have to remember later to suggest she reconsider a career in acting of some kind. "Extremely kind," he added. He looked back to Evelyn. "I don't know how we can ever repay you."

Evelyn waved her hand toward Cal. "Oh, don't even suggest it, dear. I am just happy to be a part of such a joyous reunion. Heaven knows a woman could use a touch of happiness with the gloomy state the world is in. Now, do you know where the wives' quarters are, Private Clayton?"

"Yes, I believe I do," he answered.

She nodded her head in satisfaction. "Good. Well, you go get your cute little bride settled in then."

"I will," Cal replied, trying to hide the startling sensation he felt each time he heard Kate referred to as his wife, or him as her husband. He looked toward her luggage. "Let me get those . . . er, honey," he said, trying to play the part. He reached toward the bags. "All right, sweetcakes," he continued, trying to conjure up whatever term of endearment he could think of that a husband might use for a wife. If they were going to play this game he might as well have a little fun with it. He nodded forward. "Ladies first."

Kate shot him a disarming smile and sauntered to his side, taking his arm. "Goodbye, Evelyn," Kate said in a sing-songy voice as they began their exit out the small office. "And thank you again!"

"Yes, thank you," Cal added sincerely as they walked out the door. It was terribly kind of the woman to go out on a limb for them like that, even if it was a conjured up marriage.

As soon as the door was shut and they were down the steps Kate whirled around to face Cal. "Sweetcakes?" she echoed, with laughter in her eyes.

"What? I always called you that back home."

She let out a burst of laughter. "Oh, right. Somehow I forgot that one." Looking into his eyes, the corners of her mouth turned up in an impish grin. "So, did I succeed? Were you surprised?" She was holding her chin up proudly.

Cal shook his head in disbelief. "Surprised would be an understatement," he answered, staring back into her spellbinding eyes. "What are you—"

"Shhh," she said, leaning into him a bit, raising her eyebrows and lowering her voice. "Don't give us away." Then she straightened her posture and continued a bit louder, "We can get to that later."

Cal glanced around and realized the guard at the gate wasn't that far off. He hadn't even thought of it up until now, but she was right. They needed to be careful. Other soldiers with girls back home, especially ones whose wives were actually their wives, wouldn't be too happy if they found out Cal and Kate had somehow circumvented the rules. Not only that, but he was sure he would get a mighty wrath from his lieutenant if he was to find out.

His eyes moved from the guard back to Kate. Leave it up to this brown-eyed beauty to throw the rules out the window and take matters into her hands. As much as Kate's roguish spirit went against his own nature, he knew that was one of the reasons, among a hundred others, why he found her so downright irresistible. Looking into her eyes he couldn't help but stare in awe at how adorably mischievous yet angelically beautiful she was all at once. Suddenly he couldn't stand it any longer. Almost without realizing what he was doing, he placed her suitcases down on the ground and in one swift motion took a step toward her, closing the gap between them. He reached a hand toward her face and gently tilted her chin up toward him. Their faces were mere inches away from each other. His mind flashed back to the night at the park, when they had their first kiss. The way they were standing, the way his hand was holding her face, and the way he was completely taken by her were all reminiscent of that magical evening by the lake under the stars. "You, my dear," he said, "are a force to be reckoned with."

He leaned in and brushed his lips against hers—ever so softly at first. But after a moment he moved toward her with more force, letting his inhibitions go. She wrapped her arms around his neck and returned the kiss with equal fervor. He knew the guard at the gate was likely watching them, but he didn't care. She was his wife, for all the guard knew. He had every right to kiss her passionately standing at the front gate of Camp Roberts if he darn well pleased.

After a few prolonged moments, Cal pulled back. He took a breath in an attempt to regain his steadiness, his eyes never leaving hers, still in utter awe at the turn of events that had taken place over the last ten minutes. He could be dreaming, he quickly told himself. He really could. He reached his hand up to her face and gently touched her cheek. She was too real. The kiss was too real. She was here and would be staying. For how long he still didn't know, but all that mattered now was that she was here.

But he still wasn't really even sure just why she had come. He hadn't asked permission to kiss her and hoped that it was okay. She hadn't objected; on the contrary, she seemed to have enjoyed it as much as he had. But he hoped that wasn't just part of the act. His chest suddenly tightened with the thought that this could all just be a big charade. But he quickly pushed that from his mind. They would address those details soon, and he would learn why she was here, and hopefully what she intended by it.

"Well, my dear," he said. "I would love to hear more about . . . how you got here. But we can get to that later. Let's go get you settled."

Kate nodded with a grin and linked her arm with his, and they continued forward toward the gate back into Camp Roberts.

Chapter Twenty-Six

As they walked together down the dirt walkway through the camp, arm in arm, Kate felt a rush of relief flood over her. She could hardly believe she had pulled it off! It had been a little trickier than she had initially expected, but she had been determined she would get to see Cal. Not only because she had come all this way, but because there were things she needed to say to him. She knew she could have written or even tried calling, but she much preferred the idea of talking with him in person, and now that she was actually going to be able to stay and spend time with him made it all worth it. She knew she had been bold, but she didn't care. Pretending to be his wife had actually turned out to be quite amusing and fun.

Her stomach fluttered with excitement as she looked over at him. She noticed he kept glancing down at her and smiling as they walked, making her feel secure in her decision to come. Of course she had her doubts. When she found herself at the bus station back home about to board the bus to California she had almost turned around and walked away. What if he wasn't excited to see her when she arrived? What if he had decided to move on from her? But she made the decision to stick to her plan, something deep inside telling her that if she didn't try to make amends with him and let him know how she really felt, it could be a colossal mistake. And so as elaborate of a scheme it was, feigning to be a wife that had come to visit her husband for their anniversary, clueless enough not to know that wives weren't usually permitted to visit their husbands at basic training, she went through with it.

They hadn't been able to talk much about it yet, trying to be discrete as possible, but from the way he received her warmly and simply the way he looked at her gave her high hopes that he still felt the same. And that kiss. It had been so unexpected and left her feeling as though she was floating.

As they walked she noticed the soldiers they passed were eyeing them together, especially her, as they made their way across the camp.

"The barrack I'm staying in is down that way," Cal said, pointing down a row of the white rectangular two-story buildings. She couldn't believe how many rows and rows of them there were. The camp was much larger than she expected. "You're actually not too far from me," he continued. "The wives' quarters are up on this corner of camp. I've walked past them a couple times. They're smaller than the regular barracks. I'm not really sure what the setup is like inside." He paused for a moment, a look of concern crossing his face. "I hope they're not too shabby. I want you staying in something decent."

"I'm not worried about that," she replied swiftly.

He looked down at her. "Well, I am. I'm afraid this just isn't much of a place for a lady."

Kate let out a burst of laughter. "Oh please, I'll be perfectly fine. I'd pitch a tent and camp out if I had to."

Cal gave her a wry smile. "I almost forgot who I was talking to." His face twisted a bit. "It's just . . . I'd have you staying in the nicest place in California if I could."

She felt her heart soften with his words. He had a way of making her feel genuinely cared about, even when it came to little things. "That's very sweet," she said, her mouth turning up in a smile. "But I didn't come here expecting to be pampered."

He peered at her. "I guess I'm still not exactly sure why you did come."

They stopped walking, eyes fixed on one another. With the way he was looking at her, she had the feeling he was searching for answers. She wanted to tell him more but also wanted to be able to tell him all of it. She glanced from side to side and noticed there wasn't anyone near, but at any moment there could be. And there was no telling if someone might be within hearing range. She cleared her throat. "Because," she said, "I wanted to see my husband."

"Oh, yeah. That's right," he said, letting out a chuckle. "Well, we're here." He nodded forward. They had been so involved in their conversation, she hadn't noticed they had arrived at their destination.

They were standing in front of a grouping of small barracks. They looked much like the barracks they had passed along the way, wood-walled and painted white, with a row of windows along their sides, but these barracks were only one floor tall and quite a bit smaller than the soldiers' barracks.

They knocked on the door to the closest barrack. It was answered by two women who introduced themselves as wives of officers who were currently at camp.

"Of course you are welcome to join us here," one of the women said to Kate. She was tall and thin and had thick auburn hair and large green eyes. She introduced herself as Regina. Right off the bat Kate could tell Regina would be easy to get along with. The other girl, Florence, was on the shorter side and had light, mousy hair. She seemed nice but a bit quieter than her counterpart.

Regina pointed out an available bed in the corner of the barrack, and Cal stepped in to carry Kate's things to the corner of the room. Kate followed him, observing the interior of the barrack as she walked. It was as simple on the inside as it was on the out, wood walled and wood floored. Three double beds were placed around the room with basic bedding of sheets, a pillow and a blanket over the top. She noted the simple curtains on the windows, brown linen with patterns of clusters of yellow and pale pink roses, and braided brown rugs at the doors.

"The visitor's barracks are a bit homier than ours," Cal said, glancing around while placing her things on the bed. "Curtains and rugs. Although," he added with a grin, "I'm not so sure they're on the cutting edge of fashion. But you would know about that better than me."

"Oh, sure they are," Kate rebutted. "I think I'd like to find a skirt in that pattern."

Cal laughed. "Sure you would." He cleared he throat. "I'm glad to see your washroom is actually enclosed," he said, nodding toward the door of a small walled-off room.

"Yours isn't?" she asked in surprise.

"Nope. Not much privacy here for us soldiers."

Kate had to admit she was glad for that luxury.

Regina walked over to them, standing beside Kate's bed. "Florence and I are going to head down to dinner at the visitor's mess hall. Have you eaten yet, Kate? You're welcome to join us."

Kate felt her stomach rumble with the mention of food. She hadn't eaten anything since breakfast and had forgotten how hungry she was with the excitement of arriving and all that had unfolded. "Actually, I am quiet hungry," she said, turning to Cal. "Have you eaten yet?"

He shook his head. "I was on my way to the mess hall when I . . . I got word that you had arrived."

Kate nodded and then turned back to Regina. "Sure, we'll come with you."

"Well, we're not allowed to eat with the military," Regina explained. "I don't know if someone has already gone over how things work for us visitors with you. Our husbands are still required to do everything as usual during the day with training and all, including eating their meals with their platoons. We eat our meals separately at the visitor's mess hall. Then we get to meet up with them at six o'clock when they are done for the day. We can spend the evening with them until ten o'clock when they have to report back to their barrack for lights out."

"Oh, okay," Kate replied. She was a bit disappointed. She hadn't been sure what to expect, but anticipated they'd be able to eat dinner together. It made sense that he needed to go about the training as if she wasn't there. Still, she wasn't expecting she'd have to say goodbye to him again so soon.

"I don't need dinner tonight," Cal injected. "I'll walk with you to the visitor's mess hall and wait outside while you eat."

"You don't need to do that. I don't want you going hungry. How about I go with the girls and meet you back here in a half an hour?"

A look of hesitation crossed Cal's eyes. She could tell he didn't want to be apart from her either. But they needed to be practical about things. She certainly didn't want him skipping meals for her. They would be together again very soon.

"Well . . . okay," he responded reluctantly. "But I'll at least walk you to the mess hall."

Kate couldn't help herself from smiling. "All right."

Once they were outside the barrack, they followed Regina and Florence to the mess hall. After a few steps Kate felt Cal reach his hand out and take hold of hers. Her heart fluttered with his touch. After a few moments he began stroking the back of her hand with his thumb, which was comforting and caused her stomach to dance with butterflies. A sense of contentment swept over her. She quickly realized how much she had missed just simply holding his hand.

Soon they arrived at the mess hall. The walk hadn't been nearly long enough. She didn't want to leave him just yet, didn't want to let go of his hand.

They turned toward each other. "I'll be quick, and then I'll be back," he said to her, looking intently into her eyes.

She smiled. "I'll be waiting."

He squeezed her hand once more, and then nodded and turned and walked off.

She sighed as she watched him walk away. Then she turned back toward the girls and followed them into the building.

Chapter Twenty-Seven

Cal had never eaten so fast. He shoveled the last few bites of corn into his mouth and stood. Holding his empty tray in one hand and his dinner roll in his other, he walked toward the tray drop and deposited it onto the counter. He exited the building and finished off his last bite of roll as he shuffled down the mess hall stairs.

His feet hitting the dirt ground, he jogged back to the visitors' quarters. When he reached the mess hall, he could hear talking coming from inside. He had eaten and returned back so quickly he was sure Kate would still be inside, which is what he wanted. He would wait outside of the mess hall for her to come out.

He stood on the opposite side of the dirt road that the mess hall sat on about twenty feet from its door. Leaning against a fence post with his hands in his pockets, he patiently waited. Sure enough, about five minutes later Kate emerged from the building. She was turned toward Regina, talking and laughing as she stepped out. Cal caught his breath as he watched her. How lovely she looked, her smile sparkling and full of life.

A moment later she turned forward and met his gaze. "Cal! What are you doing here?" she asked in surprise. "Didn't you eat?"

"Yes," he answered, taking a step toward her. "I'm just back already."

"Well, that was fast," she replied. She walked toward him and was soon standing directly in front of him, not leaving much space between them.

"I wanted to be here when you came out," he said, finding it difficult not to reach out to her the second she was close to him. He still couldn't believe she was actually here. All the while he was eating dinner his mind was filled with thoughts of her and all that had happened. He kept vacillating between complete amazement that he was about to spend an evening with her, to already missing her in the short time they had been apart, to chuckling to himself thinking about their encounter in the office and her convincing performance.

He noticed the corners of her mouth turning up. "I'm afraid you are too good to me."

He shook his head. "Not possible." Instinctively he took a step closer to her.

She reached out toward him, gently tugging on the sides of the jacket he was wearing. "Why the jacket?" she asked with a puzzled expression.

"You'll see."

"See you later, Kate!" a voice called from the side of them. Cal and Kate turned to see Florence and Regina walking back toward their barrack, waving at them.

Kate waved back. "See you girls!"

She turned back toward him, and Cal reached out and grabbed a hold of her hand. "Let's get out of here."

The sound of Kate's laughter was music to his ears as he whisked her down the dirt lane.

❧

Soon they arrived at the spot, the place Cal decided was far enough off the beaten path that it would be safe for them to finally talk openly. One evening after dinner he had been wandering the camp property, having felt a bit stir crazy and in need of stretching his legs and a change of scenery. During his walk around the camp, he discovered where the visitors' quarters were on the west side of the compound. On that same walk, he noticed a small grassy hill tucked up on this corner of the camp along the fence. He remembered thinking it would be a nice place to sit and relax and have some time alone. And that's just what he needed with her now. Time alone.

"Over here," he said, leading her past the visitors' quarters toward the fence. The small grassy hill had a few welcomed trees surrounding it he hadn't remembered from before, making the little spot actually have quite a secluded feel to it.

On his way to dinner at the mess hall, Cal had quickly stopped by his barrack and put on his soldier's jacket. He had gotten a few odd looks from the other privates while eating dinner probably wondering why he was wearing a jacket over his long sleeved military shirt with it being a warm summer evening. But he had retrieved the jacket with a plan in mind.

He walked toward the small hill. Swiftly pulling the jacket off his shoulders, he took hold of it with his two hands and shook it out once before laying it flat on the ground. He gestured forward, motioning for her to sit. "We're not allowed to take blankets out of our barracks, so this is the best I could do," he explained with a crooked smile.

"Clever," she said as she sat down on top of the jacket, tucking her legs to the side. "Thank you."

He sat next to her, leaving little space between the two of them. Looking ahead he noticed the sky was a mixture of hazy yellow and blue, the sun beginning to lower in sky of wispy clouds. He turned toward her. "We're alone. Finally."

She nodded. "Yes, finally."

"I believe you have some explaining to do."

Kate laughed. "I know I do." She hesitated for a moment and cast her eyes downward. Her long, dark eyelashes fluttered for a moment before she lifted her gaze back up to meet his. There was a hint of something in her eyes he didn't recognize. Something he had rarely, if ever, seen in her before. It took him a moment to pinpoint what it was, but he soon recognized it.

She was nervous.

Kate inhaled. "Well," she began, "I suppose I should start from back at home . . ."

"You mean before you decided to be my pretend wife?" he asked drolly.

"Yes," she answered with a crafty grin. "Before that." She paused for a moment and then let out a breath, her expression quickly changing from playful to serious. She looked ahead and cleared her throat. "After you left I . . . I had a really difficult time. I hated how we left things off." She shook her head. "I behaved so badly that last night we were together. After you left I was so—" He heard a catch in her voice. "So worried about you," she finished softly. Then she looked toward him, and he felt his heart drop with what he saw. Her eyes were glistening with tears.

Cal reached out to her and pulled her into him. "It's all right, my dear," he said, stroking her hair with his hand. Her head was nestled into his shoulder, the lavender scent of her suddenly enveloping him.

"I missed you so much," she murmured into his shoulder. He continued stroking her hair and then let his hand travel down to her back, gently rubbing it in slow circles. "I was filled with regret," she sighed, her words sending a tingle down his spine. "And I realized what I knew all along—that I care for you . . . so much. And knew I had to do something to make things right."

Cal's heart was racing, bounding toward encouragement and hope with every word she was saying. She had missed him. She cared for him. Cared enough that she made the effort to come all this way to tell him.

She sniffed and pulled back. Lifting her hands to her face, she brushed the tears from below her eyes with her index fingers. "I'm sorry," she said, shaking her head. "I really don't cry often, especially in front of anyone. I think it's all my emotions of the last few weeks coming to the surface."

"Don't apologize," Cal said, feeling as though his heart was slowly melting as he watched her. He reached a hand up toward her face and wiped a remaining teardrop that had trickled down to her jawline with his thumb. "So, you decided to come . . . ," he said, urging her along in her explanation.

"Yes," she continued with a smile. "And came up with the scheme of pretending to be your wife so I could get in here and see you."

"Which you play quite convincingly, I must say," Cal replied with a grin, gazing into her eyes.

"It wasn't me I was worried about. I didn't know how you would do playing along. If you would be convincing enough with you being so forthright and all."

Cal was amused. "Oh, so I'm so much of a bore that you didn't think I could pull off one simple little fib?"

"Not a bore," she quickly corrected. "Your unfailing honesty is one of the things I adore most about you."

"Adore?" he asked, raising an eyebrow.

"Yes, adore," she said with a smile.

He let out a laugh. "Well, I guess I won't argue with that."

"You shouldn't," she answered.

Cal looked down at her hand next to his. He reached out and touched her fingertips, instantly feeling the spark of her touch. Enclosing her hand in his, he slowly raised it up to his lips and placed a gentle kiss on its top. "Do you have any idea how surreal it is to have you here with me?" he asked as he lowered her hand. "I thought I would never see you again."

Emotion was suddenly rushing over him. He leaned in toward her, no longer able to restrain from continuing the kiss they had began earlier. His lips met hers tenderly, and he let all his emotions travel through him and to her. She wrapped her arms tightly around him, returning the kiss affectionately.

"Thank you for coming," he murmured when their lips parted. "I've never been happier."

She smiled. "Me neither."

He pulled her back into his chest and wrapped his arms around her, holding her close to him. He knew then what he had known for a long time but had never fully admitted to himself. He was in love with her. Overwhelmingly.

They sat on the grassy hillside the remainder of the evening, watching the sunset, talking and laughing, and simply enjoying being together.

Soon the stars were glittering above. Once again Cal found himself focusing in on one and silently making a wish. But this time his wish was twofold. He wished that he could hold her like this every night of his life. But that would have to mean two things. First, that she loved him wholeheartedly in return, enough to surmount all of her past hesitations and fears. And second—which could prove to be even more of a miracle than the first—that he would return back from the war alive.

Chapter Twenty-Eight

That afternoon Cal's platoon had finished their drill in rifle shooting. Cal had surprised everyone by hitting the bull's-eye dead center from three hundred yards away on six out of his eight rounds. The drill sergeant told Cal eventually they would be shooting from five hundred yards, and that if he could hit the bull's-eye from that length with the precision he had shown at three hundred yards, he would surely earn a sharpshooter tag.

His friends in his platoon were impressed, although Cal got more of an ironic chuckle out of it than anything else. He had always enjoyed target shooting back at home on the farm but never expected he would find himself having to use his skills out in the real world, let alone beating others at it.

Cal walked with Bernard, McKenzie, and Walker back to the mess hall for dinner.

"Where were you last night, Morgan?" Bernard asked.

Cal hadn't told his friends yet about Kate's arrival. He wasn't sure how to explain to them that first off, he had a supposed wife, and that, second, she was now visiting him there. But he knew he couldn't avoid it. They would find out soon enough with him being gone in the evenings spending time with her.

"Well . . . ," he began uneasily, "Actually, my wife came to visit me here. She arrived last night."

The men's heads all whirled around to him, their expressions ranging between puzzled to stunned.

"You're married?" Walker asked in surprise.

Cal had worried about Walker's reaction most of all. He thought back to a few weeks earlier when they had been talking after the sprint drill and Walker had told him he had been married for eight months. Cal wondered if Walker would recall the conversation and puzzle at why Cal hadn't mentioned that he was married as well.

"Yeah," Cal answered, trying to sound as confident as possible. He felt his heart rate pick up a bit. Kate was right, it wasn't in his nature to be anything but authentic.

"Oh," Walker responded, sounding confused. "But the other day when I told you about my wife, you never mentioned you were married."

"Oh yeah . . . ," Cal replied, lifting his hand to scratch his head. "Now that you say that, I don't know why I didn't mention it . . . ," he trailed off. "Well, anyway, she's here to visit for a short time."

Walker's eyebrows furrowed. "Really? I thought us GIs weren't permitted visitors."

Cal swallowed. How was he going to explain how Kate had pulled it off without Walker getting bothered that his own wife wasn't allowed to visit?

Just then Cal heard light, quick steps coming up from behind them.

"Yoo-hoo!"

The men quickly turned around, following the sing-songy voice. Cal knew who it was before even turning his head.

"Kate! What are you doing here?" he asked in surprise as he met her gaze.

"Hi, sweetheart!" she exclaimed, beaming back at him. "I was just on a walk with the girls when I spotted you walking from back there." She waved her hand behind her. "I figured you were on your way to dinner but wanted to say a quick hello."

Cal felt his mouth twitching up in a smile. "I'm glad you did," he said readily, zeroing in on her. Dressed in a flouncy yellow summer dress with her hair clipped back on one side gracefully framing her face, she looked positively radiant. This was the first he had seen her since the night before, which felt like a dream, it had been so perfect. Anxious to see her again, he had spent most of the day thinking about lying out on the grassy hillside with her under the stars and daydreaming about being with her again tonight.

"So, aren't you going to introduce me to your friends?" Kate asked impishly, eyeing him with amusement.

"Oh . . . right," Cal said with a startle, realizing he had almost forgotten about the others standing next to him along with the rather uncomfortable conversation they had just been engaged in. He cleared his throat. "Guys, this is my wife, Kate," he said, feeling an instant flush to his face. He wasn't prepared for this, hadn't expected to be introducing her to his friends as his wife. But from the playful look in Kate's eyes, she seemed to be rather enjoying watching him squirm. "Kate, these are a few of the guys in my platoon. Walker, Bernard, and McKenzie," he said, pointing out each of them.

The men and Kate exchanged hellos. As Cal watched, he couldn't help but feel a bit uneasy. He was sure Walker would resume their conversation where they had left off and wouldn't be surprised if he asked Kate upfront about how she managed to get into the camp. From what Cal could gather, Walker was a nice guy but also the type that didn't beat around the bush. Without having had a chance to warn Kate, Cal was worried how she might handle the questions.

Sure enough, Walker began. "So, how long have the two of your been married?" he asked, a hint of suspicion in his eyes.

Lands, did Walker suspect their marriage was a farce? Cal's heart rate sped up, his mind racing with the possibilities of what might happen if they were found out. The reprimand he would most definitely receive seemed almost inconsequential compared to the loss he would feel if she was suddenly ordered to leave.

"As it so happens," Kate answered without missing a beat, "our one-year anniversary is today." She smiled up at Cal. "Isn't it, sweetheart?"

Cal nodded his head in one swift movement. "That's right," he said, forcing a smile.

Today? Cal didn't know today was going to be the designated fake anniversary date. It wouldn't surprise him in the least if Kate had come up with that just now. Apparently she was going to take the act into full swing.

"Congratulations," the men replied simultaneously. McKenzie's reply was a bit louder and overly eager than the rest. Cal glanced over and noticed the man was watching Kate with an awe-like expression. Innately, the muscles in Cal's body tensed up. *He looks like a drooling puppy,* Cal thought with irritation. Taking in a breath, he quickly reminded himself that McKenzie didn't mean anything by it. The fact of the matter was the men hadn't seen a woman within close distance, and overtly attractive one at that, for weeks. But still, the way McKenzie was looking at her bothered him. She was, after all, his wife. Well, sort of.

"That's why I came here," Kate continued. "To surprise Cal for our anniversary."

"You know, I was just asking Cal here about that," Walker cut in. "I'm curious, how did you manage to get permission to stay here?"

"Well," Kate answered, "it's a rather embarrassing story." She was batting her eyelashes innocently. "But as Cal's friends, you must hear it."

Theatrically as ever, she rattled into the entire tale about how she took their savings out of the bank to buy a ticket to get to the camp and how when she arrived, clueless about the rules for visitors, she found she wouldn't be able to stay. She explained how Evelyn in the office had taken pity on her and told her that the camp actually had a shortage of visitors, and that she could pull a few strings and allow Kate to stay for a short while. Cal noticed Kate made sure to emphasize that it was pure luck she arrived when she did, because a few days sooner or later there wouldn't have been room for her. Cal wasn't sure if that was true or if she was just covering her bases to make sure the other men didn't get any ideas about trying to have their wives come out to see them, but whatever she was doing she was doing it well. Halfway into her story, Cal could tell the men were all charmed. She had them eating out of her hand just as she had Evelyn in the office.

When she finished, the men turned to Cal. "Well, I'm happy it worked out for you," Walker said, slapping his hand on Cal's back. "Can't say I don't wish it was me getting a visit from my wife. But if someone here was going to get around the rules, I'm glad it was you."

Cal immediately felt a rush of relief wash over him. Kate's charms had worked. Perhaps he wouldn't have to worry about Walker after all.

"Thanks," Cal said with a grin.

The group exchanged friendly conversation for a couple more minutes before Cal said, "You guys go ahead. I'll catch up in a minute."

The men said goodbye and began walking off toward the mess hall. When they were about ten feet away, Cal noticed McKenzie turn his head around and take one last ogle at Kate. Cal rolled his eyes. The man had some nerve.

Cal turned back to Kate and took a step closer to her, lowering his voice. "Have you had any experience in acting?" he asked, peering into her eyes with a smirk. "Hollywood isn't that far down the road, you know. You might consider making a stop down there while you're here in California."

Her eyes lit up in mock excitement. "Ooooo. I've always dreamed of being in a picture show!"

Cal let out a laugh and then shook his head. "On second thought, I don't like that idea so much. Some rich and famous actor would probably snatch you away from me."

"Yes, you're probably right," she teased back.

"I'll be at the visitor's mess hall in fifteen minutes," he said.

Kate smiled up at him. "I'll be waiting."

Chapter Twenty-Nine

The baked chicken and vegetables on her plate smelled surprisingly tasty, but the feeling of anxious excitement in Kate's stomach was suppressing her appetite. She sat across from Regina and Florence, who were both neatly cutting into the chicken on their plates with their forks and knives while Kate distractedly fiddled with her vegetables.

"Excited to see him, aren't you?"

Kate's head shot up. Regina was watching her with delight. A grin crossed Kate's lips. "I am," she admitted with a nod. And it was true. Kate could hardly wait to spend the evening with Cal. The night before had been wonderful. She was extremely happy she had made the decision to come.

The girls had questioned Kate about her and Cal's relationship while spending time together that day. Kate told them about how she and Cal first met in junior high and how they were reunited later in life and began courting. She followed fairly closely to the actual story of how it happened, leaving out the minor detail that the reuniting took place only about a month before instead of a couple years back as she had alluded to.

Kate, herself, could hardly believe all that had happened in that short amount of time. She would have never guessed someone like Cal would come into her life. Someone that she had grown to care for so deeply, someone that made her feel as though all of her past worries and inhibitions were slowly melting away. And she was surprised to admit to herself that the role of playing Cal's wife came much more naturally than she expected it to. In fact, sometimes she would momentarily forget the pretense they were playing wasn't actually the truth.

"Well, you two are a darling couple," Regina said. Florence was nodding next to her. "It's easy to tell you are in love."

Kate nearly dropped her fork. "Oh?" she asked, trying to hide the surprise coming through in her voice. She cleared her throat, trying to appear unaffected. "How so?"

Love was a word Kate had avoided since she had first began entertaining romantic interests back in her school years. Romance had always been a flirtatious game to her, but never went much deeper than that. The sound of the word had jolted her, but a strange feeling of both calmness and excitement was slowly spreading over her that was both unexpected and rather freeing.

Regina smiled. "I don't know. I guess when I've seen the two of you together, it just seems like nothing else matters." Regina glanced over at Florence, who was nodding along. "Aren't I right, Flo?"

"Yes," Florence replied readily. "And he seems to treat you very well."

Kate nodded with a smile. "He really does."

"It's great the two of you found each other," Regina continued. "When you find the right person, marriage can be a wonderful thing."

"Yes," Kate replied. But she didn't feel near as calm on the inside as she knew she was portraying. If love had been a word she had avoided in her life, marriage had been one she had practically purged herself from. The idea of matrimony had always been so boring, so mundane, but mostly, so frightening. Her former self wanted nothing to do with it. Coming into Camp Roberts she knew pretending to be Cal's wife would be the only way she'd get a chance at seeing him. At first the idea of even pretending to be married left her a bit anxious. But as it went along, she felt more and more comfortable with it. For some reason she couldn't help herself from wondering if love, and marriage, with Cal could be different. Maybe Regina was onto something. When you find the right person . . .

"Oh, and sorry about last night," Regina continued. "Flo and I meant to let Cal and you know you were welcome to have the barrack alone to yourself for the evening. But you two disappeared before we had a chance to mention it. So, anyway, plan on it tonight." She gave Kate a wink. "We'll stay out of your way."

Kate couldn't help but raise her eyebrows in surprise. "Oh . . . all right," she stumbled. It wasn't like Kate to find herself at a loss for words, but the turn in conversation was one she wasn't expecting. However, she quickly realized that as a married couple it would seem very odd if they didn't take the opportunity of having the barrack to themselves. "We'll plan on it," she added, returning the smile.

A few minutes later, Kate walked out of the mess hall. She found Cal standing outside waiting for her just as he had been the evening before. He looked dashing as ever in his soldier's uniform, and the sight of him made her heart thump within her chest. She began walking toward him, slightly nervous, but mostly curious, at how he would react to her news about their arrangements for the evening.

When she reached him, he scooped her into his arms, and she hugged him back. "I missed you," he said into her ear.

"I missed you too."

"How was your day?" he asked as he pulled back.

"Good," she replied, gazing into his striking blue eyes. She told him about how she had gone on a walk with Regina and Florence and spent some time afterward reading in the barrack. "It was quite nice and relaxing."

"I'm glad. I was afraid you'd be bored out of your socks here."

She laughed and shook her head. "No. But even if I was, it wouldn't matter. I'm just glad I'm here."

"Me too." Cal glanced from side to side. "Well, obviously there's not much of a variety of things to do around here. We could go on a walk. I could show you some of the areas we do training drills at."

Kate cleared her throat. "That sounds nice. But I, um, I think I might already have somewhere for us to be."

Cal's eyebrows knitted together. "You do?"

"Yes. The girls told me we could . . . that we could have the barrack tonight. To ourselves. I guess they sort of switch off nights, and they meant for us to have it last night but we left before they could say anything . . ." She trailed off, realizing she had been speaking rather rapidly.

Cal's face was turning a light shade of red. "Oh . . . ," he replied. "Well, I guess that makes sense." He looked down and kicked the dirt, and then looked back up at her and gave her a wry smile. "We are married, after all."

Kate smiled back at him unable to keep herself from blushing, the obvious implications lurking. "Right."

He cleared his throat. "Well, okay. We should probably go. Otherwise, I think they might . . . suspect something."

"I thought the same thing," Kate responded. "It would seem strange if we didn't."

"Right," he replied quickly.

They stood in silence for a few strained moments. Suddenly the humor of the situation struck Kate, and she couldn't help but let out a laugh. "Don't look so disappointed," she said, reaching out to him and taking his hands in hers. "The thought of being stuck alone with me for the evening can't be that scary, can it?"

He looked down at her hands. She felt him squeeze them with affection and look back up at her. He smiled, his eyes penetrating hers. "Terrifying."

She felt herself blush with his gaze and took a breath. "Well, I'd still like to walk past some of your training areas before we go back, if you'd like."

Cal nodded. "Sure. Let's go."

First he walked her by the expansive parade field. Then he led her down the dirt road to another training area where he said his platoon had done rifle shooting earlier that day. He pointed out where the targets had been set up and where they had shot from. Kate was amazed he could hit a target from so far away.

When they finished at the shooting field, it was dusk and they decided to begin the walk back to the barrack. They ambled hand in hand down the dirt road saying a few words to each other as they went, but mostly they walked in silence. Kate noticed the feeling between them wasn't relaxed as usual. There was a sort of tension building she could feel, and she knew Cal could feel it too. Her heart fluttered with anxiousness.

A few minutes later they reached the barrack. There was no one around. Kate momentarily wondered where the other girls and their husbands spent their time when it was their "off" night.

Cal gestured forward toward the door. "Ladies first."

Kate smiled and walked past him, opened the door, and stepped inside. Cal followed close behind. The open room looked just as it had when they left it earlier. It was tidy, all the beds made and everything put in place. What little light was left in the evening sky trickled through the curtain windows, casting a low-lit glow throughout the room.

Kate turned to face Cal, who was still standing close to the door. "Well, here we are."

Cal nodded and glanced around, standing still.

"You can come in. I don't bite," Kate teased.

The corner of his mouth turned up. He took a few tentative steps toward her and then stopped, still about ten feet away from her. "What are you reading?" he asked, nodding toward the small nightstand next to her bed across the room.

"Oh," she replied, looking toward the bed. "*Pride and Prejudice.*"

Cal nodded knowingly. "My sisters love that book. I wouldn't have pegged you for a Jane Austen girl, though."

"I haven't been, formally. I've tried reading it a number of times and just found it frustrating in the past. But I picked it up back at home, and for some reason this time it pulled me in." She paused for a moment and thought about how, truthfully, in the past the intrigue and romance of those types of novels hadn't interested her much. But now those feelings she read about in books seemed so much more real to her. "I guess I'm doing a lot of things differently lately than I have in the past."

"You mean like hopping on a bus and riding it across the country to pretend to be someone's wife?"

"Something like that," she replied facetiously.

Cal nodded with a smile and began glancing around the room. It was very quiet. He looked back to her and cleared his throat. She could feel his concentrated gaze piercing through her. Although they had been holding hands while walking around the camp just a few minutes earlier, now that they were alone behind closed doors it felt like much more of an intimate setting. She wanted to close the gap between them, to reach out and take a hold of his hands. Suddenly she realized her heart was beginning to pound within her chest. She gazed across the room at him, unsure of what to do, or say, next. But the moment was so still she almost didn't dare move, and she could tell he was feeling the same.

They stood there for a few moments longer. Goodness, what were they going to do in here the whole evening?

Breaking the stillness, Cal took a step forward and paused. Then he took another, and another, until they were only about a foot apart. Kate stood still, unmoving, when Cal took a final step toward her. They were now merely an inch or two apart, so close she could feel the rise and fall of his chest with each steady breath he took. Her gaze hit him just above his shoulders and she closed her eyes, savoring the feeling of him close to her, and the warmth of his breath against hair.

They continued standing this way for a few prolonged seconds. Just how long Kate wasn't sure, all she knew was she wanted the moment to last. Suddenly she felt Cal reach his hand up to her face and touch her cheek. He gently brushed her hair back from the side of her face, tucked it behind her ear, and leaned down to her level. Their lips came together with force. He reached his taut arms around her waist, pulling her close to him. Kissing each other eagerly, Kate wrapped her arms around his neck.

The kiss continued, becoming increasingly zealous with each second. Instinctively, Kate took a step backward toward her bed. She felt Cal step with her. Reaching the bed they lowered themselves to sitting onto its edge, pausing only for breaths.

Cal moved closer into Kate. His hand was clutched at her waist and slowly traveled up her side to her hair. He began combing through her locks with his fingers as he kissed her, his mouth moving from her lips to her cheek. Kate pulled herself into him even more, until there was no space left between them. Her mind was a blur of anything in the outside world. Everything was the two of them.

Then suddenly, Kate felt Cal pull back with a quick jolt. Before she knew it, he was up and off the bed. Catching her breath, Kate sat up in surprise. Standing a few feet from the bed, Cal swiftly turned away from her. He lifted his hands to his head and pressed his palms against his forehead for a moment, and then ran his hands through his hair vexingly.

He turned to her. "I just . . . we can't . . ." He paused, looking as though he wasn't sure of what to say next. He let out a rattled sigh. Taking a hesitant step forward, he lowered himself to sitting beside her on the bed. Reaching over, he took one of her hands in his. "I just, I want to do this right," he said, looking into her eyes earnestly. "Believe me, there is nothing I want more then to be with you, here tonight . . ." He paused for a moment and then shook his head. "But I can't. I made a promise to God and to myself a long time ago that I would wait for marriage."

Kate nodded. She understood, because she felt the same way.

"And not just that," he continued, "You deserve to be treated with the utmost respect. I would never want to put you in a situation that made you feel . . . compromised."

She smiled softly. "I appreciate you respecting me and caring so much, Cal." She realized she had been completely caught up in the moment. But what he was saying didn't surprise her in the least. It was the type of man he was, and she found her respect for him was deepening because of it.

Cal gripped her hand a bit more firmly, his eyes focused on her. "Kate, I love you," he said.

She felt herself inhale sharply.

"Don't feel like you need to say anything in return," he continued quickly. "But I want you to know that. I love you. I do. I love you overwhelmingly. You're all I think of. Your face is the first thing I see when I wake up in the morning. You are with me in my thoughts all day long and you are the last thing I think of at night." He reached a hand up to face and touched the hair curling above her shoulders. "You are so beautiful. But my love for you goes so much deeper than that. I care for you greatly, and that is why this is so important to me. I would never want to do anything to treat you wrong."

Kate's mind was reeling. He loved her. And even more, she believed him. He may not have been the first to tell her that, but she had always known the others didn't truly mean it. They loved her for her outward appearance, perhaps her spunk and style, and even loved the idea of her, but they didn't love her for who she really was. But Cal knew who she really was. He understood her. He accepted

173

and loved her for her good parts and bad. She found herself realizing the way he was expressing he felt was almost an echo of her own feelings for him.

Her heart was swelling. She swallowed hard. "Cal . . . I'm falling in love with you," she said back.

He blinked as if what she was telling him couldn't be true. Then a slow smile began spreading across his mouth. He leaned in and placed a gentle kiss on her lips and pulled back.

"And I understand and respect what you are saying," Kate continued, "about wanting to wait."

Cal looked back at her with a degree of relief. "I'm glad."

"I understand because I feel the same," she continued. "And I'm sorry." Her eyes fell downward, looking at her hands in his. "I don't know what came over me."

Kate shifted her gaze back up to Cal. His eyes were full of adoration as he looked at her. "No," he said, shaking his head. "It's me who should be apologizing." He paused and cleared his throat. "You know us being here, pretending to be married, getting our turn to the barrack every few nights . . . I'm afraid it's not going to get any easier." He sat quiet for a moment. "But I do believe it's best this way."

Kate nodded, looking back at him with admiration. Never before had someone stirred such emotions of attraction and love and respect in her all at once. She was most definitely falling in love with him, something she had worked so hard to keep out. But now she wanted nothing more than to grasp onto it. To not let him go.

She leaned over and rested her head against his shoulder. "You are quite possibly the most caring, selfless person I've ever known."

"No," he countered. "I'm actually quite selfish."

She pulled back and looked at him squarely in the face. "Why would you say that?"

He let out a breath. "Well, I told you I made a promise with God that I would wait for marriage."

Kate nodded.

Cal continued, "And just from tonight I know that will be the most difficult promise I've ever had to keep. I'd be lying if I said I wasn't tempted to give in. But . . . I know I have to honor you and my promise to God. Because if I get out in the war and find myself in danger I want there to be no reason on earth or in heaven of why I can't call on God and ask for His protection."

Kate sat very still, taking in what he was saying.

"If I've kept my promises and stayed true, I do believe He'll keep watch over me so I can come back to you."

Kate felt a shiver run down her spine and tears involuntarily prick her eyes. The thought of him off in some dreaded battlefield having to call on God's mercy in a moment of desperation made her stomach churn. But somehow she knew the chance of that happening was very real.

"So you see," he continued, "I'm being selfish. Because there is nothing more important to me than being able to be with you again."

She shook her head in one quick movement. "You're wrong," she said. "You're not being selfish. It's the most selfless thing you could do. Because you're doing it for me."

Chapter Thirty

How could time be so fleeting?

Cal wondered on the phenomenon while walking back to his barrack after finishing training drills for the day. Between the pervious day's drills in mortars and today's in rifle shooting, his right hand was pulsating with a dull ache. He kneaded the sore muscle in his palm absentmindedly with his other hand as he walked. The weeks of being at camp before Kate arrived had felt a decade long compared to the past two weeks since she had been there, which had gone by all too quickly. He looked forward to each evening with her with great anticipation and relished every moment they were able to spend together. But that was about to change.

A few days into her stay, Kate had been informed she would be allowed to stay a week and a half longer. Then, that had seemed like a great deal of time. But now Cal felt he had simply blinked and that time had come and gone. She was leaving tomorrow morning.

He kept wondering how they could figure a way for her to stay longer, but he knew it wasn't realistic. Not only had they been very fortunate she had been permitted to stay as long as she had, but Kate also needed to get back to Salt Lake. She had arranged with her work to be gone for two weeks and her time was up. There was no getting around it. Their blissful time together was coming to an end.

Her impending departure was causing him to feel quite dismal. If their time together had been anything short of perfect, it might not have been so difficult. But each moment had been a dream so lovely Cal didn't want to wake up.

When he was done with his dinner, Cal made his way to the wives' quarters. He was a little later this evening with afternoon drills having gone on a bit longer than usual and figured she would be back at the barrack by now. Sure enough, as he approached the barrack she shared with the other two women, the barrack they had had to themselves a handful of evenings over the past two weeks, he found Kate sitting on its steps awaiting his arrival. Her posture straightened as she saw him approaching. She slowly stood, her pale-blue skirt gently swishing against her slender legs as she stood. He could see a subdued smile rested on her lips as she watched him advance closer, her eyes twinkling in delight. But amid that delight Cal noticed a hint of sadness. He knew it was coming from the same place his was, and it made his heart throb. This would be their last night together.

They would have the barrack alone to themselves tonight, which Cal was both looking forward to and dreading. As he anticipated after their first night in the barrack, their times for the husband and wife alone time had proven to be both wonderful and trying all at once. He cherished the moments they were able to spend in privacy, immersing themselves in intimate conversation, laughter, and closeness. But keeping their passions in check hadn't come easy. Cal wanted nothing more than to show Kate the highest degree of respect. But in the moment, none of that made it any easier. If he knew how things would turn out, if he knew for certain he would return home and that Kate and him would end up together, it might be somewhat easier. But he had no guarantees. The war was claiming so many lives and there was always a chance his would be one of them.

Kate had told Cal that she was falling in love with him that first night in the barrack and repeated that she loved him over the course of their time together, but she hadn't made any promises. He hadn't asked her to. He had no idea how long he might be gone and how long the war would last, and he didn't feel he was in a position to ask her to promise to wait for him unless she offered it.

He continued walking toward her sitting on the barrack steps, clearing his head and resolving to make the most of their last night together.

"Hey, you," she said as he neared her.

"Hey," he repeated back with a smile. He was now at the base of the steps she sat on. He leaned down to her level and kissed her on the lips, feeling the heated current of the contact for a few brief moments before pulling back.

"How are you?" he asked as he lowered himself down to sit next to her on the step.

"Fine," she responded wistfully. "I've just been thinking."

"Yeah, me too."

They sat for a few moments in silence before she leaned her head against his shoulder. They sat on the porch that way a few minutes, watching the sun fade behind the horizon. Kate's mood wasn't her usual spunky, energetic self. Tonight she seemed subdued, and Cal sensed she needed comforting.

Finally he spoke. "Want to go on a walk?"

She lifted her head. "Sure."

He took her hand in his and they began meandering. They wandered down the dirt road and past some training fields, then by the parade field and up past Cal's barrack area.

Eventually they wound up back at the wives' quarters. Cal led Kate around the backside of the barracks to the grassy hill where they spent their first night together at the camp.

As they stood hand in hand, Cal spoke. "It went by too fast, didn't it?"

Kate nodded. "Much too fast."

He squeezed her hand.

They walked forward and sat down. Cal immediately pulled her back into his chest and wrapped his arms around her waist, holding her close. He felt her breathing steadily against him and wondered if he would ever get to hold her like this again. The question sent a pang through his chest. He immediately cleared his throat, trying to push away the piercing thoughts.

He swallowed hard and looked up at the dark night sky scattered with twinkling lights. "The stars are beautiful tonight," he said softly. He felt Kate nod against his chest.

Suddenly she whirled around to him. Her eyes were brimming with tears, and a look of near-panic filled her eyes. "How can I know you'll be all right?" she sputtered, her voice shaky with emotion. "You need to promise me you'll be safe. I can't stand the thought of it. Promise me you'll take care of yourself. That you'll do whatever you can—"

"Shhhh," Cal interrupted, tenderly raising a finger to touch her lips. "There's no need for you to worry like this. Everything will be fine—"

"You can't say that!" she shot back with force, pushing his hand away. Her tone had quickly transitioned from sad to angry in a matter of seconds. "You don't know what's going to happen. You can't make any guarantees."

"You're right," Cal responded, quickly realizing his mistake. She didn't want to be coddled. "There are no guarantees. But the truth is, I do believe everything will work out." He stopped and took a breath, letting himself and her take a moment to settle their emotions. "I'm not saying I know for certain I will come back," he continued carefully. "But I believe everything will turn out the way it is supposed to. God's hands are in everything."

He looked into her eyes, the emotion in them slowly transforming from confusion to hopeful.

Cal reached down and gripped her hands in his. "Kate, you don't know what you've done for me. You coming here gave a whole new meaning to my life. My first couple weeks here I didn't feel like my life had much meaning anymore. Knowing what life could be like with you and then no longer having you was almost too much to bear. But now . . ." His voice faltered, and he shook his head. He took a breath, and went on, "Now, everything has changed. You make my life worth living. And I will do all in my power, all in my will, to return to you."

A tear trickled down Kate's cheek. "I love you, Cal," she said. She grasped her arms around his neck, clinging to him. Shakily, she whispered, "Please, come back."

Chapter Thirty-One

Breathing in the balmy salty sea air, the warmth of the breeze gushed into his face as he took a step toward the railing. The wind was strong but not overbearing. He stood against the railing of the ship's upper deck looking out over the cobalt-blue ocean, the lapel of his uniform flapping against his chest with the breeze. He watched as the white-capped waves rose and fell, clapping against the side of the ship far down below.

Cal's time on the USS Robert Howze was nearing its end, which he was both anticipating and dreading. He had no idea what to expect. What island within the Philippines would they be landing on? How soon would he enter combat once hitting the beach shores? It seemed the privates were always the last to know what was going on and never knew what was coming next.

They had launched from Fisherman's Wharf in San Francisco just over a month ago. Cal thought back to the wharf's docks, lined with fishing boats and bustling with activity of seafood dealers, shellfish stands, and fishermen. As the troops approached the USS General R.L Howze, the massive transport ship they would be boarding, Cal gazed up at it astounded at the size and magnitude of the vessel.

Formally a luxury liner allocated by the US army and made into a transport ship for its speed and ability to move soldiers relatively quickly reaching speeds of up to 17 knots, the USS Howze held about five thousand soldiers on board, along with a crew of around one thousand. As the USS Howze sailed away from US shores, Cal got a view of the eerie Alcatraz prison before sailing under the striking Golden Gate Bridge.

Cal had heard rumors of men becoming profoundly seasick on the voyage, but as he walked around the ship that first day and gained an even better understanding of just how large it actually was he couldn't imagine how he would even know he was out at sea aboard the massive liner.

But soon he was proven wrong. Three days into the voyage they hit a storm late in the evening. As the winds picked up and the rain began falling, the ship lifted and plummeted with the waves so violently Cal truly wondered if the ship would go down and take them all with it. Dipping into the sea back and forth from bow to stern, literally tons and tons of water crashed onboard before receding back into the sea. The ship lurched all through the night until the storm finally calmed near morning.

The seesawing of the ship through the storm had gotten to Cal's nerves but luckily not to his stomach. He was one of the few lucky ones. From what he observed the next morning, about two-thirds of the men onboard had been cursed with stomachs that couldn't handle the seesawing of the boat in the ocean. During storms like that first one, he sometimes wondered if the men suffering from the worst of it wouldn't launch themselves overboard out of sheer desperation for the misery of the sickness to be over.

One morning while in the eating area under the main deck below water, Cal was sitting down eating his routine: bland, mushy oatmeal—the one and only option for breakfast. Suddenly the ship began swaying and the table he was sitting at began swaying back and forth. The movement didn't bother Cal other than that it made it a little difficult to eat his breakfast. But after a few minutes he noticed some of the faces of the soldiers seated near him turning a peaked shade of green. Then he heard a few low groans echoing through the hall. Suddenly Private Randall, a gangly young kid from the Midwest, stood and began hightailing it for the stairs. But before

Randall made it to the steps, he began puking. The spewing continued his whole way stumbling up the stairs to the deck. Randall's bout seemed to spur on the others and almost simultaneously what seemed to be about half of the men in the hall stood and began running to the steps, vomiting uncontrollably. They rushed to the main deck to gasp a breath of fresh air and hopefully expel their innards overboard instead of on deck.

Walking up the steps from the eating area was no fun at all on those days. But for some reason, Cal never did get seasick. Not once. But that didn't mean the voyage had been all roses for him.

The rooms the privates were assigned were five decks from the top and a deck below the waterline. Cal was about medium height but even he had to duck a good six inches to get through the squatty, low doorway into their quarters. Bunks lined the room and were stacked from floor to ceiling, making for a very crowded space. That, combined with the knowledge they were below water, made for some claustrophobic nights. The first few weeks Cal would lie awake in bed with his eyes closed, trying to push the realization from his mind that if the ship were to be attacked and hit, which was a very real possibility, they would all likely be trapped. There were far more men sleeping in the room than space to stand. If the ship was hit, the door to their room would be locked shut, a precautionary measure to keep the water out and prevent the ship from sinking. There wouldn't be time for the men to all wake and file out of the room, thus trapping them in the room.

In time Cal trained himself to push claustrophobia and concerns of attack from his thoughts and fall asleep. It was usually by focusing on the memory of Kate that he was finally able to relax and drift off. He thought of the day they stumbled into each other just before he left on his mission, when he had a girl at his side he thought he loved but realized deep down the moment he locked eyes with Kate that some way, somehow, she was the one for him. He thought of her the day he found himself at that same church house sitting beside her while she enchanted him with her eyes, her smile, and her cleverness. He thought of dancing with her those nights at the dance hall, the way she moved to the music so effortlessly and swayed in his arms. And of course he thought of his time with her at Camp Roberts, their lovely nights of endless talks, impassioned embraces, and dreamlike moments out under the stars. But perhaps one of his fondest memories of Kate, the one he found himself thinking on often, was of the two of them wandering the farm together the day before he left for California. The way she smiled up at him as they walked hand in hand. How they would stop for a kiss every so often, lingering in each other's arms before continuing their walk around the property. In that memory the world seemed right, and comfortable, and just plain happy. That's how he imagined everyday life would be like with her, and there was no thought as comforting as that.

Cal looked forward to reaching the shore for little reason other than to stretch his legs on solid earth and so he could send and receive letters from Kate. He knew the process wouldn't be a fast one, but knowing there was a means for them to communicate was paramount. He already had a stack of letters he had written while on the ship he planned to send as soon as he had a chance once they landed.

Cal sighed as he looked out over the ocean. It was difficult not to think about Christmas coming up. He was used to missing Christmases; this would be his fourth one away from home. But now, with Kate in the picture, missing this time of year was much more disheartening. He longed to be home with her. He imagined the two of them sitting next to a warm, cozy fire with his arm around her, holding her close to him. But instead he was here, out somewhere in the middle of the South Pacific Ocean, feeling the distance between them more than ever before.

Suddenly Cal heard a shout ring out from behind him. "Land port!"

Cal turned to see a soldier standing on the opposite side of the deck with his arm extended, pointing out over the railing. Cal was standing on the starboard side. "See it?" the soldier called to some others nearby him. The men began pointing and looking.

Cal walked toward the group of soldiers, squinting his eyes as he walked, trying to get a glimpse. He quickly saw the narrow strip of land off in the distance and what looked to be a few other spots of land further off behind it.

"That there's one of Fiji's islands," a crewman said, approaching them. "Hundreds of little islands make up Fiji. We'll get a little closer look at that one as we pass it in the next hour or so."

The men nodded thoughtfully.

"So where are we, exactly?" a soldier asked the crewman.

"East of Australia about twenty-five hundred miles or so," the crewman answered. "New Guinea is getting closer now, about three thousand miles out. Reckon we'll hit it in, say, five or six days."

The men nodded. They knew New Guinea was going to be a stop on the way to their final destination of the Philippines, and they knew some would get off there. Just how many they didn't know.

The crewman excused himself and went back below deck. Cal and the others stood at the railing looking out at the island in the distance. The men around him were talking on about New Guinea, what they had heard of it and what projections they had of what they might be doing once they got there. Cal found he would rather not guess and speculate of what was coming. Soon it would be here, and he would find out what was next.

"Sounds like we'll be getting to New Guinea sometime around Christmas," one of the soldiers commented. Cal knew the kid, had sat with him a handful of times at meals.

"Sure don't feel nothing like Christmas to me," another soldier responded shaking his head.

"A strange Christmas, indeed," the boy said back.

It was quiet for a few moments. Cal knew they were all thinking about what they would be doing over the holiday if they were back home. Surely they all had their own set of varying traditions of how they celebrated the Christmas season. But now they had something in common. They were here and not home. Suddenly Cal felt a pull in his chest to go retrieve his notepad and pencil and write a letter to Kate, and one to his family.

"I'm heading back down," Cal said, breaking the silence. "Have a nice evening, boys."

"You too," the men replied in unison as Cal turned to head back below the deck.

❧

"Okay guys, I have a little treat for you," Clawson said. The men exchanged curious glances. "I'm not going to tell you what it is now, but I'm going to need you to follow me up to the kitchen. And don't make a ruckus as we go. We don't want to draw any attention."

Cal couldn't help but smile as the men began following their friend through the winding passageways of the ship to the cafeteria's kitchen, trying to appear nonchalant. Clawson had gathered the group of men and told them to follow him. Cal had first gotten to know the men he was with at Sunday church services when the soldiers were allowed to break into worship groups. A small group of members of the LDS faith would meet each Sunday, and that bond of common beliefs and culture seemed to instantly join the men together as friends. Clawson was a crewman rather high up in the ranks on board and a member of the LDS church the men had gotten to know at worship services. He was a friendly fellow and sharp guy with his head on straight, but also seemed to have a touch of mischief in him. Cal wondered what he had up his sleeve.

A few minutes later they reached the kitchen. Clawson signaled to the soldiers to stay put as he quietly opened the kitchen door a notch and peered inside. He turned back to them. "Coast is clear," he said as he swung the door open and began waving the men in. One by one they filed inside.

Once they were all standing in the kitchen, Clawson said in a low voice, "Over here." The men followed as he made his way to the large white industrial GE freezer. He opened its door and reached inside. A moment later his hand emerged with a couple of white wrapped objects. It only took Cal a moment to recognize what they were.

"Ice cream bars!" one of the men shouted with excitement. He sounded like a six-year-old on Christmas morning.

"Sure are," Clawson said, eyebrows raised, appearing to be fully enjoying the sight of the men's delighted expressions. "Consider it an early Christmas present. Quick, everyone take one," he said, passing them around. "Open them and start eating fast. We can't chance taking them out of the kitchen and getting caught." The men nodded and began tearing into their wrappers. "I'd get in a heap of trouble for this," Clawson said under his breath with a wry smile on his face.

The men on the ship hadn't seen anything remotely resembling sweets, let alone ice cream, for ages.

Cal smiled back at his friend and looked down as he unwrapped his bar. As he pulled the wrapper off, he held the ice cream in his hand for a moment, staring at the icy-chocolate vision. Then he took a bite into it, the sweet and cold cocoa flavor melting on his tongue.

"If the other soldiers knew we got ice cream, they'd up and throw us overboard," mumbled one of the guys between bites.

Cal nodded. "I wouldn't doubt it," he added. They were half joking, but in all seriousness Cal could imagine the other men quite infuriated if they found out a small group of them were treated to ice cream while the others were all left with hungry stomachs. He wouldn't be at all surprised if a serious brawl would result from this if the others were to find out, not to mention trouble for Clawson by his superior crewmen, so Cal fully understood why Clawson wanted to keep it quiet.

"That's why you guys can't breathe a word of this to anyone," Clawson said, looking around at the group. "And I'm not just looking after my own behind here, but all yours too." He paused for a moment and then continued: "I just wanted to do something small to thank you all for becoming good friends. And to wish you luck as you go off."

Cal swallowed. His throat began tightening. Such a seemingly small thing, a chocolate ice cream bar. But it meant something that his friend would go out on a limb for Cal and the others so they could find a little joy amidst the despondent days on the ship and the imminent nightmare that lay ahead.

Chapter Thirty-Two

"H ot diggity-dog! Look at all them ships!"

Cal nodded in awe as he gazed out at the rows and rows of vessels lining the sandy shores of Port Moresby on the southeastern coast of New Guinea. He had been told there would be fleets of ships but hadn't begun to comprehend just how expansive and spectacular the sight of hundreds of endless liners spread across what seemed this entire side of the island would be. There were more ships than he realized were in the entire army.

"I've never seen anything like it," Cal responded with wonder to his GI friend standing beside him. The massive, intimidating steel manmade watercrafts contrasted strangely against the serene aqua blue waters and tropical greenery dotting the island's hillsides.

Cal had learned that thousands of lives had been lost in battles on these shores and throughout the island. The New Guinea campaign had been quite a large one, although not as well known as many of the other war campaigns. As the second largest island in the world, providing widespread areas for land, air and naval bases, New Guinea was a strategically important landmass to secure. For this reason, the Japanese had been after the island for nearly three years and a great deal of fighting had resulted. Allied forces had now secured Papua along with most of the island. But battles in New Guinea were still persisting, and so the ship carrying Cal and the others would stop there to send a group of reinforcements in.

Cal now knew he was not getting off here in New Guinea. He would go on to the ship's next and final destination—the island of Leyte, located in the mid-southeastern region of the Philippines.

In October, the United States, along with Filipino guerillas, had invaded Leyte and began fighting for the recapture and liberation of the Philippines after nearly three years of Japanese occupation. The invasion had been intense and began with a massive naval battle at the gulf of Leyte. Cal had overheard some crewman say the battle at the gulf of Leyte was likely the largest naval battle the war had seen.

Once allied forces secured the gulf, the United States invaded the island, and by December Leyte was secured. Leyte was now a safe zone for the States to ship in soldiers and divvy them out to where they would go next in the invasion of the Philippines.

When they reached the port, Cal and the others said goodbye to the soldiers disembarking the boat, among them a few he had become acquainted with during their time at sea. Those staying on board weren't allowed to get off. It was strange to know it was likely the last time he'd ever see those men. He wondered how many of them would make it back from the war, a morbid but realistic thought.

Cal was unsure how long they would be docked at the Port. But after the first night came and went he figured there was a good chance they would be staying another day or so. Apparently the military leaders were making plans for the invasion with other leaders stationed at New Guinea and weren't ready to move on yet.

As usual, the soldiers were the last to know what was going on, so they bided their time and waited. Cal wished they could at least get off the ship to see the island, but unless they were instructed to get off they weren't allowed to. So they stayed on board and waited. The three scanty meals they had typically been served a day had now been cut back to two: one serving of bland, mushy oatmeal in the morning and a sandwich sometime in the afternoon. He wished he had the comfort of knowing that once they reached their final destination the meals would be more substantial, but he realized the opposite was probably true.

Finally on day three, in early afternoon, Cal heard rumbles that the ship was preparing to take off. Cal set off to the top deck and watched and conversed with the men around him as the massive ship pulled out of the port and began sailing out into the sea. They were headed northbound toward the Philippines. The men, including Walker and a few of the boys from Utah, sat around a table on deck and chatted for an hour or two. Eventually Cal's legs got restless and he stood to walk to the railing of the ship. The sun was beginning its slope downward in the sky. From its placement he estimated it was about four in the afternoon. Clusters of large cotton-like clouds scattered across the sky, the puffy white juxtaposing against the bright azure-colored background.

Cal glanced downward, the sun's rays glistening off the caps of the crests of waves below. It was a lovely day at sea. These were the kind of days at sea he would have felt privileged to experience had it not been for the reason he was on the ship in the first place. He often imagined what it would be like to have Kate here with him. How he would love to gaze out over the tranquil ocean with her at his side. How much she would enjoy the ocean on a day like today. He still remembered how she had told him she loved the ocean clear back in the eighth grade.

He took in a deep breath, letting his mind linger on the daydream a bit longer. Then suddenly, something caught his eye. His vision quickly focused on the water about fifty feet ahead. Something was zipping through the ocean ten or so feet down. His eyes tried to keep up with the moving object, but it was lightning fast as it moved through the water and passed the front of the ship. It had only been a second since he first spotted it, but all at once he knew in his gut what it was.

"Torpedo!" he shouted, whirling to the men. "A torpedo just whizzed past the bow!"

The men shot out of their seats and ran to where he was standing. "You sure?" Walker asked, leaning over the rail and squinting.

"Pretty darn sure," Cal said, catching his breath. "It was right— holy mackerel!" he exclaimed. "Another one!"

This one followed the same path, and missed the front of the boat by merely a few feet.

"Cripes!" shouted Walker. "He's right! I just saw it fly past us!"

Cal turned from the railing to face the other men. "Attack!" he shouted. "Two torpedoes just missed the bow!"

It only took a few moments for the deck to turn into an uproar. Men were running all over, mostly to the railings to get a view. Cal wished he were on rotation at the gun turrets, the large firing weapons mounted on the sides of the ship. Cal took his turn sitting at a firing arm each morning for an hour. He supposed he was assigned duty on the turrets because of the sharpshooter tag he earned in training.

He had shot at a handful planes during his time on ship, but could never be quite certain if he'd sent one down or not. If one had gone down as a result of his fire, it had been too far away for him to see. It gave him a disconcerting feeling to know he could have been responsible for sending a plane down, and he often began feeling sick at the thought, but then the opposing outcome of his ship being attacked was the ill-fated alternative. While working at the turrets, he pushed thoughts of either from his mind and focused on simply doing his duties and not thinking of the results, a strange and foreign concept to someone who had always thought through his actions in life so carefully, making sure to do what was right and moral at all times. But in war right and wrong were skewed. Morality was blurred. He did what he was commanded, trusting that somehow the result of his actions would help in ending this dreadful war and ultimately returning him home.

Now Cal's fight or flight instincts were taking over. He wanted to be at the gun turrets, feeling the need to have some sort of way to combat what was happening in the waters below. As he gazed down over the open sea another flicker of an object passed speedily through the water. Less than a second later he was knocked off his feet. He hit the floor of the deck with a hard and unexpected thud. He heard yelps and hollers all around him.

"The bow was hit!" someone shouted.

Cal felt the entire ship tilting to the port side. He clamored up, regaining his footing on deck, and sprinted to the front of the ship to get a look at what had happened. The ship was still tilted, but appeared to slowly be shifting back to its upward stance.

"I saw the sub!" a soldier to his left yelled. "It's out ahead a hundred yards or so."

"Subchasers are coming!" someone shouted from behind.

Cal turned toward the stern. Sure enough, the two subchasers that had been keeping close distance to their ship since its departure from New Guinea were coming up from behind, chugging along to catch up with what was likely a Japanese sub ahead.

Cal and the others watched as the subchasers steamed ahead of the ship. A few moments later, a loud thud sounded off, sending a vibration resonating through the sea and throughout the ship up to the soles of Cal's shoes.

Cal squinted, trying to get a look at what was going on ahead. "They just dropped a bomb," he murmured. The other men looked at him in alarm. Everything went quite. The men were shocked out of their initial frenzy into a tense silence, all focusing in on the subchasers. Cal glared ahead, feeling the intensity of the situation on every nerve end of his body.

The bombs continued dropping as the subchasers advanced forward. The men had no idea what they were watching, but continued anxiously awaiting for what would happen next, knowing their fate was at stake. Slowly, the bombs began dissipating. The subchasers stayed in position, continuing on the defense. But it appeared the action had likely ceased.

"What's happening?" a young soldier asked from behind Cal, a nervous questioning in his voice.

"It's over!" a GI shouted to his right, sounding enthused. "We sucker-punched those Japs!"

"We got them?" the kid asked excitedly.

"Of course we did!" the GI exclaimed with a laugh.

Cal felt immensely relieved, but also a bit annoyed with the older GI's attitude. "We can't be sure we got them," Cal said steadily. "But either way, it appears to be over."

"Hmph," the GI breathed, shooting a hint of indignation in Cal's direction.

A chorus of excited yelps erupted all around. Many of the men began clapping. Slowly, Cal joined in the applause. Soon the crowd of men began exchanging in excited conversation, each recounting their own versions of what they saw and heard, and what they suspected went down in their first experience with naval battle.

Cal had lost track of his friends through the ruckus but spotted Walker on the starboard side after a few moments. He began making his way toward him.

"Well, that was a bit scary," said Walker as Cal approached.

Cal nodded. "I'm wondering what the situation is on the bow where that torpedo hit."

"I just asked a crewman about that," Walker replied. "He said he ran down there as soon as it happened to see what the damage was. Apparently it hit the steel part of the bow and bounced right off. Must not have hit at the right angle, or it could have been a defective torpedo. The crewmen aren't quite sure. We're just lucky it didn't hit a few more feet in, or it could have penetrated the ship and caused some real damage."

Cal let out a breath of relief.

It appeared the action was over. For now, anyway.

☙

Dearest Cal,

It was so wonderful to receive the bundle of letters you wrote me while on board the ship! They were delivered just yesterday, and I can't tell you how excited I was when the package arrived. I first told myself I would read them slowly and make them last, perhaps allow myself one a day, so I could savor each detail you penned. But after reading one I became much too impatient and ended up devouring them all in one sitting. Then I read them back over again, staying up half the night simply relishing in each word, and I've read them multiple times since. I particularly loved the last one you wrote just after you exited the ship and were about to send the letters off to me. I don't know if it was your heartfelt expressions or the knowledge that those were the most recent words you had written to me, but that letter deeply touched me and I carried it around in my pocket with me all day today. I could hardly wait to get home from work so I could sit down and write you back.

I found the details you wrote about your journey onboard the ship so exciting. How very glad I am that you didn't suffer from seasickness as so many of the men did! And how awful those tight quarters you had to stay in sounded! I can hardly stand the thought of you in such dreadful circumstances. What a miraculous blessing it was that the torpedo that hit the ship didn't do its damage! I do believe with all my heart you are being watched over and protected. That is the only comfort I have in our separation and what gets me through each day of us being apart.

I understand you are worried it might be difficult to come by paper and writing utensils out in the battlefield from what you have heard. Please don't worry about that. If I don't hear from you I will understand why. I know where your heart is without needing to receive constant letters. But when you find the opportunity to write please do, even if it's just a small note or scribble, anything you can send to let me know you are all right. Although you are so far away, just seeing your script makes me feel closer to you knowing that we have some way of connecting although we are worlds apart.

Life at home is anything but interesting. Work at the dentist's office is going just fine. I have started a new class in office management that I am finding quite interesting. I have more studying than I am used to with this class but am getting along well with it and find I don't mind being home reading or studying, anyway. I have been visiting my mother each weekend and her companionship is comforting and refreshing.

I know you said I should go out dancing with the girls as a distraction and to lift my spirits, but I can't bear the thought of entering a dance floor without you. It would be all too reminiscent of our marvelous nights spent together dancing and falling in love, and I know I would turn to my side only to find you not there and would not be able to hold myself together. I'm sure I sound all too dramatic. I'm really getting along fine. I just worry about you so, and the ache of us being apart is something that doesn't diminish with time. It only grows stronger, and I feel the hole in my heart without you is something that could never be replaced without you back with me.

Please, Cal, take care of yourself and keep out of harm's way. I don't know what type of situations you find yourself in now and if you've seen much fighting or battle yet, but if you can help it, please try your hardest to keep as far from it as possible.

I love you dearly and cannot wait to be reunited with you again.

With all my love,

Kate

Chapter Thirty-Three

JANUARY 29, 1945
Luzon, Philippines

Trudging through the rugged path with the thick, sweltering jungle surrounding him on both sides, Cal laboriously moved one foot in front of the other.

"How you doing, Abe?" Cal called to the soldier walking ahead of him.

Abe grunted. "Just swell," he answered, sarcasm seeping through his voice.

Cal let out a chuckle, although it almost pained him to do so. He was walking at the front of his mortar crew and Abe was bringing up the rear of his. They seemed to be somewhere in the middle of the one hundred man company that had been sent to continue the march from the spot where headquarters were set up three or four miles back.

Abe was a real nice guy. He was from Oregon and had also come over on the USS Howze although Cal hadn't gotten to know him until they ended up in the same company. Abe had a girl back home as well. The two men seemed to have a lot in common and Cal enjoyed passing the time talking with him. None of the men Cal had known previously from basic training or the ship voyage were in his company. He wasn't sure where they had ended up. Abe was his closest friend now.

The day before they had marched nearly twenty miles in the heat and humidity, slept on the trail, and began marching again this morning. The troops were physically worn to the bone. Cal had carried his crew's mortar weapon on his back, which was heavily weighing down on him. It was getting difficult to speak beyond anything concise.

"The blisters," Abe lamented with a groan. "They are killing me."

"Uh-huh," Cal concurred.

They weren't just blisters. They were blisters upon blisters. Cal was sure they were rubbing his feet raw. He couldn't understand how the army could give the men such awful boots and expect them to be effective soldiers, let alone win a war. Made of cheap leather, the boots had no cushion and were completely flat soled and hard as a rock. All the soldiers complained of the boots. Cal had known they were bad, but up until now he hadn't understood just how horrible they really were. If he would have been able to rotate wearing the boots with the second pair he was given at Leyte Island, he might not be in such bad off shape. But the army had failed him on that account as well. They gave him crappy boots and somehow managed to lose the second pair of crappy boots they'd given him, along with his nice new set of clothing.

When they had disembarked the USS Howze back at Leyte, the lieutenants instructed the soldiers to toss their duffle bags full of new clothing items they had just received onto the airstrip. They'd be allowed to come back for the bags later after they'd been assigned their regiments. But when they returned that afternoon the bags were gone. Cal and the others couldn't believe it. All they had were the clothes on their backs and a few personal belongings in their knapsacks. No second pair of boots or socks. No new shirts, or pants, or underwear, even. And there was no way to get a hold of more articles of clothing. They had been given all they would be allowed, and they could chalk it up as bad luck.

But dwelling on his lost clothing wouldn't do him any good now. He pushed the negativity from his mind, knowing he was letting exhaustion get the better of him. They had been marching up the island for so long, and the heat and humidity were wearing on him. They must have moved close to twenty miles and his entire body was dripping with perspiration. He barely had the strength to reach his arm up and swipe away a bead of sweat rolling down his forehead into his eyes.

There were positives to his situation, he reminded himself. He had felt very fortunate in the assignment he had been given. When they had loaded onto the battleship that would carry their regiment from Leyte to Luzon, an officer walked over to the group Cal was standing with and asked if any of them had any training in heavy weapons. Cal quickly raised his hand and responded, "I have, sir."

The officer nodded. "All right. You come on over here."

He pulled Cal aside and proceeded to tell him how he had volunteered himself to be part of a mortar crew. Cal readily agreed and explained that he had been trained in mortars during his time at Camp Roberts. The officer seemed pleased and assigned Cal to a crew right away. Cal was ecstatic and relieved. This meant he would never have to be on the front lines of battle and would hopefully never have to point a rifle and shoot anyone. This was a big break and he was thankful for it.

Ultimately, Cal had been assigned to a mortar crew in the 34th Infantry Regiment within the 24th Division of the US Army. On the battleship transporting his division to Luzon, Cal was surprised at the sight of the soldiers he was joining. He had been assigned to a regiment that needed replacements and hadn't expected the soldiers he would be fighting alongside to appear so run-down and battle-worn. The men had been through seven campaigns. Their clothes were dirty and tattered, undoubtedly the same they had worn since the very beginning. But it wasn't just the appearance of their clothing. Cal figured most of them were probably around his age, give or take a few years, but serving in the war had aged them immensely. He tried making conversation with them and a few were responsive and friendly, but most were despondent and aloof. As he looked into their glassy eyes and calloused faces, he couldn't help but wonder who the men behind the dark and altering masks of war were, and if those men would ever return.

When Cal and his battalion were about five hundred yards in from the gulf, they were instructed to de-board the battleship and climb into barges that would carry them to the shore. Riding in on the barges oscillating with the rise and fall of the waves, Cal had looked off in the distance toward the coastline with grave uncertainty. Would there be resistance once they landed? Would they find themselves in combat right away? No one knew the answer, and so the men were told to disembark prepared for anything. Moving closer and peering at the shore, Cal had felt in his soul a propelling need to offer a sincere supplication to the Lord. He had closed his eyes and silently pled with his creator. *Please, if it be Thy will, spare my life. If Thou wilt protect me, I promise to devote my entire life to Thee and Thy service.*

❧

When the troops arrived on the shores of southern Luzon, the largest most northern island of the Philippines, thankfully they were met with no opposition. Their regiment was to move along a path known as Route 7 through the rough jungle terrain of the Zambales Mountains. Further up the Japanese had control of the route and they were to fight for it.

Thus far, Cal and the soldiers surrounding him had been fortunate. They had been spared any serious damage or injuries. But now Cal had a foreboding feeling. From the attitude of his sergeant and the company lieutenants, his intuition told him that the conflict they were about to engage in would be dangerous. Cal knew at any moment they could get word the Japanese were ahead. So while he was sweltering and in pain from his blistered feet, he'd walk another twenty miles in these conditions if that meant no battle.

Beginning to trudge their way up to higher ground now, rugged jungle mountains lay ahead. Cal glanced to his sides, marveling at the density of the foliage surrounding them, imagining a person could walk ten feet off the path and get lost. It was also quite an unnerving thought, knowing the enemy could be lurking in the jungle and they would have no clue.

"Halt!"

The shout had come from up ahead. Cal and the others stopped in their tracks. For a few minutes the men stood awaiting further instruction from the Brass—a term the GIs used when referring to high-ranking officials in the military.

Abe turned to Cal. "Do you see that up there?" he murmured.

"What?" Cal responded.

"Up in the hills ahead. I think I can see some movement up there."

Cal stepped to the side, without falling out of line, to get a better look. It was difficult to tell through the heavy greenery, but sure enough, after a few moments he spotted it. There was movement up in the hills.

Suddenly, Cal heard it—the low, rumbling sound of gunfire coming from the hills above. He felt the skin on the back of his neck prickle with the sound.

Abe was still standing close by. He took a few steps toward Cal. "This is bad news," he said lowly.

Cal nodded. He glanced to his side and noticed Sergeant Williams conversing with another lieutenant. A few minutes later he approached Cal and waved in the men around him. "Our company has instructions to move forward. Apparently there is a bit of a clearing up there. They want us in the front of the column."

Cal and the soldiers around him began forward. As they moved to the front of the column Cal realized they would be the first to confront the enemy.

Once in position Cal and his crew began setting up their weapon. He couldn't help but wonder about what they were doing. Foxholes here would do little good with the Japanese still looking down on them. Why didn't they try pushing in closer to get on higher ground, which would put them in a better position? With the disadvantage in their placement, they were like sitting ducks just waiting to be pounced on.

But it wasn't Cal's place to question his superiors. Perhaps there was something he didn't understand. He sure hoped so, or he could already see the horrible aftermath of their situation playing out in his head.

Finished setting up their mortar, Cal moved to the side of the weapon, unclasped the entrenching tool off his belt and began digging into the ground to create a foxhole. They had been taught to dig a hole longer than it was deep and sideways to the front lines so they could lie flat in it, so that was what he did.

Abe began digging in next to him. "Does this make sense to

you?" Abe asked quietly as they scooped the dirt up, tossing it to the side.

Cal shook his head. "No. But I'm hoping there's something I don't understand."

"Let's hope."

Cal's heart rate was climbing and he began feeling his adrenaline kicking in. The shots from earlier had dissipated but he knew something was coming soon.

It seemed eerily quiet.

"Morgan?"

Cal turned toward the sound of Sergeant Williams' voice. "Yeah?"

Looking at the sergeant, Cal only now realized how awful he looked. Shakily digging into the ground, the man was sweating bullets. Wetness trailed into the sergeant's frantic eyes, and he didn't bother wiping it away. His face was pasty white and drained of any color.

"How can you be so calm?" the sergeant asked soberly, crouching down on the ground, sitting very still. "I am scared to death. I know I'll not make this one." His eyes were bewildered and terrified all at once.

Cal stared back at the sergeant. He wanted to tell the man that everything would be okay, that he would make it out alive, but he couldn't find the words in him to say it and knew they would be untrue even if he did.

Cal was scared for what was coming, but somehow he had with him a sense of calmness as opposed to the panic that seemed to be building around him. He couldn't put into words why that was, but knew it was because he had the Lord's help with him. He had made the decision to put his trust in God, believing that whatever was to come was all part of His plan and purpose. But Cal surely didn't know what was going to happen.

Cal sat looking back into the frantic eyes of his sergeant with empathy. He knew there was nothing he could say or do to console the man.

After a few long, silent moments, both men turned back to their holes and continued digging. Cal began digging more rapidly. He knew the further down he got the better off he'd be when the shelling started. He looked over his shoulder and noticed the Brass gathered in a circle talking, likely discussing their plan.

Cal turned back toward his foxhole and dug his entrenching tool into the thick dirt for a big scoop.

Suddenly, out of nowhere, there was a thunderous, violent explosion.

Chapter Thirty-Four

The force of the blast blew Cal forward on his face and he toppled into his foxhole. How many seconds or minutes had passed since the explosion he wasn't sure. The ground seemed to reverberate beneath him from the power of the blast. His ears were ringing and his body felt numb.

Breathing heavily, he lay still for a few minutes until the shelling stopped. Lifting his head cautiously, he peered above his foxhole. The air was filled with dark, puffy clouds of dirt and flying debris. He couldn't see anything. After a few minutes the dark swirls began to fritter away.

His eyes focused in on a massive tree trunk directly in his line of vision fifteen or so feet ahead of where he lay. The first thing he saw was a sapling on the trunk about the size of a silver dollar around. Then he noticed a peculiar red drizzle of liquid trickling down the trunk, oozing right into the sap. It only took a moment for Cal to realize what the liquid was. Blood.

But why was blood coming from the treetops? Where was it coming from? Warily, he tilted his head upward, letting his eyes trail up the trunk to the tree's branches. What he saw sent a sickening blow to his stomach. A pair of blood-spattered unattached legs draped grotesquely in the center of the tree where the trunk split out into limbs. His eyes focused on the boot of one of the legs, instantly recognizing the familiar sole of the boot. It was cut in half. He swallowed hard realizing whom the pair of legs had belonged to. Sergeant Williams had a boot sole that had been cut in half.

His head began feeling dizzy. He glanced back down, unable to look any longer. The shelling sounds had stopped, so he allowed himself to sit up in his foxhole slowly and look around. The sight he saw nearly seized the breath from his lungs. Wreckage and torn apart bodies were scattered everywhere. He looked to the area where the circle of the Brass had been gathered. Nothing was left but dead bodies and the remains of the former leaders scattered across the uneven pathway.

Crouching down, Cal quickly surveyed the area surrounding him. He couldn't see any movement. Nothing but crumpled bodies and unattached arms and legs, scattered weapons and destroyed equipment. He wanted to stop for a moment, to pay proper respect to all the men that had been killed, but he knew he didn't have time. He would need to move quickly, before the Japanese saw movement and began shooting at him.

He looked down the pathway. There was a natural ditch about one hundred feet back and to the side of the clearing. That would be a good place to take cover until he figured out what to do next.

He began standing in his foxhole, about to make a run for it, when he heard a groan to his right. Cal's head snapped to the sound. "Abe, is that you?" he called. He saw a man's body lying half in a foxhole, half out. Cal thought he saw Abe crouch up a bit. Then he heard the groan again.

Cal leapt from his foxhole and rushed over to Abe hunched over his foxhole. Cal grabbed hold of his shoulder and turned him over. "Abe!" he exclaimed, as he saw the man's eyes wide open. He noticed the rise and fall of Abe's chest. He was breathing. "You're alive!" Cal shouted, relieved his friend was okay. He pulled Abe up to sitting position. "Come on, we've got to get out of here!"

But Abe just stared back at him blankly.

"Abe?" Cal asked, shaking the man's shoulders. "Are you hurt?" He quickly scanned his friend's body and could see no bleeding, no wounds. He looked back into Abe's eyes which were uncomprehending and unable to focus. "Abe, can you hear me?" Cal asked, confused and worried. Why was his friend not answering him?

Then it hit him. He knew what was wrong. "Abe," Cal said steadily, unsure if the man could even hear or register what he was saying. But it was worth a shot. "Abe," he repeated, "you're shell shocked. But we've got to get out of here." Cal took a breath and looked from side to side, and back to Abe quickly. "Can you walk?"

Abe continued staring at him blankly.

"All right," Cal said, taking hold of the man's hand. "I'll take that as a yes."

Cal stood, pulling Abe up with him. Fortunately Abe followed his tug. "You can do this," Cal said quickly. "Now, run!"

Cal began moving as swiftly as he could, pulling Abe behind him. He couldn't run at full speed holding onto his friend's hand while maneuvering past the foxholes and debris and bodies, but Abe's feet were moving fairly quickly albeit mechanically, and Cal was grateful for that.

As they approached the area where the Brass had been gathered, Cal spotted a shiny metal gun lying in the dirt next to one of the bodies that was turned over face first on the ground. The body was covered in blood and looked as though the man had received multiple wounds through his middle. Cal squatted down, pulling Abe down with him, to get a better look at the weapon. It was a small, light handgun, the kind that was only given to higher-ups in the army. It would be much more nimble and quick to operate than his own bulky M1 rifle, the standard weapon allotted to GIs. Cal quickly grabbed for the gun and tucked it into his belt. Next he reached for the man's knapsack a few feet away and swiftly opened and dumped the ammo from the bag into his own. He was about to stand when he spotted a canteen strapped to the man's belt. He thought for a moment, feeling a bit guilty. But he quickly reminded himself that the man was dead. The canteen would be no use to him now, but for Cal it could be extremely useful. The gun and canteen could possibly end up saving his life. He reached for the canteen, unstrapped it from the dead body of the lieutenant and strapped it to his own.

"Thank you," Cal said with a nod to the deceased man. Then he turned to Abe. "Let's go."

They began running. The time it took to get across the short distance to the ditch was excruciating knowing at any moment they could both be shot down, but Cal kept telling himself not to stop. He couldn't slow down, and he couldn't look back. He just needed to keep moving.

When they reached the ditch Cal jumped in, pulling Abe in with him. After looking down and catching his breath, he lifted his head and saw four more men crouched about ten feet down the ditch from them.

"Hey!" hollered one of the men. "Glad you fellas made it."

Cal nodded breathlessly. "I wasn't sure if anyone else was left."

"I know," another soldier responded. "We've been looking up out over the ditch every so often and saw you guys coming."

"This is Abe," Cal said, turning toward his friend. "He's out of his head, shell shocked—"

"Hey, what's that dripping down your back?" the soldier interrupted. "Were you shot?"

Panic struck Cal as he reached around to his back. "I don't think so . . ." He felt the wetness that was soaking through his green shirt. He brought his hand around to his front, covered in dark reddish-purple liquid. "Is this . . . blood?" he asked. Could he really have been shot without knowing it? He quickly pulled his knapsack off his back and saw the side of it had been pierced with shrapnel. The oozy purple liquid was dribbled down the side of the bag.

Cal turned so the others could get a look at his back as he inspected the bag. He opened it up and saw the liquid was spilled all over the knapsack's inside. Then he noticed a punctured object and instantly made the connection of what had happened.

"Well, I'll be . . . " Cal said as he pulled the aluminum can out from his knapsack. "Grape jelly." He turned and held the object for all to see. The men stared in awe at the pierced ration can.

"How does it feel to know a can of grape jelly saved your life?" one of the soldiers said with a grin.

"Just swell, actually," Cal replied, shaking his head in wonder.

Over the next couple minutes the men made introductions and regrouped, and began making plans of what to do next.

"We should holler out to anyone still alive and tell them to gather here for cover," Cal said.

"Good idea."

Over the next half hour the men called what men were still alive into the ditch. Every so often shelling would start, and they would lay low and hope and pray that the Japanese troops wouldn't discover where they were hiding.

One of the men that ran into the ditch had spotted a radio that must have belonged to the Brass lying on the ground and managed to grab it on his way as he ran. The soldiers erupted excitedly when they saw the radio, but were soon deflated when they realized it didn't work.

Larry, a soldier who claimed to be handy with electronics, began fiddling with the radio. "I'll get it working," he assured the others.

Cal was hopeful. If they could get a hold of headquarters three or four miles back, perhaps they could send some extra help to get them out safely. Some extra men to help the wounded ones out, and perhaps even a truck or some sort of vehicle waiting for them around the bend to drive them back would help tremendously. It was nearing sunset and there was now a good-sized group gathered in the ditch. Some of the men had minor wounds, but most were okay.

"There's about thirty of us," Cal said to the soldier next to him. His name was Kurt, and he was the soldier Cal had first talked with when they reached the ditch. "Thirty left out of one hundred."

"Yeah," Kurt responded gravely.

They sat in silence for a moment.

"I don't think any more are coming," Kurt added.

"Me neither."

Cal sat with Abe next to him, still out of his head. Cal didn't dare let go of Abe's hand or he might stand up and wander off and be shot. So he kept a hold of Abe and made sure he stayed low.

"Hey guys!" called Larry from a few feet down the ditch. "It's working!"

Sure enough, Cal heard the static-sound of the radio.

The men all turned to Larry eagerly.

"Can you get a signal?" one of the soldiers asked.

"Working on it."

They waited anxiously as Larry fiddled with the controls. A few moments later they heard the sound of man's voice.

"Hello?" Larry shouted into the radio, clutching it desperately in his hands. "Hello, can you hear me?"

"Yes, I can hear you," a low voice responded crackly through the radio speaker.

The men all gasped in excitement and relief.

"Captain Anderson speaking," the voice continued. "Who am I speaking with?"

"This is Private Farnsworth, of the 34th Infantry Regiment," Larry responded ecstatically. "We got blistered up the road here at Zig-Zag Pass. There's a group of us gathered in a ditch. Some are wounded, but most of us are fine. We could use some help getting out of here."

There was a long pause. "I understand. How many made it?"

"About thirty, sir."

There was another long pause. Larry looked up at the group of men with a confused expression. "Are you still there, sir?" he said into the radio.

"Yes," the voice sounded through the speaker. "Can you hold for a minute?"

"Certainly," Larry responded.

The men waited anxiously for a few moments until the captain's voice returned.

"Are you there, soldier?"

"Yes, sir."

"All right. We congratulate you men for surviving such a deadly battle," the captain said. "But unfortunately, there's nothing we can do."

There was a long, heavy silence. "Excuse me, sir?" Larry finally responded. "I don't understand."

Cal closed his eyes. The second the captain put them on hold, he was worried this would happen. But his optimistic side hoped he was wrong.

"We cannot spare any more troops to come get you," the captain said through the speaker.

Larry's eyes were wide and irate. "You've gotta be kidding!" he hollered into the radio furiously. "You can't just leave us out here!"

"Unfortunately, our causalities are too high already," the captain continued through the speaker unwaveringly. "You are on your own."

Larry swore loudly. He threw the radio onto the ground and began stomping on it, crunching it beneath his foot. The men sat in disillusioned silence, watching Larry destroy the object that moments earlier seemed their saving grace, but ultimately was rendered useless. Larry let out a tirade of choice words as he picked up the smashed radio and chucked it out of the ditch.

The disappointment took a good half hour or so to set in. The men lamented over what had happened, but in the end, there was nothing they could do but make a plan of what to do next.

"So now what?" Kurt asked the group, directing the question to Cal.

"I don't think it would be wise for us to bolt anytime soon," Cal answered. "We've already drawn attention running in here. Since we have a pretty good distance to clear until the bend in the road, I'm wondering if waiting it out till early morning would be best."

Kurt nodded. "I think that sounds like a smart plan."

"We could wait till it barely starts getting light, just enough for us to see where we are going, and then make a run for it," Cal finished.

So that's what they would do.

As darkness approached, they laid low and bided their time. As the night began, there was a slight bit of light left from the setting sun's glow, but the later it got the darker it got. Eventually it became so dark that Cal held his hand in front of his face and couldn't see it. They were out in the middle of nowhere, completely alone.

Something else happened the later it got into the night. The groaning and whimpering of the dying men began—the men left out in the battlefield were too badly wounded to be saved. Cal could only guess they must have been knocked unconscious when the initial shelling began, but now, hours later, they awoke to the pain from the wounds they sustained. The men lay out there scared and bleeding to death.

The sounds of the suffering men jolted and plagued Cal all through the night. He wished there was something he could do, but he was completely helpless. He had no means of tending to their wounds, and even if he tried, there was no way he could find his way through the darkness to reach them. He and the others had to sit awake listening to the tormenting sounds of the men all night.

Cal didn't sleep a wink, not only because of the sounds of the dying men, but also because he couldn't let himself drift off or he might lose grasp of Abe. If that were to happen, Cal knew there was a good chance Abe would wander out in the darkness and that would be the end of him. Cal wasn't about to let another one of his friends die an unfair death.

When a trickle of light entered the morning sky, just barely enough to make it light enough that the men could move and know where they were going, Cal knew it was time. He roused the group and told them they needed to get moving.

"Just run," Cal said. "Run as fast as you can until you get around that bend in the road, and don't stop."

The soldiers got themselves in ready position to jump out of the ditch.

"Ready," Cal said. "Go!"

They lunged out of the ditch all at once. Cal still had his hand clutching Abe's hand, pulling him along behind him. Cal had started out at the front of the group but pulling Abe slowed him down a bit. Other soldiers began passing him up, but he and Abe kept a steady pace. Abe was still out of his mind, but at least he was moving.

They made it about halfway through the clearing when Cal heard a pinging sound coming from behind them.

"Shelling!" someone called.

They continued running, the screech of the shells zipping through the air and hitting the ground around their feet, sending dirt ricocheting up and around the men as they sprinted to the bend. Cal and Abe brought up the rear with a few of the wounded soldiers. As he ran Cal focused on the end goal of the bend ahead but allowed himself a quick look to both his sides to see if any of his friends had been shot down. So far it looked as though the group was all intact.

When they finally reached the bend, they continued running a good hundred feet before slowing. Once stopped, they hunched over huffing and gasping for air. Cal looked around quickly scanning the group of men, trying to get a count of how many there were.

"Everyone made it!" Cal heard Kurt call from the front of the group. Cal let out a deep sigh of relief.

Exhausted and in pain from their already blistered feet, the men began walking Route 7 back to headquarters. As they went they walked around and through the wreckage of army trucks, tanks, and other war machines left smoking and in ruins, which must have been hit by mortar and abandoned during battle.

Cal felt his feet were probably bleeding and torn apart inside of his wretched boots after all the walking, but it seemed so trivial to mention or even think of the pained feet now.

The group moved as quickly as possible, which was not easy in their disheveled condition.

They finally reached headquarters, weak and fatigued. As they walked into camp, their group was acknowledged casually but weren't given much notice beyond that.

Cal walked Abe over to the medic station and turned him in. He hoped the medical staff would take good care of Abe and that his friend would soon find his mind. But with his present state, Cal knew it was more than likely that Abe would end up getting sent back to the hospital at Leyte Island, or perhaps even shipped back to the hospital in California where the badly wounded soldiers were sent.

After leaving Abe, Cal found a spot on the edge of camp where he could sit and rest and be alone for a while. Finally, he was able to let his nerves settle. As he let his body and mind relax, the constant adrenal high he had been on for the past twenty-four hours let down and he was suddenly immensely overtaken with physical and mental fatigue.

But even with as tired as he was his mind wouldn't allow him to fall asleep. What his sergeant had said to him just moments before he was killed echoed in Cal's mind. *I don't know how you can be so calm.* Cal was grateful he was able to keep his wits about him throughout the whole horrendous ordeal. Seeing his friends massacred around him was horrific, but he had somehow managed, through the help of the Lord he was sure, not to let that get to his psyche.

But there was something he couldn't get from his mind. The sounds. The sounds of the wounded men left out in the clearing moaning and suffering, as they died a slow and miserable death all night long. And how completely and utterly helpless he felt. He knew those horrible sounds and feelings of helplessness would haunt him for years to come.

〜

My darling Kate,

I hope this letter finds you well. I'm so sorry it's been so long since I have been able to write. This is the first time since I wrote that letter in Leyte that I have had paper and a pencil to use. When we are on the move, we do not have access to many things other than the clothes on our backs and few supplies in our knapsacks. Although I'm not able to write you often, I'm constantly thinking of you and what I would write to you if I could. You are always on my thoughts, night and day.

I have been receiving your letters and they are what keep me going. I can't tell you how wonderful it is to read your words. It's as if a piece of heaven has been sent to me and for those few moments I am in a place of tranquility. Have I mentioned before how beautiful your script is? I don't know that I have ever seen such elegant and perfect handwriting. But that shouldn't surprise me. Every part of you is beautiful, from your smile and what's in your heart to your cursive.

We recently arrived in an area where we were sent to regroup after our company was met with some opposition in our last area. It was a difficult situation we found ourselves in and, sadly, didn't end well for some. But thankfully all is well now. And please don't worry. Things have been very routine here in this new area. We sleep in tents, which has been very nice. There are no battles on the island we are at now, as it has already been taken back over by the U.S. We are mainly regrouping and mopping up after the take over. The most exciting thing that has happened as of late was a few nights ago when a monkey fell out of a tree onto the tent me and some other fellows were sleeping in. You wouldn't think a monkey falling onto a tent could cause such noise, but we woke up thinking we were being attacked! Of course we soon discovered it was just a monkey, to which we all got a good laugh at. Watching one of the soldiers scramble out to chase the monkey off our tent and back into the jungle was a comical sight.

I will write as often as I can while I'm here, but I'm afraid once I'm sent back out it may become difficult again.

The love I feel for you is overwhelmingly strong. I anxiously look forward to the day we are reunited again. When that day comes I will be the happiest man in the world.

I love you dearly, always and forever.

Cal

Chapter Thirty-Five

MARCH 1945
Mindanao, Philippines

It was early morning and the sun was beginning to glow in the misty sky above. The clouds were low and fog-like. Lying in his foxhole, Cal could already feel the temperature around him quickly climbing. It was sure to be another sweltering, humid day. The humidity here was almost suffocating.

With temperatures and humidity high and water and food and water as scarce as it was, it was no wonder almost as many men were succumbing to the effects of dehydration and disease as they were to falling in actual battle. Cal remembered thinking he had experienced heat and humidity back in the southern United States during his mission, but this place was at a whole new level. As the men often remarked, they were living in a tropical hell. Having spent the entire night soaking wet lying in his foxhole, which he estimated had accumulated close to six inches of water throughout the heavy rainfall of the night, Cal felt the term was pretty spot on. The rainfall had been so torrential it almost looked like a snowstorm coming down. But it was either lay low in your foxhole in the water or sit up and risk getting shot down, so Cal chose staying low.

The Japanese didn't seem to rest for anything. In fact sometimes it seemed they would get more wild and brutal during the night. Each night getting drunk on Sake, they would get hooting and hollering, sneak in closer to where the American troops had dug in for the night, and suddenly Cal would hear one of them knock a grenade against their helmet to detonate it. Then Cal would anxiously wait the three seconds it took for the grenade to go off, hoping and praying it wasn't coming his way. The grenades often found their way to the holes of the soldiers. The awful sound of the grenade detonating would blast, usually failing to kill its victim right away. A few moments later the moaning would begin, and Cal and the other men around him were left to hear the agonizing sounds of the unfortunate soldier who had been hit die a slow and painful death until he finally perished. Cal always hoped the victim would go quickly, but sometimes the agonizing sounds stretched out for the better part of the night.

Many of their nights were spent this way. Fighting was on and off throughout the day, although mornings were usually fairly quiet. When the cover of dark was gone, the Japanese retreated back to their lines. But Cal and the others always needed to be on guard.

Cal often wondered about George. He worried what hardships his younger brother might be enduring and what type of combat he had faced. In the letters Cal received from home, his mother said George had seen very little combat still, but now Cal knew enough to realize that probably wasn't really the case. The soldiers usually didn't write home about battles they had fought in and things they'd endured unless wounded, and even then they would keep the details very loose, not only to keep their families from worrying but also because they were told by their leaders they needed to be careful in their letters not to disclose what was going on and especially their whereabouts in case the mail was stolen and scoured by the enemy. "Loose lips sink ships" was what they were constantly told. The soldiers knew their letters were being censored, and if they said too much part of their letter would be cut out or the letter would be discarded completely. Because of this, Cal knew George's situation was likely much more precarious than he led on. He constantly prayed his brother would be kept safe. Someday they could share with each other what they had been through.

Still lying low a few inches below ground in his foxhole, Cal could see nothing to his sides. His body was almost entirely covered in muddy water, besides his head. He shifted to his right side, feeling the sloshing of the mud through his clothes and up his back to his neck. He sat up slowly, sludge dripping off of him, and peered out of his hole. He noticed a few other soldiers around him doing the same. Movement caught his eye to his left and he watched as a man elevated himself from his foxhole, actual steam rising off his body as he stood. He looked just like a steaming hog coming out of the mud.

"Hey," Cal heard from behind. He turned to face his friend Louis, who everyone referred to as Shorty. The nickname described Louis's stature rather accurately. He was definitely on the short side, hitting Cal around his chin.

"Hey, Shorty," Cal replied. "Made it through the night without drowning?"

Shorty let out a snort. "No kidding. My mouth and eyes were barely above water. How nice would it be to actually be dry?"

Cal nodded. "I think I've almost forgotten what it would be like to wear a dry set of clothes."

"Uh-huh. Always wet, either from rain or sweat."

Cal had met Shorty a couple months earlier during his time on the island of Mindoro, a smaller island in the central part of the Philippines. Cal and his division had been sent there after losing so many at Zig-Zag Pass. They were sent to regroup and be assigned replacements. During the month they spent in Mindoro, nothing much happened. Cal never saw battle there and enjoyed the luxury of sleeping in a tent. Here in Mindanao he hadn't slept in a tent once. Constantly on the move, they didn't have time to pitch tents and they needed the protection of sleeping in foxholes.

Once Cal's division was transferred to the island of Mindanao, he soon caught onto the routine. The US troops, along with the help of the Filipino guerillas, were trying to gain ground on the Japanese. Battle was sporadic, sometimes taking place during the day and sometimes at night. The Americans and Filipinos would win and slowly push forward, gaining ground, ultimately taking it back from the Japanese. Overall the Unites States was succeeding, but battle wasn't easy. Cal guessed the Japanese had more men than the US had anticipated. Many lives were being lost each day to simply gain ground, but it had to happen.

Cal and Shorty walked to the back of the foxholes, found a spot on the ground to sit, and opened their knapsacks.

"Hmm," Shorty mumbled, pulling out a small wrapped item. "Hardtack and more hardtack." He let out a ragged breath. "I've heard it called dog biscuits and molar breakers. What do you think is the better name?"

Cal let out a chuckle. "How about molar-breaking dog biscuits?"

"Ah, there you have it. The perfect slogan." He paused for a moment. "I sure hope we get a drop of rations sometime soon."

Cal nodded. "I think we can add 'always hungry and thirsty' to the 'always wet' list. I wonder if that traveling kitchen will ever make its way to us."

"Probably best to assume it won't, and then if it does it will be a nice surprise."

"True." Cal reached into his knapsack and pulled out a long piece of yellow fruit. "At least I still have a few of these." He tossed it to his friend.

Shorty caught it reflexively. "Still have bananas left from your loot?"

Cal grinned as he pulled out another for himself. "Yep. Only one left after this."

"Mornin, guys," Cal heard from behind. He turned to see Abe walking toward them. Good old Abe. About two weeks after the Zig-Zag Pass battle, much to Cal's surprise, he had run into Abe. The men began talking and Abe seemed back to normal but he couldn't remember anything about what happened at Zig-Zag Pass. Cal had given him a quick recap of the events, but decided not to tell Abe just how out of his head he actually was. He didn't want Abe to feel embarrassed or that he owed Cal anything.

Cal reached into his sack and tossed Abe the last banana. "That's the end of my loot."

"I don't want to take your last one," Abe said, holding it back out to Cal.

Cal waved a hand toward his friend. "Nah, don't worry about it."

"You sure?"

"Don't make me say it again," Cal jokingly threatened.

Abe nodded. "Well, thanks."

The men peeled open their fruit. "Now that's a good banana," Shorty said between bites.

Cal nodded. "Best deal I ever made was trading that bar of soap for that loot of bananas. I wonder if I have anything else on me the natives would trade me some more fruit for."

"Well, I know you don't smoke, but whatever you do don't trade away your rationed cigarettes. They're way too useful in getting the leeches off."

"Isn't that the truth," Abe agreed. "I used some just the other day when we were moving through the swamps. I lit one up and twisted it onto a bloodsucker that had somehow worked its way under my pant leg and it fell right to the ground."

Cal nodded. He had been clued into the trick with the cigarettes early on and already used them many times for the same purpose. "If only there were a way to keep the mosquitoes away," Cal remarked as he swatted at one that had just landed on his arm. There were times when Cal would reach down and grab a fistful of mosquitoes off him. "I guess that's one good thing about the heavy rainfall last night. It did help the mosquitoes let up."

"Sure, but it won't be long before we're plastered all over with them again," Shorty remarked.

Cal nodded. "Hey, speaking of that, anyone hear how Thompson is doing? I heard he came down with malaria a few days ago."

"You didn't hear?" Shorty asked.

Cal shook his head.

"He passed last night," Abe said.

Cal shook his head. "Gosh. That's awful." He paused for a moment. "Didn't he get any Atabrine?" Atabrine was the anti-malaria drug the army was supplied with to give men coming down with malaria symptoms.

"He got some, but not soon enough," Shorty responded. "They're saying the malaria is spreading through the mosquitoes. A lot of guys are getting sick."

"Seems as though almost as many are falling from sickness as in battle," Cal said soberly.

They were quiet for a few moments.

"You know, I hate feeling like I'm complaining all the time,"

Shorty said, "but the thirst. It's awful. You'd think we could get a hold of some clean water, or at least some more of those water purifying tablets. They've been low on those tablets as long as we've been here. One tablet every few days to purify one canteen isn't nearly enough."

"I know," Cal agreed. "There's a lot of men getting sick from dehydration too. I have to say thirst is one thing that never occurred to me that we'd deal with out here."

Abe shook his head. "And today already seems to be cooking up to be a hot one."

&

Twenty minutes later, Cal was being led through kunai grass about ten feet tall along with the men in his platoon. There was a narrow path they were following. They rustled through the grass in a single-file line for ten minutes or so until they finally reached a clearing. The captain stopped them in front of a thick bamboo hedge about four feet tall and fifteen feet wide. The men gathered along the hedge.

"I need you five men," the captain said, pointing to a clump of soldiers in the front, "to go around this hedge into the clearing and scout out the area. See if there is anything suspicious and report back."

The men readied their rifles and began walking toward the end of the hedge. Just before they were about to turn the corner out into the clearing, the soldier in the front of the group hesitated for a moment. They all paused, exchanging wary glances.

A foreboding feeling sank in Cal's chest. Who knew what was out there. Would the soldiers be safe, or were they being sent into a death trap?

Cal noticed the soldier in front gulp nervously and turn forward again. The men began walking out together at once, turning the corner around the bamboo hedge.

Seconds later deafening gunshots began blasting. They were getting fired on.

Cal dove down to the ground. Bullets began cutting over the bamboo right above his head. The sound of the bullets whizzing above him screeched through the air. It sounded as though the bullets couldn't be missing his head by much more than an inch. All the Japs had to do was drop their shooting a notch and they would blister the whole lot of them.

The bullets kept coming continuously. Cal held his breath, knowing at any moment he could be shot in the head.

All at once, the firing stopped. Cal dared not move. He and all the other men held their positions, crouched down on the ground. Without making a sound, still and breathless, they pretended to be dead.

They stayed that way for a long time. Ten to fifteen minutes, at least.

Finally, they began standing, slowly.

Cal braced himself as he stood, expecting to be shot down at any second. But nothing happened. He glanced around to the tall grass surrounding them. There was no movement. Everything was quiet.

Somberly, without words, the men made their way to the end of the bamboo hedge and looked around the turn out into the clearing. There lay the five soldiers that had been sent out, dead and bleeding, stripped of their clothing and weapons.

A sickening feeling entered Cal's stomach. They never stood a chance.

❧

The following afternoon, Cal sat around with a group of soldiers awaiting further instructions from the Brass, continuing feeling disillusioned from what had happened with the soldiers getting killed in cold blood the day before. The image of the men lying there dead, stripped of clothes and bleeding, had haunted his dreams last night.

They were being told that the Japanese had moved further up in the hills during the night, so today there would likely be no battle. It was too hot to do much of anything but find a shady spot to sit. Moving around required using up energy and sweat, and the men didn't have much of either to spare.

As the day went on, the sun became increasingly hot and it was unbearably humid. Cal drank from his canteen sparingly and tried to ration his water to himself, but it was difficult on days like this. He had drunk the last few drops before lunch and could now think of nothing much else than water. It was one of the hottest days Cal could remember since he'd been in the Philippines. Add the humidity factor to that, and it was insanely stifling. They were all desperate with thirst.

A captain approached the area the men were gathered in and started making an announcement. "I have some good news," he began. "We have been delivered two five-gallon canisters of water." Cal saw all the men instantly perk up. "Come and form two lines over by the supply trucks. We'll be divvying out the water there."

The soldiers stood eagerly and began making their way over to the trucks. Cal was walking at a normal pace with Abe, Shorty, and Cecil. Cecil was a young guy on Cal's mortar crew and the two got along really well.

Cal soon noticed many of the men around them picking up speed, almost jogging. The overall feeling of the group was starting to feel a bit worrisome. The men were anxious, treating the walk to water almost like a race. Cal could see a look of determination that was bordering frenzy in many of the men's eyes.

When the soldiers reached the trucks Cal could see where the water canisters were set on the ground off to the side of the trucks. The men were gathering round, approaching the water like hungry wolves.

"Line up," the captain called.

The men didn't listen.

"I want my share!" a soldier hollered frantically.

"Give me my water now," another man barked, a look of fury in his eyes.

All at once the barely contained crowd of soldiers erupted. They began calling out and yelling. Before Cal knew it, men were diving toward the canisters.

"Get in line!" the captain shouted. But his shouts fell on empty ears. No one was listening.

Cal watched as a GI grabbed for one of the containers in a crazed state, began tilting it, and poured water out its side into his mouth. Cal's nerves began to curl when he saw how much water was being wasted, gushing out the side of the canister and running down the man's face. The water hit the dirt and instantly seeped into the ground.

Another soldier shouted at the man and grabbed onto the canister, yanking it from the soldier's hands. They began pulling at it back and forth. Water began spilling over the canister's sides with its jostling.

"Look what you're doing, you idiots!" one soldier yelled.

Others joined in, yelling obscenities at the men.

Cal looked to the second canister where something almost identical was taking place. Men were shouting and swearing at each other, yelling and jerking the water back and forth.

"Pass it around!" a GI shouted. "We all need our share!" He grasped the container and poured a gush into his mouth. The man next to him jerked it away and dumped water into his face, most of it pouring to the ground.

"Hey!" Cal shouted. "You guys are wasting more water than is actually being drunk!"

But no one was listening. Men were frantically grabbing for the canister, pouring water into their mouths recklessly. Almost as soon as someone began drinking, the canister would be yanked from their hands, water splashing out of the container and all over the men in the process. Far too much precious water was going to waste.

"This isn't fair," Shorty called over the ruckus to Cal. "I'm going in to get my share."

Cal nodded. "Me too." Abe and Cecil nodded.

The men rushed into the frenzied, turbulent crowd. Cal didn't want to be part of it, but he knew if he didn't act fast there would be no water left. He also knew he needed that water desperately.

Cal fought his way through the jumbled, wild throng of men. He soon lost track of his friends in the confusion of it all. The men surrounding him no longer seemed his comrades, but strangely, his enemies. They had turned from a friendly group of soldiers to men simply fighting to survive. It didn't matter that in the war they were on the same side. The innate need for the one thing a person needed more than anything to survive was all that mattered. Having been pushed to this level of dehydration and lack of nourishment, the men had become desperate and uncontrollable. They were behaving like animals.

Cal never thought he would witness such a thing. But before his eyes, the carnal nature that overtakes human beings in dire circumstances was unfolding. It was desperate, disturbing, and rather frightening all at once.

Finally, Cal found the canister in his hands. He dropped his jaw and leaned his head back, pouring a gush of water into his mouth as carefully as he could as to not let any water unnecessarily spill out. The cool, clean taste of the liquid hit the back of his throat in one fresh moment of bliss. But after a gulp the water was yanked from his hands. It was over.

Feeling defeated and realizing there was no way he was getting any more water, Cal turned and walked away from the chaotic crowd of men. He reached a point on the outskirts of the scene with a group of other soldiers looking in on how this was all playing out. He noticed that the lower the water got in the canisters the more crazed the men became. Soon the canisters were being whipped around and fought over with such anger and carelessness that no one was getting any water coming out of the canisters. It was all being splashed on the men and to the ground.

In the end, when the water was completely gone, and after the concluding fighting and arguing ended, an uncomfortable and shamed silence fell over the group of men. No one spoke. They met each other's eyes with wary glances and slowly retreated away.

Cal stood there for a long time, watching all the men walk away shamefacedly. It had been demoralizing for all of them, whether they were among those sloppily wasting water or the ones desperately trying to get an ounce.

Cal shook his head, lost in his thoughts. *I could tell this story to folks back home and no one would believe it.*

~

My dear Cal,

I'm tired as can be this evening, darling. I've been out dress shopping all day long with Lorianne (one of the girls that lives with me at the dormitory). She's going out tonight with a beau and wanted my help in finding a dress to buy. Her beau was not able to serve in the war because of a prior illness. I know it's not very good of me to think this, but all day long I couldn't help but feel jealous of her having him home. I told her that myself. How I wish it were you and I going out tonight! Sometimes I can't help but think how unfair our separation seems. But then I have to remember the noble and important cause you are fighting for. That helps, but it doesn't make being apart from you any easier.

It's been a busy week. Yesterday Dr. Carter (one of the dentists at my office) celebrated his twentieth wedding anniversary. He put me in charge of ordering a cake for a surprise celebration he was putting on for his wife with some friends and family. At first I was a little bothered he was roping me into helping with something unrelated to my office work, but it ended up being a nice diversion. He very specifically wanted twenty pink roses made out of frosting on the cake to represent each year of their marriage. Isn't that a sweet gesture? I walked down the street to the bakery and picked out the cake flavor and frosting colors myself. I hope you don't think me too presumptuous in saying this, but while there at the bakery looking at all of those elegant cakes I couldn't help but think of what our wedding cake might look like someday! I will admit I sat there daydreaming about it, which lead me to thinking about other things such as a wedding dresses, flowers, etc. I spent the better part of the day daydreaming, and my sleep last night was filled with dreams of us. I woke feeling extremely happy and content.

How very unladylike it is of me to be so forward about all of this in my writing to you! Just now I about crinkled this paper into a ball to throw in the garbage and begin a new one. But not because of it being too forward (you know that sort of thing never concerned me much) but because I worry cakes and things must sound very trivial to you compared to what is happening there. You haven't told me details but I know you must be experiencing some distressing things. But then I thought perhaps reading these things might be a nice diversion for you as it has been for me. It helped me forget, even if just momentarily, the difficulty of our situation and all the sadness and gloom going on in the world. But enough of that, I want to be a source of happiness and light for you, not one of sadness. If nothing else, at least you're sure to get some amusement out of seeing what a silly schoolgirl you have made me become! Who would have thought I'd ever be daydreaming about wedding cakes and wedding dresses and such? Certainly not I!

I love you more than words can describe and, as always, long for the day we will be together again.

All my love,
Kate

Chapter Thirty-Six

APRIL 1945

Mindanao, Philippines

Today was a day the men had been looking forward to. It was eight in the morning and excitement was brewing. The traveling kitchen was scheduled to arrive at their camp today. A cooked dinner. A real meal. It was something they'd only dreamed about up until now.

But already there was an unpleasant and rather gruesome damper on the day. Something foul was lingering in the air, literally. Dead bodies of fallen soldiers were one of the disturbing realities of war. The US troops went to great effort to bury the remains of their own men, but the bodies of the Japanese soldiers were usually left where they had perished, the surviving Japanese soldiers usually retreating to the hills following a lost battle, unable to care for their men's remains.

There had been a battle a few days before, and the fallen Japanese still laid scattered around the perimeter of the area. This morning the men had awoken to the putrid smell. The bodies were beginning to decay and the extreme heat was moving that process along quickly. Cal tried his best to breathe through his mouth so as not to inhale the stench. He noticed other men holding their noses and some gagging over the nauseating odor.

Cal was sitting with Abe, Shorty, and Cecil talking and chewing on some hardtack when the captain approached him. "Morgan, we need your help. The kitchen is setting up and the smell is nothing short of putrid." The captain had been using Cal as a sergeant since Sergeant Williams had died at Zig-Zag Pass and was constantly coming to Cal with assignments, usually in rounding up men to help carry out an order.

The captain continued. "We don't want that smell around tonight when we're eating dinner. I need you to gather a few men to help with a task. We'll need you to locate the bodies and burn them."

"Burn . . . the bodies, sir?" Cal asked.

"That's right."

Cal hesitated for a moment. He didn't want to question the captain, but he also didn't think burning the bodies was the right solution to the problem. "With all due respect, sir, I'm afraid burning the bodies would only make the smell worse."

The captain stood with his eyebrows furrowed. "Do you have experience in burning bodies, Morgan?" he asked in a challenging tone.

"Of course not, sir," Cal responded without a flinch. "But I have plenty of experience burning leaves and other things back home on the farm, and from my experience the fire takes on the smell of whatever item you are burning. In fact it usually makes it worse."

The captain's expression relaxed. He paused for a moment before continuing. "I see." He lowered his voice a bit. "Then what would you suggest for our predicament?"

Cal took a breath. "I think the only solution is to bury them, sir."

The captain swore and shook his head with indignation. "That will take a lot of work. The men aren't going to want to take the time and effort to do that."

"I realize that, sir. But I see no other way of getting rid of the smell. It's either bury them, or leave them and the stink."

The captain let out a frustrated sigh. "I suppose you're right. We'll need more men than I was originally planning on, then. I'm going to ask you to head this up. Gather twenty men or so and get this going. It will probably take you the better part of the day."

"I realize that, sir," Cal replied.

"All right. Organize it how you see best. You know where the shovels are. You have my permission to gather as many men as you need."

Cal nodded. "Will do, sir."

The captain walked away. Cal turned back to his friends. They volunteered to help before he had a chance to recruit them.

He knew this would be a lot of work, but it would be worth it to be able to enjoy the cooked meal they had all looked forward to for so long.

Soon the men had been gathered. They went to the perimeter of the camp, found the first grouping of bodies, and began the taxing task of digging up holes to bury them in. It was another day of drastic heat and humidity.

"Seeing these bodies up close sort of changes perspective, doesn't it?" Cal remarked as he tossed up a scoop of earth. Cal and his friends had been conversing as they dug.

Abe nodded. "I was just thinking the same thing."

"Like you actually feel sort of sorry for the Japs?" Shorty piped in, digging on the other side of Abe.

"Yeah," Cal replied. "Just looking at them lying here dead and lifeless, I can't help but think they are victims just like the soldiers who have died on our side. These men had just been following orders from their leaders like we do."

"True," Shorty agreed. "And tomorrow this could be us."

Cal paused for a moment. "What if it were?" he asked. He was curious what his friends thought on this matter. "What do you guys think about death and where we go from here?"

"Oh, I'd say I'll go straight to heaven," Shorty joked with a chuckle as he threw his shovel into the dirt, having just finished his hole.

Cal laughed. "I don't doubt you would. So, you believe in heaven, then?"

"Oh sure," Shorty said. "And I know you do. What about you, Abe and Cecil?"

Abe paused from his digging. "Yes. Well, I don't know if I believe it's all as clear cut as heaven and hell, but I do believe in an afterlife, if that's what you mean."

Shorty nodded. "How about you, Cec?"

Cecil had stopped digging and was listening to the men. "I don't know, sometimes I'm not really sure what I believe." At only nineteen years old, Cecil was the youngest of the group by a few years. He was a smart and thoughtful kid and Cal admired him for his maturity. He seemed to have it more together than many of the soldiers older than him there. "It does seem strange to think it would all just be over after this life," he continued. "I guess that could be, but I tend to think, or hope, that there is something more. I'm just not sure what."

Cal nodded. He could understand where Cecil's questions were coming from. Cecil went on, "I guess the hardest part is wondering if anyone really cares, you know? I mean, I know my parents care about me. But what if I die? Will I just be some strange being or spirit floating around with no purpose?"

Cal decided to speak up. "Cecil, I think it's natural to wonder about things and wonder what our purpose is in the long run. But I want you to know that I do think there is a God who knows exactly who you are and who loves you. And I don't think you'll be lost after this life. He'll be there waiting to greet you when you return. He's proud of you and loves you."

Cecil was silent for a moment. "Thanks," he responded with a slight smile. "Gives me something to think about."

The men were quiet and thoughtful as they finished digging their hole. When they finished, they placed their shovels on the ground and broke into twos to lift a body and bring it to the hole to bury.

Sometime in the late afternoon the men finally completed the assignment. Weary and exhausted, they were greatly looking forward to the dinner they had long anticipated, the smell of pork chops and potatoes now filling the air.

When the dinner was finished cooking, the men lined up and scooped their portions of meat, potatoes, and gravy into their tins. But after handling dead bodies all day, the meal didn't look as appetizing as Cal hoped it would. He wasn't sure if it was in his head, but the meat and potatoes seemed to smell a bit off. The pork chops even looked a bit discolored and spotty. From his experience on the farm, he knew that wasn't a good sign. But he told himself it was probably fine.

As he sat down on the ground among a circle of soldiers including his three friends, Cal tried to clear his mind of the bodies and focus on the meal before him. He cut into the pork chop and took his first bite. Slowly chewing, he soon realized the meat had a sour sort of taste. But he kept chewing. Maybe he was imagining it. Reluctantly, he swallowed. Then he took another bite. This time the meat tasted even more rancid. He spit it out in his tin and looked up. "Does this meat taste bad to anyone else?"

A few men nodded forlornly.

"I'm pretty sure it's rancid," Abe said.

Cal nodded. "That's what I thought."

Another man piped in. "I don't care. I'm too hungry to care." He was shoveling the food into his mouth, probably hardly chewing before swallowing.

Cal was ravenously hungry, as he knew all the men were. Cal had no way of weighing himself but his pants felt significantly looser than when he had first put them on back at Leyte Island, and he knew he had lost a few pounds on the ship over as well. He wouldn't be surprised if he weighed a good fifteen or twenty pounds less than he had when he left.

With the grossly dirt-matted clothes he wore and the beard that had grown on his face, combined with his weight loss, he figured if he were to come across a mirror he probably wouldn't recognize his own reflection.

But he couldn't stomach meat that was rancid. Even if it had looked appetizing, he didn't dare eat it. The last thing he wanted was an upset stomach and bowels tomorrow.

He looked down at the potatoes. They were covered in gravy but he was now beginning to wonder about them, too. He took a bite. Sure enough, the potatoes tasted bitter and rank. The gravy almost covered up the taste, but Cal wasn't about to eat rancid potatoes, either. He didn't want to deal with the effects later. He looked around at the men. He noticed many were forgoing their pork and eating the potatoes instead, probably because the rotten potato taste was somewhat drowned out by the gravy.

"I think the potatoes are bad too," he commented, thinking he better warn the men in case they didn't recognize the taste.

A few of the other men, including his three closest friends, nodded in reluctant agreement. Cal knew they all must be feeling the disappointment and frustration he was, especially after working hard all day to make the meal a pleasant experience.

The friends stood from the circle and in forlorn silence walked to the trash to dump their food.

Cecil finally spoke up, breaking the quiet. "Why would they feed us rotten food?"

Cal shrugged. "Maybe they didn't realize it was rancid."

"Hmph," Shorty huffed. "Somehow I doubt that."

They walked back to camp in silence for a few moments. Then Abe piped in. "They probably didn't want to disappoint us."

"Yeah, but serving rotten food to men that are starving, many of them sick already, just isn't smart," Shorty said. "They would have been better off just telling us the food was rotten and letting us deal with the disappointment."

Cal nodded. "I agree. The truth is a lot of men are going to be sick in the morning because of this." He sighed. "It's just too bad."

"And after all that digging . . ." Cecil trailed off, shaking his head.

The men built a campfire and spent the rest of the evening talking before retiring to their foxholes. It was comforting to know they would have another night free of combat until they moved on in the morning, a rarity as they had seen fighting nearly every night since being in Mindanao.

"Well, tomorrow, back to real life," Abe said. The fire was crackling and popping. "Or real life at war, I should say."

❧

The next morning as Cal woke he sat up in his foxhole. It was only an inch or so full of water this morning. The rainfall hadn't been very heavy last night. He sat up slowly, his back sore and stiff from all the digging the day before. He inhaled deeply. The air that filled his nostrils was pungent.

"What's that smell?" he murmured to himself.

He stood up, the water drizzling off his clothes as he rose. A strange snorting sound was coming from somewhere nearby. He began walking past the foxholes of the other men, most of them still sleeping, and made his way to the perimeter of the camp following where the smell and noises were coming from.

When he reached the corner of camp he saw it. A herd of wild Filipino pigs were clumped together surrounding one of the areas Cal had gotten to know all too well the day before. It was the exact spot he had labored and dug at for hours burying a large group Japanese soldiers bodies.

The boars heads were turned down, their dark, furry backsides to him. These were nothing like the pigs he knew on the farm back home. They were large, ravenous creatures, and he had a mind to usually steer clear from them. But not now.

As he moved in closer he discovered what he feared was happening was indeed taking place. The animals had dug up the buried men, eating their remains.

Cal held his breath, almost vomiting on spot at the sight. Grotesque snorts and squeals of the raving animals filled the still morning air. Anger overtook him. No man deserved this, even if it was just his remains. It didn't matter that these men hadn't been fighting on his side. These were people.

Cal picked up his pace and stomped hard and loud on the ground as he moved in closer to the animals. "Get out of here!" he shouted, waving his hands toward them, trying to scare them off, about fifteen or twenty feet from them now.

The boars lifted their heads. He could barely stomach the sight of their bloodstained faces and beady eyes staring up at him. A couple of the pigs began shuffling backward but the others seemed to care little about Cal's presence. They slung their heads back down, snorting, going back to their meal.

"Out of here!" Cal yelled again, practically screaming. He clapped his hands and stomped in closer to them now. Large and wild looking, the boars were bigger than he expected up close. But Cal wasn't worried. He was too overcome with anger to be worried.

As Cal moved in closer, the animals began recognizing his aggression. Likely startled by his close proximity and loudness, some stopped from their carnage and began to scatter and run back into the surrounding jungle. But a few stubborn pigs lingered, their heads still tilted downward to the bodies, not wanting to leave their meal.

"Out!" Cal screamed one last time, running right up to them and kicking his foot in their direction, whacking one of the boars in the backside. The kick wasn't all that hard but enough to push the pig back and give it a jolt. The animal let out a squeal as the force of the kick knocked it into the other two remaining boars. "Get outta here!" Cal yelled one more time as the remaining three scrambled away. Cal watched as they scattered off into the jungle.

When they were finally out of sight, he realized he was shaking with fury. He dropped to the ground on his knees and buried his face in his hands.

≈

Dearest Cal,

Still no word from you, but that's okay. I would write to you a million times over with no response just to know you are receiving my letters and that they may be some beacon of light to you wherever you may be.

There hasn't been much to write of going on this week. I will tell you that last weekend I went out to the ice cream parlor with Lorianne and some of the girls. While there a couple of guys approached us and asked if we wanted to go dancing at a dance hall down the road. Lorianne and the girls said they would like to, which surprised me as Lorianne has a beau, as I have mentioned before. But she assured me it was harmless and that it would be nice to go listen to some music and have a little fun. So I went along.

After a while I agreed to dance the jitterbug with one of the guys there, which seemed entirely innocent. But after the dance he kept following me around and making eyes at me, and finally I had to do something about it. I reminded him I had a beau overseas and that it just didn't feel right the way he was zeroing in on me. He laughed and joked that I was being a square, and asked, didn't I know how to have a little fun? I know he didn't mean anything by it, but it both- ered me and I started feeling fed up by the whole situation. I decided I no longer cared to be there, that I'd rather be home reading or doing something productive other than being out making meaningless small talk with pinheaded boys.

So I left and walked home myself. It was sort of nice to walk alone along the darkened streets (don't worry, it wasn't very late and people were still out and about, so it was entirely safe. Somehow I just know this would cross your mind). The walk reminded me of that first night we walked home from the Coconut Grove together. Although it may seem like a small, insignificant event to most, to me it is a beautiful memory. That night stands out as a special one in my mind. I believe it was the beginning of my falling in love with you, although I wouldn't admit it to myself yet at the time.

Anyhow, my experience the other night made me grateful for you all the more. I'm afraid you have ruined me against all other men. They all seem frivolous and dim-witted to me now! It makes me realize even more how wonderful you are and how thankful I am that we connect on so many levels. Maybe all couples feel this way, but I think it's quite extraordinary. I told you this story not to make you jealous, of course, but because I want to reassure you that although we've been apart for some time now there are no other men in my life and won't be. No one else can even begin to compare!

I'm not sure how much news you get from the outside world, but I'm sure you've heard talk of the war nearing the end in Europe. Such wonderful news! This must mean things will be ending where you are soon too? I certainly hope so.

I hesitate to write this because as I have said before I want my letters to be uplifting to you, but I also thought you would want to know of this if you don't already. Have you heard of some of the things being reported about the way the Nazis have treated the Jewish people these past years during the war? When the newspapers first began reporting these things, it all sounded all very outlandish and I think most assumed it was propaganda.

But just a few days ago there was a radio broadcast given by Edward Murrow (the reputable CBS journalist) about a place in Buchenwald, Germany, that was a camp of some sorts where the Nazis kept the Jewish people. I can't bring myself to write about the horrendous things he reported happened there, but many were treated unthinkably and died or were killed. It was all very disturbing. Reporters are saying this was happening in multiple camps across Germany. I feel so horribly for those people and can't fathom how human beings could treat other human beings that way.

How grateful I am that this evil is coming to an end. You are fighting for the triumph over the evil that has been enveloping the world and that we are hopefully now breaking free from, and I couldn't be more proud of you.

As hard as it is to be apart, I know you are doing your duty and the right thing.

You are always on my thoughts and I pray for you each and every day. May God watch over and protect you and return you to me, my dearest.

With all my love,
Kate

Chapter Thirty-Seven

MAY 1945

Mindanao, Philippines

Cal watched as dark puffs of smoke rose into the air from the ground of the valley below. Swallowing hard, Cal looked back at his mortar crew. His captain had just instructed him to take his crew, along with their mortar weapon, down the hillside to get in touch with the company engaged in battle and see if they needed help.

Cal knew this was going to be dangerous. The Japanese would likely see their movement down the hillside. But he had instructions to follow.

"All right, guys, let's go," he said back to his fatigued-ridden crew.

The men moved forward reluctantly. It was taxing to always be on guard, knowing your life was constantly on the line.

They started weaving down the hill with Cal leading the group. Sweet potato vines were growing all over the hillside, wild and out of control. The trail they were following made a narrow path through the foliage. Cal gazed down the slope of the hill to the bottom of the gulch where a pretty little stream twisted and turned its way along the valley floor. The battle appeared to be taking place right around

233

the stream. Cal was dismayed at the thought that its waters would soon be running with streaks of blood.

The further down the hill they moved, the higher the vines grew around them. They were almost as high as Cal's shoulders now.

Just as he glanced back at his men, he heard a popping sound resounding off the hillside.

"Get down!" he yelled as he dove to the ground.

He looked back at his men. They had followed his lead and were diving down. Within a second, bullets were flying over their heads.

"It wasn't an inch from nailing me!" Cecil hollered.

Cal recognized the popping of the Japanese machine guns going off. The bullets seemed to be coming from above. There must have been a nest of Japanese hiding up there. The bullets persisted whizzing by, coming in waves. Although the vines wouldn't protect them by any means, they were giving the men a way to stay hidden. Fortunately, the Japanese were aiming too high, at least for now.

"Stay low!" Cal hollered back to the men.

He had to think fast. Should they turn around and go back up the hill, or continue down? What would be the smartest way to move to avoid getting blistered?

They were nearly two-thirds of the way down the hill now. If they moved upward the Japanese would have a closer shot at them. If they continued down they would make it further away and might be able to lose them.

"Let's continue down," Cal called back to his men. "Move fast and stay low."

The men began to crawl, dragging their weapons behind them. The gunshots continued darting over their heads, missing them by inches. Every few moments the firing would slow down, but Cal knew better than to think they were out of danger yet.

About five minutes into the crawl, the shots stopped. "Don't get up yet," Cal said back to the others. "They want us to think they've given up. Just keep crawling."

They continued on. Sure enough, a minute or so later the shots began again. Cal figured the Japanese could see a slight rustle in the potato vines as they crawled but just couldn't get their shots quite low enough.

The men reached the bottom of the gulch still scooting along the ground, the bullets persistently whizzing over their heads. They needed to move fast. If they stayed still for too long the Japanese would have a better aim at them. It seemed that as long as they kept moving, hidden in the foliage, they had a better chance of surviving.

Cal quickly scanned the area. There was a clearing about twenty feet wide a couple yards ahead where the potato vines stopped. The small stream he had been admiring from above ran through the middle of the clearing. On the other side of the clearing, more potato vines were growing tall and wild along the base of the gulch and up the opposite hillside. To the north, the direction where the battle was taking place about a half mile up, the foliage was low. If they headed that direction there would be nowhere to take cover. Easy targets. If they headed south and bolted deep in the flora on the other side of the wash they might stand a chance of losing their predators.

"What next?" Cecil asked from behind.

Cal turned his head to face his crew. Lying flat on his stomach, it was an awkward position and difficult to communicate. Cecil and the others were lying flat, their noses practically in the dirt, breathing heavily.

"I think the best chance we have is to cross the clearing," Cal huffed. "If we dive into the vine on the other side and move along the base of that opposite hill, we'll eventually lose them." He paused, catching his breath. "What do you think?"

"Sounds good," Cecil replied. "We can't turn back. It would be a death trap."

"Agreed," another crewman spoke up.

The others were nodding.

Crossing the clearing would be dangerous. They would be left completely exposed for those few seconds. Realistically Cal knew the chances of at least one of them, and probably more, getting hit was very high. But they couldn't go back and they couldn't just stay here like sitting ducks. He could see no other viable option.

"It's going to be dicey," he said to the men. "I think it best if we go one at a time. That way if one of us . . . goes down, there's a better chance more will make it."

The men nodded gravely.

"I'll go first," Cal said. He turned his head back toward the clearing. Having been crawling for such a long time, he glanced down and noticed his hands were caked in dirt and mud. For the first time he realized his palms felt numb and were throbbing. They were likely bleeding beneath all the mud, his weight bearing down on them for so long. He hadn't stopped long enough to notice.

He looked back up and continued crawling forward. Soon he reached the point where the vines came to an end. He closed his eyes for a moment, offering a silent prayer. Then he crouched onto his feet in a squatting position, paused for a moment to take a deep breath, and bolted.

Almost instantly the popping began. He moved his feet as rapidly as he could, his eyes focused on the vines ahead. The bullets were flying behind him. He felt one zip past the back of his head so close he could feel the whip of the air against his scalp. He was almost there. Only a few more feet to go.

As he reached the end of clearing, he dove into the vines, just in time to feel more bullets fly past him. Once in the foliage he shimmied along the ground quickly to get a few yards further away from the clearing. But he knew he wouldn't have to go far. As soon as another one of the soldiers began crossing all the shots would be focused on him.

Cal turned so that he could see the others make their way across.

First Cecil left the protection of the vines. Cal watched in dread as Cecil's face contorted and twisted as he ran with all his might, swinging his arms vigorously, willing himself across. It seemed a hundred bullets were flying past him. Cal was amazed that not one met Cecil's body. Cecil dove forward into the foliage, gasping for air as he hit the ground hard.

Cal reached his hand out to him. "Nice work."

Cecil nodded breathlessly. "Let's hope to God the others make it."

The men crouched down low as they watched the remaining four men cross the clearing. Each time was just as nerve wracking as the last, and just as amazing when they all made it without being shot.

When they were all gathered together again, Cal gave instructions for everyone to move as quickly as they could through the vines down the gulch, and to keep moving until the shots were long gone.

The men agreed and took off.

Miraculously, they all made it back to their company intact.

❧

That evening as the sun was beginning to set, Cal stood around with a few men talking over what had happened that day. His usual comrades weren't around, likely digging their holes for the night. Today the company down in the gulch had won the battle and advanced forward. Cal's company had stayed on higher ground and hadn't met any resistance. They chose a spot to dig in and were getting ready to retire for the night.

"I hope those Japs' feet are rotting and that their skin is getting eaten alive by these blasted mosquitoes as bad as we're getting it," one soldier said, grabbing a fistful of mosquitoes off his pant leg and throwing it into the air.

"I hope they're getting it worse," another man said.

"Yeah, no kidding," the man replied bitterly.

"I hope they are starving," another guy said. "I was so hungry today I started eating leaves off those potato vines that are all over the place."

"Hey, I've been doing that all along," another said.

"The hunger I can get past somewhat," Cal piped in. "But the thirst . . . it's unbearable." His mouth was dry and his throat burned. His canteen was empty again. He continually had dizzy spells fall over him, and he knew it was from lack of food and water.

The men all grunted in agreement.

"It's enough to drive a man mad," a soldier added.

The group fell silent for a few moments.

"Wonder if we'll have combat tonight?" one soldier said.

A few of them shrugged.

"Every night I hear them hitting those blasted grenades against their helmets before tossing them in our men's holes I wish I could catch one and throw it right back into their yellow faces," said the man that had first begun the conversation about mosquitoes, with animosity in his eyes. "I'd just love to see the look on their face right before it blew them to bits."

Cal flinched. He hated being here, hated the combat, and hated what the Japanese were doing as much as anyone. But he couldn't find in himself the degree of abhorrence for the Japanese soldiers that many of the soldiers around him seemed to have. At the core they were all people, human beings, and he couldn't help but realize that at the end of the day they were all just men following orders.

A few moments later Cal heard a rustling in the trees about fifty feet behind where the group of them was standing. He and the men turned toward the sound. A few seconds later a group of Japanese soldiers emerged from the trees. Cal quickly counted there were eight of them. They were holding their rifles up above their heads. Cal instantly realized the Japanese soldiers were entering their area without opposition. They were intending to surrender.

"Don't shoot!" an officer called out from behind Cal and the others. But almost as soon as the words escaped the officer's mouth shots began blasting out, piecing Cal's ears. He turned back toward the Japanese soldiers only to witness them being blown apart. One by one each of them dropped to the ground in cold blood.

Bewildered, Cal whirled around, looking back and forth to both his sides at the men he was standing with. Every one of them had their rifles drawn, aimed at the soldiers. They all had been shooting. Some had halted now, but some were still blasting off shots at the bodies lying on the ground.

"That's enough!" the officer yelled.

A few last shots rang out before the men lowered their weapons.

Cal stared at the men in shock. As he met the malicious yet blank stares of his fellow soldiers, he was filled with a strange combination of revulsion and pity. They were past feeling. It wasn't right and it sickened him, but after all they'd witnessed and been through, he couldn't entirely blame them.

Cal dropped his eyes and walked away.

He wandered to his foxhole and sat down, feeling an overwhelming sinking feeling inside. He sat quietly for a long time. Finally he lay down on his back in his foxhole. The sky was dark and for once clear of clouds. He gazed up at the stars in night sky watching their twinkling lights. As disheartened as he felt, watching the stars always gave him a flicker of hope. They made what he was going through seem small in the grand scheme of things, which wasn't necessarily a bad thing. It helped him keep the big picture. It reminded him that although he sometimes felt he was living in the depths of a dark abyss, the war would be a distant memory someday. He still had so much left to live for. The world had good left in it. He knew it did.

Somewhere, far away from war, there was still happiness, if he could only make his way to it.

He remembered the many times he and Kate had watched the stars together, and his heart ached with longing. He felt a million worlds away from her. Time was crawling, and he was suddenly overtaken with a distressing thought, the same thought that had come to him numerous times during battles and sometimes out of nowhere while traipsing through these wretched jungles. What if he didn't survive? What if he never had the opportunity to be with her again? He could have very well been killed today and she would have forever been gone to him, and him to her.

He sighed with angst and turned onto his side, closing his eyes. He couldn't let that happen. He had to return to her. He had to make it past this wretched war and back home. And he knew that only through the help of God that could happen.

❧

Dearest Kate,

I woke today to quite a miracle. A captain entered our camp announcing he had been delivered a supply of paper and pencils for us to use to write home. Last night was a difficult one, and after praying for the better part of the night asking God for strength and protection, the paper being delivered this morning felt like a blessing sent straight to me from above reassuring me that I am not forgotten. It might sound a small thing, but for me it was very comforting. I only got divvied out three papers and plan to use two to write to you and one to my parents. How wonderful it is to be holding a pencil in my hand! It makes me feel more normal than I have felt in a long time.

I have been receiving your letters and they are nothing short of heaven sent. Reading your words and seeing your handwriting brings me so much happiness. What I love most of all is how I can almost hear your voice speaking to me as I read your letters. I love how your tenacity and passion seep through in the words you write. Reading them has only made me fall all the more in love with you, if that was even possible.

Thank you for reassuring me that you aren't going with any other men. I do appreciate you telling me that, as I'd be lying to say the question hasn't entered my mind. I'm grateful to hear that you aren't entertaining any other beaus and even more relieved to hear that any you have come across seem "dim-witted," as you put it. I laughed out loud at that one.

I couldn't agree more that our love is something extraordinary, and believe it with all my heart. You are my morning and my night, my moon and my stars. You are my everything. I see you everywhere I go and you are always in my thoughts and dreams. If it weren't for you, I do believe I would have perished by now. You are what keeps me remembering there is good and love in the world past the darkness that surrounds me.

As I alluded to earlier, there have been some events lately that have left me feeling downhearted. I would rather not write of the things I have experienced here. Someday I will share them with you, but like you've said, I wish to keep our correspondence hopeful and uplifting. Please don't worry, though, as I am safe and believe I am being protected.

I have been acting as sergeant over my crew for some time now, although I haven't officially been given my sergeant stripes yet. As an acting sergeant I am able to call some of the orders for my squad and I am constantly being asked to head up small missions and projects. Acting in this position helps me to feel I have some say in what is going on and that I have some control in the situations I find myself in, which is a comforting feeling rather than always being at the mercy of others decisions.

I do have a couple of stories to share that I thought you might find interesting. The first is more amusing than anything. Awhile back we came to an area that had a Filipino man nearby who was a banana grower. Have I ever told you bananas are my favorite fruit? I've loved them since I was a little boy. So when I heard of these fresh bananas, I had to get ahold of some. I approached the man with a bar of soap and asked if he'd be interested in trading me some bananas for the soap. He didn't speak English so I had to hold up the soap and point to it and slowly say b-a-n-a-n-a while pointing to his surrounding banana trees. Eventually he understood what I was talking about and nodded his head eagerly. He left to go fetch the bananas and came back with a gigantic bushel of them. I never expected to get that many! There were about fifty in all. At first I felt a little guilty taking all those bananas from him, but then I decided if he thought it a fair trade I might as well too! The bananas were delicious, so fresh and sweet, almost like candy. My friends and I hauled them back to my foxhole and luckily we were stationed in that a spot for longer than usual, about a week. It was quite a funny sight having my foxhole filled with bananas. When I would crawl in it I was practically swimming in them. My friends and I were able to eat off those bananas for the better part of a week. That's actually a fond memory I'll return with from this place.

Also, a couple weeks back my crew was put in charge of scouring an abandoned Filipino village to make sure there weren't any Japanese soldiers left hiding there. I led the crew in and we searched the area. Eventually we heard some rustling coming from inside a house and pinpointed it to a cellar dug out below the ground. What we found surprised us. A young Filipino girl of about twelve or thirteen years old was hiding there inadequately dressed, dirty, and scared. She spoke broken English and said she was lost and didn't know where her family was. She had been hiding there for some time piecing off what little food there was left in the cellar, scared to leave in fear the Japanese would capture her. We took her with us and found the nearest Filipino village and turned her over to them. They said they would take care of her and look for her family (I hope there is something left of them). I was grateful we could return an innocent child to safety. I was happy to have the opportunity to help someone. It's not often I feel my actions here are worthy and just. Although I know I'm fighting for the right side, in war right and wrong are skewed, and sometimes it becomes difficult to feel I am making any real difference or doing any good. But at least in this instance I felt for certain we had a positive impact on someone's life.

I am running short on room but would write you twenty more pages if I had the means. My love for you is ever strong and grows with each passing day. Your talk of weddings left me with a smile on my face all day long that I couldn't be rid of. I can't tell you how happy it makes me that you are beginning to entertain these thoughts. I know you have come a long way in that regard. You know the mere thought or possibility of that outcome makes me the happiest (and luckiest) man in the world.

I hope it won't be long until I am able to write you again. Until then take care, my love, and know my thoughts are always with you. I love you.

Yours forever and always,

Cal

Chapter Thirty-Eight

Mindanao, Philippines

Large, stubborn green leaves swung relentlessly into the soldier's faces as they struggled to push forward in the overpowering heat. The men had spent most of the day fighting their way through the acres upon acres of tightly woven, thick-stemmed abaca plants looming fifteen to twenty feet off the ground. Visibility was limited and Cal had to use the entire weight of his body to push forward through the plants.

The troops were told they were on their way to the city of Ula on the outskirts of the larger city of Davao. Throughout the day, many men had fallen from heat exhaustion. Rarely able to see more than ten feet ahead, Cal willed himself to not allow the stifling hotness and consuming feeling of being trapped in an endless jungle of giant plants overtake both his physical strength and psyche. Machetes or some sort of long bladed weapon to cut through the plants would have made the march significantly easier but they were only equipped with rifles and small switchblades, so they relied on their hands and body weight to push through the plants.

Finally, after hours of marching through the wretched plants, the densely formed greenery began to thin out and Cal had some visibility ahead. The men decided to take a rest for some food and water. They all sat down on the ground opening their knapsacks and pulling out what food rations they had to snack on.

Cal and Cecil sat next to each other. A few minutes into their meal, Abe and Shorty walked upon them. "There you guys are," Shorty said. "We've been looking for you."

"Sit down and have a piece of this meat here," Cal said, lifting the can toward them.

"Nah, you've been saving that," Abe said as he sat next to Cal. "We all have stuff we can piece on."

"How'd you guys handle those abaca fields?" Shorty asked with dread in his voice as he sat beside Cal.

The men all shook their heads in disdain.

"It was like a blasted oven in there," Cecil said.

"Pure torture," Abe agreed. "I stumbled a few times and wasn't sure if I would be able to get back up, but somehow did."

"Same here," Cal said. "I can hardly imagine anything worse. Except battling in there."

Shorty groaned. "That would be awful."

"Speaking of battle, anyone know what we are doing here?" Abe asked.

Cal shrugged. "Don't know. But it looks like we're setting up for something. I'd guess there's a Japanese stronghold up ahead we're going to try and break through."

"Hopefully we won't have any fighting till morning," Shorty said. "We all need some rest."

The men nodded warily, chewing on their rations. They could hardly imagine battling after being so fatigued.

After the soldiers had rested for a time the commanders started rounding up their men. They were instructed to dig foxholes to take cover for the night. They were told to make a battalion perimeter, which was a bit unusual. Usually perimeters were formed as a company. Cal and Cecil found a spot with a hole that was already partially dug. They dug in a bit deeper and wider, making room to keep the mortar weapon in the hole, plus room for the two of them to lie on both sides of the weapon.

When nightfall came the soldiers began retiring to their foxholes.

Just as Cal was beginning to get situated for the evening, the battalion commander approached their hole. "Morgan, can you come with me for a minute?"

"Sure," Cal replied, surprised the commander had sought him out, let alone at this time of night.

He stood and followed the commander. They weaved out and around the foxholes to the rear of the camp where the Brass was set up along with some army vehicles. The commander led Cal to an army truck. He opened its back swinging doors and reached for a small army green backpack placed in the storage area of the vehicle.

Holding the bag in his hands, the captain turned to Cal. "You can probably tell there's some things being orchestrated here at Route 1-D. I can't tell you much, but I will tell you this. The Japanese have a long defense line set up ahead going east to west blocking the route. We need to get past them, but it's not going to be easy."

Cal nodded, taking in what the commander was saying.

The commander reached into the bag and pulled out two phones connected with an extremely long electric wire of sorts. "You may have seen others using these connecting phones," he said. "Typically, we only trust high ranking soldiers with them." He paused for a moment, and continued. "I need you to take it tonight and keep it with you in your hole. There may be instructions I have for you late into the night or early tomorrow morning, and with this phone I'll be able to reach you at anytime."

"Yes, sir," Cal responded.

The captain quickly showed Cal how to operate his end of the phone. It was very simple.

"All right," the commander said once he finished his instructions. "Let's go put one phone in my hole and string the line from there to yours so you have the other one."

Cal followed the commander to his foxhole and watched as he placed one of the phones in his hole, and then strung the phone line all the way to Cal's foxhole a couple hundred feet ahead.

When they reached it, Cal noticed Cecil lying on his side in the hole, appearing to have already dozed off to sleep. Cal didn't blame him for being tired. It had been an exhausting day.

The commander handed Cal the connecting phone. "Make sure to keep it close to you so you'll hear my call."

Cal nodded. "I will, sir."

"Oh, and one more thing," the commander said.

"Yes?" The phone was already quite a surprise. He wondered what else the commander might have up his sleeve.

"I wanted you to know that I put in for your sergeant stripes today."

Cal was briefly taken back. He figured this was coming but wasn't expecting the topic to come up now. "Thank you," he replied.

"I know it's been a long time coming," the commander continued. "You've been a dutiful and brave soldier, and I wanted you to know we've noticed and appreciated it."

"Just doing my duty, sir," Cal responded steadily.

A look of fondness crossed the commander's eyes. "Thank you, Morgan. You have carried out that duty well." He paused for a moment and cleared his throat. "Very well. You may go back to your post now. Keep that phone close. I'll likely be contacting you at some point."

"Will do, sir."

The commander turned and began walking away. Cal was glad the commander trusted him enough to give him the phone and appreciated that he was getting his sergeant stripes, but he couldn't help but notice a difference in the way the commander had conducted himself tonight, as if he knew something was coming.

❧

Cal had been lying awake with his shoulders and head propped against the edge of his foxhole all night long. He was holding the phone the captain had given him in his hands and trying to relax, but it wasn't possible. Knowing he could be getting a call at any moment, along with the strange foreboding feeling he got from the commander earlier, had left him alert as a bird all night. He'd been awake so long now he was beginning to wonder if what the commander had alluded to was no longer going to happen. Perhaps there had been a change in plans. It had to be close to five in the morning and still no phone call or sign of action.

Cal could see a trickle of light beginning to outline the tops of the hillsides in the distance. Everything was quiet other than the gentle rustling of the trees and bushes in the subtle breeze. There had been no rain last night, and appeared to be none this morning. Not yet, at least.

Suddenly something startled Cal from his thoughts. A low and distant sputtering echoed through the darkened sky. He instantly recognized it as the far-off sound of gunfire. The shots started out irregular, but then picked up. A few moments later, return fire was going off. Up the road, a battle was beginning.

The men began stirring in their foxholes. Suddenly a ringing sound went off. Swiftly, Cal grabbed the receiver off the phone in his hand and lifted it to his ear. "Hello?"

"Morgan, it's me." It was the commander. "The Japs are approaching our front lines. We can't get our front men out of their holes in time and they're moving right in on them."

Cal understood the dire nature of the frontline men's situation. Soon they would be trapped. "What do we do?" Cal asked.

"If you let off some rounds, it should distract the Japs and give us time to get some of our machine guns into action."

"Will do, sir. I'll shoot off twenty rounds."

"Perfect. Thanks, Morgan."

"You're welcome." Cal didn't wait for further response. He knew he had to move fast. He clicked the receiver onto the phone, sat it down next to him, and stood to move over to Cecil, who appeared to have just woken up.

"They are moving in on our front lines," Cal told Cecil. "We need to let off fire."

Cecil nodded. "I'll load the ammo. The other guys can stay in their holes."

"Thanks," Cal replied.

The two men readied themselves beside their mortar weapon. Cecil retrieved the ammo and loaded it into the firearm. Within moments they were ready.

"Here it goes," Cal said. He pulled back on the trigger and began shooting off the booming rounds. One, two, three, four, five . . . He continued firing until he had thrown off twenty.

When he finished everything was dead quiet. Cal kneeled down and began counting the shells from the ammo. Cecil was crouched down a few feet to the side of him.

Cal was about halfway through counting the shells when out of nowhere a tremendous blast went off. Instantly, the strong force of the blast threw Cal backward off his feet. He felt himself launched into the air. A moment later he hit the ground with a hard thud. The breath instantly seized in his lungs. He tried opening his eyes, but everything was blurry. Mustering up all the energy he had, he lifted his head slightly off the ground. For a brief moment his eyes focused in on his chest in front of him. He was covered in blood.

His eyes lost focus and his head fell backward onto the hard dirt ground.

This must be it, he thought.

And then everything was dark.

Chapter Thirty-Nine

Images and flashes of light and color were fluttering before him like a random movie reel. One moment it was Kate sitting under the large wispy willow tree near her home. She was glowing against the dimly lit evening sky, gazing at him angelically. An inquisitive look rested upon her features, and her eyes looked as though she was silently asking him something.

Abruptly she was gone and Cal was seeing his mother. She was in the front yard of his home standing below the apple tree he had climbed so many times as a young boy. She reached toward the tree and tugged at a piece of fruit. It gently snapped off the tree. Holding the green fruit in her fingers, she slowly turned her eyes toward Cal. On her face was the same curious expression Kate had.

Suddenly he was out walking through the tall, wild grass of the fields of his father's farm, his hands brushing against the tops of the grass. Then he was walking along the streets of downtown Salt Lake City, holding Kate's hand and watching her throw back her head in laughter. Next he was riding a bus across the country, looking out the window at the endless miles and miles of land wiz past him.

The images and memories began flooding in faster and faster, until they were all a blur of colors and sounds and light.

He gasped in a gulp of air, choking on his own breath. There was only darkness. A soft, high-pitched buzzing was ringing in his ears. Gradually the ringing became louder and louder until it stopped and was replaced by a jumble of garish noises. Blasting, screaming, shooting, yelling.

Cal struggled to open his extremely heavy eyelids. An image, the outline of a person, was standing over him. After a few moments his eyes adjusted and he could see it was a man wearing a medic uniform. The man was holding something in his hands and looking down at Cal's wounds.

Cal opened his mouth to talk. Nothing came out but a dry, choked sound. He looked down to see a hole in the left side of his chest filled with gauze. Then he saw his left arm had a long, red tube running into it.

"What . . . what's that?" Cal managed to stammer in a horse whisper.

The medic looked down at him. "You're awake. I've been giving you blood. Just finishing off three pints."

Cal's head felt heavy and fogged. He let it fall back to the ground. Suddenly he felt a searing jolt of pain in his right arm.

"Ouch," he moaned. He looked up to see the medic pushing down on his upper right arm near the bicep area. Some gauze was placed there, soaked through with blood.

"I know you must be in pain," the medic said. "I wish I had some pain medicine I could shoot into you, but we're out."

Cal nodded with a grimace.

"You were hit with shrapnel," he continued. "The wound on your chest is a large one. It was bleeding out the most. This one on your right arm is pretty bad, too." He paused for a moment, focusing on replacing the gauze on Cal's arm. "That blood I gave you brought you back. You should be okay."

"How . . . how long was I out?" Cal managed to ask.

"I'm not sure. Ten, fifteen minutes, maybe? This area was hit with a huge explosion. I don't know how you weren't blown apart. We didn't expect to find anyone alive up here."

Cal inhaled sharply. "My crew?"

The man shook his head regretfully. "I don't think anyone survived."

Cal closed his eyes tightly. He could hear blasting sounds off in the distance. It appeared they were far enough back to be out of the warzone, but it didn't sound too far off.

A few seconds later Cal heard the voice of his captain. "Morgan?" he asked, the shuffle of his boots moving along the ground nearing them. "You're alive?" Soon he was standing over Cal. "I can hardly believe you survived that blast. Amazing!"

Cal couldn't respond.

"We need to get him out of here," he heard the medic say.

"With all this debris I don't think we can get any trucks in here," the captain replied.

"Can we get some men to carry him out?"

The captain hesitated. "I don't know. I'll see what I can do." He turned his attention down to Cal. "I'm going to find a way to get you out of here."

Cal exerted a great deal of energy to nod.

The captain reached down and patted him on the shoulder. "Good to see you alive, soldier." Then he stood and walked off.

As the medic took the tube out of Cal's arm, Cal mustered all the strength he had to turn his head to look to his side and survey the battlefield. It was dark and difficult to make out his surroundings, but what he saw was barely recognizable to what the area looked like just minutes before. The scene was one of pure chaos. The ground was torn up and debris and bodies were scattered everywhere. As he looked to his other side he was immediately met with a sickening sight. It was Cecil, or what was left of the young man's bloodied body, not much more than an arm's length away.

Cal turned his head back, closing his eyes tight. He felt his breath seize within his chest. His eyes began to burn, and he felt a tear prick at one of his eyelids and roll down the side of his temple. Cecil was gone. In one swift blast, the smart, thoughtful boy Cal had come to think so highly of was gone.

"All right, you're finished up," the medic said, tying off some bandages to Cal's arm where the blood had been pumped into him.

Just then Cal heard the rumbling sound of a motor running.

"A truck!" the medic exclaimed. "Looks like we'll be getting you out of here quickly."

The truck pulled up near them and some men jumped out.

Together they carried Cal to the truck. They laid him down flat in the back of it. Soon they were off.

Lying beside other wounded men, Cal felt the bumps of the ride rock and sway him back and forth as he fell in and out of sleep on the way to wherever they were going. He felt pain radiating through his entire body with each jolt of the truck, but he wasn't sure where it was coming from or what was worse—the physical pain he felt, or the pain of knowing that Cecil and so many of his friends were dead. He thought of Abe and Shorty and wondered when and if he would find out what their fate had been.

The next thing he knew, he was being loaded onto a stretcher and rolled into a large tent structure. Groggily, Cal looked up at the man pushing him. "Where am I?"

"A mass unit," the man answered. "This is where all the wounded are brought."

Cal nodded and closed his eyes again.

He must have fallen back to sleep, because the next time he opened his eyes, he looked around to see his stretcher was parked alongside dozens of others. He couldn't tell if the men on the stretchers were dead or alive. They lay there lifeless, shrouded with wounds, their green uniforms blackened with dirt and mud and covered in blood.

Too weak to get up off his stretcher, Cal lay there for hours without contact from any medics. Once in awhile he'd see someone run across the area or push another stretcher in, but not a word was spoken to any of the soldiers. Obviously the medics were overrun with more wounded men than they could handle.

Cal was desperately thirsty and hungry, but no water or food had been brought to him. He began wondering how many men around him were now no longer but corpses now. It felt like he was lying in the middle of a morgue.

Well into the day, probably sometime in the afternoon he guessed, Cal was awoken with an acute pain coming from the wound in his chest. His eyes opened to see a medic standing over him. Cal looked down at his chest and could see a man's fingers penetrating into the wound, fiddling around inside of him.

"Wow," the man said in an awed tone. "It looks like a piece of shrapnel went straight through your chest and out your back." The expression on his face bothered Cal. It wasn't so much concerned as it was careless and aloof. "It feels like there are still some pieces in there."

Cal could feel the man's fingers boring deeper into the wound, fumbling with the skin and flesh. Cal immediately had the impression that the medic had no clue what he was doing. Anger and frustration began welling up inside of him. He had somehow managed to survive that terrible blast. The last thing he needed was some ignorant medic worsening his condition.

Cal opened his mouth, letting out the words as loudly and poignantly as he could muster. "If you don't know what you're doing," he uttered sharply, "then don't touch it."

The man's expression immediately changed from careless to surprised, and then to affronted. Slowly, he pulled his fingers out of Cal's chest, turned, and walked away.

Chapter Forty

With the sterilized hospital smell penetrating his nostrils, Cal focused on breathing through his mouth to diffuse the chemically doused aroma. Disinfecting alcohol and iodine seemed to always linger in the air here, often leaving him with a grating headache. The nurses and medics were constantly sterilizing the hospital from its floors, to the equipment, to the tools the doctors used. Disease was rampant within these walls and those working here had to do all they could to keep it from spreading and contracting diseases themselves.

Cal had been at the hospital in Leyte for three weeks now. After spending a full day and night in the mass unit in Mindanao, he had been flown out the next morning on a small two-engine airplane. Once arriving in Leyte, he was admitted to the army hospital, where he was to undergo surgery to remove the shrapnel in his chest.

By the end of his first day at the mass unit in Mindanao, he had been conscious enough to realize he had wounds all over his body, some larger than others. Fragments of shrapnel had cut into him all over. Particularly bad was his right ear, which was torn up and bloodied, and his right arm, where the shrapnel pierced through his lower bicep near his elbow. The pain was awfully deep and severe. But worst of all was the wound in the left side of his chest. Medics continually commented it was a miracle he was alive. An inch to the right and it would have gone straight through his heart.

He underwent the surgery to remove the shrapnel from his chest the morning he arrived in Leyte. The nurse shot anesthetic into his arm and he was immediately out. When he began coming to, he strained to open his eyes but they were incredibly heavy, like a ton of bricks. He tried wiggling his fingers and toes but his body wouldn't respond with his brain. After quite some time of struggling to rouse himself he was finally able to crack open his eyes. As he glanced around the room, he noticed men lying in their beds around him eating a meal.

His voice throaty and strained, he had managed to say, "What's for dinner?"

A soldier in a bed next to him looked over. "You're awake."

"Seems so," Cal replied, his voice hoarse.

"Welcome back. And we're not eating dinner; we're eating breakfast. You've been out for twenty-four hours."

"We were starting to wonder if you were ever going to wake up," a man a couple beds down had added.

Cal was shocked he had been out a full day. He wondered if the nurses shot him up with a bit more anesthesia than he actually needed. He counted himself lucky he'd actually woken up.

After coming out of the anesthesia, he also noticed his other wounds had been tended to. Someone had removed the remaining shrapnel pieces lodged in his skin, cleaned up the dried blood, and bandaged him up. He had been dressed in a nice, clean pair of pajamas. He had briefly wondered what they had done with his disgustingly dirty army greens and welcomed the thought of them being thrown into the trash.

Cal soon found out they were unable to get to the shrapnel in his right arm. It was a small piece but had gone through the muscle and lodged into the bone close to the elbow. The nurse told him they had decided not to take it out because the doctor thought it was very close to a nerve, and if that nerve was accidentally pierced in the process, it would cause permanent damage. They told him the shrapnel shard was small enough that his arm should be able to heal with it left inside him. The bone would likely grow around it.

But the pain in his arm didn't subside. He could never find a comfortable position to rest it. If he straightened the arm, it caused him a great deal of pain, so he resorted to holding it up bent at the elbow, resting his elbow on his bed with his hand straight up in the air. Keeping it this way seemed to be the only way to stop the pain. He propped it like this day and night.

Following his surgery, the doctors put him on the new antibiotic drug, penicillin, which had successfully kept him from developing any infection in his wounds. He was beginning to be able to stand on his own, and could even take a few steps. The nurses said he would be able to walk soon. He worked at it a little bit each day. Once he could walk he would most likely get sent back to the States to finish up his recovery there.

Now he sat in his hospital bed reading over his most recent letter from Kate for about the tenth time, his arm propped in its usual position. He was finally able to write Kate letters as frequently as he wanted to. The hospital had paper and pencils he could use at any time. It still took weeks for their letters to reach each other, but it was wonderful to be able to write out his thoughts and feelings to her and have her respond back about them. He felt their time apart had deepened their relationship, which he would never have thought possible.

As he read, engrossed in the letter, imagining what Kate might be doing this very instant and wondering just how long it would be until he would be able to see her again, he heard footsteps clicking down the hallway outside his door. He glanced up to see a doctor walking past his room. As the doctor strode by, he turned his head and glanced into the door at Cal. He continued walking, but then Cal heard the clicking of the footsteps abruptly come to a halt. Suddenly the doctor's head was peering back through the door.

"Why are you holding your arm up like that?" the doctor asked.

Surprised at the question, Cal quickly glanced to his sides, making sure the doctor was addressing him. He realized the doctor was indeed addressing him and must be talking about his right arm. "Oh, this? Because it hurts to straighten it out," he answered matter-of-factly.

The doctor looked at Cal curiously and took a step into the room. "And why is that?" His dress shoes clicked on the floor with each measured step he took.

Cal had never talked to or seen this doctor before, but he could tell he was an agreeable enough fellow. He conducted himself in a professional, no-nonsense manner, and struck Cal as a man who knew what he was talking about.

"A piece of shrapnel went through the muscle to the bone here," Cal answered, pointing to his elbow with the finger from his other hand.

The doctor nodded and walked toward Cal's bed. "And you're not using it?"

Cal shook his head. "No."

"How long has it been this way?"

"A few weeks."

"I see," the doctor said, looking at Cal's arm. He examined it a few seconds longer and then turned his attention back to Cal. "Do you want to be able to use it again?"

The question struck Cal with surprise. "Of course," he answered. "I don't just want to use it again, I *need* to use it again." His livelihood as a farmer depended on that arm.

The doctor nodded understandingly and stepped in close to Cal. He reached a hand out to Cal's right hand and tugged it forward.

Cal grimaced. The arm moved slightly, but mostly remained stiffly in place.

The doctor exhaled. "That's what I thought," he murmured under his breath. "It's not healing correctly. I'm afraid your arm needs to be re-broken or you'll never have use of it. It will be stuck in this position for the rest of your life."

Cal's eyes widened. "Then it needs to be done," he replied without hesitation. "I'm a farmer. I need use of this arm."

"Okay, then," the doctor said conclusively. He grabbed hold of Cal's arm firmly with his two hands, lifted his knee up, and pressed it down on Cal's chest.

Cal quickly realized the doctor was going to do it here and now. He took a deep breath and closed his eyes.

"Brace yourself," the doctor warned.

Cal closed his eyes. The next thing he knew he felt his arm

yanked forward strongly and swiftly. The movement was followed by a loud snap. Instantly, an excruciating blow of pain jolted through his arm and reverberated through his entire body. A shrill bellow exited his lips.

Chapter Forty-One

MID AUGUST 1945
Pacific Ocean

I couldn't bear to think about it; and yet, somehow, I couldn't think about nothing else. Those were the words of Huckleberry Finn Cal had read a few weeks before, and since then the prose had been on the forefront of his mind. As he had come across that sentence while reading good old Huck's story, Cal felt it described, spot on, how he was feeling. He could hardly bear to recall the horrors he had seen in the war, and even more, the sound of the men moaning and dying throughout the nights. But when those sights and sounds had been so engraved in his mind over the past several months, how on earth could he rid his memory of them?

His active duty in the Philippines had lasted about six months, but it had felt like a lifetime. He had been in the hospital in Leyte for about a month. It took him that entire month to be able to hobble around on his own. Soon after he was well enough to walk, he was informed that he would be boarding a large hospital ship that would transport him, along with many other wounded soldiers, back to an army hospital in California. There he would finish up the remainder of his recovery.

He wished he could simply go home when landing in California. He was feeling a hundred times better. He could walk, albeit slowly, but the last thing he wanted was to be holed up any longer in another wretched hospital. He wanted to be home. He wanted to be with Kate and with his family.

He had been told he would likely get some furloughs home during his time at the hospital in California, but he wasn't allowed to go home until he was officially released. He mused about buying a bus ticket home after landing and never going back, but he knew it wasn't a realistic option. Not worth getting into trouble. Regretfully, he would have to bide his time until they let him go.

They were nearing the end of the voyage now. The voyage from Leyte to San Francisco had been a long and tedious one of nearly a month and a half. After the arm re-breaking incident back in Leyte the doctor had told him to make sure he moved and rotated it every day. He had done just that, but it proved to be severely painful. He couldn't help from cringing in pain as he performed the simple arm movements the doctor had instructed him to do, but it had to be done.

He hadn't bothered trying to make any friends on board the vessel. He wasn't sullen or cranky or unfriendly, but simply didn't care to reach out to anyone. He was too tired and too worn out for new friendships. He simply wanted to keep to himself and be left alone. Although he didn't speak much to the other men on board, he could tell most of them felt the same. They were all exhausted. Too physically and emotionally weary to socialize and banter the way they all likely did on their voyage over.

He often thought of the friends he had made in the war. As far as he knew Shorty and Abe were still back fighting in the Philippines. He prayed they were okay and hoped to someday enter into some sort of correspondence with them. But Cecil, well, Cal had seen all too closely what had happened to him. It was strange how quickly friendships in war could rise and fall, whether ending in sudden separation due to wounds, or because of death.

The one positive aspect of this voyage home was that the ship had a fantastic library. Cal had spent most of his waking moments on the boat reading. He never knew he enjoyed reading so much. He had read over twenty books during his time on the boat. Mostly classics. His favorites had been Mark Twain's *Tom Sawyer* and *Huckleberry Finn*. Those boys seemed like old friends now. Old friends that had helped pass the slow ticking of the clock until he returned to California, and then, finally, home.

❧

As the ship glided forward into the fog-filled San Francisco Bay, Cal was surprised at the feelings of both immense excitement and relief he was experiencing. He gazed over the railing of the top level of the vessel, his favorite spot on both this ship and the one he had traveled to the Philippines on. How wonderful to be entering a port of the country he was born in, his homeland, and not a port filled with foreboding uncertainty. He never realized, until this moment, just how much he appreciated his country and the freedom he enjoyed and had been fighting for overseas.

As the ship moved forward to its final stretch into the dock, the fog parted like a dream, revealing dozens of people standing on the pier waving and cheering them in. Although Cal knew none of his friends or family would be there to greet him, he still felt joy as he looked into the euphoric faces of those standing on the docks welcoming in their beloved soldiers.

Shuffling off the ship bare-footed, wearing the same pajamas he had been given in the hospital back in Leyte, along with all the other pajama-wearing men, Cal finally stepped foot back on American ground.

❧

My dear Cal,

I am so relieved to know you are back safe in the U.S.! What a wonderful gift it was to receive the package of letters you sent that you wrote during your ship ride back to California. It was very reminiscent of when I received the letters you wrote on your journey to the Philippines, but reading the letters this time was also very different as there was no uncertainty in them or in my thoughts as I read them of what your experiences at war would be. Isn't it wonderful to know there are no longer unknowns? The war is now behind us and soon we will be together again! It almost seems to good to be true and I often have to remind myself that it's not all just a dream.

It's so nice that our letters can now travel back and forth to each other so quickly. I know you say for me not to come and visit you in the hospital, that you will get a furlough home very soon, but I can hardly stand knowing you are just a bus or train ticket away and that I'm not on my way there now.

Will you please reconsider?

As you know from my coming to Camp Roberts, I am not afraid of going places I may not necessarily be permitted and working the situation to my advantage. But I can see how it might not be ideal if there is truly nowhere for me to stay and if we weren't able to spend much time together. I can't imagine there isn't a spare hospital bed somewhere I can sleep on, but if the place is brimming full of men as you say it is and those in charge are strict, I can see how it might be tricky. If we must wait for your furlough, I hope that it comes as quickly as possible. If you see any change in situation or chance of my visiting working out, please let me know and I will come running.

I'm so glad to hear that your injuries are continuing to heal. How wonderful that you are able to walk fairly steadily now and that your arm mobility is coming back. I nearly fainted reading about how the doctor had to re-break your arm. I can't imagine how painful that must have been! I wish you would have told me about it sooner but I know you wanted to keep me from unpleasant details. However, I am very glad you told me. How much you've had to endure, and I know you have only told me a small part of it. I greatly admire your strength, faith, and courage.

It's wonderful the war has come to an end now in all areas of the world. As you know, news has spread of Japan's surrender, which I understand is a great relief for you to know your friends in the Philippines will no longer be engaged in combat. Also, I am glad to hear that your brother has returned home safely.

I'm so glad it's all over, but the explosive the U.S. dropped on Japan to will them to surrender sounds as though it was nothing short of horrific. How much sadness, destruction, and casualty this war has caused. But of course you know that from a personal standpoint better than most. I hope your thoughts and memories of the war do not plague you. I have heard of some men coming home from the war out of their minds and overcome with grief. But in reading your letters I get the sense that you have somehow been able to keep your mind and spirits well through all of this. I'm very grateful for that, although I know it must still be difficult. I hope someday you will feel able to share with me the things you experienced. I would like to know this part of you, but also so that you have someone to talk to and share about it with.

I wish we could know when your furlough will be, but until then I will be here anxiously awaiting it, hoping for it to come soon. I can't wait to see you and speak with you face to face. It's so exciting, but also rather nerve racking. Do you feel that way, too? Over the course of our time apart I feel as though I've written a lot of heartfelt things, a lot of dramatic things, and a lot of silly things in my letters I've sent you (if I were to read them back I'd probably be embarrassed), but I hope above all I have adequately explained how much you mean to me. I imagine and hope that everything will be as wonderful and magical as ever when we are reunited.

I love you dearly and can't wait for your return.
All my love,
Kate

Chapter Forty-Two

SEPTEMBER 1945
DeWitt General Hospital, California

There she was, looking his way again. Cal quickly dropped his eyes and grabbed for the book off his lap. He flipped it open, hoping his apparent reading would encourage her to walk on by. The attractive blonde nurse had been making eyes at him ever since he was admitted to the hospital, but lately she had been trying to strike up conversation with him more frequently when making her rounds. He always ignored her flirtatious tone and tried acting nonchalant, but he was beginning to wonder if she was taking that as a challenge.

Absorbed again in his reading, he was startled a bit when he heard a female's voice speak up to his side. "Hi, Private Morgan."

It was her. Cal smiled politely, "Hi," he replied, looking up and closing his book. "Here to check my blood pressure?"

Her eyes dropped downward. "Um, no, actually. I just wanted to tell you that if you ever need someone to help you take a longer walk around the halls or even out on the hospital grounds to get some fresh air, just let me know. I'd be happy to accompany you and help you keep steady."

Cal was unsure how to answer, sensing there was more behind

her willingness to accompany him than simply trying to help him get his walking back to normal.

"Thanks, I'll remember that," he said, looking back down to his book, hoping she would take the cue for their conversation to be finished.

But she still stood there, not walking away. "Do you even know my name?" she asked playfully.

Cal looked back up at her. Now that she mentioned it, he really wasn't sure. "No, I can't say that I do."

Her eyes were studying him. "It's Judy." She paused for a moment and then continued in a more hushed tone, "You might be the one guy in here who doesn't know my name, or that . . . doesn't seem to notice me." She hesitated for a moment. "The funny thing is, you're the one guy here who I'd actually be interested in getting to know better."

Cal was taken back by her sudden forwardness. For a moment he wasn't sure how to respond. Finally he decided it was best to just be honest. "Judy, you're very nice, and a very pretty girl. And I'm sure there are a lot of guys here who would feel lucky to have your . . . special interest." He turned toward the table next to his bed. Propped up against a couple of books he had stacked was a photo of Kate. Pointing to it, he continued, "Do you see that girl right there?" Judy turned her head toward the photo and nodded. "That is the girl I am going to marry. My heart is with her, and it just wouldn't feel right for me to go on a walk as you say, or to carry on with you, when I know the girl I love is waiting for me back home."

"Hmm," she replied. "I see." She looked back at him. "But you know, there are a lot of men around here who have girls back home. Some are even married. But they talk and flirt with me, just having fun. It doesn't have to lead to anything real, you know."

Cal considered what she was saying. "I'm sure that's true," he responded. "But that just isn't me."

She stood looking at him for a moment, a somewhat mysti-fied expression resting on her face. But he also thought he noticed a glint of admiration, or maybe it was respect, in her eyes. "Well, that's a first," she said with a wry smile. She nodded toward the photo of Kate. "She's a lucky girl." She stood a little straighter and rocked back on her foot, as if preparing to leave. "I hope she knows that." Then she offered him a cordial smile, turned, and walked away.

Inwardly, Cal let out a sigh of relief. He was glad that conversation was over. He suspected it had needed to happen for a while now. He was also pleased he could do something to show his devotion to Kate, in this place where loyalty to the soldiers' women back home didn't always seem to be upheld as it should be.

As chock-full as the hospital was, it was a lonely place. Many of the men here seemed dispirited and aloof. Their injuries ranged from everything as simple as a broken bone to very precarious ones such as blown off or amputated limbs and recovering from serious surgeries. Now that the war was over, all the men just wanted to go home. But for those that were injured and recovering it wasn't that easy. They had to finish out their recovery in the military hospital they were sent to. For some, home was a lot further off than others and it was discouraging to know that men who weren't injured were able to return home while they were left biding their time in a hospital bed. Time away from their loved ones was dragging on and sometimes felt as if it would never end.

Cal was grateful he had Kate's letters to keep him company. As well, he had made quite a close friend that he had much in common with. He was a fellow by the name of Charles. Charles had also come home on the ship from Leyte to California, although the two men had never spoken until the day they disembarked in San Francisco. As they walked off the ship and around the wharf, the men began making casual conversation. They quickly made the connection that they were both Utah boys. Cal learned that Charles was from Sandy, the neighboring town north of Cal's hometown of Crescent. After recovering from the initial disbelief that they had grown up just a few mere miles away from each other, Charles explained he was in search of a birthday present for his wife. Cal happily tagged along with Charles as he searched out a gift to send home to his beloved. Cal told Charles all about Kate and the men planned to take their gals out for dinner together when they returned home, and perhaps dancing if their injuries allowed for it. In the hospital Cal and Charles ended up being only a few beds away from each other in the large open hospital floor of men recovering. It was nice to have a friend nearby.

Cal had learned that DeWitt General Hospital was a large facility ran by the US War Department. It opened in February of 1944 with the purpose of treating soldiers wounded in the war. Currently, the hospital was at full capacity with 2,300 patients.

The war was now officially over. On the European front the Germans had surrendered in late April. By early May all of Europe was celebrating the war's end. In the Pacific the Japanese held out longer, but Japan announced their surrender on August 14, with the formal surrender taking place September 2.

Thankfully, George had made it through the war safe and uninjured. He had returned home in June. Since Cal had been in the hospital, the brothers had written back and forth a couple times, their letters including generalities about the war and some encouraging words, but no details as to what they personally experienced yet. Someday they would get to that. It was just too fresh on their minds now and for the time being Cal knew they'd both rather forget those details than relive them.

Cal's wounds were healing up well. He was able to walk increasingly steadily and faster and care for himself more and more each day. He was constantly frustrated at the fact that he had to wait out his time here. Kate had written him early on asking if she could come to California to visit him. He had to convince her that it wouldn't be worth the money and time for the visit. There wouldn't be anything for her to do here, and the hospital was no place she'd want to hang around.

Camp Roberts had been one thing, but this place was at full capacity and packed to the brim. There would be nowhere for her to stay and he didn't know how or where they would even be able to spend any alone time together. He explained that soon enough he would be able to get a furlough home, and that would be a much more ideal reunion.

And that time had finally almost come. In just a week Cal would be getting his furlough. Initially when he found out he was going to be able to go home for a visit, he thought it would be fun to surprise Kate and show up without telling her he was coming. But he was unable to contain his excitement. He had written her six days ago to tell her and she had written him back quickly, for he had received a letter, just yesterday, expressing her excitement to see and be with him again. This year had been the longest of his life. But he was finally almost back to her.

Kate hadn't fully declared she wanted to marry him, but their letters always talked of their future together. Cal hadn't written asking her to promise anything because he wanted to have that conversation in person. He couldn't imagine anything going wrong at this point. When he returned, if everything went as well as he imagined, he would take what little money he had out of the bank, buy a ring for her, and propose. Then, moving forward, in their letters they could openly talk of their marriage and begin planning for the future.

Lying in his hospital bed, Cal had opened his book back up to read, but he let his mind get lost in all his thoughts and anticipation of being home with Kate again.

"Private Morgan?"

Cal looked up and was surprised to see a nurse standing over him. He hadn't even heard her coming.

She reached out her hand, holding a letter toward him.

"A delivery for you. It looks rather official."

Cal nodded and took the letter in his hand. "Thank you," he said.

The nurse nodded, turned, and walked away.

He glanced at the letter, which was obviously some sort of correspondence from the military. The return address listed *Headquarters 24th Infantry Division*—Cal's infantry division.

He carefully opened the envelope and pulled out the letter.

"Well, I'll be," he murmured to himself as he read the letter over.

He never expected to receive acclamation for his actions in the war. The letter cited his heroic achievement and selfless performance of duty in the battle at Ula, Mindanao, which was that last battle that nearly took his life. It also said his actions were an inspiration to his fellow soldiers. He was being awarded a Bronze Star.

Chapter Forty-Three

Gazing out the window as they soared through the sky, Cal's stomach fluttered with the bumps of the small airplane as it jetted through the clouds. A rush of anticipation and excitement ran through his veins. The plane ride was invigorating and made him feel as free as a bird. Finally, he was homebound.

He had been on a plane ride once before, when he was injured in Mindanao and was flown from the mass unit early in the morning to the hospital in Leyte to get surgery on his chest. Because of his injuries he'd had to lie down flat on the plane's floor, and had been in great pain, leaving him barely conscious enough to realize he was on an airplane at all, let alone enjoy the ride. But this was completely different. He was greatly enjoying it. A large part of that had to do with the destination it was taking him to. He felt purely elated.

Cal originally planned to take a bus or train home for his furlough. But then he heard of some soldiers who had gone to the Air Force base near the hospital and managed to catch rides home on planes scheduled to go to cities near their hometowns. Cal figured it was worth a shot. He went to the Air Force base a week before his furlough and asked if any planes were going to Salt Lake City anytime soon. Sure enough, a plane was scheduled to Salt Lake the following Tuesday afternoon. His furlough was to begin Monday and last two weeks, but he figured it was worth waiting the extra day to catch a ride on the airplane. The travel time would be much faster, he would practically make up any lost time, and it wouldn't cost him a penny. Any little bit of money he could save and put toward a ring for Kate would be helpful.

Riding behind the pilot and copilot in a jump seat, Cal was the only other person on the plane. As he looked out the window he saw they were now soaring over the Oquirrh Mountain Range—the mountains making up the southwestern side of the Salt Lake Valley. In the distance he could see the miles and miles of shallow, salty water and wetlands that made up the Great Salt Lake. The Salt Lake Airport was situated on the south side of the expansive lake. The plane should begin descending any moment.

But as they moved forward the plane wasn't dropping any lower. Cal watched as they soared right over the airport. He gulped. Maybe they would be making a turn around and then touching down. He hoped there hadn't been some sort of misunderstanding on where the plane was heading. He hadn't spoken to the pilot or copilot once they'd been on board. The plane was very noisy and loud, and they seemed busy working with the plane's controls.

Cal wondered what Kate and his family would think if he didn't show up at the airport tonight. When he found out he would be coming home on the plane, he had written to Kate and his family telling them he was flying into the Salt Lake airport on Tuesday evening, and an approximate time of when he would arrive. He wasn't sure if they would get the letters soon enough for him to receive a response, but he received letters back from both Kate and his mother on Monday saying the two of them had spoken. His family and Kate were planning to drive to the airport together to meet and welcome him home.

He joyed at the thought of seeing all his loved ones gathered together as he walked off the plane. But now he was beginning to worry. The plane was continuing northbound and didn't appear to be turning around. The Salt Lake airport was far behind them now.

Cal began feeling the opposite of how he was feeling just

moments before. Where were they headed? What would he tell Kate and his family?

About five minutes later, he felt the plane begin to tilt downward. They were definitely descending. But where were they landing?

Just then the copilot turned his head around to Cal and shouted, "We're starting the decent into the base now."

The base? What base?

Then it hit Cal. Hill Air Force Base was located about thirty miles north of Salt Lake City, near Ogden, Utah. There must have been a miscommunication when they told him they were flying into Salt Lake City. They were actually headed to Hill.

Cal nodded. He decided not to tell the men of the misunderstanding and his impending predicament. He would simply have to catch a bus or find a ride back home.

❧

An hour later Cal was walking along the road from Hill Air Force Base toward the highway. He had settled on trying to hitchhike. He only had his small army knapsack with him and wouldn't be much trouble to anyone that might pick him up. Luckily, back at the hospital, he had gotten a hold of a nice new pair of army greens to wear home. Otherwise now he would have looked like a crazy person in pajamas wandering the roads at night. If he could at least catch a ride into Salt Lake, he could hop on a bus to Sandy, which was the nearest bus station to home. He had no idea what the bus schedule was and if he would be able to catch one tonight. It was just after seven o'clock and would be getting dark by eight. If he had to he could sleep the night in a field, or perhaps find an inexpensive hotel room in Salt Lake if he made it that far.

His family and Kate probably figured he hadn't made the flight. He wished there was some way to get a hold of them, but with no phone there was no way for him to contact them.

The small road that he was walking down now had hardly any travelers. One man stopped and asked where he was heading, but unfortunately the man was on his way up north, the opposite direction of where Cal needed to go. Cal figured once he reached the highway there would be more cars headed toward Salt Lake.

He came upon the highway, which didn't look as busy as he had hoped. In fact so far he hadn't seen a single vehicle pass. He sighed as he turned and began walking along the roadside. After a few seconds he heard the sound of a motor approaching from behind. He turned to see a car coming up quickly from behind him. He stuck out his thumb, but the car zoomed right past him. Again, another car came, but with the same result. A few seconds later he heard the rumble of a third engine approaching. He turned to see a pickup truck approaching, much like the one his family owned. He stuck out his thumb and the truck began slowing and pulled up behind him.

"Where you headed, soldier?" the man asked with a drawl. He was around Cal's father's age and was likely a farmer as well.

"Out south to Crescent," Cal answered. "But I'm hoping to at least make it to Salt Lake tonight."

The man smiled. "Just so happens I'm headed to Bluffdale myself."

Cal was floored. Bluffdale was a town just south of Crescent. Cal could hardly expect to get any closer to his hometown unless the man happened to be traveling to his parents' front doorstep.

"Reckon I could take you as far as you're needin' to go," the man concluded.

Cal grinned widely. "That would be great."

A little over an hour later, the pickup Cal was riding in pulled up the dirt driveway of Cal's parents' home and came to a stop.

"Thanks again," Cal said to the man, who he had gotten to know quite well over the last hour.

"No problem," he man replied. "Have a nice visit home."

Cal smiled. "I will."

Cal stepped out of the pickup, shut the door, and waved good-bye to the man as he backed out of the darkened drive. He turned around and allowed himself to pause for a brief moment and soak in the comforting image of the home he grew up in. It was dark out and light glowed through the windows of the front room of the home creating a cozy, welcoming air. He wondered who would be inside. Would it only be his family, or would Kate be there too?

He took a deep breath and began walking toward the front doorstep.

Chapter Forty-Four

The creaking sound of the door was the first thing Cal was met with. As he pushed it fully open, he saw the surprised faces of his mother and father sitting on chairs directly across the room. Next he saw his sisters and brothers scattered throughout the room, their eyes immediately on him. But the one person who hadn't witnessed his entrance was sitting on the couch that faced the opposite direction of the door. With her soft, brown curls falling down the back of her neck, Cal immediately knew who it was. Elation rushed over his body. She was here.

"Cal!" his mother called out from across the room. "You're home!"

Cal watched as Kate's head swiftly turned to face him, her hair swishing with the movement. Meeting his gaze, the sight of her nearly left him breathless. She looked as lovely and as radiant as ever. The first thing he noticed was her eyes—those deep chocolate-brown eyes he had dreamed of so many times. His gaze moved to her mouth where a dazzling smile was curled on her lips.

"Yes," Cal managed, moving his attention to his mother and the rest of the group. "I made it." He was addressing the whole group but couldn't keep from looking back to Kate.

Before he knew it his mother was at his side, wrapping her arms around him. Next George approached him and gave him a firm hug. Almost instantly he was surrounded by his family members hollering with excitement and giving him hugs.

"Why weren't you at the airport?"

"How did you get here?"

"How are you feeling?"

"You look so thin!"

Cal laughed as all the questions and comments came flying at him. "I'll explain everything," he said with a smile as he looked around at the faces of those he loved.

"Give your brother some room!" his mother hollered, waving everyone back. "Now, let's get him into the kitchen and fed. He can tell us all about it then."

Everyone agreed and began dispersing. Cal gave his two sisters hugs and they turned and followed his mother into the kitchen. Everyone began funneling in after them talking over each other excitedly.

Still standing in the entryway, Cal looked back to the couch where Kate had been sitting. She hadn't run up to him as all his family had. Standing beside the couch, she was wearing a lilac colored dress that beautifully complicated the softness of her features and contrasted stunningly against her dark hair. She wore stylish matching heels and a becoming bright red shade of lipstick. Her eyes looked as though she could hardly believe he was standing in front of her. He knew how she felt. He felt the very same way.

He took a step toward her, but before he knew it, she had closed the short distance between them and thrown her arms around him. He dropped the knapsack he was still holding in his hand to the floor and wrapped both his arms around her. He closed his eyes, soaking in everything about this moment: the feeling of holding her in his arms, the softness of her cheek against his, the lavender smell radiating off her. But mostly the incredible sense of relief and gratitude he felt having her back in his arms again.

"I can't believe you're finally here," Kate said shakily into his ear.

Cal felt his heartstrings tug with her words. He could feel water pricking at the corners of his eyes. He opened his mouth to say something but was afraid he wouldn't be able to hold in his emotions if he did. He thought of the many nights he spent stuck in his foxhole, soaking wet, praying he wouldn't get blown to pieces. He thought of the horrible battles he'd lived through and all the fatalities he had witnessed. He thought of the countless medics who had commented it was a miracle he had survived the shrapnel piercing through his chest. He knew it was nothing short of a miracle he was standing here with her now.

"Neither can I," he finally replied gruffly.

He continued holding her in his arms, not wanting to let her go.

Interrupting the tenderness of the moment, a whistle came from the kitchen door. "Come on in here, you two lovebirds!" Cal's brother Jack hollered.

Still holding onto Kate, Cal slowly pulled back. He sniffed and wiped the corners of his eyes and watched Kate adoringly as she did the same thing.

He reached his hand down and took hold of her hand. Relishing the feeling of wrapping his fingers around hers, together they walked into the kitchen.

❧

The air was crisp but not cold. It was a pleasant, fall evening. Cal had retrieved one of his jackets from his closet and wrapped it around Kate to keep her warm. They sat on the back porch swing, Cal's arm around Kate's shoulder holding her close.

They had spent an hour or so in the kitchen with his family. As his mother served him her savory beef stew and delicious biscuits, everyone gathered around to hear the explanation of how he had gotten home. Cal explained how the airplane he thought was headed to Salt Lake actually ended up at Hill Air Force Base. Everyone laughed as he told of the pit in his stomach as they flew over the Salt Lake City airport leaving him wondering where in the world they were headed.

They asked about his wounds and how he was feeling. He assured them he was healing up very well. They wanted to know in more detail than he had provided in letters what is was like where he had been in the Philippines. He told them of the jungle foliage and rough landscape.

"You didn't talk of battles much in your letters," Jack said. "Did you see much fighting other than that time that you were wounded?"

Cal hesitated. He glanced over to Kate. Her eyes were wide with concern. "Yes," he finally answered, looking back at Jack. "More than I wish I had, I'm afraid."

The room fell silent.

Breaking the quiet, George spoke up. "So, tell us more about your ship ride home," he said. "Was it a big liner or a smaller ship?" Cal looked at George, a little puzzled by the abrupt shift in conversation. George's voice had been nonchalant but his eyes were willing Cal on, and instantly Cal recognized the empathy in his brother's gaze. He knew what George was doing. Cal was unsure how much battle George had seen, but he obviously knew enough to understand why Cal wouldn't want to speak of it, especially tonight when his happy reunion was finally taking place.

"It was huge," Cal responded, readily taking his brother's cue. Their eyes were locked for a few moments, and in those short moments a mutual understanding and respect was exchanged. Cal offered his brother a slight smile of thanks that no one else in the group likely even caught onto and continued, "Even bigger than the ship we went over on." Cal noticed George's face instantly relax, pleased he had helped his brother in turning the conversation from a troubling direction.

Cal went on with more details about the ship. George responded with some specifics about the liners he had rode on during his time in the war, and soon they were on to other nonthreatening war-related topics.

The entire evening Kate sat next to Cal at the table. He couldn't keep his focus from going back to her as he was relaying his stories. She had been relatively quiet, letting everyone else in the room get in questions. Cal enjoyed the evening catching up with his family very much, but more than anything he had wanted a chance to be alone with Kate.

Now, sitting on the back porch swing with her, they were finally alone. Cal felt so much love and eagerness toward her, he could hardly contain himself from getting down on his knee and asking her to marry him. But he had to remind himself that he needed to be one hundred percent sure that her feelings were the same. She had for so long been opposed to marriage. Her letters seemed to say she now felt the opposite, along with the way she was acting tonight. But he didn't want to be presumptuous. Not only that, he wanted the moment he proposed to be memorable and special. He was an old-fashioned romantic, and wanted to surprise her with the ring and the engagement. So tonight he had resolved not to let his excitement and emotions overtake him. He would enjoy this evening with her and hopefully get a read if she was on the same page as him without actually having to tell her he wanted to propose. If she was, he wouldn't waste any time. He would go out ring shopping tomorrow.

"I can't tell you how happy I was to see you when I walked through that door," he said, holding her close. "Thanks for coming tonight."

"Of course," Kate replied tenderly, looking into his eyes. "I wouldn't have missed it."

Cal smiled.

"But I almost did miss it," she continued before he could respond. "Because *you* almost didn't show up."

Cal tipped his head back and chuckled. "Oh, Kate. I'm glad you haven't changed. You sure know how to keep me on my toes."

She smiled back at him, looking pleased.

Suddenly a thought entered Cal's head. "Do you want to go on a walk?" he asked. "I know it's dark out, but the stars are bright enough that we'll be able to make our way around the property."

"Sure," Kate replied enthusiastically. "A walk sounds lovely."

They lingered in the swing facing each other for a moment before standing. They had not yet kissed since Cal had returned. But as Cal sat staring at her, he was finding it difficult to keep his focus from zeroing in on her lips. He wanted to move in toward her now but quickly thought better of it. He would have to wait a few more minutes, but it would be worth it.

He stood and pulled her up by her hands. Then, holding hands, they walked off the back porch and out onto the grass. "We've spent the whole evening talking about me," he said as they began wandering around the property. "But all I've really wanted to talk about is you."

Kate smiled softly. "Nothing much has gone on that I haven't told you in my letters," she paused contemplatively for a moment. "You know I'm still working at the dentist's office."

Cal nodded.

"And . . ." She glanced over at him with a reluctant expression. "I don't think I mentioned this to you yet, but I gave up my room at the Beehive House. I'm moving home."

Cal could feel the surprised expression fill his face. "Oh?" he asked. "But I thought you loved living downtown."

"Well, I did. But after you left I began tiring of it a bit. Going out with the girls and all that just started getting, I don't know, a little meaningless. I stayed living downtown to be with my friends. But a month or so ago when I found out you'd be coming home soon, I thought I might as well move back home, so I could be closer to you."

Cal felt his heart pick up pace with her words. She wanted to be close to him.

"Plus," she continued. "Living at home I'll be able to save money, which will be helpful for the future . . . for us . . ." She trailed off. Her cheeks reddened.

He immediately realized what she was inferring to—their future together. He looked over at her blushing. She looked so very beautiful. Every urge within him wanted to drop to his knee and ask her to marry him. But he couldn't. He needed a ring in his hand for that moment.

"You don't know how much it means to me to hear you say that," he said, looking over at her intently as he took a slow and steady step.

She smiled back at him bashfully through her long eyelashes.

They continued walking. "I don't have anything much else exciting or new to tell you since my last letter," she said. "Except that my beau just returned home from the war."

Cal was amused. "Oh, really. And how do you feel about this beau of yours being home?"

The corners of Kate's lips turned up as she gazed up at the night sky. "Hmm, it's kind of hard to say . . . ," she answered with an impish smile. Then she sighed, turned toward him, and stopped walking. "Honestly, I couldn't be happier."

Cal felt his heart thudding loudly inside his chest. He didn't know why but she still made him nervous. Not a bad nervous. It was lovely and electrifying, and he had a feeling that with Kate that feeling would never leave or go away.

"Neither could I," he replied. He reached out and took both her hands in his. "I'm still having a hard time believing I'm actually here with you, and that this isn't just a dream," he said, gazing into her eyes.

Kate squeezed his hands in response. "I know. You know, this walk sort of reminds me of our nightly walks around Camp Roberts."

Cal nodded. "Me too." He had often wondered something and wanted to ask her now. "Do you ever look back and think you were crazy for going out to California?" he asked.

"Of course not," Kate responded without hesitation. "If anything I've wondered why I didn't go sooner. And wish I would have found a way to stay longer."

Her response was exactly what he was hoping to hear. He took a breath. "You'll never know how much you coming there meant to me," he responded. "You gave me hope and a reason to live."

"You gave me the very same thing," she responded. "Hope."

Cal closed his eyes and took in a breath of the fresh, crisp air. This night was turning out to be everything he had hoped for.

He opened his eyes and lifted her hand to his lips, placing a gentle kiss on it. Then he took a step in closer to her. "Do you know why I wanted to go on a walk around the property tonight?"

Kate shook her head.

"Because when I was out in the war, I had a single memory that brought me more hope and comfort each day than any other."

Kate's eyebrows pinched. "What was that?"

Cal smiled. "When we walked around this property together, the night before I left."

Recollection filled her eyes.

"But there is a reason that memory was the one I always thought of," he continued. "It was because being here with you was the happiest I have ever been. Having you with me at home, picturing you in my everyday life, was more wonderful than I could have imagined." He paused for a moment. He hadn't planned to say these things, but they were flowing out of him now. And he wanted to say them. He wanted her to understand how much she meant to him. "Kate, you are my home. I can't imagine ever being without you."

"I feel the very same," she responded, her eyes looking into his intently, filled with adoration.

He leaned in closer to her and kissed her on the cheek. Lingering near her ear, he whispered, "Do you know where we are standing?"

She shook her head.

He smiled as he leaned back a bit to meet her eyes. "We're in the very spot we first kissed that night when we were walking around the property."

Her eyes glanced around for a brief moment before looking back at him. "You're right, it is," she replied with a grin.

He reached a hand up to her cheek and stroked his thumb from her cheek down to the corner of her lower lip. He took a step in closer to her. With his face merely an inch away from hers, he whispered, "Kate, I missed you." He moved toward her the remainder of the way and met her soft, velvety lips. He wrapped his arms around her waist. Immediately she reached her hands up around his neck and pulled herself in close to him, returning his kiss with fervor.

It was too good to be true. They were reunited again, beneath the stars. As Cal held her in his arms, he told himself that nothing could ever again come between them.

Chapter Forty-Five

In that strange place somewhere between asleep and awake, Cal twisted and turned his body in his uncomfortable state. His mind was fogged and he couldn't seem to think of anything except for how cold he felt. He was sopping wet. Shivering, he groaned with pain. His head was pounding and his body throbbing. It wasn't a searing pain like his wounds from battle, but a dull, achy pain that seemed to radiate from his core to his limbs.

A moment later he felt incredibly hot. Boiling even. He clawed at his shirt to tear it off but couldn't see or feel it. He felt claustrophobic.

I must be drowning, he thought. Drowning in his foxhole. The sloshy mud and water were sucking him under, consuming him.

But then snippets of moments of the day before began flickering in his mind. There was a plane ride. And his family. And Kate. And before that there was a hospital. And a ship ride back to the States.

He couldn't be in a foxhole. Unless, of course, that had all been a dream.

He remembered what he would do back when he was a child having a nightmare. He focused on closing his eyes tightly and then began counting to five in his head. When he reached five, he flung his eyes open.

He inhaled deeply. Thank goodness. He was lying in his bed in his room at home.

But something wasn't right. He was shivering, and his head felt heavy and achy. He looked toward the window of his room. Light was pouring through the part in the curtains. Immediately the brightness hit his eyes and an incredibly intense pounding began stabbing at his head. Shielding his eyes from the light with one hand, he felt his shirt with his other hand and found it was, indeed, wet.

Slowly, he sat up and lifted his legs over the side of the bed. With every movement his head throbbed. He felt off balance and was having a difficult time thinking clearly.

He stood and staggered out of bed to his door. He looked down the hallway but everything was quiet. He opened his mouth. "Mother?" he called out, his voice crackly, barely above a whisper. No one answered.

Maybe someone would be downstairs. He walked toward the staircase and braced himself as he took hold of the railing and began shakily descending its steps. He reached the bottom of the staircase and turned a corner. Feeling as though he was moving through a dream, he could hardly make sense of where he was in the very home he grew up in. Soon he found himself at the door to the kitchen. He pushed it open and went straight for the kitchen table. Unable to retain the weight of his body on his aching legs any longer, he fell into a chair and sat slumped over, utterly exhausted.

A few moments later he heard the door from the back porch to the kitchen swing open, but his head was too heavy to turn it to the side to see who it was.

"Cal, you're up!" the cheery voice of his mother said. "I figured you needed the extra sleep, so I didn't wake you." He heard her rustling around with something at the kitchen counter. "Now here's a nice glass of orange ju—Cal?" Her voice sounded startled. "Is something wrong, dear? You don't look well."

Cal could feel his entire body shivering. "I don't feel very well," he answered, looking up to see her standing over him.

"Your hair and shirt are wet," his mother said. "And your face is quite red." She placed a hand on his forehead. "Oh, goodness. Your temperature feels very high."

Cal was trying to hold back the jittering.

"You must have come down with something."

Cal nodded.

"Can you stop the shaking, dear?" she asked.

"I-I think so," he stuttered.

She looked at him with concern. "Well, do you think you can eat? Some food might do you some good. Then we'll get you back into bed."

He really didn't feel like eating. He was afraid it might upset his stomach. But she was probably right. "Maybe just a slice of bread and butter."

"Of course," she replied.

A moment later she placed a slice of buttered bread in front of him, along with a glass of orange juice.

Over the next couple minutes he nibbled at his bread and took a couple sips of the juice. But he wasn't feeling any better. If anything, he was feeling worse. He probably picked up some sort of sickness back in the hospital.

Then a thought struck him. These symptoms were familiar. The pounding head, the achy body, the high fever; he had witnessed soldiers over in the Philippines lament about these very ailments. Malaria. Of course that's what it was. All the symptoms were there. The disease must have been dormant in his body, deterred by the medicine the army had given him, but it had now come back. He had heard that could happen.

In the Philippines, if the men were given Atabrine—the anti-malaria drug—soon enough, it would stop the disease. But if they waited too long, it could be deadly.

Without thinking, he stood up abruptly from his chair, rattling the table and nearly knocking over his orange juice. He had to get to a hospital.

His mother's head snapped over to him. "What's wrong, dear?"

"I, um . . ." He couldn't tell his mother he thought he had malaria. He didn't want to worry her. As long as he got the Atabrine he would be okay. "I think I might have picked up something that was going around in the hospital back in California. I know the type of medicine the doctors can give me that will take care of it. I think I just need to get to a doctor and I'll be fine."

"Then let's go out to the truck and I'll drive you over to Doctor Caldwell's," she replied.

Cal had already thought this through. He knew the local doc, Doctor Caldwell, wouldn't have the medicine he needed. He was sure he would need to go to a major hospital for them to know how to treat a foreign disease like malaria.

"The thing is, I think I might need to go to a bigger place that has dealt with this type of illness before. Maybe the hospital up at the University."

His mother looked at him worriedly and nodded. "All right, then. I can drive you—"

"No," Cal interrupted. "I don't want to take you away from the things you need to do around here today. If you could just give me a ride to the bus station, I'll catch a bus up to the hospital."

His mother looked at him as if he were crazy. "No, son. I will take you. It's not a problem."

But Cal didn't think it best that she go with him. He appreciated her concern and care, but he was afraid that once she heard him tell the doctors he was sure it was malaria she would be worried sick. And there was no need for that. He knew he'd be fine once he got that medicine.

"Ma, please. I'm feeling a little better already," he lied. "I'll be fine. But it's still probably best I go up there to get the medicine. I don't want to take you away all day. I'm sure it will just be a quick appointment with a doctor and then I'll be on my way home."

She stood watching him uneasily. After a few moments, she reluctantly nodded her head. "Well, you're a grown man now. I suppose I can't argue with you. But you remember that we have a phone now. I want you to call me once you are up there and let me know that you made it okay, and let me know if you need me to come up there. After you see the doctor, call and let me know when you are headed back so I can pick you up from the bus station."

He nodded his head, which was feeling increasingly heavy. He strained to stand straight and keep from shaking to appear as though he was feeling better than he actually was. He was now vacillating from feeling shivering cold to very hot, and could feel beads of sweat forming on his forehead.

"I will, Mother. Don't worry. I'll be just fine."

An hour later Cal was staggering into the University of Utah hospital emergency wing's front doors. The hospital was the most reputable medical center in the Salt Lake Valley.

His head was pounding and he felt extremely cold again. He wasn't even trying to stop the shaking now.

He began walking toward the front desk. The woman sitting behind it looked up at him. "What can I help you with?" she asked.

"I've been home from f-fighting in the war in the Philippines about a-a month now," he began, having a difficult time delivering the words. During the bus ride he had fallen in and out of sleep and felt dizzy and lightheaded the entire way. The shaking was now causing his teeth to chatter, making it difficult to keep from stuttering. "I-I believe I am having s-symptoms of malaria."

The woman's eyes widened. She immediately sent for a nurse to get a wheelchair.

Two nurses arrived. They sat Cal in a wheelchair and pushed him to a room at the very end of the hallway. As soon as he was wheeled through the doors of the room, his eyes were pierced by sunlight beating through a large window that took up nearly the entire outer wall of the room. Cal groaned. The sunlight was like daggers to his aching head. The room was very warm. He no longer felt cold but now incredibly hot.

The nurses got a read of his temperature. "One hundred and five," one of the nurses said, exchanging glances with the other.

Cal wanted to ask questions, but between the sun beating through the window and the fogginess of his head, he was having a hard time articulating what he wanted to say. "Have . . . have you had any experience with malaria?" he managed. "At this hospital, I mean?"

The nurse who seemed to be in charge hesitated and then cleared her throat. "I can't answer that, sir. But I'm sure one of our doctors will know what to do."

He was becoming skeptical. From the moment he uttered the word *malaria* the hospital staff had looked at him as if he were a foreigner and treated him with trepidation.

The nurses said they needed to check on some other patients but that the doctor would be in to see him soon.

Cal sat in the sun-filled room waiting. He thought of what he really wanted to be doing today—ring shopping for Kate. But here he sat. He worried his plans for today, and the remainder of this furlough, were going awry.

He had arrived at the hospital at nine o'clock. He watched the hands of the clock on the wall move slowly as he sat in the room burning up and sweating. Soon it was ten o'clock. The one spot his wheelchair had been parked that had been protected from the sun had now lost its shade. The entire room appeared to be filled with sun except one tiny spot in the corner. He pushed himself out of the wheelchair, weak and dizzy, and stumbled across the room to sit in the corner. He sat there with his knees tucked up to him and his head slung forward, resting it on his knees. He sat that way for a very long time.

He looked up it at the clock. It read eleven. Still no visit from a doctor. Frustration and anger began to rise up inside of him. He lay on the ground, trying to soak out any coolness from the hard tile floor.

They did realize that malaria was a deadly disease if not treated quickly, didn't they? Were they just going to leave him here to shrivel up and die? A couple hours ago he would have laughed at the thought.

But now he was beginning to wonder.

Finally, he heard the door squeak open. "Mr. Morgan?" a woman's voice said. He looked up to see the nurse again. He lifted himself from his lying position to sitting.

"What are you doing on the floor?" she asked.

"Trying to find a way to get c-comfortable in this darned sunroom," he answered, not caring that his irritation was coming through in his voice. "I-is there any other room . . . less sunny . . . that I c-can be transferred to?"

"I'm afraid not," she answered. "The staff wants you to stay down at the end of the hall."

Cal stared back at her blankly. "I'm in here b-burning up and you can't switch me rooms?"

"Not with your . . . condition, sir."

He shook his head in disbelief. "Do you realize I've been sitting in here for t-two hours? Where is a doctor?"

"I'm terribly sorry," she replied with sympathy. "We are trying to find a doctor who is familiar with . . . your situation."

Cal's blood was boiling. "You mean to tell me there isn't one doctor h-here who knows about malaria?" He was raising his voice now. "Don't you have any Atabrine?"

The nurses' eyes looked startled, and a bit frightened. "I can't answer that, sir."

Cal again shook his head and buried his face in his knees.

"We're working on it, sir."

He looked back up as she was walking out the door.

Another hour passed and still no sign of a doctor.

His room was on ground level. Right outside his window he could see a grouping of large pine trees. If he could just get outside he could sit under those trees in the shade and the fresh air. He knew it would do him a world of good.

He used every ounce of strength he had to stand up and walk across the room to the window. He unlatched the window and slid it open as far as it would go. Then he lifted his foot and climbed out of it. He crawled over to the trees and sprawled out on the cool grass under the shade. This was a million times better than that furnace of a room they had banished him to.

He lay there for another half hour or so with his eyes closed, but not sleeping, when suddenly he heard someone approaching him.

"What are you doing out here?" the low voice of a man barked.

Cal opened his eyes to see what appeared to be a doctor in a white jacket standing in front of him.

"Did someone give you permission to open that window and come out here?" the doctor asked, raising his voice condescendingly.

Cal was furious. He took a deep breath and pushed himself up off the grass so he was standing face-to-face with the doctor. "What does it look like I'm doing out here? Your staff goes and puts me in the hottest room in the hospital with a temperature of one hundred and five degrees and leaves me in there roasting for three hours!" he yelled. "I could have passed out and died in there and they wouldn't have known the difference!" The doctor flinched. "Now I'm through with this pigsty of a place you call a hospital. I want my papers ready so I can get out of here and back to the hospital in California!"

Affronted, the doctor looked him over and opened his mouth but didn't seem to be able to choke out his words.

"When I was wounded fighting in the Philippines, I spent over a month in a hellhole of a hospital over there and was never treated with the disregard and rudeness that I have here."

He knew that wasn't entirely true. The time immediately after he had been wounded and sent to the mass unit, he had been basically ignored the entire day. But there was reason for it there. The medics were dealing with hundreds of injuries and casualties and were too busy to keep anything straight. Here they had no excuse.

The doctor again opened his mouth, this time managing to spit out his words. "I apologize," he said quickly. "I can understand your frustration. Now, let's get you back inside and we'll get you taken care of."

Reluctantly, Cal let the doctor take hold of his arm and lead him inside the hospital.

Chapter Forty-Six

Standing in front of the mirror hanging on the wall in her bedroom, Kate brushed through her hair one last time. Placing the brush on the dresser table, she stood observing her reflection for a moment. She couldn't help but notice how purely happy she looked. Her face was glowing, and she couldn't keep from smiling. He was finally home and their reunion couldn't have been more perfect.

She loved him, there was no doubt about it in her mind, and she knew he returned that love wholeheartedly. She had never known how comforting and freeing that knowledge could be. Knowing she was going to spend the rest of her life with him was more elating than she had ever imagined, more than all of her previous aspirations of leaving small-town Utah behind and living in a big city. She had always been searching for something she was never quite able to find—contentment. She thought she might find it somewhere far off in a life different than the one she had always led. But she knew now that was a way of running away from something she was afraid of. Now all her hopes and dreams were with Cal, and she couldn't imagine living her life any other way. She still wanted a life of passion and excitement, but she knew that with Cal, no matter where they lived or what they were doing, that was what she would have.

She heard a knock at the door and glanced at the clock. It was six forty-five. Cal said he would pick her up tonight at seven, giving her time to get home from work and get ready for the evening. But perhaps he had arrived a little early. She turned excitedly and dashed out of her room and quickly down the stairs. Reaching the front door, she swung it open with anticipation.

Her eyes met the person on the other side of the door with puzzle. "Mrs. Morgan!" she exclaimed. "What are you doing here?" She quickly realized the face of the mother of her beau appeared troubled.

"Kate, I have some bad news," Mrs. Morgan answered.

Kate stood staring back at her in alarm. What on earth could she be talking about?

"I'm afraid something has happened," she continued. "Cal spent the day up the University Hospital and is now on a train headed back to California."

Kate's eyes widened in disbelief. "I don't understand," she stammered. "What is wrong?"

Mrs. Morgan took a breath. "I'm sorry, dear. Cal has come down with malaria."

❧

Cal was sprawled out across his seat on the train and the seat next to him, faint and dazed. Luckily the seat next to him had been unoccupied and he was able to use the extra space to lie down, unable to sit and hold the weight of his head up for more than a few seconds. Shaking uncontrollably he was now extremely cold and wished he had a blanket or something to pull over him to keep him warm. But he hadn't thought of asking his mother to grab a blanket when he called to tell her he needed to be picked up and taken to a bus or a train station to get back to California.

Once the doctor had admitted to Cal that they weren't familiar with malaria at the hospital and had been unable to find Atabrine, Cal had again demanded for his papers to get him out of there and on his way. He called his mother and could find no other way around it but to tell her about the malaria. She made a few calls to find the quickest way to get him back to California. Soon after, she picked him up from the hospital and took him to the train station.

After hugging his mother goodbye and reassuring her again that once he got the Atabrine he would be just fine, he staggered onto the train. He hoped what he had told his mother was true. As he had walked aboard the train he was greeted by the conductor's startled expression. He didn't blame the man; Cal was sure he looked a frightful sight. He had worried that when the conductor saw him he would forbade him from riding on the train. But luckily that hadn't been the case. As Cal's bloodshot, weary eyes met the conductor's he stuttered, "I-I don't know how I'll be when we g-get to Auburn . . . " He figured it was fairly obvious he wasn't sure if he would be awake or asleep or passed out by that time. "B-but it's very important I get to the army h-hospital there."

The conductor looked Cal over—wearing his army greens—with sympathy. "I'll make sure you get there," the conductor replied with an understanding nod.

Cal had now been riding the train for what seemed like days and he was so cold, nauseated, and miserable. But in reality it had only been a few hours. It was a night train and it was dark now. He wished he could fall into a deep restful slumber, but instead his sleep was uncomfortable and fitful. He lay there, swaying with the movement of the passenger car, hoping and praying he would arrive in California in time for the Atabrine to be effective.

His mother said she would stop by Kate's home and explain what had happened. He felt guilty about how Kate might worry for him and was so very disappointed in how his plans had with her had deteriorated. Finally, he had returned home to her only to be pulled away again and wasn't even able to say goodbye. He had hoped they would be engaged tonight, but instead here he was being carted back to the military hospital once again.

But he was determined to beat this. He would arrive in California and make a fast turnaround. He wouldn't let the malaria stop him when he had already made it through so much. He wasn't about to lose her now.

Chapter Forty-Seven

Well, Cal, you're looking well."

Cal nodded back at the doctor, encouraged. As bad as he had gotten, barely able to walk in his state of acute illness and confusion by the time he'd stumbled off that train, he had made great strides over the past week in the hospital. It was amazing what modern medicine could do. The doctor came to check on him once or twice daily, and Cal felt in good hands.

"I'm feeling a great deal better," Cal replied. "My strength is really coming back."

Cal had been able to keep food and water down for a few days now, and was beginning to be able to walk long distances down the hospital hallways all on his own. He didn't feel completely back to normal, still experiencing flu-like symptoms. The doctor said it could take up to a month for those symptoms to completely go away. But Cal was functioning and was just grateful to be alive.

"However," the doctor continued, "I'm afraid I have some rather discouraging news, although I think it's best you are aware of it."

The change in conversation had Cal distraught. He was doing so well. What could the doctor be referring to?

The doctor went on. "Even once your body has fully recovered from this bout, with the type of malaria you contracted it is probable the symptoms will reoccur for years to come."

Cal was dubious. "You mean to tell me I'm going to have to go through all this again?"

The doctor's face was regretful. "I'm afraid there's a good chance of it."

Cal was at a loss for words.

"But keep in mind, reoccurring bouts aren't usually as severe as the original manifestation of the disease. They'll probably happen yearly. But with proper and prompt treatment, the symptoms can be lessened. In my experience and from what the experts say, you'll likely come down with the symptoms for the next fourteen years or so."

Cal let out a breath. The doctor was right—this wasn't good news. In the farming business it wouldn't be easy to have the malaria symptoms come back. He let out a breath. "Well, I suppose I just need to be grateful that it didn't get me altogether," he finally replied.

The doctor smiled ruefully. "You're absolutely right. You are lucky you've recovered so well, especially considering the delay in treatment."

Cal nodded.

They talked for a few more minutes before the doctor excused himself to check on another patient.

Although this week in the hospital had been positive considering his quick turnaround, it was another frustrating delay keeping him from the life he longed for back home. His wounds were still healing, and now with the malaria on top of his injuries, the nurses alluded that his release date would likely be prolonged due to his contracting of the disease.

But he focused on the positive. He had escaped death both with his battle wounds and in contracting the disease. He had a body that functioned normally, and his prognosis going forward was good. With all the men that had perished in the war and suffered debilitating injuries, he knew he was one of the lucky ones. And back home he had the girl of his dreams waiting for him. As much as he hoped and prayed and wished upon every star he ever saw in the night sky in the Philippines that he would end up with Kate, it always almost seemed too good to be true. But now life with her was so close within his grasp, and he couldn't wait for it to begin.

Unbeknownst to him at the time, the day he arrived back to the hospital, Kate had called the administration desk and asked to speak with him. They told her he was unable to take phone calls. She called back again later that day demanding to at least have the chance to speak a quick word to him or she would travel to the hospital herself to do it. The hospital discouraged visitors, especially those who weren't family, so they sent someone to Cal's room. They told him his girlfriend back home was on the phone. Doing a little better, he nodded weakly and told them that yes, he indeed wanted to take the call. They wheeled him to the administration office.

He reached the phone to his ear and breathed, "Kate?"

"Cal! How are you?" she exclaimed shakily. "Are you okay? How are you feeling?"

Cal mustered a smile, although very fatigued and ill. "I'm doing a little better," he said hoarsely.

"Do they have you on the medicine?" she asked poignantly.

"Yes. They put me on it right away."

"Good," she sighed. "Well, I'm coming to see you. I told the office I could work until Friday but that I would be leaving for the weekend and wouldn't be back next week."

"No, please, Kate. You don't understand—"

"Yes, I do understand, Cal. You are sick and I should be there. I should have been at the hospital here in Salt Lake to take care of you. I felt horrible when I found out what happened." He could hear her voice beginning to tremble.

"Kate, please don't feel bad. There was nothing you could have done."

"That doesn't matter! I wanted to be there. I want to be there with you now."

He took a breath. "Trust me, I want to be with you too, but this place is not what you think. I want the next time we are together to be wonderful, but here we'll hardly have any time together and I'll only be recovering. It wouldn't be worth the time away, or the money."

"I knew you would say that," she said under her breath. "I should have just bought my train ticket and come without telling you."

Cal couldn't help but let out a chortle at the zest in her voice that he admired and loved. "Kate, I want to be with you more than you know. But I'll be back soon, I promise."

There was a long pause on the other end, followed by a sigh. "Well, I don't want to argue with you now. I'm sure I have kept you on the phone much longer than I should have in your condition. But . . . I suppose you probably know best. I'll stay, if that's what you want."

Cal was deeply relieved. Of course he would love to see her, but he knew the reality was it was best this way.

He had written her a letter yesterday saying he was doing a great deal better, but still not able to do much. Of course this wasn't entirely true. He had made a fairly rapid recovery. He attributed it to having so much to look forward to when he returned home.

But he wanted her to think it was taking him longer to recover than it actually was. He had a plan up his sleeve.

Chapter Forty-Eight

Walking along the streets of downtown Salt Lake City, Cal felt the small box in the pocket of his slacks clank against his leg. Nervousness, excitement, and anticipation were flooding over him.

Kate had no idea he was back in town yet. He arrived on the early train the day before and spent the morning visiting with her mother. He knew Kate would be away at work and wanted to ask her mother's permission for her hand. Kate's mother told Cal she would be proud to call him her son-in-law. Cal asked Kate's mother to promise not to breathe a word about him being in town.

He spent that afternoon shopping for rings and brought his sister along to help. Eventually he found the perfect one. It was classic and elegant, just like Kate, and he felt certain she would like it. He wished he could afford a bigger diamond and decided that someday he would replace it with something larger.

He had written Kate the day before he left telling her he would be getting a furlough home the following week. All along he had kept her about a week behind in his recovery process, wanting to surprise her with his arrival.

Arriving at Huddart Floral, the flower shop in downtown Salt

Lake his sisters told him about, he reached for the doorknob and pushed it open. The chime of the shop bell jingled as he walked through the door. Immediately the fresh, perfume fragrance of flowers struck his nostrils. He inhaled deeply, taking in the lovely scent. He quickly glanced around at the vibrant colors of dozens of bouquets and flower arrangements decorating the shop. The little flower shop was a sensory overload.

"Welcome!" a cheerful voice of an older man called to him.

Cal looked over to see a man standing behind the counter in the front of the shop.

"Hello," Cal answered, tipping his fedora hat to him.

"May I help you?" the man asked, stepping out from behind the counter.

Cal glanced around. He had never purchased a bouquet of flowers before and was now realizing there were many more options than he realized. "Some help would be great," he replied.

Ten minutes later he emerged from the shop with a striking bouquet of a dozen red roses dotted with a touch of baby's breath and greenery wrapped with white paper around the stems, tied with an elegant red bow. There were so many exquisite arrangements of flowers in varying colors that it was difficult to pick, but in the end he had chosen the red roses. They were the obvious and perfect choice for today.

He turned the corner and walked the few blocks down the street to where he had parked the truck. Gently placing the roses on the passenger seat next to him, he turned the ignition and began the drive back to the south end of the valley. Soon, he would be at Kate's doorstep.

❧

With the bouquet of roses in his hands, he paused in front of Kate's mother's beige brick home for a moment. He took in a breath. This was it.

His shoes crunched against the gravel drive as he walked toward the front door. He walked up the steps to the porch, reached his hand forward, and knocked.

With his heart pounding, he waited for a few seconds before the door swung open. It was Kate's mother. "Hello, Cal," she said softly yet excitedly. She looked down at the roses in his hands and back up at him with a smile spread across her face. "My, what beautiful flowers. I'll call for Kate."

Cal nodded. "That would be great."

"Kate!" her mother called. "Someone's at the door for you!"

She turned to Cal and winked at him with a delighted smile.

A moment later Cal heard Kate's steps coming down the stairs. He took in another deep breath, trying to calm the nervous flutters in his stomach.

Just then Kate appeared at the door in front of him. Their eyes met and she gasped, a startled expression filled her face. "Cal!" she exclaimed. For a brief moment she seemed to be stunned in her place. But then she rushed toward him and flung her arms around his neck. "You're home!"

He wrapped his arms around her. "I am," he replied with a chuckle.

"But what are you doing here?" she asked with a surprised expression, leaning back to look him in the face.

"I came home a little early," he answered with a wry grin.

She let out a breath. "I can see that." She leaned back into his chest, hugging him tightly. "How are you feeling?" she asked.

"Never better," he said, still holding her in his arms.

They clung to each other for a few seconds longer before Cal took a step back. Still holding the roses in his hand, he reached them toward her. "These are for you."

She took the bouquet in her hands, a wide smile forming on his lips. "Oh my, they are beautiful," she replied. He watched as she lifted the roses to her nose and inhaled. "And they smell divine." She looked back up at him with affection in her eyes. "Thank you."

Cal nodded. "Of course."

"They really are stunning," Kate's mother piped in from behind. "Would you like me to put them in vase with water?"

Cal glanced back to Mrs. Clayton. He had forgotten she was even standing there.

"Oh, I can do that," Kate replied.

"Well, actually," Cal piped in, "I was wondering if you'd like to go for a little walk before the sun sets."

Kate raised her eyebrows in slight surprise. "Of course," she replied. "It is a pleasant evening. A walk sounds lovely."

Mrs. Clayton stepped toward Kate and took the bouquet in her hands. "I'll have these in water and set on the kitchen counter so you can enjoy them when you get back."

"Thank you, mother," Kate replied.

As Kate stepped out of the doorway Cal admired how perfectly enchanting she looked. She was wearing a lacy pale pink dress that gathered at her waist and fanned out in soft folds. "You look beautiful," he said as he reached for her hand.

She smiled. "Thank you."

Holding hands the pair walked down the steps. "Do you have a destination in mind?" Kate asked.

"Actually, yes," he replied. "The willow tree."

She smiled. "There couldn't be a more perfect place to watch the sun set."

"Exactly."

As they walked Kate asked Cal all sorts of questions he thought he had already answered in his letters to her about his recovery, but she claimed he hadn't provided enough detail. So he told her more about what those first days in the hospital were like, what the doctors told him, and how thankful he was for his speedy turnaround. "Another miracle allowing me to be here, really," he said.

She agreed earnestly.

They continued meandering down the dirt road hand in hand, conversing and enjoying each other's company and the mild fall evening. The trees were filled with luminous fall colors in the dimming evening sky. Light, wispy clouds were beginning to glow with soft oranges and pinks scattered above, stretching over the grassy fields to the horizon.

As they approached Kate's favorite spot, the willow tree, Cal could hardly believe how heavenly the scene looked. It was more than he could have hoped for. The leaves of the large, drooping tree had transformed into an exquisite golden color. The radiance of the tree contrasting against the low lit pastel sky looked like something out of a picture book.

"This is breathtaking," Kate said, as they approached the tree. They paused a few feet in front of its weeping branches.

"It couldn't be more perfect."

She nodded in agreement.

"Just like you," he added.

"Oh, Cal," she countered with a laugh, shaking her head. "Don't be silly."

"I'm not," he replied sincerely. "You are." He was gazing intently into her eyes.

"Well now you're going to make me blush," she replied with an impish grin.

Quickly he made a decision. His anticipation was outweighing all of his nervousness now. He didn't want to delay any longer. He reached toward her so he was holding both her hands in his and took a step in closer to her. "Kate," he said, "my dear Kate." He paused for a moment and lifted one of her hands up to his lips, placing a kiss on its top. He lowered it back down and continued, "You had my heart from the first time I laid eyes on you in the eighth grade. When I saw you that day at the church house before my mission, I knew you were the one for me, I just had no idea how it would happen. But we were finally brought together by a divine power greater than anything I can imagine, I believe." He paused for a moment, watching the emotion filling her face. "While I was serving in the war you were what got me through. I would think about you and how your eyes make me feel like a new person every time I look into them. I'd think about your smile and how it brings the kind of joy into my heart that I never imagined possible. I'd think of the incredible woman you are and I knew there was something good in the world left for me to live for. I can't tell you how many times I dreamt about us and what our future together could bring." He inhaled unevenly. "We've been through so much, so many bumps that could have pulled us apart, and yet here we are together again."

Kate nodded, her eyes brimming with tears.

"You make me happier than I ever imagined possible, and you make me the person I want to be. I love you."

He let go of one of her hands and slyly reached into his pocket, pulling out the ring box, and dropped to one knee.

Kate let out a surprised gasp.

He was still holding onto one of her hands lightly with his spare hand. He watched as realization began to emerge in her eyes. Soon they were filled with tears, and a slow smile began forming on her lips.

Gently letting go of her hand, he slipped open the lid to the small box he was holding revealing the sparkling diamond ring. His hands shaking, he lifted the box up toward her to see. "Kate Clayton, will you marry me?"

Kate smiled radiantly through her tears. "Yes!" she exclaimed. "Of course I will marry you."

Shakily, he took the ring out of the box and slid it onto her ring finger. She gazed at it beaming, then reached down to him and pulled him up onto his feet. She stepped toward him and placed a kiss on his lips. He kissed her back, so elated he felt like he was floating.

Later, as they walked back to Kate's house, the sun had set and the stars were beginning to shine in the night sky. Cal thought of the many times he had looked up at the stars and made a wish, a wish that seemed so distant and impossible knowing all that he would face going off to war, and all else that could come between them. But now that wish had come true.

Unable to keep his eyes off her, Cal glanced over at Kate again for the hundredth time, completely in awe that Kate Clayton, the girl of his dreams, was truly his forever.

Epilogue

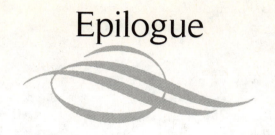

Rooted to my chair, I sat in awe as Cal finished the last beautiful piece to the tapestry of his enchanting story.

"That was . . . amazing," I said for lack of a word that could better describe my thoughts and feelings on all he had told me.

"Well, if you say so," Cal replied, his twinkling blue eyes and the creases in their corners smiling back at me. "I don't know how amazing an old codger like me could be."

Cal wasn't the type to revel in himself or his triumphs for one second unless it was to talk about Kate and how he had won her over; that much I had learned as he unraveled his story to me. But I felt compelled to let him know that his story was something beyond ordinary. It was extraordinary. Something to be proud of.

"Cal," I said, looking at him directly. "You have lived through so much. Your youth, the war, you and Kate's love story, just everything. It truly is remarkable and inspiring. It's something I wish everyone could hear."

Cal smiled modestly with a chuckle.

But I think he was beginning to believe me.

After talking with him for a few more minutes, I looked at the time on my cell phone and realized it was almost five o'clock. I had been sitting with him for nearly four hours.

I thanked him again before leaving and told him I'd love to come back and visit him again sometime soon.

Walking away from that charming old house, I felt refreshed and invigorated. I began thinking about how astounding it was that a person I grew up living down the street from for the better part of my life could have such a remarkable story to tell. It was one that simply shouldn't be forgotten.

As I drove away from the house, lost in my thoughts of Cal and the war and Kate, a thought struck me: *Wouldn't that make a wonderful novel.*

Afterword

Cal and Kate were married January 10, 1946. Kate moved to California after their marriage and obtained a job as a secretary for the army at Camp Lockett where Cal was transferred to finish his recovery. After nine months in California between his stay at DeWitt General Hospital and Camp Lockett, Cal was finally released and allowed to return home to Utah.

Cal and Kate knew they wanted children from the get-go, and they began their role as parents quickly. On December 12, 1946, Kate gave birth to their first child, a baby boy. Immediately following the delivery, she looked up at Cal and said, "He will be our only child, because I'm *never* doing that again!" She went on to have four more children.

Kate was a loving and dedicated mother to four boys and one girl. She found passion in raising her children and watching them learn and grow. In addition to their five children, Cal and Kate took in one of their son's friends in high school who lived with them until he was married, and who still considers himself a member of their family today.

Cal continued pursuing his livelihood as a farmer and eventually ran a successful farming business and sold farming equipment as well. As he promised, forever in debt to his heavenly creator for sparing him in the war, Cal dedicated his life to the service of God. He served in many clergy and leadership positions within the LDS church, giving countless hours of his time to the service of God and others.

Just as the doctor at DeWitt General Hospital predicted, every fall for fourteen years Cal came down with symptoms of malaria. After those fourteen years it never came back. He fully recovered from all his battle wounds, but still, to this day, the piece of shrapnel from the deadly blast at the battle of Ula is embedded in the bone of his right elbow.

As attested to by Cal, his children, and neighbors that lived near the Morgans and knew the family intimately, Cal and Kate lived a love story that never died. A neighbor relayed an account from when Cal had been the bishop of the congregation in their area sometime around 1960. Cal was sitting on the stand behind the pulpit in the chapel in front of the congregation when Kate walked in halfway through the service, having just arrived back in town from visiting a relative in California. When Cal saw her walk through the doors, he jumped out of his seat on the stand, ran into the aisle to meet her halfway, and gave her a hug and a kiss in front of the entire congregation. When asked about that story Cal simply said he missed her so much while she was gone he couldn't help but greet her when she walked through the chapel doors.

Cal and Kate were married for sixty-two years. Kate passed away on April 22, 2008.

As of June 2014, Cal continues living on his own in the home he and Kate raised their family in. To date, he and Kate have twenty-three grandchildren and twenty great-grandchildren.

Cal greatly looks forward to the time when he and Kate will be reunited again.

Author's Note

Everyone has a story to tell, but once in a while, perhaps even once in a lifetime, we run across a story that we know can't be forgotten. Feeling this way, I am extremely pleased that the story I was in awe of, and instantly fell in love with, will be able to be shared with others through this novel inspired by a true story. Through many visits and interviews with the man whose experiences inspired this novel, I was privileged to learn about his life and will forever be grateful for the friendship we formed and the story he allowed me to write and share.

Writing a novel inspired by a true story proved to be tricky at times, but mostly it was a lot of fun. Nonetheless, I'd be lying if I said that going into it I wasn't intimidated. I knew I would love creating and weaving the story together, but the research required in writing a historical novel was something I had never done before. Furthermore, writing about war and making war scenes believable was a daunting thought. But because I felt so compelled to write the story, I decided to give it a shot, and I ended up being surprised how much I enjoyed the research and learning more about the era, the war, and even writing war scenes. However, I don't claim to be a historian by any means and realize there is a chance there could be a discrepancy I am unaware of. Having said this, I put countless hours into research and fact-checking and made every effort to make certain historical details are correct.

It is important to note that while this novel was inspired by a true story, names have been changed, as its central character humbly wishes to remain anonymous. While the basis of the story is true and a large amount of the details are factual, I would like to reiterate that it is historical fiction inspired by a true story, meaning conversations, scenes, and some details are fictionalized.

I feel it necessary to mention a few of the largest fictionalizations in the story, which mainly have to do with Kate's character (I will refer to the characters as Kate and Cal, although those names are fictional). First, parents of the person whom Kate's character is based on were not divorced in reality, although she most definitely was afraid of marriage and had decided to never marry prior to meeting Cal. It is unclear why she felt this way, although we do know her family life wasn't simple due to her parents' marriage being second marriages for both. I felt writing her parents' divorce into the novel would explain this fear and also be relatable to many readers.

Secondly, Kate's place of residence during the time she and Cal were courting. I thought it would be fun to use a tidbit from my grandmother's history by placing her in downtown Salt Lake City at the Beehive House, although the person her character is based on didn't actually reside there. The Beehive House was indeed used as a dormitory for young women at the time, and my grandmother lived there. I thought having Kate there would pull in a fun historical element to the novel, as well as conveniently place her in downtown Salt Lake City, as she and Cal spend a lot of time there while courting. Outside of those details, the broad basis of the story is true.

One of the questions I have been most frequently asked from early readers of the novel is: Did Kate really visit Cal at Camp Roberts and pretend to be his wife? The answer is yes! She somehow managed to stay there for a couple weeks pretending to be his wife. In fact, while researching Camp Roberts I called the administration office that handles the historical affairs of the camp with a few questions. When I told them about the novel I was writing and how the man's girlfriend stayed at the camp pretending to be his wife, they told me that that couldn't be possible. It was very rare for wives to be allowed to visit their husbands at the camp, even if married to a high-ranking officer within the military. It sometimes happened, but only under extenuating circumstances. I told them it indeed happened, and I think they were having a hard time understanding how that could be. I have to chalk it up to Kate's determination and charisma, and of course her devotion to Cal and to seeing him one last time before he left overseas.

I also would like to note that when it comes to the war, every battle scene, confrontation, and experience (outside of fictionalized conversations) actually happened. I was fascinated with this man's war experiences and what everyday life was like as a soldier. Through learning about his service in the war and the research I did, I gained a much greater understanding and appreciation for not only the soldiers that served in WWII, but for our soldiers that work to defend our freedoms today.

If you would like to learn more about the story and the process of writing it, I will be posting additional information on my website at www.lindsaybferguson.com.

I hope you enjoyed Cal and Kate's story. Thank you for reading!

Discussion Questions

1 In Cal and Kate's school years, Cal tended to be on the quiet, reserved side, while Kate was outgoing and popular by nature. Which character were you more like as a youth, or were you somewhere in between?

2 Kate has some fears and insecurities but does a good job at hiding them. Do you think people often try to portray they are something they may not entirely be? Why do you suppose people have a tendency to do this?

3 Cal felt an instant connection with Kate that never waned, while she took a lot longer to reciprocate those feelings. Do you believe love at first sight can really happen? Why does it take longer for some people to develop those feelings? Does it break down to situations, personalities, or maybe even destiny?

4 Why do you think it took Cal leaving for Kate to realize her true feelings for him? What does her going to Camp Roberts show us about how she is changing?

5 What does Cal's commitment to his morals and to God show us about his character? Do you find these qualities admirable?

6 When reading the letters written between Cal and Kate while Cal was at war, what stood out to you the most? Did you find the contrast between their letters surprising?

7 What were your thoughts as you read about how the soldiers reverted to primal instincts at times during the war? For example, the scene when they were fighting over water?

8 Is it possible to find compassion instead of hate for our enemies? What does Cal's reaction to the Japanese soldiers entering the US campground to surrender tell us about his view of humanity?

9 What were your feelings when Cal and Kate met yet another roadblock when he came down with malaria?

10 It is often said that hardships and trials can strengthen and deepen love. Do you think this was true in Cal and Kate's relationship?

Bonus Question: Does knowing that Cal and Kate's story was inspired by a true story make you feel more connected to it? Do you think there are many seemingly "ordinary" people that may have "extraordinary" stories to tell if they were willing to share and we were willing to listen?

About the Author

Lindsay Ferguson has been immersing herself in stories since her childhood days of sneaking a flashlight into her room and staying up reading The Babysitters Club series way past her bedtime, writing spinoffs of *The Twelve Dancing Princesses*, and imagining herself in fascinating, far-off places. She still dreams of traveling the world one day, and finds getting lost in a good book almost as absorbing as penning her own stories and experiencing them unfold. A communication graduate from the University of Utah, she worked as a PR and marketing writer for a computer software company for several years before resigning to focus on raising her family. She has also contributed lifestyle articles to various media outlets. When she felt the itch to attempt novel writing, a fascination with history created a natural inclination toward historical fiction—with a romantic flare, of course. She lives in a suburb of Salt Lake City with her husband and four children. *By the Stars* is her first novel.

0 26575 18151 7